Praise for *The Essential Patricia A. McKillip*

"Reading McKillip is the closest you will come to entering a waking dream. Her prose seduces and enchants, blurring the line between the real and imagined, as her characters take you down paths both perilous and familiar. She shaped a generation of writers' imaginations, and no fantasy collection is complete without her unique voice."
—Leigh Bardugo, *New York Times* bestselling author of the *Grishaverse* series

"McKillip was a singular, arguably the best, proponent of a gentle, lyrical style of storytelling that embraced the reader with warmth and hope, even when she tackled darker subjects."
—Charles de Lint, author of the *Newford* series

"Patricia McKillip is indeed essential. If you want to read the very best fantastical fiction that has ever been written, you have to include McKillip on your list."
—Theodora Goss, author of *Letters from an Imaginary Country*

"McKillip's stories are as stately, luminous, and tightly woven as figures in the margins of an illuminated manuscript and as full of secrets trembling on the edge of knowing."
—Kathleen Jennings, World Fantasy Award–winning author of *Kindling*

"Patricia McKillip is the single writer whose work I treasure above all others. Her books have shaped the way I think about the art of writing fantasy: how to create fully realized imaginary worlds, even in the brief space of a short story."
—Terri Windling, author of *The Wood Wife*

Also by Patricia A. McKillip

Novels and Novellas

The House on Parchment Street (1973)
The Forgotten Beasts of Eld (1974)
The Night Gift (1976)
Stepping from the Shadows (1982)
Fool's Run (1987)
The Changeling Sea (1988)
Brian Froud's Faerielands: Something Rich and Strange (1994)
The Book of Atrix Wolfe (1995)
Song for the Basilisk (1998)
The Tower at Stony Wood (2000)
Ombria in Shadow (2002)
In the Forests of Serre (2003)
Alphabet of Thorn (2004)
Od Magic (2005)
The Bell at Sealey Head (2008)
The Bards of Bone Plain (2010)
Kingfisher (2016)

The Quest of the Riddle-Master

The Riddle-Master of Hed (1976)
Heir of Sea and Fire (1977)
Harpist in the Wind (1979)

Kyreol

Moon-Flash (1984)
The Moon and the Face (1985)

Cygnet

The Sorceress and the Cygnet (1991)
The Cygnet and the Firebird (1993)

Winter Rose

Winter Rose (1996)
Solstice Wood (2006)

Collections

Harrowing the Dragon (2005)
Wonders of the Invisible World (2012)
Dreams of Distant Shores (2016)

THE ESSENTIAL
PATRICIA A. McKILLIP

TACHYON + SAN FRANCISCO

The Essential Patricia A. McKillip

This is a work of fiction. All events portrayed in this book are fictitious, and any resemblance to real people or events is purely coincidental. All rights reserved, including the right to reproduce this book or portions thereof in any form without the express permission of the author and the publisher. No part of this book may be used or reproduced in any manner for the purpose of training artificial intelligence technologies or systems.

Introduction copyright © 2025 by Ellen Kushner
Interior and cover design by Elizabeth Story
Cover art by Thomas Canty

Tachyon Publications LLC
1459 18th Street #139
San Francisco, CA 94107
415.285.5615
www.tachyonpublications.com
tachyon@tachyonpublications.com

Series editor: Jacob Weisman
Project Editor: Jaymee Goh

Print ISBN: 978-1-61696-448-1
Digital ISBN: 978-1-61696-449-8

Printed in the United States by Versa Press, Inc.

First Edition: 2025
9 8 7 6 5 4 3 2 1

"Lady of the Skulls" copyright © 1993 by Patricia A. McKillip. First published in *Strange Dreams*, edited by Stephen R. Donaldson (Bantam Spectra: New York).

"Wonders of the Invisible World" copyright © 1995 by Patricia A. McKillip. First published in *Full Spectrum 5*, edited by Jennifer Hershey, Tom Dupree, and Janna Silverstein (Bantam Spectra: New York).

"The Lion and the Lark" copyright © 1995 by Patricia A. McKillip. First published in *The Armless Maiden and Other Takes for Childhood's Survivors*, edited by Terri Windling (Tor: New York).

"The Harrowing of the Dragon of Hoarsbreath" copyright © 1982 by Patricia A. McKillip. First published in *Elsewhere* Vol. II, edited by Terri Windling and Mark Arnold (Ace Books: New York).

"Out of the Woods" copyright © 2006 by Patricia A. McKillip. First published in *Flights: Extreme Visions of Fantasy, Volume II*, edited by Al Sarrantonio (Roc: New York).

"The Fortune-Teller" copyright © 2007 by Patricia A. McKillip. First published in *The Coyote Road: Trickster Tales*, edited by Ellen Datlow and Terri Windling (Viking: New York).

"The Witches of Junket" copyright © 1996 by Patricia A. McKillip. First published in *Sisters in Fantasy II*, edited by Susan Shwartz and Martin H. Greenberg (Roc: New York).

"Byndley" copyright © 2003 by Patricia A. McKillip. First published in *Firebirds*, edited by Sharyn November (Firebird: New York).

"Jack O'Lantern" copyright © 2006 by Patricia A. McKillip. First published in *Firebirds Rising*, edited by Sharyn November (Firebird: New York).

"The Stranger" copyright © 1993 by Patricia A. McKillip. First published in *Temporary Walls*, edited by Greg Ketter and Robert T. Garcia (DreamHaven Books: Minneapolis).

"The Gorgon in the Cupboard" copyright © 2004 by Patricia A. McKillip. First published in *To Weave a Web of Magic*, edited by Susan Allison (Berkley Books: New York).

"Mer" copyright © 2016 by Patricia A. McKillip. First published in *Dreams of Distant Shores*, edited by Jacob Weisman (Tachyon Publications: San Francisco).

"Weird" copyright © 2014 by Patricia A. McKillip. First published in *Unconventional Fantasy*, edited by Peggy Rae Sapienza, Jean Marie Ward, Bill Campbell, and Sam Lubell (Baltimore Washington WorldCon Association, Inc.: Baltimore).

"Hunter's Moon" copyright © 2002 by Patricia A. McKillip. First published in *The Green Man: Tales from the Mythic Forest*, edited by Ellen Datlow and Terri Windling (Viking: New York).

"Undine" copyright © by Patricia A. McKillip 2004. First published in *The Faery Reel*, edited by Ellen Datlow and Terri Windling (Viking: New York).

"Knight of the Well" copyright © 2008 by Patricia A. McKillip. First published in *A Book of Wizards*, edited by Marvin Kaye (Science Fiction Book Club: Garden City, New York).

"What Inspires Me: Guest of Honor Speech at WisCon28, 2004" copyright © 2004. First print publication in *Wonders of the Invisible World*, edited by Jacob Weisman (Tachyon Publications: San Francisco).

"Writing High Fantasy" copyright © 2002 by Patricia A. McKillip. First published in *The Writer's Guide to Fantasy Literature*, edited by Philip Martin (Kalmbach Publishing Company: Waukesha, Wisconsin).

TABLE OF CONTENTS

Introduction by Ellen Kushner i

Lady of the Skulls 2
Wonders of the Invisible World 12
The Lion and the Lark 23
The Harrowing of the Dragon of Hoarsbreath 43
Out of the Woods 62
The Fortune-Teller 75
The Witches of Junket 82
Byndley 104
Jack O'Lantern 117
The Stranger 131
The Gorgon in the Cupboard 145
Mer 199
Weird 216
Hunter's Moon 224
Undine 236
Knight of the Well 243

What Inspires Me: *Guest of Honor Speech at WisCon28, 2004* 292
Writing High Fantasy 299

INTRODUCTION
Ellen Kushner

I THINK OF PAT McKILLIP.

It is my first summer out of college. I want to be a writer, but I need to earn a living. I am trying to get a job in publishing, but I keep flunking the typing test. A cheap apartment in a bad part of New York City. A grey and a rainy day. The library has a new book by Patricia A. McKillip, the woman who wrote *The Forgotten Beasts of Eld*. I stretch out on my roommate's ratty, burlap-covered chaise longue, and open *The Riddle-Master of Hed*. In a few chapters, the world has changed. Fantasy has become less fantastical, more real—and yet, and yet . . . the True Magic runs through the book with this woman's voice and language.

I think of Pat McKillip.

Against all odds, I have gotten the job of Assistant Editor at a major Science Fiction & Fantasy (SFF) publisher. I meet Pat at my first World Science Fiction Convention. Later I find her, her arms full of books, waiting patiently in a long autograph line to get Isaac Asimov to sign them. "Why are you waiting in line?" I say. "*You* don't have to do that!"

She is embarrassed, but easily bullied by a wiry tornado just out of her teens.

I think of Pat McKillip.

Now an Associate Editor, I've been sent to a convention in San Francisco, Pat's town. Boldly, I ask if we can get together. She invites me for the evening to her small, cozy apartment. Her voice is always soft, always amused. A baby grand piano takes up most of the room off the kitchen. We're at the kitchen table, in soft lamplight. She's not the chattiest person in the world. There are pauses between sentences. I find out she trained as a classical pianist, and beg her to play for me. Was it Chopin? Schubert? I wish I'd written these things down! It was gorgeous.

I confide that I, too, want to write fantasy—but the years are slipping by: I'll be *twenty-five* next year. She breaks into peals of laughter. "That's so young!" she says.

I am softly crushed. Patricia A. McKillip laughed at my earnest angst. By the time I was the age she was during that visit, I think it's funny, too—but I had learned an important lesson. I try never to laugh when anyone younger thinks they're getting old. It's all a matter of perspective. (When I did quit my job to write my first novel, Pat would let me sleep on the floor of her hotel room as I impecuniously continued to attend SFF conventions.)

Of course, at twenty-five McKillip had already published two much-praised children's fantasies. Then, in 1974, came *The Forgotten Beasts of Eld*, with its mythical creatures, its matter-of-fact prose, and most important, its revolutionary heroine.

Like every fantasy fan who came of age in the 1950s and 1960s, McKillip grew up reading the fantasy masterworks of male authors such as T.H. White and J.R.R. Tolkien, written always from the male point of view. In a post for "Fantasy Cafe" (April 15, 2013), she remembers sitting down to create *The Forgotten Beasts of Eld*, and:

> I didn't question the point of view that came out of my pen. It seemed very natural to me to wonder why in the world a woman couldn't be a witch or a wizard, or why, if she did, she had to be virginal as well. Or why, if she was powerful and not a virgin, she was probably the evil force the male hero had to overcome. Such was my experience reading about women in fantasy, back then. So I wrote

from the point of view of a powerful female wizard, who, even after she married, was the hero of her own story, and whose decisions, for better and for worse, were her own.

McKillip's first short story for the adult fantasy market was commissioned by the visionary young editor Terri Windling for her groundbreaking anthology series *Elsewhere*, which she co-edited in 1982. You'll find it in this volume: "The Harrowing of the Dragon of Hoarsbreath." The title alone shows how inseparable were music and language to this pianist/writer. Say it aloud, and you'll hear it: *Hhhharrrowing . . . . Hhhhoarrsbreath*. This is the language of the Old Magic.

We think of Pat McKillip.
Terri Windling went on to edit any number of McKillip short stories, many found within these pages. I asked Terri to talk with me about her longtime friend and colleague. She begins with this perspective:
"In my view, Pat's distinctive prose places her firmly in the mythopoeic tradition of fantasy writers from William Morris, Hope Mirrlees, and Sylvia Townsend Warner to Alan Garner, John Crowley, and Susanna Clarke—by which I mean writers for whom the magic of their tales is inextricably bound to language they use to conjure it: a language that holds (however faintly) the cadence and rhythm of the mythic, Romantic, and oral folk traditions. Pat's other writing skills were also formidable, of course: her ability to create psychologically complex characters, intricate plots, and richly textured fantasy worlds; but it is her language that makes me return to reread her books again and again."
"It's the language of a musician," I respond. "There's a beat that is recognizably hers that shifts to fit the needs of any particular narrative. The sounds of the words themselves, with their long vowels, their short vowels, singing their way across the page amongst crisp or hissing consonants . . . I love it when McKillip writes about music and musicians, making the music the magic, sometimes, and sometimes just making her characters be working musicians in a fantasy world. She's always so good at the nitty-gritty."

"So many of her stories are ultimately about love," I muse. "Finding the right person—getting the right people together in just the right way—was so important to her."

"It was," Terri agrees. "And yet love, in a Patricia McKillip story, is never easy, simple, or safe. These are not cozy rom-coms with a fantasy twist. There is always a wonderfully subversive quality to Pat's art, a gentle but deliberate overturning of readers' expectations. Her tales are full of enchantment, wonder, and romance, yes; but they can also be sly, sharp, and tricky. They can knock you sideways."

True! "The protean nature of her work really shows in the short fiction," I say. "From one story to the next, you're bounding around in a Victorian artist's garden, or you're slowly riding a barge into a city bound by magic rituals . . . each one always perfect in every detail, and perfectly convincing. She's a master of the double helix: the magical city has perfectly ordinary, even grouchy people in it—and the ordinary English garden contains myth and magic. Pat always walks with exquisite balance that tightrope stretching over the mundane on one side and the numinous on the other."

"Pat was a prolific reader," Terri points out, "with a wide range of literary interests, and she brought those disparate influences into her own work. Readers who only know The *Riddle-Master* trilogy, for example, tend to think of her solely as a writer of classic high fantasy—but, as you've noted, her work is more protean than that. She actually moved easily between many genres and forms, including science fiction, historical fantasy, dark fantasy on the border of horror, adult fairy tales in the Angela Carter tradition, and contemporary works where magic intrudes into the real world or hovers at edge of sight."

She did.

I think of Pat McKillip.

In 1996, when Delia Sherman and I plighted our troth in a huge "party with a ceremonial interruption," as we called it, Pat was there, with the gift of two vintage china teacups for us to drink out of happily ever after.

She'd left San Francisco for the Catskills by then, on the trail of an old love that brought her into a whole new community. And then, one day, there was Dave. David Lunde, a poet, teaching at the State University of New York at Fredonia. They'd met at ICFA, the annual International Conference on the Fantastic in the Arts, where academics and novelists mingle freely.

Pat, David, Delia and I met up annually at the peripatetic World Fantasy Convention for a quiet lunch away from the crowds. In 2000, in Corpus Christi, I found just the sort of cool, off-the-road fish shack travelers dream of, and dragged the four of us there. But the food was taking forever to come. We had panels we needed to get back to. This was all my fault! I was getting desperate for conversation to distract us. But hey: I had the annual undivided attention of Patricia A. McKillip! So I leaned over the rough-hewn table and asked: "What inspires *you* to write?"

She just looked at me and said, "I dunno. I'd have to think about it."

I think of Pat McKillip.

She didn't much like being the center of attention. She did her best to avoid being on panels where she had to talk about her writing. But when she had enough warning to put words and thoughts together, she was eloquent.

For many attendees, the high point of the annual feminist convention WisCon is the Saturday night Guest of Honor speeches. It was 2004, and Pat was the honoree. She walked up to the brightly lit podium, took out her text, and began:

> A friend asked me recently, "What inspires you to write?"
>
> She is a writer herself, so I knew she wasn't asking me, 'Where do you get your ideas?' She would know that ideas are as random as shooting stars; they come while you're cleaning the bathtub, or watching *Four Weddings and a Funeral* for the ninth time, or in the morning when the last bit of your dream is fraying away, just before you open your eyes. You see it, then, what you've been searching for all these weeks or months, clear as day; you look at it and

think, "Oh. Yeah," and open your eyes. That wasn't what she was asking. And that was why I couldn't answer; I could only sit and stare at her with my mouth hanging gracelessly open, because all the answers that sprang immediately to mind answered the question she hadn't asked . . .

I'm glad the entire speech is printed here (as "What Inspires Me") because I was too busy choking and gasping to take it all in at the time: I was the "friend," and I am answered at last.

Her romance with David was such a solid partnership, even when his career meant they were living in different places. When Dave finally retired in 2001, they were able at last to fulfil their dream of moving together to the Oregon Coast, where they proceeded to live happily ever after—until Death, master of us all, ender of all stories, came for Pat on May 6, 2022.

It wasn't until May 10th that the awful news swept through the SFF world. We were so shocked, so stunned, so sad . . . We hadn't known Pat was ill. We hadn't had the chance to say goodbye.

The internet was full of tributes. On her blog "Myth & Moor," Terri Windling wrote:

> I admired Pat professionally, loved her personally, and have been profoundly influenced by her artistically . . . [H]er books have been lodestars for me—demonstrating, over and over again, the timeless power of myth and fairy tale tropes when wielded by a master writer. And a master of fantasy she certainly became: one of the very best of our age, as well as one of the most influential in the mythopoeic end of the fantasy field.

That night, for my own post in response to the news, I helplessly wrote:

> Far away, a sun has gone out.
> The light of the star

Introduction

bright in the night sky
Reaches us still
And will
For years to come.

You'll have noted by now that this introduction has said very little about the specific stories in this volume. That is because they are not mine to tell: they are yours, now: Pat speaking to you directly, letting you into one of her many worlds, inviting you to be her companion there.

Turn the page, and see where she takes you.

Ellen Kushner
New York City
October 2025

LADY OF THE SKULLS

THE LADY saw them ride across the plain: a company of six. Putting down her watering can, which was the bronze helm of some unfortunate knight, she leaned over the parapet, chin on her hand. They were all armed, their warhorses caparisoned; they glittered under the noon sun with silver-edged shields, jeweled bridles and sword hilts. What, she wondered as always in simple astonishment, did they imagine they had come to fight? She picked up the helm, poured water into a skull containing a miniature rosebush. The water came from within the tower, the only source on the entire barren, sun-cracked plain. The knights would ride around in the hot sun for hours, looking for entry. At sunset, she would greet them, carrying water.

She sighed noiselessly, troweling around the little rosebush with a dragon's claw. If they were too blind to find the tower door, why did they think they could see clearly within it? They, she thought in sudden impatience. They, they, they . . . they fed the plain with their bleached bones, they never learned. . . .

A carrion bird circled above her, counting heads. She scowled at it; it cried back at her, mocking. *You*, its black eye said, *never die. But you bring the dead to me.*

"They never listen to me," she said, looking over the plain again, her eyes prickling dryly. In the distance, lightning cracked apart the sky; purple clouds rumbled. But there was no rain in them, never any rain; the sky was as tearless as she. She moved from skull to skull along the parapet wall, watering things she had grown stubbornly from seeds that blew from distant, placid gardens in peaceful kingdoms. Some were grasses, weeds, or wildflowers. She did not care; she watered anything that grew.

The men below began their circling. Their mounts kicked up dust, snorting; she heard cursing, bewildered questions, then silence as they paused to rest. Sometimes they called her, pleading. But she could do nothing for them. They churned around the tower, bright, powerful, richly armed. She read the devices on their shields: three of Grenelief, one of Stoney Head, one of Dulcis Isle, one of Carnelaine. After a time, one man dropped out of the circle, stood back. His shield was simple: a red rose on white. Carnelaine, she thought, looking down at him, then realized he was looking up at her.

He would see a puff of airy sleeve, a red geranium in an upside-down skull. Lady of the Skulls, they called her, clamoring to enter. Sometimes they were more courteous, sometimes less. She watered, waiting for this one to call her. He did not; he guided his horse into the tower's shadow and dismounted. He took his helm off, sat down to wait, burrowing idly in the ground and flicking stones as he watched her sleeve sometimes, and sometimes the distant storm.

Drawn to his calm, the others joined him finally, flinging off pieces of armor. They cursed the hard ground and sat, their voices drifting up to her in the windless air as she continued her watering.

Like others before them, they spoke of what the most precious thing of the legendary treasure might be, besides elusive. They had made a pact, she gathered: If one obtained the treasure, he would divide it among those left living. She raised a brow. The one of Dulcis Isle, a dark-haired man wearing red jewels in his ears, said, "Anything of the dragon for me. They say it was a dragon's hoard once. They say that dragon bones are wormholed with magic, and if you move one bone the rest will follow. The bones will bring the treasure with them."

"I heard," said the man from Stoney Head, "there is a well and a fountain rising from it, and when the drops of the fountain touch ground they turn to diamonds."

"Don't talk of water," one of the three thick-necked, nut-haired men of Grenelief pleaded. "I drank all mine."

"All we must do is find the door. There's water within."

"What are you going to do?" the man of Carnelaine asked. "Hoist the water on your shoulder and carry it out?"

The straw-haired man from Stoney Head tugged at his long moustaches. He had a plain, blunt, energetic voice devoid of any humor. "I'll carry it out in my mouth. When I come back alive for the rest of it, there'll be plenty to carry it in. Skulls, if nothing else. I heard there's a sorceress's cauldron, looks like a rusty old pot—"

"May be that," another of Grenelief said.

"May be, but I'm going for the water. What else could be most precious in this heat-blasted place?"

"That's a point," the man of Dulcis Isle said. Then: "But, no, it's dragon bone for me."

"More to the point," the third of Grenelief said, aggrieved, "how do we get in the cursed place?"

"There's a lady up there watering plants," the man of Carnelaine said, and there were all their faces staring upward; she could have tossed jewels into their open mouths. "She knows we're here."

"It's the Lady," they murmured, hushed.

"Lady of the Skulls."

"Does she have hair, I wonder."

"She's old as the tower. She must be a skull."

"She's beautiful," the man of Stoney Head said shortly. "They always are, the ones who lure, the ones who guard, the ones who give death."

"Is it her tower?" the one of Carnelaine asked. "Or is she trapped?"

"What's the difference? When the spell is gone, so will she be. She's nothing real, just a piece of the tower's magic."

They shifted themselves as the tower's shadow shifted. The Lady took a sip of water out of the helm, then dipped her hand in it and ran it over her face. She wanted to lean over the edge and shout at them all: Go home, you silly, brainless fools. If you know so much, what are you doing here sitting on bare ground in front of a tower without a door waiting for a woman to kill you? They moved to one side of the tower, she to the other, as the sun climbed down the sky. She watched the sun set. Still the men refused to leave, though they had not a stick of wood to burn against the dark. She sighed her noiseless sigh and went down to greet them.

The fountain sparkled in the midst of a treasure she had long ceased to notice. She stepped around gold armor, black, gold-rimmed dragon bones, the white bones of princes. She took the plain silver goblet beside the rim of the well, and dipped it into the water, feeling the cooling mist from the little fountain. The man of Dulcis Isle was right about the dragon bones. The doorway was the dragon's open yawning maw, and it was invisible by day.

The last ray of sunlight touched the bone, limned a black, toothed opening that welcomed the men. Mute, they entered, and she spoke.

"You may drink the water, you may wander throughout the tower. If you make no choice, you may leave freely. Having left, you may never return. If you choose, you must make your choice by sunset tomorrow. If you choose the most precious thing in the tower, you may keep all that you see. If you choose wrongly, you will die before you leave the plain."

Their mouths were open again, their eyes stunned at what hung like vines from the old dragon's bones, what lay heaped upon the floor. Flicking, flicking, their eyes came across her finally, as she stood patiently holding the cup. Their eyes stopped at her: a tall, broad-shouldered, barefoot woman in a coarse white linen smock, her red hair bundled untidily on top of her head, her long skirt still splashed with the wine she had spilled in the tavern so long ago. In the torchlight it looked like blood.

They chose to sleep, as they always did, tired by the long journey, dazed by too much rich, vague color in the shadows. She sat on the steps and watched them for a little. One cried in his sleep. She went to the top of the tower after a while, where she could watch the stars. Under the moon, the flowers turned odd, secret colors, as if their true colors blossomed in another land's daylight, and they had left their pale shadows behind by night. She fell asleep naming the moon's colors.

In the morning, she went down to see who had had sense enough to leave.

They were all still there, searching, picking, discarding among the treasures on the floor, scattered along the spiraling stairs. Shafts of light from the narrow windows sparked fiery colors that constantly caught their eyes, made them drop what they had, reach out again. Seeing her, the one from Dulcis Isle said, trembling, his eyes stuffed with riches, "May we ask questions? What is this?"

"Don't ask her, Marlebane," the one from Stoney Head said brusquely. "She'll lie. They all do."

She stared at him. "I will only lie to you," she promised. She took the small treasure from the hand of the man from Dulcis Isle. "This is an acorn made of gold. If you swallow it, you will speak all the languages of humans and animals."

"And this?" one of Grenelief said eagerly, pushing next to her, holding something of silver and smoke.

"That is a bracelet made of a dragon's nostril bone. The jewel in it is its petrified eye. It watches for danger when you wear it."

The man of Carnelaine was playing a flute made from a wizard's thighbone. His eyes, the odd gray-green of the dragon's eye, looked dream-drugged with the music. The man of Stoney Head shook him roughly.

"Is that your choice, Ran?"

"No." He lowered the flute, smiling. "No, Corbeil."

"Then drop it before it seizes hold of you and you choose it. Have you seen yet what you might take?"

"No. Have you changed your mind?"

"No." He looked at the fountain, but, prudent, did not speak.

"Bram, look at this," said one brother of Grenelief to another. "Look!"

"I am looking, Yew."

"Look at it! Look at it, Ustor! Have you ever seen such a thing? Feel it! And watch: It vanishes, in light."

He held a sword; its hilt was solid emerald, its blade like water falling in clear light over stone. The Lady left them, went back up the stairs, her bare feet sending gold coins and jewels spinning down through the crosshatched shafts of light. She stared at the place on the horizon where the flat dusty gold of the plain met the parched dusty sky. Go, she thought dully. Leave all this and go back to the places where things grow. Go, she willed them, go, go, go, with the beat of her heart's blood. But no one came out the door beneath her. Someone, instead, came up the stairs.

"I have a question," said Ran of Carnelaine.

"Ask."

"What is your name?"

She had all but forgotten; it came to her again, after a beat of surprise. "Amaranth." He was holding a black rose in one hand, a silver lily in the other. If he chose one, the thorns would kill him; the other, flashing its pure light, would sear through his eyes into his brain.

"Amaranth. Another flower."

"So it is," she said indifferently. He laid the magic flowers on the parapet, picked a dying geranium leaf, smelled the miniature rose. "It has no smell," she said. He picked another dead leaf. He seemed always on the verge of smiling. It made him look sometimes wise and sometimes foolish. He drank out of the bronze watering helm; it was the color of his hair.

"This water is too cool and sweet to come out of such a barren plain," he commented. He seated himself on the wall, watching her. "Corbeil says you are not real. You look real enough to me." She was silent, picking dead clover out of the clover pot. "Tell me where you came from."

She shrugged. "A tavern."

"And how did you come here?"

She gazed at him. "How did you come here, Ran of Carnelaine?"

He did smile then, wryly. "Carnelaine is poor; I came to replenish its coffers."

"There must be less chancy ways."

"Maybe I wanted to see the most precious thing there is to be found. Will the plain bloom again, if it is found? Will you have a garden instead of skull-pots?"

"Maybe," she said levelly. "Or maybe I will disappear. Die when the magic dies. If you choose wisely, you'll have answers to your questions."

He shrugged. "Maybe I will not choose. There are too many precious things."

She glanced at him. He was trifling, wanting hints from her, answers couched in riddles. Shall I take rose or lily? Or wizard's thighbone? Tell me. Sword or water or dragon's eye? Some had questioned her so before.

She said simply, "I cannot tell you what to take. I do not know myself. As far as I have seen, everything kills." It was as close as she could come, as plain as she could make it: Leave.

But he said only, his smile gone, "Is that why you never left?" She stared at him again. "Walked out the door, crossed the plain on some dead king's horse and left?"

She said, "I cannot." She moved away from him, tending some wildflowers she called wind-bells, for she imagined their music as the night air tumbled down from the mountains to race across the plain. After a while, she heard his steps again, going down.

A voice summoned her: "Lady of the Skulls!" It was the man of Stoney

Head. She went down, blinking in the thick, dusty light. He stood stiffly, his face hard. They all stood still, watching.

"I will leave now," he said. "I may take anything?"

"Anything," she said, making her heart stone against him, a ghost's heart, so that she would not pity him. He went to the fountain, took a mouthful of water. He looked at her, and she moved to show him the hidden lines of the dragon's mouth. He vanished through the stones.

They heard him scream a moment later. The three of Grenelief stared toward the sound. They each wore pieces of a suit of armor that made the wearer invisible: one lacked an arm, another a thigh, the other his hands. Subtly their expressions changed, from shock and terror into something more complex. Five, she saw them thinking. Only five ways to divide it now.

"Anyone else?" she asked coldly. The man of Dulcis Isle slumped down onto the stairs, swallowing. He stared at her, his face gold-green in the light. He swallowed again. Then he shouted at her.

She had heard every name they could think of to shout before she had ever come to the tower. She walked up the stairs past him; he did not have the courage to touch her. She went to stand among her plants. Corbeil of Stoney Head lay where he had fallen, a little brown patch of wet earth beside his open mouth. As she looked, the sun dried it, and the first of the carrion birds landed.

She threw bones at the bird, cursing, though it looked unlikely that anyone would be left to take his body back. She hit the bird a couple of times, then another came. Then someone took the bone out of her hand, drew her back from the wall.

"He's dead," Ran said simply. "It doesn't matter to him whether you throw bones at the birds or at him."

"I have to watch," she said shortly. She added, her eyes on the jagged line the parapet made against the sky, like blunt, worn dragon's teeth, "You keep coming, and dying. Why do you all keep coming? Is treasure worth being breakfast for the carrion crows?"

"It's worth many different things. To the brothers of Grenelief it means adventure, challenge, adulation if they succeed. To Corbeil it was something to be won, something he could have that no one else could get. He would have sat on top of the pile and let men look up to him, hating and envying."

"He was a cold man. Cold men feed on a cold fire. Still," she added, sighing,

"I would have preferred to see him leave on his feet. What does the treasure mean to you?"

"Money." He smiled his vague smile. "It's not in me to lose my life over money. I'd sooner walk empty-handed out the door. But there's something else."

"What?"

"The riddle itself. That draws us all, at heart. What is the most precious thing? To see it, to hold it, above all to recognize it and choose it—that's what keeps us coming and traps you here." She stared at him, saw, in his eyes, the wonder that he felt might be worth his life.

She turned away; her back to him, she watered bleeding heart and columbine, stonily ignoring what the crows were doing below. "If you find the thing itself," she asked dryly, "what will you have left to wonder about?"

"There's always life."

"Not if you are killed by wonder."

He laughed softly, an unexpected sound, she thought, in that place. "Wouldn't you ride across the plain if you heard tales of this tower, to try to find the most precious thing in it?"

"Nothing's precious to me," she said, heaving a cauldron of dandelions into shadow. "Not down there, anyway. If I took one thing away with me, it would not be sword or gold or dragon bone. It would be whatever is alive."

He touched the tiny rose. "You mean, like this? Corbeil would never have died for this."

"He died for a mouthful of water."

"He thought it was a mouthful of jewels." He sat beside the rose, his back to the air, watching her pull pots into shadow against the noon light. "Which makes him twice a fool, I suppose. Three times a fool: for being wrong, for being deluded, and for dying. What a terrible place this is. It strips you of all delusions, and then it strips your bones."

"It is terrible," she said somberly. "Yet those who leave without choosing never seem to get the story straight. They must always talk of the treasure they didn't take, not of the bones they didn't leave."

"It's true. Always, they take wonder with them out of this tower and they pass it on to every passing fool." He was silent a little, still watching her. "Amaranth," he said slowly. "That's the flower in poetry that never dies. It's apt."

"Yes."

"And there is another kind of Amaranth, that's fiery and beautiful and it dies. . . ." Her hands stilled, her eyes widened, but she did not speak. He leaned against the hot, crumbling stones, his dragon's eyes following her like a sunflower following the sun. "What were you," he asked, "when you were the Amaranth that could die?"

"I was one of those faceless women who brought you wine in a tavern. Those you shout at, and jest about, and maybe give a coin to and maybe not, depending how we smile."

He was silent, so silent she thought he had gone, but when she turned, he was still there; only his smile had gone. "Then I've seen you," he said softly, "many times, in many places. But never in a place like this."

"The man from Stoney Head expected someone else, too."

"He expected a dream."

"He saw what he expected: Lady of the Skulls." She pulled wild mint into a shady spot under some worn tapestry. "And so he found her. That's all I am now. You were better off when all I served was wine."

"You didn't build this tower."

"How do you know? Maybe I got tired of the laughter and the coins and I made a place for myself where I could offer coins and give nothing."

"Who built this tower?"

She was silent, crumbling a mint leaf between her fingers. "I did," she said at last. "The Amaranth who never dies."

"Did you?" He was oddly pale; his eyes glittered in the light as if at the shadow of danger. "You grow roses out of thin air in this blistered plain; you try to beat back death for us with our own bones. You curse our stupidity and our fate, not us. Who built this tower for you?" She turned her face away, mute. He said softly, "The other Amaranth, the one that dies, is also called Love-lies-bleeding."

"It was the last man," she said abruptly, her voice husky, shaken with sudden pain, "who offered me a coin for love. I was so tired of being touched and then forgotten, of hearing my name spoken and then not, as if I were only real when I was looked at and just something to forget after that, like you never remember the flowers you toss away. So I said to him: No, and no, and no. And then I saw his eyes. They were amber with thorns of dark in them: sorcerer's eyes. He said, 'Tell me your name.' And I said, 'Amaranth,' and he laughed and laughed and I could only stand there, with the wine I had brought him overturned on my tray, spilling down my skirt. He said, 'Then you shall make a tower of your name, for the tower is already built in your heart.'"

"Love-lies-bleeding," he whispered.

"He recognized that Amaranth."

"Of course he did. It was what died in his own heart."

She turned then, wordless, to look at him. He was smiling again, though his face was still blanched under the hard, pounding light, and the sweat shone in his hair. She said, "How do you know him?"

"Because I have seen this tower before and I have seen in it the woman we all expected, the only woman some men ever know . . . And every time we come expecting her, the woman who lures us with what's most precious to us and kills us with it, we build the tower around her again and again and again. . . ."

She gazed at him. A tear slid down her cheek and then another. "I thought it was my tower," she whispered. "The Amaranth that never dies but only lives forever to watch men die."

"It's all of us," he sighed. In the distance, thunder rumbled. "We all build towers, then dare each other to enter. . . ." He picked up the little rose in its skull-pot and stood abruptly; she followed him to the stairs.

"Where are you going with my rose?"

"Out."

She followed him down, protesting, "But it's mine!"

"You said we could choose anything."

"It's just a worthless thing I grew, it's nothing of the tower's treasure. If you must take after all, choose something worth your life!"

He glanced back at her, as they rounded the tower stairs to the bottom. His face was bone-white, but he could still smile. "I will give you back your rose," he said, "if you will let me take the Amaranth."

"But I am the only Amaranth."

He strode past his startled companions, whose hands were heaped with this, *no this*, and *maybe this*. As if the dragon's magical eye had opened in his own eye, he led her himself into the dragon's mouth.

WONDERS OF THE INVISIBLE WORLD

I AM THE ANGEL sent to Cotton Mather. It took me some time to get his attention. He lay on the floor with his eyes closed; he prayed fervently, sometimes murmuring, sometimes shouting. Apparently the household was used to it. I heard footsteps pass his study door; a woman—his wife Abigail?—called to someone: "If your throat is no better tomorrow, we'll have Phillip pee in a cup for you to gargle." From the way the house smelled, Phillip didn't bother much with cups. Cotton Mather smelled of smoke and sweat and wet wool. Winter had come early. The sky was black, the ground was white, the wind pinched like a witch and whined like a starving dog. There was no color in the landscape and no mercy. Cotton Mather prayed to see the invisible world.

He wanted an angel.

"O Lord," he said, in desperate, hoarse, weary cadences, like a sick child talking itself to sleep. "Thou hast given angelic visions to Thy innocent children to defend them from their demons. Remember Thy humble servant, who prostrates himself in the dust, vile worm that I am, forsaking food and comfort and sleep, in humble hope that Thou might bestow upon Thy humble servant the blessing and hope at this harsh and evil time: a glimpse of Thy shadow, a flicker of light in Thine eye, a single word from Thy mouth. Show me Thy messengers of good who fly between the visible and invisible worlds. Grant me, O God, a vision."

I cleared my throat a little. He didn't open his eyes. The fire was dying down. I wondered who replenished it, and if the sight of Mather's bright, winged creature would surprise anyone, with all the witches, devils and demented goldfinches perched on rafters all over New England. The firelight spilling across the wide planks glowed just beyond his outstretched hand. He lay in dim lights and fluttering shadows, in the long, long night of history, when no one could ever see clearly after sunset, and witches and angels and living dreams trembled just beyond the fire.

"Grant me, O God, a vision."

I was standing in front of his nose. He was lost in days of fasting and desire, trying to conjure an angel out of his head. According to his writings, what he expected to see was the generic white male with wings growing out of his shoulders, fair-haired, permanently beardless, wearing a long white nightgown and a gold dinner plate on his head. This was what intrigued Durham, and why he had hired me: he couldn't believe that both good and evil in the Puritan imagination could be so banal.

But I was what Mather wanted: something as colorless and pure as the snow that lay like the hand of God over the earth, harsh, exacting, unambiguous. Fire, their salvation against the cold, was red and belonged to Hell.

"O Lord."

It was the faintest of whispers. He was staring at my feet.

They were bare and shining and getting chilled. The ring of diamonds in my halo contained controls for light, for holograms like my wings, a map disc, a local-history disc in case I got totally bewildered by events, and a recorder disc that had caught the sudden stammer in Mather's last word. He had asked for an angel; he got an angel. I wished he would quit staring at my feet and throw another log on the fire.

He straightened slowly, pushing himself off the floor while his eyes traveled upward. He was scarcely thirty at the time of the trials; he resembled his father at that age more than the familiar Pelham portrait of Mather in his sixties, soberly dressed, with a wig like a cream puff on his head, and a firm, resigned mouth. The young Mather had long dark hair, a spare, handsome, clean-shaven face, searching, credulous eyes. His eyes reached my face finally, cringing a little, as if he half expected a demon's red, leering face attached to the angel's body. But he found what he expected. He began to cry.

He cried silently, so I could speak. His writings are mute about much of the angel's conversation. Mostly it predicted Mather's success as a writer, great reviews and spectacular sales in America and Europe. I greeted him, gave him the message from God, quoted Ezekiel, and then got down to business. By then he had stopped crying, wiped his face with his dusty sleeve and cheered up at the prospect of fame.

"There are troubled children," I said, "who have seen me."

"They speak of you in their misery," he said gratefully. "You give them strength against evil."

"Their afflictions are terrible."

"Yes," he whispered.

"You have observed their torments."

"Yes."

"You have taken them into your home, borne witness to their complaints, tried to help them cast out their tormentors."

"I have tried."

"You have wrestled with the invisible world."

"Yes."

We weren't getting very far. He still knelt on the hard floor, as he had done for hours, perhaps days; he could see me more clearly than he had seen anything in the dark in his life. He had forgotten the fire. I tried to be patient. Good angels were beyond temperament, even while at war with angels who had disgraced themselves by exhibiting human characteristics. But the floorboards were getting very cold.

"You have felt the invisible chains about them," I prodded. "The invisible, hellish things moving beneath their bedclothes."

"The children cannot seem to stand my books," he said a little querulously, with a worried frown. "My writing sends them into convulsions. At the mere act of opening my books, they fall down as dead upon the floor. Yet how can I lead them gently back to God's truth if the truth acts with such violence against them?"

"It is not against them," I reminded him, "but against the devil, who," I added, inspired, "takes many shapes."

He nodded, and became voluble. "Last week he took the shape of thieves who stole three sermons from me. And of a rat—or something like a hellish rat—we could feel in the air, but not see."

"A rat."

"And sometimes a bird, a yellow bird, the children say—they see it perched on the fingers of those they name witches."

"And since they say it, it is so."

He nodded gravely. "God made nothing more innocent than children."

I let that pass. I was his delusion, and if I had truly been sent to him from God, then God and Mather agreed on everything.

"Have they"—this was Durham's suggestion—"not yet seen the devil in the shape of a black horse who spews fire between its teeth, and is ridden by three witches, each more beautiful than the last?"

He stared at me, then caught himself imagining the witches and blinked. "No," he breathed. "No one has seen such a thing. Though the Shape of Goody Bishop in her scarlet bodice and her lace had been seen over the beds of honest married men."

"What did she do to them?"

"She hovered. She haunted them. For this and more she was hanged."

For wearing a color and inciting the imagination, she was hanged. I refrained from commenting that since her Shape had done the hovering, it was her Shape that should have been hanged. But it was almost worth my researcher's license. "In God's justice," I said piously, "her soul dwells." I had almost forgotten the fire; this dreary, crazed, malicious atmosphere was more chilling than the cold.

"She had a witchmark," Mather added. "The witch's teat." His eyes were wide, marveling; he had conjured witches as well as angels out of his imagination. I suppose it was easier, in that harsh world, to make demons out of your neighbors, with their imperfections, tempers, rheumy eyes, missing teeth, irritating habits and smells, than to find angelic beauty in them. But I wasn't there to judge Mather. I could hear Durham's intense voice: *Imagination. Imagery. I want to know what they pulled out of their heads. They invented their devil, but all they could do was make him talk like a bird? Don't bother with a moral viewpoint. I want to know what Mather saw. This was the man who believed that thunder was caused by the sulfurous farts of decaying vegetation. Why? Don't ask me why. You're a researcher. Go research.*

Research the imagination. It was as obsolete as the appendix in most adults, except for those in whom, like the appendix, it became inflamed for no reason. Durham's curiosity seemed as aberrated as Mather's; they both craved visions. But in his world, Durham could afford the luxury of being crazed. In this world, only the crazed, the adolescent girls, the trial judges, Mather himself, were sane.

I was taking a moral viewpoint. But Mather was still talking, and the recorder was catching his views, not mine. I had asked Durham once, after an exasperating journey to some crowded, airless, fly-infested temple covered with phallic symbols to appear as a goddess, to stop hiring me; the Central Research Computer had obviously got its records mixed when it recommended me to him. Our historical viewpoints were thoroughly incompatible. "No, they're not," he had said obnoxiously, and refused to elaborate. He paid well. He paid very well. So here I was, in frozen colonial New England, listening to Cotton Mather talk about brooms.

"The witches ride them," he said, still wide-eyed. "Sometimes three to a besom. To their foul Witch's Sabbaths."

Their foul Sabbaths, he elaborated, consisted of witches gathering in some boggy pasture where the demons talked with the voices of frogs, listening to a fiendish sermon, drinking blood, and plotting to bring back pagan customs like dancing around a maypole. I wondered if, being an angel of God, I was supposed to know all this already, and if Mather would wonder later why I had listened. Durham and I had argued about this, about the ethics and legalities of me pretending to be Mather's delusion.

"What's the problem?" he had asked. "You think the real angel is going to show up later?"

Mather was still speaking, in a feverish trance caused most likely by too much fasting, prayer and mental agitation. Evil eyes, he was talking about, and "things" that were hairy all over. They apparently caused neighbors to blame one another for dead pigs, wagons stuck in potholes, sickness, lust and deadly boredom. I was getting bored myself, by then, and thoroughly depressed. Children's fingers had pointed at random, and wherever they pointed, they created a witch. So much for the imagination. It was malignant here, an instrument of cruelty and death.

"He did not speak to the court, neither to defend his innocence nor confess his guilt," Mather was saying solemnly. "He was a stubborn old man. They piled stones upon him until his tongue stuck out and he died. But he never spoke. They had already hanged his wife. He spoke well enough then, accusing her."

I had heard enough.

"God protect the innocent," I said, and surprised myself, for it was a prayer to something. I added, more gently, for Mather, blinking out of his trance, looked worried, as if I had accused him, "Be comforted. God will give you strength to bear all tribulations in these dark times. Be patient and faithful, and in the fullness of time, you will be rewarded with the truth of your life."

Not standard Puritan dogma, but all he heard was "reward" and "truth." I raised my hand in blessing. He flung himself down to kiss the floor at my feet. I activated the controls in my halo and went home.

Durham was waiting for me at the Researchers' Terminus. I pulled the recorder disc out of my halo, fed it to the computer, and then stepped out of the warp chamber. While the computer analyzed my recording to see if I had broken any of one thousand, five hundred and sixty-three regulations, I took off my robe and my blond hair and dumped them and my halo into Durham's arms.

"Well?" he said, not impatient, just intent, not even seeing me as I pulled a skirt and tunic over my head. I was still cold, and worried about my researcher's license, which the computer would refuse to return if I had violated history. Durham had eyes like Cotton Mather's, I saw for the first time: dark, burning, but with a suggestion of humor in them. "What did you find? Speak to me, Nici."

"Nothing," I said shortly. "You're out several million credits for nothing. It was a completely dreary bit of history, not without heroism but entirely without poetry. And if I've lost my license because of this—I'm not even sure I understand what you're trying to do."

"I'm researching for a history of imaginative thought."

Durham was always researching unreadable subjects. "Starting when?" I asked tersely, pulling on a boot. "The cave paintings at Lascaux?"

"No art," he said. "More speculative than that. Less formal. Closer to chaos." He smiled, reading my mind. "Like me."

"You're a disturbed man, Durham. You should have your unconscious scanned."

"I like it the way it is: a bubbling little morass of unpredictable metaphors."

"They aren't unpredictable," I said. "They're completely predictable. Everything imaginable is accessible, and everything accessible has been imagined by the Virtual computer, which has already researched every kind of imaginative thought since the first bison got painted on a rock. That way nothing like what happened in Cotton Mather's time can happen to us. So—"

"*Wonders of the Invisible World*," Durham interrupted. He hadn't heard a word. "It's a book by Mather. He was talking about angels and demons. We would think of the invisible in terms of atomic particles. Both are unseen yet named, and immensely powerful—"

"Oh, stop. You're mixing atoms and angels. One exists, the other doesn't."

"That's what I'm trying to get at, Nici—the point where existence is totally immaterial, where the passion, the belief in something creates a situation completely ruled by the will to believe."

"That's insanity."

He smiled again, cheerfully. He tended to change his appearance according to what he was researching; he wore a shimmering bodysuit that showed all his muscles, and milk-white hair. Except for the bulky build of his face and the irreverence in his eyes, he might have been Mather's angel. My more androgynous face worked better. "Maybe," he said. "But I find the desire, the passion, coupled with the accompanying imagery, fascinating."

"You are a throwback," I muttered. "You belong to some barbaric age when people imagined things to kill each other for." The computer flashed a light; I breathed a sigh of relief. Durham got his tape, and the computer's analysis; I retrieved my license.

"Next time—" Durham began.

"There won't be a next time." I headed for the door. "I'm sick of appearing as twisted pieces of people's imagination. And one of these days I'm going to find myself in court."

"But you do it so well," he said softly. "You even convince the Terminus computer."

I glared at him. "Just leave me alone."

"All right," he said imperturbably. "Don't call me, I'll call you."

I was tired, but I took the tube-walk home, to get the blood moving in my feet, and to see some light and color after that bleak, dangerous world.

The moving walkway, encased in its clear tube, wound up into the air, balanced on its centipede escalator and station legs. I could see the gleaming city domes stretch like a long cluster of soap bubbles toward the afternoon sun, and I wondered that somewhere within the layers of time in this place there was a small port town on the edge of a vast, unexplored continent where Mather had flung himself down on his floorboards and prayed an angel out of himself.

He could see an angel here without praying for it. He could be an angel. He could soar into the eye of God if he wanted, on wings of gold and light. He could reach out, even in the tube-walk, punch in a credit number, plug into his implant or his wrist controls, and activate the screen above his head. He could have any reality on the menu, or any reality he could dream up, since everything imagined and imaginable and every combination of it had been programmed into the Virtual computer. And then he could walk out of the station into his living room and change the world all over again.

I had to unplug Brock when I got home; he had fallen asleep at the terminal. He opened heavy eyelids and yawned.

"Hi, Matrix."

"Don't call me that," I said mechanically. He grinned fleetingly and nestled deeper into the bubble-chair. I sat down on the couch and pulled my boots off again. It was warm, in this time; I finally felt it.

Brock asked, "What were you?"

Even he knew Durham that well. "An angel."

"What's that?"

"Look it up."

He touched the controls on his wrist absently. He was a calm child, with blue, clinical eyes and angelic hair that didn't come from me. He sprouted wings and a halo suddenly, and grunted. "What's it for?"

"It talks to God."

"What God?"

"In God We Trust. That God."

He grunted again. "Pre-Real."

I nodded, leaned back tiredly, and watched him, wondering how much longer he would be neat, attentive, curious, polite, before he shaved his head, studded his scalp and eyebrows with jewels and implants, got eye-implants that held no expression whatsoever, inserted a CD player into his earlobe, and never called me Matrix again. Maybe he would go live with his father. I hadn't seen him since Brock was born, but Brock knew exactly who he was, where he was, what he did. Speculation was unnecessary, except for aberrants like Durham.

The outercom signaled; half a dozen faces appeared onscreen: Brock's friends who lived in the station complex. They trooped in, settled themselves around Brock, and plugged into their wrists. They were playing an adventure game, a sort of space-chase, where they were intergalactic thieves raiding alien zoos of rare animals and selling them to illegal restaurants. The computer played the team of highly trained intergalactic space-patrollers. The thieves were constantly falling into black holes, getting burnt up speeding too fast into strange atmospheres, and ambushed by the wily patrollers. One of them, Indra, tried to outwit the computer by coming up with the most bizarre alien species she could imagine; the computer always gave her the images she wanted. I watched for a while. Then an image came into my head, of an old man in a field watching his neighbors pile stones on him until he could no longer breathe.

I got up, went into my office, and called Durham.

"I could have stopped it," I said tersely. He was silent, not because he didn't know what I was talking about, but because he did. "I was an angel from God. I could have changed the message."

"You wouldn't have come back," he said simply. It was true. I would have been abandoned there, powerless, a beardless youth with breasts in a long robe raving about the future, who would have become just one more witch for the children to condemn. He added, "You're a researcher. Researchers don't get emotional about history. There's nothing left of that time but some old bones in a museum from where they dug them up to build a station complex. A gravestone with an angel on it, a little face with staring eyes, and a pair of cupid wings. What's to mope about? I put a bonus in your account. Go spend it somewhere."

"How much?"

He was silent again, his eyes narrowed slightly. "Not enough for you to go back. Go get drunk, Nici. This is not you."

"I'm haunted," I whispered, I thought too softly for him to hear. He shook his head, not impatiently.

"The worst was over by then, anyway. Heroics are forbidden to researchers. You know that. The angel Mather dreamed up only told him what he wanted to hear. Tell him anything else and he'd call you a demon and refuse to listen. You know all this. Why are you taking this personally? You didn't take being a goddess in that Hindu temple personally. Thank God," he added with an obnoxious chuckle. I grunted at him morosely and got rid of his face.

I found a vegetable bar in the kitchen, and wandered back into the living room. The space-thieves were sneaking around a zoo on the planet Hublatt. They were all imaging animals onscreen while their characters studied the specimens. "We're looking for a Yewsalope," Brock said intently. "Its eyeballs are poisonous, but if you cook them just right, they look like boiled eggs to whoever you're trying to poison."

The animals were garish in their barred cells: purple, orange, cinnamon, polka-dotted, striped. There were walking narwhales, a rhinoceros horn with feet and eyes, something like an octopus made out of elephant trunks, an amorphous green blob that constantly changed shape.

"How will you know a Yewsalope when you see it?" I asked, fascinated with their color combinations, their imagery. Brock shrugged slightly.

"We'll know."

A new animal appeared in an empty cage: a tall, two-legged creature with long golden hair and wings made of feathers or light. It held on to the bars with its hands, looking sadly out. I blinked.

"You have an angel in your zoo."

I heard Brock's breath. Indra frowned. "It could fly out. Why doesn't it fly? Whose is it? Anyway, this zoo is only for animals. This looks like some species of human. It's illegal," she said, fastidiously for a thief, "on Hublatt."

"It's an angel," Brock said.

"What's an angel? Is it yours?"

Brock shook his head. They all shook their heads, eyes onscreen, wanting to move on. But the image lingered: a beautiful, melancholy figure, half-human, half-light, trapped and powerless behind its bars.

"Why doesn't it just fly?" Indra breathed. "It could just fly. Brock—"

"It's not mine," Brock insisted. And then he looked at me, his eyes wide, so calm and blue that it took me a moment to transfer my attention from their color to what they were asking.

I stared at the angel, and felt the bars under my hands. I swallowed, seeing what it saw: the long, dark night of history that it was powerless to change, to illumine, because it was powerless to speak except to lie.

"Matrix?" Brock whispered. I closed my eyes.

"Don't call me that."

When I opened my eyes, the angel had disappeared.

THE LION AND THE LARK

There was once a merchant who lived in an ancient and magical city with his three daughters. They were all very fond of each other, and as happy as those with love and leisure and wealth can afford to be. The eldest, named Pearl, pretended domesticity. She made bread and forgot to let it rise before she baked it; she pricked her fingers sewing black satin garters; she inflicted such oddities as eggplant soup and barley muffins on her long-suffering family. She was very beautiful, though a trifle awkward and absent-minded, and she had suitors who risked their teeth on her hard, flat bread as boldly as knights of old slew dragons for the heart's sake. The second daughter, named Diamond, wore delicate, gold-rimmed spectacles, and was never without a book or a crossword puzzle at hand. She discoursed learnedly on the origins of the phoenix and the conjunctions of various astrological signs. She had an answer for everything and was considered by all her suitors to be wondrously wise.

The youngest daughter, called Lark, sang a great deal but never spoke much. Because her voice was so like her mother's, her father doted on her. She was by no means the fairest of the three daughters; she did not shine with beauty or wit. She was pale and slight, with dark eyes, straight, serious brows, and dark braided hair. She had a loving and sensible heart, and she adored her family, though they worried her with their extravagances and foolishness. She wore Pearl's crooked garters, helped Diamond with her crossword puzzles, and heard odd questions arise from deep in her mind when she sang. *What is life?* she would wonder. *What is love? What is man?*

This last gave her a good deal to ponder, as she watched her father shower his daughters with chocolates and taffeta gowns and gold bracelets. The young gentlemen who came calling seemed especially puzzling. They sat in their velvet shirts and their leather boots, nibbling burnt cakes and praising Diamond's mind, and all the while their eyes said other things. Now, their eyes said. Now. Then: *Patience, patience.* "You are flowers," their mouths said, "You are jewels, you are golden dreams." Their eyes said: *I eat flowers, I burn with dreams, I have a tower without a door in my heart, and I will keep you there . . .*

Her sisters seemed fearless in the face of this power—whether from innocence or design, Lark was uncertain. Since she was wary of men and seldom spoke to them, she felt herself safe. She spoke mostly to her father, who only had a foolish, doting look in his eyes, and who of all men could make her smile.

One day their father left on a long journey to a distant city where he had lucrative business dealings. Before he left, he promised to bring his daughters whatever they asked for. Diamond, in a riddling mood, said merrily, "Bring us our names!"

"Oh, yes," Pearl pleaded, kissing his balding pate. "I do love pearls." She was wearing as many as she had, on her wrists, in her hair, on her shoes. "I always want more."

"But," their father said with an anxious glance at his youngest, who was listening with her grave, slightly perplexed expression, "does Lark love larks?"

Her face changed instantly, growing so bright she looked almost beautiful. "Oh, yes. Bring me my singing name, Father. I would rather have that than all the lifeless, deathless jewels in the world."

Her sisters laughed; they petted her and kissed her, and told her that she was still a child to hunger after worthless presents. Someday she would learn to ask for gifts that would outlast love, for when love had ceased, she would still possess what it had once been worth.

"But what is love?" she asked, confused. "Can it be bought like yardage?" But they only laughed harder and gave her no answers.

She was still puzzling ten days later when their father returned. Pearl was in the kitchen baking spinach tea cakes, and Diamond in the library, dozing over the philosophical writings of Lord Thiggut Moselby. Lark heard a knock at the door, and then the lovely, liquid singing of a lark. Laughing, she ran down the hall before the servants could come and swung open the door to greet their father.

He stared at her. In his hands he held a little silver cage. Within the cage, the lark sang constantly, desperately, each note more beautiful than the last, as if, coaxing the rarest, finest song from itself, it might buy its freedom. As Lark reached for it, she saw the dark blood mount in her father's face, the veins throb in his temples. Before she could touch the cage, he lifted it high over his head, dashed it with all his might to the stone steps.

"No!" he shouted. The lark fluttered within the bent silver; his boot lifted over cage and bird, crushed both into the stones.

"No!" Lark screamed. And then she put both fists to her mouth and said nothing more, retreating as far as she could without moving from the sudden, incomprehensible violence. Dimly she heard her father sobbing. He was on his knees, his face buried in her skirt. She moved finally, unclenched one hand, allowed it to touch his hair.

"What is it, Father?" she whispered. "Why have you killed the lark?"

He made a great, hollow sound, like the groan of a tree split to its heart. "Because I have killed you."

In the kitchen, Pearl arranged burnt tea cakes on a pretty plate. The maid who should have opened the door hummed as she dusted the parlor and thought of the carriage driver's son. Upstairs, Diamond woke herself up mid-snore and stared dazedly at Lord Moselby's famous words and wondered, for just an instant, why they sounded so empty. *That has nothing to do with life*, she protested, and then went back to sleep. Lark sat down on the steps beside the mess of feathers and silver and blood, and listened to her father's broken words.

"On the way back . . . we drove through a wood . . . just today, it was . . . I had not found you a lark. I heard one singing. I sent the post boy looking one way, I searched another. I followed the lark's song, and saw it finally, resting on the head of a great stone lion." His face wrinkled and fought itself; words fell like stones, like the tread of a stone beast. "A long line of lions stretched up the steps of a huge castle. Vines covered it so thickly it seemed no light could pass through the windows. It looked abandoned. I gave it no thought. The lark had all my attention. I took off my hat and crept up to it. I had it, I had it . . . singing in my hat and trying to fly. . . . And then the lion turned its head to look at me."

Lark shuddered; she could not speak. She felt her father shudder too.

"It said, 'You have stolen my lark.' Its tail began to twitch. It opened its stone mouth wide to show me its teeth. 'I will kill you for that.' And it gathered its body into a crouch. I babbled—I made promises—I am not a young man to run from lions. My heart nearly burst with fear. I wish it had . . . I promised—"

"What," she whispered, "did you promise?"

"Anything it wanted."

"And what did it want?"

"The first thing that met me when I arrived home from my journey." He hid his face against her, shaking her with his sobs. "I thought it would be the cat! It always suns itself at the gate! Or Columbine at worst—she always wants an excuse to leave her work. Why did you answer the door? Why?"

Her eyes filled with sudden tears. "Because I heard the lark."

Her father lifted his head. "You shall not go," he said fiercely. "I'll bar the doors. The lion will never find you. If it does, I'll shoot it, burn it—"

"How can you harm a stone lion? It could crash through the door and drag me into the street whenever it chooses." She stopped abruptly, for an odd, confused violence tangled her thoughts. She wanted to make sounds she had never heard from herself before. *You killed me for a bird!* she wanted to shout. *A father is nothing but a foolish old man*! Then she thought more calmly, *But I always knew that.* She stood up, gently pried his fingers from her skirt. "I'll go now. Perhaps I can make a bargain with this lion. If it's a lark it wants, I'll sing to it. Perhaps I can go and come home so quickly my sisters will not even know."

"They will never forgive me."

"Of course they will." She stepped over the crushed cage, started down the path without looking back. "I have."

But the sun had begun to set before she found the castle deep in the forest beyond the city. Even Pearl, gaily proffering tea cakes, must notice an insufficiency of Lark, and down in the pantry, Columbine would be whispering of the strange, bloody smear she had to clean off the porch. . . . The stone lion, of pale marble, snarling a warning on its pedestal, seemed to leap into her sight between the dark trees. To her horror, she saw behind it a long line of stone lions, one at each broad step leading up to the massive, barred doors of the castle.

"Oh," she breathed, cold with terror, and the first lion turned its ponderous head. A final ray of sunlight gilded its eye. It stared at her until the light faded.

She heard it whisper, "Who are you?"

"I am the lark," she said tremulously, "my father sent to replace the one he stole."

"Can you sing?"

She sang, blind and trembling, while the dark wood rustled around her, grew close. A hand slid over her mouth, a voice spoke into her ear. "Not very well, it seems."

She felt rough stubbled skin against her cheek, arms tense with muscle; the voice, husky and pleasant, murmured against her hair. She turned, amazed, alarmed for different reasons. "Not when I am so frightened," she said to the shadowy face above hers. "I expected to be eaten."

She saw a sudden glint of teeth. "If you wish."

"I would rather not be."

"Then I will leave that open to negotiation. You are very brave. And very honest to come here. I expected your father to send along the family cat or some little yapping powder puff of a dog."

"Why did you terrify him so?"

"He took my lark. Being stone by day, I have so few pleasures."

"Are you bewitched?"

He nodded at the castle. Candles and torches appeared on steps now. A row of men stood where the lions had been, waiting, while a line of pages carrying light trooped down the steps to guide them. "That is my castle. I have been under a spell so long I scarcely remember why. My memory has been turning to stone for some time, now. . . . I am only human at night, and sunlight is dangerous to me." He touched her cheek with his hand; unused to being touched, she started. Then, unused to being touched, she took a step toward him. He was tall and lean, and if the mingling of fire and moonlight did not lie, his face was neither foolish nor cruel. He was unlike her sisters' suitors; there was a certain sadness in his voice, and hesitancy and humor that made her want to hear him speak. He did not touch her again when she drew closer, but she heard the pleased smile in his voice. "Will you have supper with me?" he asked. "And tell me the story of your life?"

"It has no story yet."

"You are here. There is a story in that." He took her hand then and drew it under his arm. He led her past the pages and the armed men, up the stairs to the open doors. His face, she found, was quite easy to look at. He had tawny hair and eyes, and rough, strong, graceful features that were young in expression and happier than their experience.

"Tell me your name," he asked, as she crossed his threshold.

"Lark," she answered, and he laughed.

His name, she discovered over asparagus soup, was Perrin. Over salmon and partridge and salad, she discovered that he was gentle and courteous to his servants, had an ear for his musicians' playing, and had lean, strong hands that moved easily among the jeweled goblets and gold-rimmed plates. Over port and nuts, she discovered that his hands, choosing walnuts and enclosing them to crack them, made her mouth go dry and her heart beat. When he opened her palm to put a nut into it, she felt something melt through her from throat to thigh, and for the first time in her life she wished she were beautiful. Over candlelight, as he led her to her room, she saw herself in his eyes. In his bed, astonished, she thought she discovered how simple life was.

And so they were married, under moonlight, by a priest who was bewitched by day and pontifical by night. Lark slept until dusk and sang until morning. She was, she wrote her sisters and her father, entirely happy. Divinely happy. No one could believe how happy. When wistful questions rose to the surface of her mind, she pushed them under again ruthlessly. Still they came—words bubbling up—stubborn, half-coherent: *Who cast this spell and is my love still in danger? How long can I so blissfully ignore the fact that by day I am married to a stone, and by night to a man who cannot bear the touch of sunlight? Should we not do something to break the spell? Why is even the priest, who preaches endlessly about the light of grace, content to live only in the dark?* "We are used to it," Perrin said lightly, when she ventured these questions, and then he made her laugh, in the ways he had, so that she forgot to ask if living in the dark, and in a paradox, was something men inherently found more comfortable than women.

One day she received letters from both sisters saying that they were to be married in the same ceremony, and she must come, she could not refuse them, they absolutely refused to be married without her; and if their bridegrooms cast themselves disconsolately into a dozen millponds, or hung themselves from a hundred pear trees, not even that would move them to marry without her presence.

"I see I must go," she said with delight. She flung her arms around Perrin's neck. "Please come," she pleaded. "I don't want to leave you. Not for a night, nor for a single hour. You'll like my sisters—they're funny and foolish, and wiser, in their ways, than I am."

"I cannot," he whispered, loath to refuse her anything.

"Please."

"I dare not."

"Please."

"If I am touched by light as fine as thread, you will not see me again for seven years except in the shape of a dove."

"Seven years," she said numbly, terrified. Then she thought of lovely, clumsy Pearl and her burnt tea cakes, and of Diamond and her puzzles and earnest discourses on the similarities between the moon and a dragon's egg. She pushed her face against Perrin, torn between her various loves, gripping him in anguish. "Please," she begged. "I must see them. But I cannot leave you. But I must go to them. I promise: no light will find you, my night-love. No light, ever."

So her father sealed a room in his house so completely that by day it was dark as night, and by night as dark as death. By chance, or perhaps because, deep in the most secret regions of his mind he thought to free Lark from her strange, enchanted husband and bring her back to light and into his life, he used a piece of unseasoned wood to make a shutter. While Lark busied herself hanging pearls on Pearl, diamonds on Diamond, and swathing them both in yards of lace, Sun opened a hair-fine crack in the green wood where Perrin waited.

The wedding was a sumptuous, decadent affair. Both brides were dressed in cloth of gold, and they carried huge languorous bouquets of calla lilies. So many lilies and white irises and white roses crowded the sides of the church that, in their windows and on their pedestals, the faces of the saints were hidden. Even the sun, which had so easily found Perrin in his darkness, had trouble finding its way into the church. But the guests, holding fat candles of beeswax, lit the church with stars instead. The bridegrooms wore suits of white and midnight blue; one wore pearl buttons and studs and buckles, the other diamonds. To Lark they looked very much alike, both tall and handsome, tweaking their mustaches straight, and dutifully assuming a serious expression as they listened to the priest, while their eyes said: *at last, at last, I have waited so long, the trap is closing, the night is coming.* . . . But their faces were at once so vain and tender and foolish that Lark's heart warmed to them. They did not seem to realize that one had been an ingredient in Pearl's recipes that she had stirred into her life, and the other a three-letter solution in Diamond's crossword puzzle. At the end of the ceremony, when the bridegrooms had searched through cascades of heavy lace to kiss their brides' faces, the guests blew out their candles.

In the sudden darkness a single hair-fine thread of light shone between two rose petals.

Lark dropped her candle. Panicked without knowing why, she stumbled through the church, out into light, where she forced a carriage driver to gallop madly through the streets of the city to her father's house. Not daring to let light through Perrin's door, she pounded on it.

She heard a gentle, mournful word she did not understand.

She pounded again. Again the sad voice spoke a single word.

The third time she pounded, she recognized the voice.

She flung open the door. A white dove sitting in a hair-fine thread of light fluttered into the air, and flew out the door.

"Oh, my love," she whispered, stunned. She felt something warm on her cheek that was not a tear, and touched it: a drop of blood. A small white feather floated out of the air, caught on the lace above her heart. "Oh," she said again, too grieved for tears, staring into the empty room, her empty life, and then down the empty hall, her empty future.

"Oh, why," she cried, wild with sorrow, "have I chosen to love a lion, a dove, an enchantment, instead of a fond foolish man with waxed mustaches whom nothing, neither light nor dark, can ever change? Someone who could never be snatched away by magic? Oh, my sweet dove, will I ever see you? How will I find you?"

Sunlight glittered at the end of the hall in a bright and ominous jewel. She went toward it thoughtlessly, trembling, barely able to walk. A drop of blood had fallen on the floor, and into the blood, a small white feather.

She heard Perrin's voice, as in a dream: Seven years. Beyond the open window on the flagstones another crimson jewel gleamed. Another feather fluttered, caught in it. On the garden wall she saw the dove turn to look at her.

Seven years.

This, its eyes said. *Or your father's house, where you are loved, and where there is no mystery in day or night. Stay. Or follow.*

Seven years.

By the end of the second year, she had learned to speak to animals and understand the mute, fleeting language of the butterflies. By the end of the third year, she had walked everywhere in the world. She had made herself a gown of soft white feathers stained with blood that grew longer and longer as she followed the dove. By the end of the fifth year, her face had grown familiar to the stars, and the moon kept its eye on her. By the end of the sixth year, the gown of feathers and her hair swept behind her, mingling light and dark, and she had become, to the world's eye, a figure of mystery and enchantment. In her own eyes she was simply Lark, who loved Perrin; all the enchantment lay in him.

At the end of the seventh year she lost him.

The jeweled path of blood, the moon-white feathers stopped. It left her stranded, bewildered, on a mountainside in some lonely part of the world. In disbelief, she searched frantically: stones, tree boughs, earth. Nothing told her which direction to go. One direction was as likely as another, and all, to her despairing heart, went nowhere. She threw herself on the ground finally and wept for the first time since her father had killed the lark.

"So close," she cried, pounding the earth in fury and sorrow. "So close—another step, another drop of blood—Oh, but perhaps he is dead, my Perrin, after losing so much blood to show me the way. So many years, so much blood, so much silence, so much, too much, too much . . ." She fell silent finally, dazed and exhausted with grief. The wind whispered to her, comforting; the trees sighed for her, weeping leaves that caressed her face. Birds spoke.

Maybe the dove is not dead, they said. *We saw none of ours fall dying from the sky. Enchantments do not die, they are transformed. . . . Light sees everything. Ask the sun. Who knows him better than the sun who changed him into a dove?*

"Do you know?" she whispered to the sun, and for an instant saw its face among the clouds.

No, it said in words of fire, and with fire, shaped something out of itself. *It's you I have watched, for seven years, as constant and faithful to your love as I am to the world. Take this. Open it when your need is greatest.*

She felt warm light in her hand. The light hardened into a tiny box with jeweled hinges and the sun's face on its lid. She turned her face away disconsolately; a box was not a bird. But she held it, and it kept her warm through dusk and nightfall as she lay unmoving on the cold ground.

She asked the full moon when it rose above the mountain, "Have you seen my white dove? For seven years you showed me each drop of blood, each white feather, even on the darkest night."

It was you I watched, the moon said. *More constant than the moon on the darkest night, for I hid then, and you never faltered in your journey. I have not seen your dove.*

"Do you know," she whispered to the wind, and heard it question its four messengers, who blew everywhere in the world. No, they said, and No, and No. And then the sweet South Wind blew against her cheek, smelling of roses and warm seas and endless summers. Yes.

She lifted her face from the ground. Twigs and dirt clung to her. Her long hair was full of leaves and spiders and the grandchildren of spiders. Full of webs, it looked as filmy as a bridal veil. Her face was moon pale; moonlight could have traced the bones through it. Her eyes were fiery with tears.

"My dove."

He has become a lion again. The seven years are over. But the dove changed shape under the eyes of an enchanted dragon, and when the dragon saw lion, battle sparked. He is still fighting.

Lark sat up. "Where?"

In a distant land, beside a southern sea. I brought you a nut from one of the trees there. It is no ordinary nut. Now listen. This is what you must do . . .

So she followed the South Wind to the land beside the southern sea, where the sky flashed red with dragon fire, and its fierce roars blew down trees and tore the sails from every passing ship. The lion, no longer stone by daylight, was golden and as flecked with blood as Lark's gown of feathers. Lark never questioned the wind's advice, for she was desperate beyond the advice of mortals. She went to the seashore and found reeds broken in the battle, each singing a different, haunting note through its hollow throat. She counted. She picked the eleventh reed and waited. When the dragon bent low, curling around itself to roar rage and fire at the lion gnawing at its wing, she ran forward quickly, struck its throat with the reed.

Smoke hissed from its scales, as if the reed had seared it. It tried to roar; no sound came out, no fire. Its great neck sagged; scales darkened with blood and smoke. One eye closed. The lion leaped for its throat.

There was a flash, as if the sun had struck the earth. Lark crouched, covering her face. The world was suddenly very quiet. She heard bullfrogs among the reeds, the warm, slow waves fanning across the sand. She opened her eyes.

The dragon had fallen on its back, with the lion sprawled on top of it. A woman lay on her back, with Perrin on top of her. His eyes were closed, his face bloody; he drew deep, ragged breaths, one hand clutching the woman's shoulder, his open mouth against her neck. The woman's weary face, upturned to the sky above Perrin's shoulder, was also bloodstained; her free hand lifted weakly, fell again across Perrin's back. Her hair was as gold as the sun's little box; her face as pale and perfect as the moon's face. Lark stared. The waves grew full again, spilled with a languorous sigh across the sand. The woman drew a deep breath. Her eyes flickered open; they were as blue as the sky.

She turned her head, looked at Perrin. She lifted her hand from his back, touched her eyes delicately, her brows rising in silent question. Then she looked again at the blood on his face.

She stiffened, began pushing at him and talking at the same time. "I remember. I remember now. You were that monstrous lion that kept nipping at my wings." Her voice was low and sweet, amused as she tugged at Perrin. "You must get up. What if someone should see us? Oh, dear. You must be hurt." She shifted out from under him, made a hasty adjustment to her bodice, and caught sight of Lark. "Oh, my dear," she cried, "it's not what you think."

"I know," Lark whispered, still amazed at the woman's beauty and at the sight of Perrin, whom she had not seen in seven years, and never in the light, lying golden-haired and slack against another woman's body. The woman bent over Perrin, turned him on his back.

"He is hurt. Is there water?" She glanced around vaguely, as if she expected a bullfrog to emerge in tie and tails, with water on a tray. But Lark had already fetched it in her hands, from a little rill of fresh water.

She moistened Perrin's face with it, let his lips wander over her hands, searching for more. The woman was gazing at Lark.

"You must be an enchantress or a witch," she exclaimed. "That explains your—unusual appearance. And the way we suddenly became ourselves again. I am—we are most grateful to you. My father is King of this desert, and he will reward you richly if you come to his court." She took a tattered piece of her hem, wiped a corner of Perrin's lips, then, in afterthought, her own.

"My name is Lark. This man is—"

"Yes," the princess said, musing. Her eyes were very wide, very blue; she was not listening to Lark. "He is, isn't he? Do you know, I think there was a kind of prophecy when I was born that I would marry a lion. I'm sure there was. Of course they kept it secret all these years, for fear I might actually meet a lion, but—here it is. He. A lion among men. Do you think I should explain to my father what he was, or do you think I should just—not exactly lie, but omit that part of his past? What do you think? Witches know these things."

"I think," Lark said unsteadily, brushing sand out of Perrin's hair, "that you are mistaken. I am—"

"So I should tell my father. Will you help me raise him? There is a griffin just beyond those rocks. Very nice; in fact we became friends before I had to fight the lion. I had no one else to talk to except bullfrogs. And you know what frogs are like. Very little small talk, and that they repeat incessantly." She hoisted Perrin up, brushing sand off his shoulders, his chest, his thighs. "I don't think my father will mind at all. About the lion part. Do you?" She put her fingers to her lips suddenly and gave a piercing whistle that silenced the frogs and brought the griffin, huge and flaming red, up over the rocks. "Come," she said to it. Lark clung to Perrin's arm.

"Wait," she said desperately, words coming slowly, clumsily, for she had scarcely spoken to mortals in seven years. "You don't understand. Wait until he wakes. I have been following him for seven years."

"Then how wonderful that you have found him. The griffin will fly us to my father's palace. It's the only one for miles, in the desert. You'll find it easily." She laid her hand on Lark's. "Please come. I'd take you with us, but it would tire the griffin—"

"But I have a magic nut for it to rest on, while we cross the sea—"

"But you see we are going across the desert, and, anyway, I think a nut might be a little small." She smiled brightly but very wearily at Lark. "I feel I will never be able to thank you enough." She pushed the upright Perrin against the griffin's back, and he toppled facedown between the bright, uplifted wings.

"Perrin!" Lark cried desperately, and the princess, clinging to the griffin's neck, looked down at her, startled, uncertain. But the thrust of the griffin's great wings tangled wind and sand together and choked Lark's voice. She coughed and spat sand while the princess, cheerful again, waved one hand and held Perrin tightly with the other.

"Good-bye . . ."

"No!" Lark screamed. No one heard her but the frogs.

She sat awake all night, a dove in speckled plumage, mourning with the singing reeds. When the sun rose, it barely recognized her, so pale and wild was her face, so blank with grief her eyes. Light touched her gently. She stirred finally, sighed, watching the glittering net of gold the sun cast across the sea. They should have been waking in a great tree growing out of the sea, she and Perrin and the griffin, a wondrous sight that passing sailors might have spun into tales for their grandchildren. Instead, here she was, abandoned among the bullfrogs, while her true love had flown away with the princess. What would he think when he woke and saw her golden hair, heard her sweet, amused voice telling him that she had been the dragon he had fought, and that at the battle's end, she had awakened in his arm? An enchantress—a strange, startling woman who wore a gown of bloodstained feathers, whose long black hair was bound with cobweb, whose face and eyes seemed more of a wild creature's than a human's—had wandered by at the right moment and freed them from their spells.

And so. And therefore. And of course what all this must mean was, beyond doubt, their destiny: the marriage of the dragon and the lion. And if they were very lucky—wouldn't it be splendid—the enchantress might come to see them married.

"Will he remember me?" Lark murmured to the bullfrogs. "If he saw me now, would he even recognize me?" She tried to see her face reflected in the waves, but of the faces gliding and breaking across the sand, none seemed to belong to her, and she asked desperately, "How will he recognize me if I cannot recognize myself?"

She stood up then, her hands to her mouth, staring at her faceless shadow in the sand. She whispered, her throat aching with grief, "What must I do? Where can I begin? To find my lost love and myself?"

You know where he is, the sea murmured. *Go there.*

"But she is so beautiful—and I have become so—"

He is not here, the reeds sang in their soft, hollow voices. *Find him. He is again enchanted.*

"Again! First a stone lion, and then a dove, and then a real lion—now what is he?"

He is enchanted by his human form.

She was silent, still gazing at her morning shadow. "I never knew him fully human," she said at last. "And he never knew me. If we meet now by daylight, who is to say whether he will recognize Lark, or I will recognize Perrin? Those were names we left behind long ago."

Love recognizes love, the reeds murmured.

Her shadow whispered, *I will guide you.*

So she set her back to the sun and followed her shadow across the desert.

By day the sun was a roaring lion, by night the moon a pure white dove. Lion and dove accompanied her, showed her hidden springs of cool water among the barren stones, and trees that shook down dates and figs and nuts into her hands. Finally, climbing a rocky hill, she saw an enormous and beautiful palace, whose immense gates of bronze and gold lay open to welcome the richly dressed people riding horses and dromedaries and elegant palanquins into it.

She hurried to join them before the sun set and the gates were closed. Her bare feet were scraped and raw; she limped a little. Her feathers had grown frayed; her face was gaunt, streaked with dust and sorrow. She looked like a beggar, she knew, but the people spoke to her kindly and even tossed her a coin or two.

"We have come for the wedding of our princess and the Lion of the Desert, whom it is her destiny to wed."

"Who foretold such a destiny?" Lark asked, her voice trembling.

"Someone," they assured her. "The king's astrologer. A great sorceress disguised as a beggar, not unlike yourself. A bullfrog, who spoke with a human tongue at her birth. Her mother was frightened by a lion just before childbirth, and dreamed it. No one exactly remembers who, but someone did. Destiny or no, they will marry in three days, and never was there a more splendid couple than the princess and her lion."

Lark crept into the shadow of the gate. "Now what shall I do?" she murmured, her eyes wide, dark with urgency. "With his eyes full of her, he will never notice a beggar."

Sun slid a last gleam down the gold edge of the gate. She remembered its gift then and drew the little gold box out of her pocket. She opened it.

A light sprang out of it, swirled around her like a storm of gold dust, glittering, shimmering. It settled on her, turned the feathers into the finest silk and cloth of gold. It turned the cobwebs in her hair into a long, sparkling net of diamonds and pearls. It turned the dust on her feet into soft golden leather and pearls. Light played over her face, hiding shadows of grief and despair. Seeing the wonderful dress, she laughed for the first time in seven years, and, with wonder, she recognized Lark's voice.

As she walked down the streets, people stared at her, marveling. They made way for her. A man offered her his palanquin, a woman her sunshade. She shook her head at both, laughing again. "I will not be shut up in a box, nor will I shut out the sun." So she walked, and all the wedding guests slowed to accompany her to the inner courtyard.

Word of her had passed into the palace long before she did. The princess, dressed in fine, flowing silks the color of her eyes, came out to meet the stranger who rivaled the sun. She saw the dress before she saw Lark's face.

"Oh, my dear," she breathed, hurrying down the steps. "Say this is a wedding gift for me. You cannot possibly wear this to my wedding—no one will look at me! Say you brought it for me. Or tell me what I can give you in return for it." She stepped back, half-laughing, still staring at the sun's creation. "Where are my manners? You came all the way from—from—and here all I can do is—Where are you from, anyway? Who in the world are you?" She looked finally into Lark's eyes. She clapped her hands, laughing again, with a touch of relief in her voice. "Oh, it is the witch! You have come! Perrin will be so pleased to meet you. He is sleeping now; he is still weak from his wounds." She took Lark's hand in hers and led her up the steps. "Now tell me how I can persuade you to let me have that dress. Look how everyone stares at you. It will make me the most beautiful woman in the world on my wedding day. And you're a witch, you don't care how you look. Anyway, it's not necessary for you to look like this. People will think you're only human."

Lark, who had been thinking while the princess chattered, answered, "I will give you the dress for a price."

"Anything!"

Lark stopped short. "No—you must not say that!" she cried fiercely. "Ever! You could pay far more than you ever imagined for something as trivial as this dress!"

"All right," the princess said gently, patting her hand. "I will not give you just anything. Though I'd hardly call this dress trivial. But tell me what you want."

"I want a night alone with your bridegroom."

The princess's brows rose. She glanced around hastily to see if anyone were listening, then she took Lark's other hand. "We must observe a few proprieties," she said softly, smiling. "Not even I have had a whole night in my lion's bed—he has been too ill. I would not grant this to any woman. But you are a witch, and you helped us before, and I know you mean no harm. I assume you wish to tend him during the night with magic arts so that he can heal faster."

"If I can do that, I will. But—"

"Then you may. But I must have that dress first."

Lark was silent. So was the princess, who held her eyes until Lark bowed her head. *Then I have lost*, she thought, *for he will never even look at me without this dress.*

The princess said lightly, "You were gracious to refuse my first impulse to give you anything. I trust you, but in that dress you are very beautiful, and you know how men are. Or perhaps, being a witch, you don't. Anyway, there is no need at all for you to appear to him like this. And how can I surprise him on our wedding day with this dress if he sees you in it first?"

You are like my sisters, Lark thought. *Foolish and wiser than I am.* She yielded, knowing she wanted to see Perrin with all her heart, and the princess only wanted what dazzled her eyes. "You are right," she said. "You may tell people that I will stay with Perrin to heal him if I can. And that I brought the dress for you."

The princess kissed her cheek. "Thank you. I will find you something else to wear, and show you his room. I'm not insensitive—I fell in love with him myself the moment I looked at him. So I can hardly blame you for—and of course he is in love with me. But we hardly know each other, and I don't want to confuse him with possibilities at this delicate time. You understand."

"Perfectly."

"Good."

She took Lark to her own sumptuous rooms and had her maid dress Lark in something she called "refreshingly simple" but which Lark called "drab," and knew it belonged not even to the maid, but to someone much farther down the social strata who stayed in shadows and was not allowed to wear lace.

I am more wren or sparrow than Lark, she thought sadly, as the princess brought her to Perrin's room.

"Till sunrise," she said; the tone of her voice added, *And not a moment after.*

"Yes," Lark said absently, gazing at her sleeping love. At last the puzzled princess closed the door, left Lark in the twilight.

Lark approached the bed. She saw Perrin's face in the light of a single candle beside the bed. It was bruised and scratched; there was a long weal from a dragon's claw down one bare shoulder. He looked older, weathered, his pale skin burned by the sun, which had scarcely touched it in years. The candlelight picked out a thread of silver here and there among the lion's gold of his hair. She reached out impulsively, touched the silver. "My poor Perrin," she said softly. "At least, as a dove, for seven years, you were faithful to me. You shed blood at every seventh step I took. And I took seven steps for every drop you shed. How strange to find you naked in this bed, waiting for a swan instead of Lark. At least I had you for a little while, and at long last you are unbewitched."

She bent over him, kissed his lips gently. He opened his eyes.

She turned away quickly before the loving expression in them changed to disappointment. But he moved more swiftly, reaching out to catch her hand before she left.

"Lark?" He gave a deep sigh as she turned again, and eased back into the pillows. "I heard your sweet voice in my dream . . . I didn't want to wake and end the dream. But you kissed me awake. You are real, aren't you?" he asked anxiously, as she lingered in the shadows, and he pulled her out of darkness into light.

He looked at her for a long time, silently, until her eyes filled with tears.

"I've changed," she said.

"Yes," he said. "You have been enchanted, too."

"And so have you, once again."

He shook his head. "You have set me free."

"And I will set you free again," she said softly, "to marry whom you choose."

He moved again, too abruptly, and winced. His hold tightened on her hand. "Have I lost all enchantment?" he asked sadly. "Did you love the spellbound man more than you can love the ordinary mortal? Is that why you left me?"

She stared at him. "I never left you—"

"You disappeared," he said wearily. "After seven long years of flying around in the shape of a dove, due to your father's appalling carelessness, I finally turned back into a lion, and you were gone. I thought you could not bear to stay with me through yet another enchantment. I didn't blame you. But it grieved me badly—I was glad when the dragon attacked me, because I thought it might kill me. Then I woke up in my own body, in a strange bed, with a princess beside me explaining that we were destined to be married."

"Did you tell her you were married?"

He sighed. "I thought it was just another way of being enchanted. A lion, a dove, marriage to a beautiful princess I don't love—What difference did anything make? You were gone. I didn't care any longer what happened to me." She swallowed, but could not speak. "Are you about to leave me again?" he asked painfully. "Is that why you'll come no closer?"

"No," she whispered. "I thought—I didn't think you still remembered me."

He closed his eyes. "For seven years I left you my heart's blood to follow . . ."

"And for seven years I followed. And then on the last day of the seventh year, you disappeared. I couldn't find you anywhere. I asked the sun, the moon, the wind. I followed the South Wind to find you. It told me how to break the spell over you. So I did—"

His eyes opened again. "You. You are the enchantress the princess talks about. You rescued both of us. And then—"

"She took you away from me before I could tell her—I tried—"

His face was growing peaceful in the candlelight. "She doesn't listen very well. But why did you think I had forgotten you?"

"I thought—she was so beautiful, I thought—and I have grown so worn, so strange—"

For the first time in seven years, she saw him smile. "You have walked the world, and spoken to the sun and wind . . . I have only been enchanted. You have become the enchantress." He pulled her closer, kissed her hand and then her wrist. He added, as she began to smile, "What a poor opinion you must have of my human shape to think that after all these years I would prefer the peacock to the Lark."

He pulled her closer, kissed the crook of her elbow and then her breast. And then she caught his lips and kissed him, one hand in his hair, the other in his hand.

And thus the princess found them, as she opened the door, speaking softly, "My dear, I forgot, if he wakes you must give him this potion—I mean, this tea of mild herbs to ease his pain a little—" She kicked the door shut and saw their surprised faces. "Well," she said frostily. "Really."

"This is my wife," Perrin said.

"Well, really." She flung the sleeping potion out the window, and folded her arms. "You might have told me."

"I never thought I would see her again."

"How extraordinarily careless of you both." She tapped her foot furiously for a moment and then said slowly, her face clearing a little, "That's why you were there to rescue us! Now I understand. And I snatched him away from you without even thinking—and after you had searched for him so long, I made you search—oh, my dear." She clasped her hands tightly. "What I said. About not spending a full night here. You must not think—"

"I understand."

"No, but really—tell her, Perrin."

"It doesn't matter," Perrin said gently. "You were kind to me. That's what Lark will remember."

But she remembered everything, as they flew on the griffin's back across the sea: her father's foolish bargain, the fearsome stone lion, the seven years when she followed a white dove beyond any human life, the battle between dragon and lion, and then the hopeless loss of him again. She turned the nut in her palm, and questions rose in her head: *Can I truly stand more mysteries, the possibilities of more hardships, more enchanting princesses between us? Would it be better just to crack the nut and eat it? Then we would all fall into the sea, in this moment when our love is finally intact. He seems to live from spell to spell. Is it better to die now, before something worse can happen to him? How much can love stand?*

Perrin caught her eyes and smiled at her. She heard the griffin's labored breathing, felt the weary catch in its mighty wings. She tossed the nut high into the air and watched it fall a long, long way before it hit the water. And then the great tree grew out of the sea, to the astonishment of passing sailors, who remembered it all their lives, and told their incredulous grandchildren of watching a griffin red as fire drop out of the blue to rest among its boughs.

THE HARROWING OF THE DRAGON OF HOARSBREATH

Once, on the top of a world, there existed the ring of an island named Hoarsbreath, made out of gold and snow. It was all mountain, a grim, briny, yellowing ice world covered with winter twelve months out of thirteen. For one month, when the twin suns crossed each other at the world's cap, the snow melted from the peak of Hoarsbreath. The hardy trees shrugged the snow off their boughs and sucked in light and mellow air, pulling themselves toward the suns. Snow and icicles melted off the roofs of the miners' village; the snow tunnels they had dug from house to tavern to storage barn to mine shaft sagged to the ground; the dead white river flowing down from the mountain to the sea turned blue and began to move again. Then the miners gathered the gold they had dug by firelight out of the chill, harsh darkness of the deep mountain and took it downriver, across the sea to the mainland, to trade for food and furs, tools and a liquid fire called wormspoor because it was gold and bitter, like the leavings of dragons. After three swallows of it, in a busy city with a harbor frozen only part of the year, with people who wore rich furs, kept horses and sleds to ride in during winter, and who knew the patterns of the winter stars since they weren't buried alive by the snow, the miners swore they would never return to Hoarsbreath. But the gold waiting in the dark secret places of the mountain island drew at them in their dreaming, lured them back.

For two hundred years after the naming of Hoarsbreath, winter followed winter, and the miners lived their rich, isolated, precarious lives on the pinnacle of ice and granite, cursing the cold and loving it, for it kept lesser folk away. They mined, drank, spun tales, raised children who were sent to the mainland when they were half-grown, to receive their education and find easier, respectable lives. But always a few children found their way back, born with a gnawing in their hearts for fire, ice, stone, and the solitary pursuit of gold in the dark.

Then two miners' children came back from the great world and destroyed the island.

They had no intention of doing that. The younger of them was Peka Krao. After spending five years on the mainland, boring herself with schooling, she came back to Hoarsbreath to mine. At seventeen, she was good-natured and sturdy, with dark eyes and dark, braided hair. She loved every part of Hoarsbreath, even its chill, damp shafts at midwinter and the bone-jarring work of hewing through darkness and stone to unbury its gold. Her instincts for gold were uncanny; she seemed to sense it through her fingertips touching bare rock. The miners called her their good luck. She could make wormspoor, too, one of the few useful things she had learned on the mainland. It lost its bitterness, somehow, when she made it: it aged into a rich, smoky gold that made the miners forget their sore muscles and inspired marvelous tales out of them that whittled away at the endless winter.

She met the Dragon Harrower one evening at a cross section of tunnel between her mother's house and the tavern. She knew all the things to fear in her world: a rumble in the mountain, a guttering torch in the mines, a crevice in the snow, a crack of ice underfoot. There was little else she couldn't handle with a soft word or her own right arm. So when he loomed out of the darkness unexpectedly into her taper-light, she wasn't afraid. But he made her stop instinctively, like an animal might stop, faced with something that puzzled its senses.

His hair was dead white, with strands bright as wormspoor running through it; his eyes were the light, hard blue of dawn during suns-crossing. Rich colors flashed out of him everywhere in her light: from a gold knife hilt and a brass pack buckle; from the red ties of his cloak that were weighted with ivory, and the blue-and-silver threads in his gloves. His heavy fur cloak was closed, but she felt that if he shifted, other colors would escape from it into the cold, dark air. At first she thought he must be ancient: the taper-fire showed her a face that was shadowed and scarred, remote with strange experience, but no more than a dozen years older than hers.

"Who are you?" she breathed. Nothing on Hoarsbreath glittered like that in midwinter; its colors were few and simple: snow, damp fur and leather, fire, gold.

"I can't find my father," he said. "Lule Yarrow."

She stared at him, amazed that his colors had their beginnings on Hoarsbreath. "He's dead." His eyes widened slightly, losing some of their hardness. "He fell in a crevasse. They chipped him out of the ice at suns-crossing, and buried him six years ago."

He looked away from her a moment, down at the icy ridges of tramped snow. "Winter." He broke the word in two, like an icicle. Then he shifted his pack, sighing. "Do they still have wormspoor on this ice-tooth?"

"Of course. Who are you?"

"Ryd Yarrow. Who are you?"

"Peka Krao."

"Peka. I remember. You were squalling in somebody's arms when I left."

"You look a hundred years older than that," she commented, still puzzling, holding him in her light, though she was beginning to feel the cold. "Seventeen years you've been gone. How could you stand it, being away from Hoarsbreath so long? I couldn't stand five years of it. There are so many people whose names you don't know, trying to tell you about things that don't matter, and the flat earth and the blank sky are everywhere. Did you come back to mine?"

He glanced up at the gray-white ceiling of the snow tunnel, barely an inch above his head. "The sky is full of stars, and the gold wake of dragon-flights," he said softly. "I am a Dragon Harrower. I am trained and hired to trouble dragons out of their lairs. That's why I came back here."

"Here. There are no dragons on Hoarsbreath."

His smile touched his eyes like a reflection of fire across ice. "Hoarsbreath is a dragon's heart."

She shifted, her own heart suddenly chilled. She said tolerantly, "That sounds like a marvelous tale to me."

"It's no tale. I know. I followed this dragon through centuries, through ancient writings, through legends, through rumors of terror and deaths. It is here, sleeping, coiled around the treasures of Hoarsbreath. If you on Hoarsbreath rouse it, you are dead. If I rouse it, I will end your endless winter."

"I like winter." Her protest sounded very small, muted within the thick snow-walls, but he heard it. He lifted his hand, held it lightly against the low ceiling above his head.

"You might like the sky beyond this. At night it is a mine of lights and hidden knowledge."

She shook her head. "I like close places, full of fire and darkness. And faces I know. And tales spun out of wormspoor. If you come with me to the tavern, they'll tell you where your father is buried and give you lodgings, and then you can leave."

"I'll come to the tavern. With a tale."

Her taper was nearly burned down, and she was beginning to shiver. "A dragon." She turned away from him. "No one will believe you anyway."

"You do."

She listened to him silently, warming herself with wormspoor, as he spoke to the circle of rough, fire-washed faces in the tavern. Even in the light, he bore little resemblance to his father, except for his broad cheekbones and the threads of gold in his hair. Under his bulky cloak, he was dressed as plainly as any miner, but stray bits of color still glinted from him, suggesting wealth and distant places.

"A dragon," he told them, "is creating your winter. Have you ever asked yourselves why winter on this island is nearly twice as long as winter on the mainland twenty miles away? You live in dragon's breath, in the icy mist of its bowels, hoarfrost cold, that grips your land in winter the way another dragon's breath might burn it to flinders. One month out of the year, in the warmth of suns-crossing, it looses its ring-grip on your island, slides into the sea, and goes to mate. Its ice-kingdom begins to melt. It returns, loops its length around its mountain of ice and gold. Its breath freezes the air once more, locks the river into its bed, you into your houses, the gold into its mountain, and you curse the cold and drink until the next dragon-mating." He paused. There was not a sound around him. "I've been to strange places in this world, places even colder than this, where the suns never cross, and I have seen such monsters. They are ancient as rock, white as old ice, and their skin is like iron. They breed winter and they cannot be killed. But they can be driven away, into far corners of the world where they are dangerous to no one. I'm trained for this. I can rid you of your winter. Harrowing is dangerous work and usually I am highly paid. But I've been looking for this ice-dragon for many years, through its spoor of legend and destruction. I tracked it here, one of the oldest of its kind, to the place where I was born. All I ask from you is a guide."

He stopped, waiting. Peka, her hands frozen around her glass, heard someone swallow. A voice rose and faded from the tavern kitchen; sap hissed in the fire. A couple of the miners were smiling; the others looked satisfied and vaguely expectant, wanting the tale to continue. When it didn't, Kor Flynt, who had mined Hoarsbreath for fifty years, spat worm-spoor into the fire. The flame turned a baleful gold, and then subsided. "Suns-crossing," he said politely, reminding a scholar of a scrap of knowledge children acquired with their first set of teeth, "causes the seasons."

"Not here," Ryd said. "Not on Hoarsbreath. I've seen. I know."

Peka's mother Ambris leaned forward. "Why," she asked curiously, "would a miner's son become a Dragon Harrower?" She had a pleasant, craggy face; her dark hair and her slow, musing voice were like Peka's. Peka saw the Dragon Harrower ride between two answers in his mind. Meeting Ambris's eyes, he made a choice, and his own eyes strayed to the fire.

"I left Hoarsbreath when I was twelve. When I was fifteen, I saw a dragon in the mountains east of the city. Until then, I had intended to come back and mine. I began to learn about dragons. The first one I saw burned red and gold under the suns' fire; it swallowed small hills with its shadow. I wanted to call it, like a hawk. I wanted to fly with it. I kept studying, meeting other people who studied them, seeing other dragons. I saw a night-black dragon in the northern deserts; its scales were dusted with silver, and the flame that came out of it was silver. I saw people die in that flame, and I watched the harrowing of that dragon. It lives now on the underside of the world, in shadow. We keep watch on all known dragons. In the green midworld belt, rich with rivers and mines, forests and farmland, I saw a whole mining town burned to the ground by a dragon so bright I thought at first it was sun-fire arching down to the ground. Someone I loved had the task of tracking that one to its cave, deep beneath the mine shafts. I watched her die, there. I nearly died. The dragon is sealed into the bottom of the mountain, by stone and by words. That is the dragon which harrowed me." He paused to sip wormspoor. His eyes lifted, not to Ambris, but to Peka. "Now do you understand what danger you live in? What if one year the dragon sleeps through its mating time, with the soft heat of the suns making it sluggish from dreaming? You don't know it's there, wrapped around your world. It doesn't know you're there, stealing its gold. What if you sail your boats full of gold downriver and find the great white bulk of it sprawled like a wall across your passage? Or worse, you find its eye opening like a third, dead sun to see your hands full of its gold? It would slide its length around the mountain, coil upward, and crush you all, then breathe over the whole of the island and turn it dead-white as its heart, and it would never sleep again."

There was another silence. Peka felt something play along her spine like the thin, quavering, arthritic fingers of wind. "It's getting better," she said, "your tale." She took a deep swallow of wormspoor and added, "I love sitting in a warm, friendly place listening to tales I don't have to believe."

Kor Flynt shrugged. "It rings true, lass."

"It is true," Ryd said.

"Maybe so," she said. "And it may be better if you just let the dragon sleep."

"And if it wakes unexpectedly? The winter killed my father. The dragon at the heart of winter could destroy you all."

"There are other dangers. Rockfalls, sudden floods, freezing winds. A dragon is simply one more danger to live with."

He studied her. "I saw a dragon once with wings as softly blue as a spring sky. Have you ever felt spring on Hoarsbreath? It could come."

She drank again. "You love them," she said. "Your voice loves them and hates them, Dragon Harrower."

"I hate them," he said flatly. "Will you guide me down the mountain?"

"No. I have work to do."

He shifted, and the colors rippled from him again, red, gold, silver, spring-blue. She finished the wormspoor, felt it burn in her like liquid gold. "It's only a tale. All your dragons are just colors in our heads. Let the dragon sleep. If you wake it, you'll destroy the night."

"No," he said. "You will see the night. That's what you're afraid of."

Kor Flynt shrugged. "There probably is no dragon, anyway."

"Spring, though," Ambris said; her face had softened. "Sometimes I can smell it from the mainland, and I always wonder . . . Still, after a hard day's work, sitting beside a roaring fire sipping dragon-spit, you can believe anything. Especially this." She looked into her glass at the glowering liquid. "Is this some of yours, Peka? What did you put into it?"

"Gold." The expression in Ryd's eyes made her swallow sudden tears of frustration. She refilled her glass. "Fire, stone, dark, wood smoke, night air smelling like cold tree bark. You don't care, Ryd Yarrow."

"I do care," he said imperturbably. "It's the best wormspoor I've ever tasted."

"And I put a dragon's heart into it." She saw him start slightly; ice and hoarfrost shimmered from him. "If that's what Hoarsbreath is." A dragon beat into her mind, its wings of rime, its breath smoldering with ice, the guardian of winter. She drew breath, feeling the vast bulk of it looped around them all, dreaming its private dreams. Her bones seemed suddenly fragile as kindling, and the gold wormspoor in her hands a guilty secret. "It's a tale."

"Oh, go with him, lass," her mother said tolerantly. "There may be no dragon, but we can't have him swallowed up in the ice like his father. Besides, it may be a chance for spring."

"Spring is for flatlanders. There are things that shouldn't be wakened. I know."

"How?" Ryd asked.

She groped, wishing for the first time for a flatlander's skill with words. She said finally, "I feel it," and he smiled. She sat back in her chair, irritated and vaguely frightened. "Oh, all right, Ryd Yarrow, since you'll go with or without me. I'll lead you down to the shores in the morning. Maybe by then you'll listen to me."

"You can't see beyond your snow-world," he said implacably. "It is morning."

They followed one of the deepest mine shafts and clambered out of it to stand in the snow halfway down the mountain. The sky was lead gray; across the mists ringing the island's shores, they could see the ocean, a swirl of white, motionless ice. The mainland harbor was locked. Peka wondered if the ships were stuck like birds in the ice. The world looked empty and somber.

"At least in the dark mountain there is fire and gold. Here, there isn't even a sun." She took out a skin of wormspoor, sipped it to warm her bones. She held it out to Ryd, but he shook his head.

"I need all my wits. So do you, or we'll both end up preserved in ice at the bottom of a crevasse."

"I know. I'll keep you safe." She corked the skin and added, "In case you were wondering."

But he looked at her, startled out of his remoteness. "I wasn't. Do you feel that strongly?"

"Yes."

"So did I, when I was your age. Now I feel very little." He moved again. She stared after him, wondering how he kept her smoldering and on edge.

She said abruptly, catching up with him, "Ryd Yarrow."

"Yes."

"You have two names. Ryd Yarrow and Dragon Harrower. One is a plain name this mountain gave you. The other you got from the world, the name that gives you color. One name I can talk to, the other is the tale at the bottom of a bottle of wormspoor. Maybe you could understand me if you hadn't brought your past back to Hoarsbreath."

"I do understand you," he said absently. "You want to sit in the dark all your life and drink wormspoor."

She drew breath and held it. "You talk but you don't listen," she said finally. "Just like all the other flatlanders." He didn't answer. They walked in silence a while, following the empty bed of an old river. The world looked dead, but she could tell by the air, which was not even freezing spangles of breath on her hood fur, that the winter was drawing to an end. "Suns-crossing must be only two months away," she commented surprisedly.

"Besides, I'm not a flatlander," he said abruptly, surprising her again. "I do care about the miners, about Hoarsbreath. It's because I care that I want to challenge that ice-dragon with all the skill I possess. Is it better to let you live surrounded by danger, in bitter cold, carving half-lives out of snow and stone, so that you can come fully alive for one month of the year?"

"You could have asked us."

"I did ask you."

She sighed. "Where will it live, if you drive it away from Hoarsbreath?"

He didn't answer for a few paces. In the still day, he loosed no colors, though Peka thought she saw shadows of them around his pack. His head was bowed; his eyes were burning back at a memory. "It will find some strange, remote place where there is no gold, only rock; it can ring itself around emptiness and dream of its past. I came across an ice-dragon unexpectedly once, in a land of ice. The bones of its wings seemed almost translucent. I could have sworn it cast a white shadow."

"Did you want to kill it?"

"No. I loved it."

"Then why do you—" But he turned at her suddenly, almost angrily, waking out of a dream. "I came here because you've built your lives on top of a terrible danger, and I asked for a guide, not a gadfly."

"You wanted me," she said flatly. "And you don't care about Hoarsbreath. All you want is that dragon. Your voice is full of it. What's a gadfly?"

"Go ask a cow. Or a horse. Or anything else that can't live on this forsaken, frostbitten lump of ice."

"Why should you care, anyway? You've got the whole great world to roam in. Why do you care about one dragon wrapped around a tiny island on the top of nowhere?"

"Because it's beautiful and deadly and wrapped around my heartland. And I don't know—I don't know at the end of things which of us will be left on Hoarsbreath." She stared at him. He met her eyes fully. "I'm very skilled. But that is one very powerful dragon."

She whirled, fanning snow. "I'm going back. Find your own way to your harrowing. I hope it swallows you."

His voice stopped her. "You'll always wonder. You'll sit in the dark, drinking wormspoor twelve months out of thirteen, wondering what happened to me. What an ice-dragon looks like, on a winter's day, in full flight."

She hovered between two steps. Then, furiously, she followed him.

They climbed deeper into mist, and then into darkness. They camped at night, ate dried meat and drank wormspoor beside a fire in the snow. The night sky was sullen and starless as the day. They woke to gray mists and traveled on. The cold breathed up around them; walls of ice, yellow as old ivory, loomed over them. They smelled the chill, sweaty smell of the sea. The dead riverbed came to an end over an impassable cliff. They shifted ground, followed a frozen stream downward. The ice walls broke up into great jewels of ice, blue, green, gold, massed about them like a giant's treasure hoard. Peka stopped to stare at them.

Ryd said with soft, bitter satisfaction, "Wormspoor."

She drew breath. "Wormspoor." Her voice sounded small, absorbed by cold. "Ice jewels, fallen stars. Down here you could tell me anything and I might believe it. I feel very strange." She uncorked the wormspoor and took a healthy swig. Ryd reached for it, but he only rinsed his mouth and spat. His face was pale, his eyes red-rimmed, tired.

"How far down do you think we are?"

"Close. There's no dragon. Just mist." She shuddered suddenly at the soundlessness. "The air is dead. Like stone. We should reach the ocean soon."

"We'll reach the dragon first."

They descended hillocks of frozen jewels. The stream they followed fanned into a wide, skeletal filigree of ice and rock. The mist poured around them, so painfully cold it burned their lungs. Peka pushed fur over her mouth, breathed through it. The mist or wormspoor she had drunk was forming shadows around her, flickerings of faces and enormous wings. Her heart felt heavy; her feet dragged like boulders when she lifted them. Ryd was coughing mist; he moved doggedly, as if into a hard wind. The stream fanned again, going very wide before it met the sea. They stumbled down into a bone-searing flow of mist. Ryd disappeared; Peka found him again, bumping into him, for he had stopped. The threads of mist untangled above them, and she saw a strange black sun, hooded with a silvery web. As she blinked at it, puzzled, the web rolled up. The dark sun gazed back at her. She became aware then of her own heartbeat, of a rhythm in the mists, of a faint, echoing pulse all around her: the icy heartbeat of Hoarsbreath.

She drew a hiccup of a breath, stunned. There was a mountain cave ahead of them, from which the mists breathed and eddied. Icicles dropped like bars between its grainy white surfaces. Within it rose stones or teeth as milky white as quartz. A wall of white stretched beyond the mists, vast, earthworm round, solid as stone. She couldn't tell, in the blur and welter of mist, where winter ended and the dragon began.

She made a sound. The vast, silvery eyelid drooped like a parchment unrolled, then lifted again. From the depths of the cave came a faint rumbling, a vague, drowsy waking question: Who?

She heard Ryd's breath finally. "Look at the scar under its eye," he said softly. She saw a jagged track beneath the black sun. "I can name the Harrower who put that there three hundred years ago. And the broken eyetooth. It razed a marble fortress with its wings and jaws; I know the word that shattered that tooth, then. Look at its wing scales. Rimed with silver. It's old. Old as the world." He turned, finally, to look at her. His white hair, slick with mists, made him seem old as winter. "You can go back now. You won't be safe here."

"I won't be safe up there, either," she whispered. "Let's both go back. Listen to its heart."

"Its blood is gold. Only one Harrower ever saw that and lived."

"Please." She tugged at him, at his pack. Colors shivered into the air: sulfur, malachite, opal. The deep rumble came again; a shadow quickened in the dragon's eye. Ryd moved quickly, caught her hands. "Let it sleep. It belongs here on Hoarsbreath. Why can't you see that? Why can't you see? It's a thing made of gold, snow, darkness—" But he wasn't seeing her; his eyes, remote and alien as the black sun, were full of memories and calculations. Behind him, a single curved claw lay like a crescent moon half-buried in the snow.

Peka stepped back from the Harrower, envisioning a bloody moon through his heart, and the dragon roused to fury, coiling upward around Hoarsbreath, crushing the life out of it. "Ryd Yarrow," she whispered. "Ryd Yarrow. Please." But he did not hear his name.

He began to speak, startling echoes against the solid ice around them. "Dragon of Hoarsbreath, whose wings are of hoarfrost, whose blood is gold—" The backbone of the hoar-dragon rippled slightly, shaking away snow. "I have followed your path of destruction from your beginnings in a land without time and without seasons. You have slept one night too long on this island. Hoarsbreath is not your dragon's dream; it belongs to the living, and I, trained and titled Dragon Harrower, challenge you for its freedom." More snow shook away from the dragon, baring a rippling of scale and the glistening of its nostrils. The rhythm of its mist was changing. "I know you," Ryd continued, his voice growing husky, strained against the silence. "You were the white death of the fishing island Klonos, of ten Harrowers in Ynyme, of the winter palace of the ancient lord of Zuirsh. I have harried nine ice-dragons—perhaps your children—out of the known world. I have been searching for you for many years, and I came back to the place where I was born to find you here. I stand before you armed with knowledge, experience, and the dark wisdom of necessity. Leave Hoarsbreath, go back to your birthplace forever, or I will harry you down to the frozen shadow of the world."

The dragon gazed at him motionlessly, an immeasurable ring of ice looped about him. The mist out of its mouth was for a moment suspended. Then its jaws crashed together, spitting splinters of ice. It shuddered, wrenched itself loose from the ice. Its white head reared high, higher, ice booming and cracking around it. Twin black suns stared down at Ryd from the gray mist of the sky. Before it roared, Peka moved.

She found herself on a ledge above Ryd's head without remembering how she got there. Ryd vanished in a flood of mist. The mist turned fiery; Ryd loomed out of it like a red shadow, dispersing it. Seven crescents lifted out of the snow, slashed down at him, scarring the air. A strange voice shouted Ryd's name. He flung back his head and cried a word. Somehow the claw missed him, wedged deep into the ice.

Peka sat back. She was clutching the skin of wormspoor against her heart; she could feel her heartbeat shaking it. Her throat felt raw; the strange voice had been hers. She uncorked the skin, took a deep swallow, and another. Fire licked down her veins. A cloud of ice billowed at Ryd. He said something else, and suddenly he was ten feet away from it, watching a rock where he had stood freeze and snap into pieces.

Peka crouched closer to the wall of ice behind her. From her high point she could see the briny, frozen snarl of the sea. It flickered green, then an eerie orange. Bands of color pinioned the dragon briefly like a rainbow, arching across its wings. A scale caught fire; a small bone the size of Ryd's forearm snapped. Then the cold wind of the dragon's breath froze and shattered the rainbow. A claw slapped at Ryd; he moved a fraction of a moment too slowly. The tip of a talon caught his pack. It burst open with an explosion of glittering colors. The dragon hooded its eyes; Peka hid hers under her hands. She heard Ryd cry out in pain. Then he was beside her instead of in several pieces, prying the wormspoor out of her hands.

He uncorked it, his hands shaking. One of them was seared silver.

"What are they?" she breathed. He poured wormspoor on his burned hand, then thrust it into the snow. The colors were beginning to die down.

"Flame," he panted. "Dragon-flame. I wasn't prepared to handle it."

"You carry it in your pack?"

"Caught in crystals, in fire-leaves. It will be more difficult than I anticipated."

Peka felt language she had never used before clamor in her throat. "It's all right," she said dourly. "I'll wait."

For a moment, as he looked at her, there was a memory of fear in his eyes. "You can walk across the ice to the mainland from here."

"You can walk to the mainland," she retorted. "This is my home. I have to live with or without that dragon. Right now there's no living with it. You woke it out of its sleep. You burnt its wing. You broke its bone. You told it there are people on its island. You are going to destroy Hoarsbreath."

"No. This will be my greatest harrowing." He left her suddenly and appeared flaming like a torch on the dragon's skull, just between its eyes. His hair and his hands spattered silver. Word after word came out of him, smoldering, flashing, melting in the air. The dragon's voice thundered; its skin rippled and shook. Its claw ripped at ice, dug chasms out of it. The air clapped nearby, as if its invisible tail had lifted and slapped at the ground. Then it heaved its head, flung Ryd at the wall of mountain. Peka shut her eyes. But he fell lightly, caught up a crystal as he rose, and sent a shaft of piercing gold light at the upraised scales of its underside, burrowing toward its heart.

Peka got unsteadily to her feet, her throat closing with a sudden whimper. But the dragon's tail, flickering out of the mist behind Ryd, slapped him into a snowdrift twenty feet away. It gave a cold, terrible hiss; mist bubbled over everything, so that for a few minutes Peka could see nothing beyond the lip of the ledge. She drank to stop her shivering. Finally, a green fire blazed within the white swirl. She sat down again slowly, waited.

Night rolled in from the sea. But Ryd's fires shot in raw, dazzling streaks across the darkness, illuminating the hoary, scarred bulk of dragon in front of him. Once, he shouted endless poetry at the dragon, lulling it until its mist-breath was faint and slow from its maw. It nearly put Peka to sleep, but Ryd's imperceptible steps closer and closer to the dragon kept her watching. The tale was evidently an old one to the dragon; it didn't wait for an ending. Its head lunged and snapped unexpectedly, but a moment too soon. Ryd leaped for shelter in the dark, while the dragon's teeth ground painfully on nothingness. Later, Ryd sang to it, a whining, eerie song that showered icicles around Peka's head. One of the dragon's teeth cracked, and it made an odd, high-pitched noise. A vast webbed wing shifted free to fly, unfolding endlessly over the sea. But the dragon stayed, sending mist at Ryd to set him coughing. A foul, ashy-gray miasma followed it, blurring over them. Peka hid her face in her arms. Sounds like the heaving of boulders and the spattering of fire came from beneath her.

She heard the dragon's dry roar, like stones dragged against one another. There was a smack, a musical shower of breaking icicles, and a sharp, anguished curse. Ryd appeared out of the turmoil of light and air, sprawled on the ledge beside Peka.

His face was cut, with ice, she supposed, and there was blood in his white hair. He looked at her with vague amazement.

"You're still here."

"Where else would I be? Are you winning or losing?"

He scooped up snow, held it against his face. "I feel as if I've been fighting for a thousand years . . . Sometimes, I think I tangle in its memories, as it thinks of other Harrowers, old dragon-battles, distant places. It doesn't remember what I am, only that I will not let it sleep . . . Did you see its wingspan? I fought a red dragon once with such a span. Its wings turned to flame in the sunlight. You'll see this one in flight by dawn."

She stared at him numbly, huddled against herself. "Are you so sure?"

"It's old and slow. And it can't bear the gold fire." He paused, then dropped the snow in his hand with a sigh and leaned his face against the ice-wall. "I'm tired, too. I have one empty crystal, to capture the essence of its mist, its heart's breath. After that's done, the battle will be short." He lifted his head at her silence, as if he could hear her thoughts. "What?"

"You'll go on to other dragons. But all I've ever had is this one."

"You never knew—"

"It doesn't matter that I never knew it. I know now. It was coiled all around us in the winter, while we lived in warm darkness and firelight. It kept out the world. Is that such a terrible thing? Is there so much wisdom in the flatlands that we can't live without?"

He was silent again, frowning a little, either in pain or faint confusion. "It's a dangerous thing, a destroyer."

"So is winter. So is the mountain, sometimes. But they're also beautiful. You are full of so much knowledge and experience that you forgot how to see simple things. Ryd Yarrow, miner's son. You must have loved Hoarsbreath once."

"I was a child, then."

She sighed. "I'm sorry I brought you down here. I wish I were up there with the miners, in the last peaceful night."

"There will be peace again," he said, but she shook her head wearily.

"I don't feel it." She expected him to smile, but his frown deepened. He touched her face suddenly with his burned hand.

"Sometimes I almost hear what you're trying to tell me. And then it fades against all my knowledge and experience. I'm glad you stayed. If I die, I'll leave you facing one maddened dragon. But still, I'm glad."

A black moon rose high over his shoulder and she jumped. Ryd rolled off the ledge into the mists. Peka hid her face from the peering black flare. Blue light smoldered through the mist, the moon rolled suddenly out of the sky, and she could breathe again.

Streaks of dispersing gold lit the dawn sky like the sunrises she saw one month out of the year. Peka, in a cold daze on the ledge, saw Ryd for the first time in an hour. He was facing the dragon, his silver hand outstretched. In his palm lay a crystal so cold and deathly white that Peka, blinking at it, felt its icy stare into her heart.

She shuddered. Her bones turned to ice; mist seemed to flow into her veins. She breathed bitter, frozen air as heavy as water. She reached for the wormspoor; her arm moved sluggishly, and her fingers unfolded with brittle movements. The dragon was breathing in short, harsh spurts. The silver hoods were over its eyes. Its unfolded wing lay across the ice like a limp sail. Its jaws were open, hissing faintly, but its head was reared back, away from Ryd's hand. Its heartbeat, in the silence, was slow, slow.

Peka dragged herself up, icicle by icicle. In the clear wintry dawn, she saw the beginning and the end of the enormous ring around Hoarsbreath. The dragon's tail lifted wearily behind Ryd, then fell again, barely making a sound. Ryd stood still; his eyes, relentless, spring-blue, were his only color. As Peka watched, swaying on the edge, the world fragmented into simple things: the edges of silver on the dragon's scales, Ryd's silver fingers, his old-man's hair, the pure white of the dragon's hide. They faced one another, two powerful creatures born out of the same winter, harrowing one another. The dragon rippled along its bulk; its head reared farther back, giving Peka a dizzying glimpse of its open jaws. She saw the cracked tooth, crumbled like a jewel she might have battered inadvertently with her pick, and winced. Seeing her, it hissed, a tired, angry sigh.

She stared down at it; her eyes seemed numb, incapable of sorrow. The wing on the ice was beginning to stir. Ryd's head lifted. He looked bone-pale, his face expressionless with exhaustion. But the faint, icy smile of triumph in his eyes struck her as deeply as the stare from the death-eye in his palm.

She drew in mist like the dragon, knowing that Ryd was not harrowing an old, tired ice-dragon, but one out of his memories who never seemed to yield. "You bone-brained dragon," she shouted, "how can you give up Hoarsbreath so easily? And to a Dragon Harrower whose winter is colder and more terrible than yours." Her heart seemed trapped in the weary, sluggish pace of its heart. She knelt down, wondering if it could understand her words or only feel them. "Think of Hoarsbreath," she pleaded, and searched for words to warm them both. "Fire. Gold. Night. Warm dreams, winter tales, silence—" Mist billowed at her and she coughed until tears froze on her cheeks. She heard Ryd call her name on a curious, inflexible note that panicked her. She uncorked the wormspoor with trembling fingers, took a great gulp, and coughed again as the blood shocked through her. "Don't you have any fire at all in you? Any winter flame?" Then a vision of gold shook her: the gold within the dragon's heart, the warm gold of wormspoor, the bitter gold of dragon's blood. Ryd said her name again, his voice clear as breaking ice. She shut her eyes against him, her hands rising through a chill, dark dream. As he called the third time, she dropped the wormspoor down the dragon's throat.

The hoods over its eyes rose; they grew wide, white-rimmed. She heard a convulsive swallow. Its head snapped down; it made a sound between a bellow and a whimper. Then its jaws opened again and it raked the air with gold flame.

Ryd, his hair and eyebrows scored suddenly with gold, dove into the snow. The dragon hissed at him again. The stream beyond him turned fiery, ran toward the sea. The great tail pounded furiously; dark cracks tore through the ice. The frozen cliffs began to sweat under the fire; pillars of ice sagged down, broke against the ground. The ledge Peka stood on crumbled at a wave of gold. She fell with it in a small avalanche of ice-rubble. The enormous white ring of dragon began to move, blurring endlessly past her eyes as the dragon gathered itself. A wing arched up toward the sky, then another. The dragon hissed at the mountain, then roared desperately, but only flame came out of its bowels, where once it had secreted winter. The chasms and walls of ice began breaking apart. Peka, struggling out of the snow, felt a lurch under her feet. A wind sucked at her hair, pulled at her heavy coat. Then it drove down at her, thundering, and she sat in the snow. The dragon, aloft, its wingspan the span of half the island, breathed fire at the ocean, and its husk of ice began to melt.

Ryd pulled her out of the snow. The ground was breaking up under their feet. He said nothing; she thought he was scowling, though he looked strange with singed eyebrows. He pushed at her, flung her toward the sea. Fire sputtered around them. Ice slid under her; she slipped and clutched at the jagged rim of it. Brine splashed in her face. The ice whirled, as chunks of the mountain fell into the sea around them. The dragon was circling the mountain, melting huge peaks and cliffs. They struck the water hard, heaving the ice-floes farther from the island. The mountain itself began to break up, as ice tore away from it, leaving only a bare peak riddled with mine shafts.

Peka began to cry. "Look what I've done. Look at it." Ryd only grunted. She thought she could see figures high on the top of the peak, staring down at the vanishing island. The ocean, churning, spun the ice-floe toward the mainland. The river was flowing again, a blue-white streak spiraling down from the peak. The dragon was over the mainland now, billowing fire at the harbor, and ships without crews or cargo were floating free.

"Wormspoor," Ryd muttered. A wave ten feet high caught up with them, spilled, and shoved them into the middle of the channel. Peka saw the first of the boats taking the swift, swollen current down from the top of the island. Ryd spat out seawater, and took a firmer grip of the ice. "I lost every crystal, every dragon's fire I possessed. They're at the bottom of the sea. Thanks to you. Do you realize how much work, how many years—"

"Look at the sky." It spun above her, a pale, impossible mass of nothing. "How can I live under that? Where will I ever find dark, quiet places full of gold?"

"I held that dragon. It was just about to leave quietly, without taking half of Hoarsbreath with it."

"How will we live on the island again? All its secrets are gone."

"For fourteen years I studied dragons, their lore, their flights, their fires, the patterns of their lives and their destructions. I had all the knowledge I thought possible for me to acquire. No one—"

"Look at all that dreary flatland."

"No one," he said, his voice rising, "ever told me you could harrow a dragon by pouring wormspoor down its throat!"

"Well, no one told me, either!" She slumped beside him, too despondent for anger. She watched more boats carrying miners, young children, her mother, down to the mainland. Then the dragon caught her eye, pale against the winter sky, somehow fragile, beautifully crafted, flying into the wake of its own flame.

It touched her mourning heart with the fire she had given it. Beside her, she felt Ryd grow quiet. His face, tired and battered, held a young, forgotten wonder, as he watched the dragon blaze across the world's cap like a star, searching for its winter. He drew a soft, incredulous breath.

"What did you put into that wormspoor?"

"Everything."

He looked at her, then turned his face toward Hoarsbreath. The sight made him wince. "I don't think we left even my father's bones at peace," he said hollowly, looking for a moment less a Dragon Harrower than a harrowed miner's son.

"I know," she whispered.

"No, you don't," he sighed. "You feel. The dragon's heart. My heart. It's not a lack of knowledge or experiences that destroyed Hoarsbreath, but something else I lost sight of: you told me that. The dark necessity of wisdom."

She gazed at him, suddenly uneasy, for he was seeing her. "I'm not wise. Just lucky—or unlucky."

"Wisdom is a flatlander's word for your kind of feeling. You put your heart into everything—wormspoor, dragons, gold—and they become a kind of magic."

"I do not. I don't understand what you're talking about, Ryd Yarrow. I'm a miner; I'm going to find another mine—"

"You have a gold mine in your heart. There are other things you can do with yourself. Not harrow dragons, but become a Watcher. You love the same things they love."

"Yes. Peace and quiet and private places—"

"I could show you dragons in their beautiful, private places all over the world. You could speak their language."

"I can't even speak my own. And I hate the flatland." She gripped the ice, watching it come.

"The world is only another tiny island, ringed with a great dragon of stars and night."

She shook her head, not daring to meet his eyes. "No. I'm not listening to you anymore. Look what happened the last time I listened to your tales."

"It's always yourself you are listening to," he said. The gray ocean swirled the ice under them, casting her back to the bewildering shores of the world. She was still trying to argue when the ice moored itself against the scorched pilings of the harbor.

OUT OF THE WOODS

The scholar came to live in the old cottage in the woods one spring. Leta didn't know he was there until Dylan told her of the man's request. Dylan, who worked with wood, cut and sold it, mended it, built with it, whittled it into toothpicks when he had nothing better to do, found the scholar under a bush, digging up henbane. From which, Dylan concluded, the young man was possibly dotty, possibly magical, but, from the look of him, basically harmless.

"He wants a housekeeper," he told Leta. "Someone to look after him during the day. Cook, wash, sew, dust, straighten. Buy his food, talk to peddlers, that sort of thing. You'd go there in the mornings, come back after his supper."

Leta rolled her eyes at her brawny, comely husband over the washtub as she pummeled dirt out of his shirts. She was a tall, wiry young woman with her yellow hair in a braid. Not as pretty or as bright as some, but strong and steady as a good horse, was how her mother had put it when Dylan came courting her.

"Then who's to do it around here?" she asked mildly, being of placid disposition.

Dylan shrugged, wood chips from a stick of kindling curling under his knife edge, for he had no more pressing work. "It'll get done," he said. He sent a couple more feathery chips floating to his feet, then added, "Earn a little money for us. Buy some finery for yourself. Ribbon for your cap. Shoe buckle."

She glanced down at her scuffed, work-worn clogs. Shoes, she thought with sudden longing. And so the next day she went to the river's edge and then took the path downriver to the scholar's cottage.

She'd known the ancient woman who had died there the year before. The cottage needed care; flowers and moss sprouted from its thatch; the old garden was a tangle of vegetables, herbs and weeds. The cottage stood in a little clearing surrounded by great oak and ash, near the river and not far from the road that ran from one end of the wood to the other. The scholar met her at the door as though he expected her.

He was a slight, bony young man with pale thinning hair and gray eyes that seemed to look at her, through her and beyond her, all at the same time. He reminded Leta of something newly hatched, awkward, its down still damp and all askew. He smiled vaguely, opened the door wider, inviting her in even before she explained herself, as though he already knew.

"Dylan sent me," she said, then gazed with astonishment at the pillars and piles of books, scrolls, papers everywhere, even in the rafters. The cauldron hanging over the cold grate was filthy. She could see a half-eaten loaf on a shelf in the open cupboard; a mouse was busily dealing with the other half. There were cobwebs everywhere, and unwashed cups, odd implements she could not name tossed on the colorful, wrinkled puddles of clothes on the floor. As she stood gaping, an old, wizened sausage tumbled out of the rafters, fell at her feet.

She jumped. The scholar picked up the sausage. "I was wondering what to have for breakfast." He put it into his pocket. "You'd be Leta, then?"

"Yes, sir."

"You can call me Ansley. My great-grandmother left me this cottage when she died. Did you know her?"

"Oh, yes. Everyone did."

"I've been away in the city, studying. I decided to bring my studies here, where I can think without distractions. I want to be a great mage."

"Oh?"

"It is an arduous endeavor, which is why I'll have no time for—" He gestured.

She nodded. "I suppose when you've become a mage, all you'll have to do is snap your fingers or something."

His brows rose; clearly, he had never considered the use of magic for housework. "Or something," he agreed doubtfully. "You can see for yourself what I need you for."

"Oh, yes."

He indicated the vast, beautifully carved table in a corner under a circular window from which the sunny river could be seen. Or could have been seen, but for the teetering pile of books blocking the view. Ansley must have brought the table with him. She wondered how he had gotten the massive thing through the door. Magic, maybe; it must be good for something.

"You can clear up any clutter in the place but that," he told her. "That must never be disturbed."

"What about the moldy rind of cheese on top of the books?"

He drew breath, held it. "No," he said finally, decisively. "Nothing on the table must be touched. I expect to be there most of the time anyway, learning spells and translating the ancient secrets in manuscripts. When," he asked a trifle anxiously, "can you start?"

She considered the various needs of her own husband and house, then yielded to his pleading eyes. "Now," she said. "I suppose you want some food in the place."

He nodded eagerly, reaching for his purse. "All I ask," he told her, shaking coins into her hand, "is not to be bothered. I'll pay whatever you ask for that. My father did well with the tavern he owned; I did even better when I sold it after he died. Just come and go and do whatever needs to be done. Can you manage that?"

"Of course," she said stolidly, pocketing the coins for a trip to the market in the village at the edge of the woods. "I do it all the time."

She spent long days at the cottage, for the scholar paid scant attention to time and often kept his nose in his books past sunset despite the wonderful smells coming out of his pots. Dylan grumbled, but the scholar paid very well, and didn't mind Leta taking leave in the late afternoons to fix Dylan's supper and tend for an hour to her own house before she went back to work. She cooked, scrubbed, weeded and washed, got a cat for the mice and fed it too, swept and mended, and even wiped the grime off the windows, though the scholar never bothered looking out. Dylan worked hard, as well, building cupboards and bedsteads for the villagers, chopping trees into cartloads of wood to sell in the market for winter. Some days, she heard his ax from dawn to dusk. On market days, when he lingered in the village tavern, she rarely saw his face until one or the other of them crawled wearily into bed late at night.

"We never talk anymore," she murmured once, surprisedly, to the dark when the warm, sweaty, grunting shape that was Dylan pushed under the bedclothes beside her. "We just work and sleep, work and sleep."

He mumbled something that sounded like "What else is there?" Then he rolled away from her and began to snore.

One day when Ansley had gone down to the river to hunt for the details of some spell, Leta made a few furtive passes with her broom at the dust under his worktable. Her eye fell upon a spiral of gold on a page in an open book. She stopped sweeping, studied it. A golden letter, it looked like, surrounded by swirls of gold in a frame of crimson. All that richness, she marveled, for a letter. All that beauty. How could a simple letter, this undistinguished one that also began her name, be so cherished, given such loving attention?

"One little letter," she whispered, and her thoughts strayed to earlier times, when Dylan gave her wildflowers and sweets from the market. She sighed. They were always so tired now, and she was growing thinner from so much work. They had more money, it was true. But she had no time to spend it, even on shoes, and Dylan never thought of bringing her home a ribbon or a bit of lace when he went to the village. And here was this letter, doing nothing more than being the first in a line of them, adorned in red and gold for no other reason than that it was itself—

She touched her eyes, laughed ruefully at herself, thinking, I'm jealous of a letter.

Someone knocked at the door.

She opened it, expecting Dylan, or a neighbor, or a tinker—anyone except the man who stood there.

She felt herself gaping, but could not stop. She could only think crazily of the letter again: how this man too must have come from some place where people as well as words carried such beauty about them. The young man wore a tunic of shimmering links of pure silver over black leather trousers and a pair of fine, supple boots. His cloak was deep blue-black, the color of his eyes. His crisp dark curls shone like blackbirds' wings. He was young, but something, perhaps the long, jeweled sword he wore, made both Dylan and Ansley seem much younger. His lean, grave face hinted of a world beyond the wood that not even the scholar had seen.

"I beg your pardon," he said gently, "for troubling you." Leta closed her mouth. "I'm looking for a certain palace of which I've heard rumors all my life. It is surrounded by a deadly ring of thorns, and many men have lost their lives attempting to break through that ensorceled circle to rescue the sleeping princess within. Have you heard of it?"

"I—" Leta said, and stuck there, slack-jawed again. "I—I—"

Behind the man, his followers, rugged and plainly dressed, glanced at one another. That look, less courteous than the young man's, cleared Leta's head a bit.

"I haven't," she brought out finally. "But the man I work for is a—is trying to be—a mage; he knows a thousand things I don't."

"Then may I speak with him?"

"He's out—" She gestured, saw the broom still in her hand and hid it hastily behind her. "Down by the river, catching toads."

"Toads."

"For his—his magic."

She heard the faint snort. One of the followers pretended to be watching a crow fly; the other breathed, "My lord, perhaps we should ask farther down the road."

"We'll ride to the river," the young lord said, and turned to mount his horse again. He bowed graciously to Leta from his saddle. "Thank you. We are grateful."

Blinking at the light spangling off his harness and jewels, she watched him ride through the trees and toward the water. Then, slowly, she sat down, stunned and witless with wonder, until she heard Ansley's voice as he walked through the doorway and around her.

"I found five," he announced excitedly, putting a muddy bucket on his table. "One of them is pure white!"

"Did you see—?" Her voice didn't come. She was sitting on the floor, she realized then, with the broom across her knees. "Did you see the—? Them?"

"Who?" he asked absently, picking toads out of the bucket and setting them on his papers.

"The traveler. I sent him to talk to you." She hesitated, finally said the word. "I think he is a prince. He is looking for a palace surrounded by thorns, with a sleeping princess inside."

"Oh, him. No. I mean yes, but no I couldn't help him. I had no idea what he was talking about. Come here and look at this white one. You can do so many things with the white toads."

She had to wait a long time before Dylan came home, but she stayed awake so that she could tell him. As he clambered into bed, breathing a gust of beer at her, she said breathlessly, "I saw a prince today. On his way to rescue a princess."

He laughed and hiccuped at the same time. "And I saw the Queen of the Fairies. Did you happen to spot my knife too? I set it down yesterday when I was whittling, and it must have strolled away."

"Dylan—"

He kissed her temple. "You're dreaming, love. No princes here."

The days lengthened. Hawthorn blossoms blew everywhere like snow, leaving green behind. The massive oaks covered their tangled boughs with leaves. An early summer storm thundered through the woods one afternoon. Leta, who had just spread Ansley's washing to dry on the hawthorn bushes around the cottage, heard the sudden snarl of wind, felt a cold, hard drop of rain on her mouth. She sighed. The clothes were wet anyway; but for the wild wind that might steal them, she could have left them out. She began to gather them back into her basket.

She heard voices.

They sounded like wind at first, one high, pure, one pitched low, rumbling. They didn't seem human, which made Leta duck warily behind a bush. But their words were human enough, which made her strain her ears to listen. It was, she thought bewilderedly, like hearing what the winds had to say for themselves.

"Come into my arms and sleep, my lord," the higher voice crooned. "You have lived a long and adventurous life; you may rest now for a while."

"No," the deeper voice protested, half-laughing, half-longing, Leta thought. "It's not time for me to sleep, yet. There are things I still must teach you."

"What things, my heart?"

"How to understand the language of beetles, how to spin with spindrift, what lies hidden in the deepest place in the ocean and how to bring it up to light."

"Sleep a little. Teach me when you wake again."
"No, not yet."
"Sleep."

Leta crept closer to the voices. The rain pattered down now, great, fat drops the trees could not stop. Through the blur of rain and soughing winds stirring up the bracken, she saw two figures beneath an oak. They seemed completely unaware of the storm, as if they belonged to some enchanted world. The woman's long, fiery, rippling hair did not notice the wind, nor did the man's gray-white beard. He sat cradled in the oak roots, leaning back against the trunk. His face looked as harsh and weathered, as ancient and enduring as the wood. The woman stood over him, close enough for him to touch, which he did now and then, his hand caressing the back of her knee, coaxing it to bend. They were both richly dressed, he in a long, silvery robe flecked with tiny jewels like points of light along the sleeves, the hem. She wore silk the deepest green of summer, the secret green of trees who have taken in all the light they can hold, and feel, somewhere within them, summer's end. His eyes were half-closed. Hers were very wide as she stared down at him: pale amber encircling vivid points of black.

Leta froze. She did not dare move, lest those terrible eyes lift from his and search her out behind the bush with Ansley's trousers flapping on it.

"Sleep," the woman murmured again, her voice like a lightly dancing brook, like the sough of wind in reeds. "Sleep."

His hand dropped from her knee. He made an effort, half lifting his eyelids. His eyes were silver, metallic like a knife blade.

"Not yet, my sweet Nimue. Not yet."

"Sleep."

He closed his eyes.

There was a crack as though the world had been torn apart. Then came the thunder. Leta screamed as she felt it roll over her, through her, and down beneath her into the earth. The ancient oak, split through its heart, trailing limbs like shattered bone, loosed sudden, dancing streams of fire. Rain fell then in vast sheets as silvery as the sleeper's eyes. Leta couldn't see anything; she was drenched in a moment and sinking rapidly into a puddle. Rising, she glimpsed the light shining from the cottage windows. She stumbled out of the mysterious world toward it; wind blew her back through the scholar's door, then slammed the door behind her.

"I saw—I saw—" she panted.

But she did not know what she saw. Ansley, his attention caught at last by something outside his books—the thunder, maybe, or the lake she was making on his floor—looked a little pale in the gloom.

"You saw what?"

But she had only pieces to give him, nothing whole, nothing coherent. "I saw his eyes close. And then lightning struck the oak."

Ansley moved then. "Oh, I hope it won't topple onto my roof."

"His eyes closed—they were like metal—she put him to sleep with her eyes—"

"Show me the tree."

She led him eagerly through the rain. It had slowed a little; the storm was moving on. Somewhere else in the wood strange things were happening; the magic here had come and gone.

They stood looking at the broken heart of the oak, its wood still smoldering, its snapped boughs sagging, shifting dangerously in the wind. Only a stand of gnarled trunk was left, where the sleeper had been sitting.

"Come away," Ansley said uneasily. "Those limbs may still fall."

"But I saw two people—"

"They had sense enough to run, it seems; there are no bodies here. Just," he added, "a lot of wet clothes among the bushes. What exactly were those two doing?"

"They're your clothes."

"Oh."

She lingered, trying to find some shred of mystery left in the rain, some magic smoldering with the wood. "He closed his eyes," she whispered, "and lightning struck the oak."

"Well, he must have opened them fast enough then," Ansley said. "Come back into the house. Leave the laundry; you can finish all that later." His voice brightened as he wandered back through the dripping trees. "This will send the toads out to sun. . . ."

She did not even try to tell Dylan, for if the young scholar with all his books saw no magic, how could he?

Days passed, one very like the next. She cooked, washed, weeded in the garden. Flowers she had rescued from wild vines bloomed and faded; she picked herbs and beans and summer squashes. The scholar studied.

One day the house was full of bats, the next full of crows. Another day he made everything disappear, including himself. Leta stepped, startled, into an empty cottage. Not a thing in it, not even a stray spider. Then she saw the scholar's sheepish smile forming in the air; the rest of his possessions followed slowly. She stared at him, speechless. He cleared his throat.

"I must have mistranslated a word or two in that spell."

"You might have translated some of the clutter out of the door while you were at it," she said. What had reappeared was as chaotic as ever. She could not imagine what he did at nights while she was at home. Invented whirlwinds, or made his pots and clothes dance in midair until they dropped, it looked like.

"Think of magic as an untamed creature," he suggested, opening a book while he rained crumbs on the floor chewing a crust he had found on his table. "I am learning ways to impose my will upon it, while it fights me with all its cunning for its freedom."

"It sounds like your garden," she murmured, tracking down her gardening basket, which was not on the peg where she hung it, but, for some reason, on a shelf, in the frying pan. The scholar made an absent noise, not really hearing her; she had gotten used to that. She went outside to pull up onions for soup. She listened for Dylan's ax while she dug; he had said he was cutting wood that day. But she didn't hear it, just the river and the birds and the breeze among the leaves.

He must have gone deeper than usual into the woods, she thought. But she felt the little frown between her brows growing tighter and tighter at his silence. For no reason her throat grew tight too, hurt her suddenly. Maybe she had misunderstood; maybe he had gone into the village to sell wood instead. That made the ache in her throat sharper. His eyes and voice were absent, those days. He looked at her, but hardly saw her; he kissed her now and then, brief, chuckling kisses that you'd give to a child. He had never gone to the village so often without her before; he had never wanted to go without her, before . . .

She asked him tentatively that night, as he rolled into bed in a cloud of beer fumes and wood smoke, "Will you take me with you, next time?"

He patted her shoulder, his eyes already closed. "You need your rest, working so hard for two houses. Anyway, it's nothing; I just have a quick drink and a listen to the fiddling, then I'm home to you."

"But it's so late."

He gave her another pat. "Is it? Then best get to sleep."

He snored; she stared, wide-eyed, back at the night.

She scarcely noticed when the leaves first began to turn. Suddenly there were mushrooms and berries and nuts to gather, and apples all over the little twisty apple tree in her own garden. The days were growing shorter, even while there seemed so much more to do. She pulled out winter garments to mend where the moths had chewed; she replenished supplies of soap and candles. Her hands were always red; her hair, it seemed, always slightly damp with steam from something. The leaves grew gold, began to fall, crackle underfoot as she walked from one house to the other and back again. She scarcely saw the two men: the scholar hunched over a book with his back to her, her husband always calling good-bye as he went to chop or sell or build. Well, they scarcely saw her either, she thought tiredly; that was the way of it.

She stayed into evening at the scholar's one day, darning his winter cloak while the stew she had made of carrots and potatoes and leeks bubbled over the fire. He was at his table, staring into what looked like a glass ball filled with swirling iridescent fires. He was murmuring to it; if it answered him, she didn't hear.

At least not for some time. When she began to hear the strange, crazed disturbance beneath the wind rattling at the door, she thought at first that the sound came from within the globe. Her needle paused. The noise seemed to be coming closer: a disturbing confusion of dogs barking, horns, faint bells, shouting, bracken and fallen limbs crackling under the pounding of many hooves. She stared at the glass ball, which was hardly bigger than the scholar's fist. Surely such an uproar couldn't be coming from that?

The wind shrieked suddenly. The door shook on its hinges. She froze, midstitch. The door sprang open as if someone had kicked it. All the confusion in the night seemed to be on the scholar's doorstep and about to roil into his cottage.

She leaped to her feet, terrified, and clung to the door, trying to force it shut against the wind. A dark current was passing the house: something huge and nameless, bewildering until her eyes began to find the shapes in the night. They appeared at random, lit by fires that seemed to stream from the nostrils of black horses galloping past her. The flames illumined great hounds with eyes like coals, upraised sword blades like broken pieces of lightning, cowled faces, harnesses strung with madly clamoring bells.

She stared, unable to move. One of the hooded faces turned toward her as his enormous horse, its hooves sparking fire, cleared her potato rows. The rider's face was gaunt, bony, his hair in many long braids, their ends secured around clattering bones. He wore a crown of gold; its great jewel reflected fire the color of a splash of blood. White moons in the rider's eye sockets flashed at Leta; he opened his jaws wide like a wolf and laughed.

She could not even scream, her voice was that shriveled with fear. She could only squeak. Then the door was taken firmly out of her hands, closed against the night.

The scholar grumbled, returning to his work, "I couldn't hear a thing with all that racket. Are you still here? Take a lamp with you when you go home."

She went home late, terrified at every step, every whine of wind and crackle of branch. Her cold hands woke Dylan as she hugged him close in their bed for warmth and comfort. He raised his head, breathing something that may have been a name, and maybe not. Then his voice came clear.

"You're late." He did not sound worried or angry, only sleepy. "Your hands are ice."

"Dylan, there was something wicked in the woods tonight."

"What?"

"I don't know—riders, dark riders, on horses with flaming breath—I heard horns, as if they were hunting—"

"Nobody hunts in the dark."

"Didn't you hear it?"

"No."

"Were you even here?" she asked incredulously. He turned away from her, settled himself again.

"Of course. You weren't, though, so I went to bed."

"You could have come to fetch me," she whispered. "You could have brought a lamp."

"What?"

"You could have wondered."

"Go to sleep," he murmured. "Sleep."

Winter, she thought as she walked to the scholar's cottage the next morning. There wouldn't be so much work then, with the snow flying. No gardens to tend, no trees to chop, with their wood damp and iron-clad. She and Dylan would see more of one another, then. She'd settle the scholar and come home before dark; they'd have long evenings together beside the fire. Leaves whirled around her. The brightly colored autumn squashes were almost the last things still unpicked in the garden, besides the root vegetables. One breath of frost, and the herbs would be gone, along with most of the green in the world.

"You'll need wood for winter," she reminded the scholar. "I'll have Dylan bring you some."

He grunted absently. She sighed a little, watching him, as she tied on her apron.

I've grown invisible, she thought.

Later, she caught herself longing for winter, and didn't know whether to laugh or cry.

Dylan stacked the scholar's wood under the eaves. The squashes grew fat as the garden withered around them. The air smelled of rain and sweet wood smoke. Now and then the sky turned blue; fish jumped into sunlight; the world cast a glance back at the season it had left. On one of those rare days Leta spread the washing on the bushes to dry. Drawn to the shattered oak, she left her basket and walked through the brush to look at it, search for some sign that she had truly seen—whatever she had seen.

The great, gnarled stump, so thick that two or maybe three of her might have ringed it with her arms, stood just taller than her head. Only this lower, rooted piece of trunk was left intact, though lightning had seared a black stain on it like a scar. It stood dreaming in the sunlight, revealing nothing of its secrets. Just big enough, she thought, to draw a man inside it, if one had fallen asleep against it. In spring, living shoots would rise like his dreams out of the trunk, crown it with leaves, this still-living heart big enough to hide a sleeping mage. . . .

Something moving down the river caught her eyes.

She went through the trees toward it, unable to see clearly what it was. An empty boat, it seemed, caught in the current, but that didn't explain its odd shape, and the hints of color about it, the drift of cloth that was not sail.

She ran down the river path a ways to get ahead of it, so that she could see it clearly as it passed. It seemed a fine, delicate thing, with its upraised prow carved into a spiral and gilded. The rest of it, except for a thin line of gold all around it, was painted black. Some airy fabric caught on the wind, drifted above it, and then fell back into the boat. Now the cloth was blue, now satiny green. Now colors teased at her: intricately embroidered scenes she could not quite make out, on a longer drift of linen. She waited, puzzled, for the boat to reach her.

She saw the face within and caught her breath.

It was a young woman. She lay in the boat as though she slept, her sleeves, her skirt, the tapestry work in her hands picked up by passing breezes, then loosed again. Her hair, the color of the dying leaves, was carefully coiled and pinned with gold. Leta started to call to her. Words stopped before they began. That lovely face, skin white as whitest birch, held nothing now: no words, no expressions, no more movement than a stone. She had nothing left to tell Leta but her silence.

The boat glided past. Golden oak leaves dropped gently down onto the still figure, as though the trees watched with Leta. She felt sorrow grow in her throat like an apple, a toad, a jewel. It would not come out in tears or words or any other shape. It kept growing, growing, while she moved because she still could—walk and speak and tell and even, with a reason, smile—down the river path. She followed the boat, not knowing where it was going, or what she was mourning, beginning to run after a while when the currents quickened and the trees thinned, and the high slender towers of a distant city gleamed in the light of the waning day.

THE FORTUNE-TELLER

Merle saw the silk trailing out from under the toothless pile of rags snoring in a muddy alley. She glanced around. Most in the busy marketplace were buried under hoods and shawls, eyes squinched against the drizzling rain. They paid her no attention. She knelt swiftly, tugged at the silk. Cards came with it; she felt them as she stuffed the plunder under her shawl and strode away. Oversize, they were, like her mother's cards, and knotted in threads spun by little worms on the far side of the world. The sleeping lump had probably stolen them herself, and there was no reason why Merle shouldn't have them instead. She, after all, wasn't wasting the day facedown in the mud. Fortune favored those who recognized her, and Merle had watched her mother read the cards often enough to know what to do with them.

She worked quickly and efficiently through the crowd, a tall, thin, unremarkable figure swathed against the rain like everyone, with only her eyes visible and wide open. Her long fingers caught the change rattling into a capacious coat pocket as its distracted owner bit into the sausage roll he had just purchased. Farther down among the stalls, she slid a lovely square of linen and lace, perfumed against the smells of the street, out of a lady's gloved fingers. The lady had stopped to laugh at a parrot inviting her to "Have a dance, luv, have a dance." Opening her bag to find the one-armed sailor a coin, she gave a sudden exclamation. Merle left her searching the cobbles for her lace, and disappeared back into the crush.

Another carelessly unguarded pocket in a great coat caught her eye, its shiny brass button dangling free of its loop and winking at her. She drew up close, dipped a hand in. Faster than thought another hand followed, closed around her fingers.

She drew a startled breath, gathered her wits and more breath in the next instant to raise an indignant and noisy complaint against the ruffian who had grabbed a poor, honest young girl going about her business.

Then she saw the face between the upraised coat collar and the hat. Her tirade whooshed into a laugh.

"Ansel! You gave me a moment, there."

He didn't look amused; his lean, comely face, his jade eyes were hard. "Someone will give you more than a moment," he warned, "if you don't stop this."

She shrugged that away, more interested in his clothes. "Where did you steal the coat?"

"I didn't. I'm a working man. I drive a carriage now. You—"

"I'm a working girl," she interrupted before he could get started.

"You're a thief."

"I'm a fortune-teller. Look. I even have cards now." She opened her cloak, gave him a glimpse of the cards in their silk tucked into her waistband. "I found them this morning."

He gave a sour laugh. "You stole them."

"Nobody else was using them."

"You said you were going to—"

"You know I can earn my way, telling fortunes. I've done it before. I told yours. Remember?" She shifted the shawl wrapped up under her almond-shaped eyes to remind him of the full lips and sweet, stark jawline beneath, a trifle wolfish, maybe, but then she was ravenous half the time. His own lips parted; his eyes grew vague with memory. "Remember? The day we met. You saw me and followed me to my tent; I told your fortune with tea leaves and coins made of candle wax. You stole bread and sausages and cheese for our supper. Now that I have cards, I can build a reputation like my mother had—at least when my father stayed in one place long enough."

"You told me," he reminded her softly, "that I'd meet a stranger with storm-gray eyes I'd follow forever. I thought, that night, I had."

She shrugged slightly. "You liked me well enough then. But you didn't stay forever."

"You promised me you'd stop this magpie life. I stopped, but you didn't."

"Now I can," she said, tightening her cloak around the cards again. But he only made a sound between a sigh and a groan, and stepped back impatiently.

"You'll never change."

"Come and see. You know where to find me."

"Wherever they lock you away, most likely, one of these days. You can't play your tricks on the world forever."

"I'll stop, I promise," she told him, half-laughing again. He shook his head wordlessly, turning away, and so did she, with another shrug. She had coins for a meal, lace to sell; she could spend some time studying the cards now. She made her way back to her tent, pocketing a stray meat pie from a baker's busy stall along the way. Why should she pay for what the world put in her way for free?

Her fortune-teller's tent was makeshift: an abandoned shell of a wagon on the edge of the marketplace. It had a broken axle and two barrels propping up the corners where the wheels were missing. A discarded sail nailed over the ribs kept it dry. Merle had brightened the inside with dyed muslin and sprigged lawn skirts she'd separated from their drying lines. Fine shawls with gold threads, ribbons, beads of crystal and jet, left unattended in carriages or dangling too far over a lady's arm, she'd appropriated from their careless owners. She picked apart the seams and wound the swaths around the wagon ribs to make a colorful cave of embroidery, lace, ribbons, flowing cloth. She collected candle ends wherever she found them, to scatter around her while she worked. The tent was guarded by an old raven she'd found protecting a blind beggar who had fallen dead in the street. She'd coaxed it to eat; it came home with her. It had a malevolent eye, a sharp beak, and a vocabulary of two words—"Help! Murder!"—which it loosed with an ear-splitting squall when it was alone and faced with a stranger.

It greeted Merle with a rustle of wind and a faint, throaty chuckle. She lit candles and shared bits of the meat pie with the bird. Then she reached outside to hang her painted sign above the wagon steps, and draped a long, dark, beaded veil over her hair and shoulders. She unwrapped the cards.

The silk was snagged and frayed, with a spill of wine along one edge. The cards themselves were creased, flecked with candle wax, and so thumbed with use that some of the images were blurring. She began to lay them out.

Scarecrow. Old Woman. Sea. Gypsy Wagon.

She paused, studying them. It was an odd deck, not at all like her mother's with its bright paintings of cups and swords, kings and queens. Those had once belonged to Merle's great-grandmother; her mother cherished them, wrapped them in spotless silk and tucked them into a cedar and rosewood box between readings. These, well-drawn and colored despite their age, said nothing at all familiar. She laid out a few more and gazed at them, perplexed. There seemed to be a lot of crows. And what would a snake curled into a hoop and rolling itself down a road possibly signify?

The curtains trembled. Merle glimpsed fingers, pale and slender, heard whisperings outside on the steps. She drew the veil across her face. No sense in getting herself into unnecessary trouble if someone happened to recognize her. When the whispering didn't go away, she lit more candles around her and waited.

The curtains opened finally. Three young women, as neatly and fashionably dressed as they could afford, stared at her anxiously.

"Come in."

Something—the exotic veil, her deep voice, which made her sound older and possibly wiser than she was, the flames weaving a mystery of light and glittering dark around her—reassured them. They ducked under the canopy, seated themselves on pilfered carriage cushions, the golden-haired one in front, the other two behind. They spent a moment eyeing the fortune-teller, the cards she had gathered up again, the motionless raven, the drifts of silk and muslin above their heads.

The one in front spoke. "I need to know my fortune."

Merle, shuffling the deck, supposed that anyone with that pretty, tired, worried face probably needed all the good news she could get.

She named her price, and when the coin lay between them, she began to turn the cards, laying them into a pattern: the rainbow arc of life and fortune.

"Wolf. Sun. Old Woman. Well." Again, nothing was familiar; she had to guess at what they should be called, keeping her voice calm and certain, no matter what showed its face. "Spider. The Blind Man. The Masked Lovers." She hesitated briefly. Who on earth was this? A blue-eyed grinning skeleton with a full head of red-gold hair, cloaked in blue and crowned, rode a pitchfork with three blackbirds clinging to the tines.

"Lady Death," she guessed wildly, and the young women made various distraught noises.

One suggested timidly, "Three of crows?" which made sense when Merle remembered the other crows in the deck.

But she answered smoothly, "When a card falls into the arc of life, it no longer belongs to a suit. Don't be afraid. She doesn't always signify death. Let's see what falls after her . . ." She turned another card, hoping it wasn't more crows. Pockmarked puddles came up; that was plain enough. "Rain." She turned the next and decided it would be the last: best to end with a cheerful face. "Fool." She put the deck down. "This is good. Very good."

"It is?" the young woman who had paid said incredulously. "But it says so little about love."

Love. Of course.

"Oh, but it says a great deal." Improvising rapidly, she led the rapt watchers through it, card by card. "Wolf, at the beginning of the arc, signifies a messenger. Sun is, of course, a fortuitous message. The Old Woman in conjunction with the Well is someone you will meet who will give you strength and power—that's the well water—to achieve your heart's desire. Spider may be good or bad. When it appears in the arc, it's the web that signifies, and here it means something well planned, successful."

And so on. She could chart a fortune through twigs and broken eggshells, if she had to. Where she saw a pattern, she could find a fortune. She'd learned that much from her mother before she'd escaped from her eternally traveling family to the city. Even she couldn't see a fortune in a tinker's wagon.

"But what about Lady Death?" the young woman whispered, mesmerized by the card. "Who will die?"

"In this arc," Merle explained glibly, "Lady Death signifies protection. She guards against misfortune, malice, bad influences. Rain follows her. A little stormy weather will hamper the lovers, but that is natural in the course of true love. In the end the Fool, who signifies the wisdom of innocence, will guide your heart to achieve its innermost dreams."

The young woman, whose mouth was hanging by now, closed it with a click of teeth. She sighed and began to smile; the faces behind her brightened. "So he will love me in spite of everything."

"So the cards have shown," Merle answered solemnly, sweeping them together and palming the coin at the same time. She wondered briefly what obstacles the cards had missed. The rival lover? The deluded husband? The betrayed wife? Lack of money to wed? Mismatched circumstances: she a seamstress, he a noble who had admired too closely the shape of her lips? Merle had a hunch that, under other eyes, the cards would have suggested a darker, more ambiguous future. But the young woman had paid for hope, and Merle had earned her pay.

You see? she told Ansel silently as the women went back into the rain. I have a profession, too. Soon, with these strange cards, I'll even have a reputation. Then I can afford to be honest.

Ansel came to her that night as she knew he would. In spite of himself, she guessed wryly, taking note of his dour, reluctant expression. But she knew tricks to make him smile, others to make him laugh, which he did at last, though he sobered up too soon after that.

"You've learned a few things on the street since I saw you last," he commented, rolling onto his back in her meager bed, and stroking her hair as she laid her cheek on his chest.

"Knowledge is free," she said contentedly.

"Is it?"

"At least I don't have to steal it. Don't—" she pleaded as he opened his mouth. "Don't go back to glowering at me. You like what I learned."

She felt him draw breath, but he didn't lecture. He didn't say anything, just smoothed her hair, drew it out across his chest to watch it gleam in the candlelight, onyx dark, raven dark, true black without a trace of color in it. He laughed a little, gently, as at a memory.

"You're growing so beautiful . . . All I could see of that the few months ago I met you was in your eyes. You were such a scrawny girl, all bones and sharp edges, and those huge eyes, the color of a mist that I wanted to walk through to see what I would find."

"And what did you find?"

He was silent again; she listened drowsily to his heartbeat. "Someone like me," he said finally. "Which was fine until I started not liking what I was . . . So I made myself into someone more to my liking."

Within the little cave he had made of her hair, her eyes opened. She felt a sudden, odd hollow inside her. As though he had tricked her, taken something from her that she didn't know she had until he showed her.

"So now you like me less," she said softly, and pulled herself over him until they were eye to eye in the dark fall of her hair. "But I'm going to make myself respectable with my cards."

"You stole them."

She laughed. "From some old biddy lying dead drunk in an alley. Besides, I'll hardly be the first to turn myself respectable with stolen goods. I didn't rob a bank, after all. They're only cards."

"Are they?" He eased out from under her and sat up, reaching for his trousers. "I've got to go. I'm stealing time, myself, from my job."

"Come tomorrow?"

He gave her a wide-eyed, almost startled look, as though she'd suggested leaping off a roof together, or rifling through his employer's house.

"I don't know." His face disappeared under his shirt. "I doubt that I'll have time." He reappeared. "You haven't heard a word I said."

"What word didn't I hear?" she demanded. "Tell me."

But he was withdrawing again, going away from her, even before he left the wagon.

She sighed, sitting on her pallet, naked and alone but for the raven, feeling again that strange hollow where something should have been but wasn't any longer.

"You'll come back," she whispered and reached abruptly for the cards in their stained silk to find him in her future. She shuffled them and dealt the arc: Old Woman, Spider, Rain, the Masked Lovers, Lady Death . . .

She gave a cry and flung the deck down. Candlelight glided across the Old Woman's raddled face; she seemed to smile up at Merle.

You stole a poor old woman's only means to earn a coin, the smile said. *You stole her hope. And now you want to twist her cards, make them lie to you, show you how lovable you still are . . .*

The raven rustled on its perch, made a sound like a soft chuckle. Merle gathered the cards together with icy, trembling fingers, wanting to cry, she felt, but not remembering how to start. She pulled on clothes, flung her cloak around her, and splashed barefoot into the rain, not sure where to find the old woman, only certain that until she returned the cards she could not change her future of webs and rain and fools and the Old Woman's knowing eyes.

THE WITCHES OF JUNKET

GRANNY HEATHER was out on the lawn digging up night crawlers by flashlight when she saw the black spot on the moon. She heard the tide, though the sea was twenty miles away, and she saw the massive rock just offshore south of Crane Harbor open vast black eyes and stare at her. Three huge birds flew soundlessly overhead, looking like pterodactyls, glowing bluish white, like ghosts might. She didn't know if she was in the past or future. In the future, the sea might eat its way through the wrinkled old coast mountains, across the pastures where the sheep grazed, to her doorstep. In the past, those dinosaur birds might have flown over Junket, or whatever was there before the town was. She stopped tugging at a night crawler that was tugging itself back into its hole, and she turned the flashlight off. She made herself as small as possible, hunkering down on her old knees in the damp grass. Her hair felt too bright; she wondered if, under the moonlight, it glowed like the ghost birds. She heard her thin blood singing.

"So," she whispered, "you're awake."

For a moment she felt stared at, as if the full moon were an eye. It could see into her frail bones, find the weakest places where a tap might shatter her. She felt luminous, exposed, her old bones shining like the bones of little fish down in the darkest realms of the sea.

Then it was over, she was disregarded, the moon was no longer interested in her.

She stood up in the dark, tottery, her heart hammering, and made her way back into her house.

The next morning, she took her pole and her night crawlers and her lawn chair down the road to where the old pump house straddled a branch of the Junket River, where the bass liked to feed. She pleated a worm onto her hook and added an afterthought: a green marshmallow. No telling, she thought. She cast her line into the still water.

A trout rose up out of the water, danced on its tail, and said, "Call Storm's children."

It vanished back into the water as she stared, and took the worm clean off the hook, leaving the marshmallow.

She reeled in, sighing. "It's easy," she grumbled to the trout, "for you to say. You don't have to put up with them."

But she had to admit it was right.

Still and all, Storm's children being what they were, she got a second opinion.

She drove her twenty-year-old red VW Beetle over to Poppy and Cass's house, adding another 3.8 miles to the 32,528.9 she had turned over in twenty years. Cass was in the yard, polishing a great wheel of redwood burl. His work shed, which was a small warehouse left over from when the nearly invisible town of Raventree actually had a dock for river traffic, was cluttered with slabs of redwood and smaller, paler pieces of myrtle. He smiled at Heather, but he didn't speak. He was a shy, untidy giant, with hair that needed pruning and a nicotine-stained mustache. He jerked his head at the house to tell Heather where Poppy was, and Heather, feeling damp in her bones, creaked to the door, stuck her head inside.

"Poppy?"

Poppy came out of the kitchen, wiping her hands on a dish towel. "Why, Heather, you old sweet thing. I didn't hear you drive up. Come on in and sit down. I'll get us some tea." Turning briskly back to the kitchen, she caused whirlwinds: plants moved their faces, table legs clattered, framed photos on the wall slid askew. Heather waited until things quieted, then eased into one of Cass's burl chairs. It had three legs like a stool and a long skinny back with a face, elongated and shy, peering out of the wood grain. A teakettle howled; Poppy came back again carrying mugs of water with mint leaves floating in them. Heather preferred coffee, but she preferred nearly anything to Poppy's coffee. Anyway, she liked chewing on mint leaves.

Poppy settled into a chair with wide arms that had holes for plant pots;

delicate strings-of-hearts hung their runners over the sides almost to the floor. Poppy was a tall, big-boned woman who wore her yellow-gray hair in a long braid over one shoulder. Her eyes were wide-set, smoky gray; her brows were still yellow in her smooth forehead. She favored eye-smacking colors and clunky jewelry. Abalone, turquoise, hematite, and coral danced on her fingers. She wore big myrtle wood loops in her ears; a chunk of amber on a chain bounced on her bosom. She was the age Storm would have been, if Storm hadn't skidded into a tree on a rainy night. Heather had looked to Poppy after that, someone for her bewildered eyes to rest on after Storm had vanished, and Poppy had let her, coaxing her along as patiently as if Heather had been one of her ailing plants.

Heather took a sip of tea and spent a moment working a mint leaf out from behind one tooth, while Poppy meandered amiably about her married daughter and her new grandson. "Chance, they named him," she said. "Might as well have named him Luck or Fate or—Still and all, it's kind of catching."

"Poppy," Heather said, having finally swallowed the mint leaf, "I got to send for Storm's children."

Poppy put her mug down on the chair arm. Her brows pinched together suddenly, as if a tooth had jabbed her. "Oh, no."

"I've been told to."

"Who told you?"

"A trout, under Tim Greyson's pump house."

"Well, why, for goodness' sake?"

Heather sighed, feeling too old and very frail. "You know what's inside Oyster Rock." Poppy gave a nod, silent. "Well, it's not going to stay there."

Poppy swallowed. She stared at nothing a moment, her sandal tapping—she preferred the cork-soled variety, which lifted her up even taller and slapped her feet as she walked. "Oh, Lord," she muttered. "Are you sure? It's been down there for eight hundred years, ever since that Klamath woman drove it back into the rock. You'd think it could have stayed there a few more years."

"You'd think so. But—"

"Maybe we don't have to send for Storm's children. Maybe we could handle it ourselves. Still, Annie's up north with her daughter and Tessa has to get her legs worked on, and Olivia's at the mud caves in Montana, rejuvenating her skin—"

"That leaves you and me," Heather said dryly. "Unless you're busy, too."

"Well—"

"The point is, that thing's not going to ask us if we have time for it. It's not going to wait around for Annie to get home or Olivia to get the mud off her face. It's coming out. I felt it, Poppy. I saw the warnings. None of us was around eight hundred years ago to know exactly what it does, so if a trout says get help, how're you going to argue with it?"

Poppy drew a breath, held it. "Did you catch the trout?" she asked grimly.

"No."

"Pity. I'd like to deep-fry it." She kicked moodily at the planter again; the ficus in it shivered and dropped a leaf. "Are you sure what's inside the rock isn't the lesser of the two evils?"

"Poppy! Those are my grandchildren you're talking about. Besides," she added, "they're older now. Maybe they've settled down a little."

"Last time they came, they threw a keg party in the church parking lot."

"That was seven years ago, and, anyway, it was at Evan's funeral," Heather said stubbornly. She kicked at the planter herself, feeling the chill at her side where Evan wasn't anymore. "And it was more like a wake. Even I had a sip of beer."

Poppy smiled, patting Heather's hand soothingly, though her brows still tugged together. "Evan would have enjoyed the party," she said. "It's a wonder he didn't shuffle back out of his grave."

"He always was an irreligious old poop. Poppy, I got to do it. I can't ignore what I saw. I can't ignore advice given by water."

"No." Poppy sighed. "You can't. But you can't bring Storm's children back here without explaining why, either. We'd better have a meeting. I'd like to know what we're dealing with. Inside the rock, that is. It had another name, that rock, didn't it? Some older name . . . Then people settling around Crane Harbor renamed it; the old name didn't make any sense to them."

"I don't remember."

"Well, of course it was years before even you were born—Mask. That's what it was. Mask-in-the-Rock."

Heather felt her face wrinkle up, in weariness and perplexity. "Mask. They were right—it doesn't make much sense." Her legs tensed to work herself to her feet. But she didn't move. She wanted to stay in Poppy's house, where the chairs had shy faces and lived in a green forest hidden away from anything called Mask. "Things get old," she said half to herself. "Maybe this Mask-thing got a little tired in eight hundred years."

"More likely," Poppy said, "it had an eight-hundred-year nap." The door opened; Cass came in, and her face changed quickly. She rose, smiling, flashing amber and mother-of-pearl, chattering amiably as she picked up Heather's mug. "Heather and I are going to take a little ride, honey. Maybe do a little shopping, go watch some waves, have a bite to eat at Scudder's. Is there anything you want me to pick up for you?"

"I don't think so," Cass said, smoothing his mustache. His hand, broad, solid, muscular, like something he might have carved out of wood, moved with deliberation from his mustache to Poppy's purple shoulder. He smiled at her, seeing her a moment. Then his eyes filled up again with burls, boles, shapes embedded in wood grain. He gave her shoulder an absent pat. "Have fun."

"Fun," Poppy said, grim again, as she fired up Heather's VW and careened onto the two-lane road that ran along the Junket River into Crane Harbor. "Heather, I feel like I'm sitting in a tin can. Is this thing safe?"

"I've had it for twenty years and I never even dinged it," Heather said, clutching the elbow rest nervously. "You be careful with my car, Poppy McCarey. If you land us in the river—"

"Oh, honey, this car would float like a frog egg."

"Maybe," Heather said grumpily. "But you don't got to go so fast—that thing's been in there for eight hundred years."

The road hugged the low, pine-covered mountain on one side and gave them a view of the Junket Valley on the other, with the slow river winding through green fields, the sheep on them white as dandelion seed. Occasionally, they passed small herds of cows, which made Heather remember the old farm back in Nebraska, before the drought boiled the ground dry as a rusty pot.

"There's that Brahman bull," she said as they rounded a curve. She liked looking at it, humpy and gray among the colored cows.

"There's llamas," Poppy said, "over by Port James. Have you seen them?"

"Over by the cranberry bogs?"

"Yeah."

"Yeah."

Poppy weighed down on the gas suddenly to pass a pickup pulling a horse trailer, and Heather closed her eyes. She must have taken a little nap, with the sun flicking in and out of the trees, light and dark chasing each other over her face, for when she opened them again, they were passing the slough, and there were no more hills left in front of them. Then there was no more land left; they had come to the edge of the world. She put her window down to smell the sea.

The air was chilly; the sea, its morning mist rolling away in a dark gray band across the horizon, looked turquoise. The tide heaved against the pilings along the harbor channel; foam exploded like bed ticking into the bright air.

"Tide's in." Poppy turned away from the harbor onto a road that ambled along the cliffs and beaches toward Oyster Rock. Fishers stood at the edge of the tide, casting into the surf.

"Bet the perch are biting now," Heather said wistfully.

Poppy, who hated to fish, said nothing. They passed the Sandpiper Hotel, pulled into a viewpoint parking lot behind it. Poppy turned off the engine.

They sat silently. From that angle on the cliff, they could see the grassy knoll on top of Oyster Rock, and the white-spattered ledges where the cormorants nested. The tide boiled around the rock, tried to crawl up it. Gulls circled it, like they circled trawlers and schools of fish, wheedling plaintively. To Heather, their cries seemed suddenly cries of alarm, of warning, at something they had felt stirring beneath their bird feet, inside the massive rock.

"Looks quiet enough," Poppy said after a while.

"Maybe," Heather said, feeling small again, cold. "But it doesn't make me quiet in my bones. Always did before, always whenever we'd drive here to look at it—me and Evan, or me alone after Evan died—in the morning, in the moonlight. You watched the waves, curling around that old rock with the birds on its head, and you feel like as long as that rock stands there, so will the world. Now, it don't feel that way. It just feels—hollow."

Poppy nodded, the myrtle loops rocking in her ears. "The cormorants have all gone," she said suddenly, and Heather blinked. So they had. The dark shadows on the splotched wall where the birds had nested for years were nothing but that—splits in the rock, or maybe shadows of the birds that the birds had left behind, escaping. Poppy's mouth tightened; her ringed hand fiddled nervously with amber. She reached out abruptly and started the engine. "We've got to make some phone calls."

"Where we going to meet?"

"Your house, of course. Nobody but the cats there to listen in."

"You better get me home then. I got to dust."

Poppy spun to a halt in the gravel. She stared at Heather a second before she laughed. "Listen to you! I swear you wouldn't go to your own funeral unless you cleaned out your refrigerator first."

"I probably won't," Heather retorted. "Now, between this and that and Storm's children coming, I'll never get my tomatoes planted."

"That's another thing you have to do."

"What?"

"Call Storm's children."

"Oh, fiddle," Heather said crossly. "Damn!"

Sarah Ford came that night, and Tessa, walking with her canes, and Laura Field, who was even older than Heather, from the Victorian mansion across the street, and Dawn Singleton, who was only nineteen, and Rachel Coulter, who always found the thread on the carpet, the stain on the coffee cup, the dust on the whatnot shelf. Heather took oatmeal cookies out of the freezer and jars of Queen Anne cherries from her tree out of the pantry. Olivia Bogg was out of state, Vi Darnelle was down with the flu, and Annie Turner had gone to Portland to visit her daughter. But, considering the notice they'd been given, it was a good gathering, Heather thought. She watched Rachel turn a cookie over to examine a burned spot on it, and she wanted to take one of Tessa's canes and smack Rachel in the shin. Rachel bit into the cookie dubiously; her heavy, frowning face quivered like custard. How Poppy, in an orange sweater, orange lipstick, tight jeans, high-heeled sandals, and what looked like half the dime store jewelry in Junket, managed to look remotely glamorous at her age was more than Heather could understand.

They finished their coffee and dessert and gossip; little pools of silence spread until they were all silent, curious faces turning toward Poppy, who was perched on the arm of the sofa, and toward Heather, who was gazing at an old oval black-and-white picture of Evan as a little boy, wearing a sailor suit and shoes that buckled like a girl's. How, she wondered, always with the same astonishment, did he get from being that little long-haired boy to that old man in his grave? How does that happen?

Then the cuckoo sprang out of its doorway nine times, and Heather blinked and saw the faces turned toward her, waiting.

"Who called this meeting?" Tessa asked in her deep, strong voice.

"I did," Heather said.

"For what reason?" Dawn Singleton's young voice wavered a little out of nervousness; her black high-tops stirred the nap on Heather's carpet.

"I've been warned."

"By what?" old Laura Field asked, her voice as sweet and quavery as Dawn's. Poppy almost hadn't got her; she'd been on her way out the door to visit her husband, who had been in a coma at the Veterans Hospital in Slicum Bay for nine years.

"By the moon. By birds. By water."

There was a short silence; even Rachel was looking a little bug-eyed. Then Rachel cleared her throat. "What warning was given?"

"The thing inside Oyster Rock is coming out."

Even the cuckoo clock went silent then. It seemed a long slow moment from the movement of its pendulum back to the movement of its pendulum forth. Dawn's high-tops crept together, sought comfort from each other. Poppy moved, fake clusters of diamonds sparkling in her ears. It was her turn to ask one question.

"What must be done?"

They came to life a little at her voice. Rachel blinked; Laura Field cleared her throat softly; Sarah Ford, her mouth still open, shifted her coffee cup.

"I have been advised."

"What advice was given?" Sarah asked faintly. Middle-aged, plump, pretty, she looked constantly harried, as if she were trying to catch up with something always blown just out of reach. Having half a dozen boys would do that, Heather guessed. The cuckoo clock stretched time again, suspending Heather's thoughts between its tick and its tock.

"I got to call Storm's children."

Somebody's cup and saucer crashed onto the floor. Heather opened her eyes. Dawn's hands were over her mouth; her eyes looked half-shocked, half-smiling. Rachel, of all people, had dropped her coffee on the floor. Luckily she was sitting over in the kitchen area, where there was nothing to spill it on. Laura Field's eyes looked enormous, stricken; she was patting her hair as if a wind had blustered through the room. Tessa closed her own eyes, looking as if she were praying, or counting to ten.

"Who in hell," Tessa demanded, "gave that advice?"

Rachel, standing beside Poppy while Poppy wiped up the mess, gave Tessa a reproving glance. But no one else seemed to think the profanity unjustified. Heather sighed. Storm had been born out of blistering sun, dust storms, blizzards so thick they had swallowed houses, barns, light itself. But Storm had been the aftermath, the memory of what had passed. She had swallowed the storms, had them inside her, returned them as gifts her children carried—lightning bolts, icicles, streaks of hot brown wind—across the threshold of the world.

"A fish," Heather said.

Tessa pressed her lips together. She was ten years younger than Heather, but heavy and slow; the veins in her legs nearly crippled her. She had kept books for the lumber mill for thirty years. Whenever it closed down, depending on whether the political outcry was for live trees or lumber, she fiddled with an article about how things got named up and down the river between Junket and Crane Harbor, along the coast between Port James and Slicum Bay. She'd be fiddling in her grave, Heather thought privately; she viewed bits of information as suspiciously as she might have viewed something furry in her refrigerator.

Dawn opened her mouth, her young face looking perplexed, as well it might. "What is inside Oyster Rock?" she asked. There was a short silence.

"Don't know; nobody knows. Mask, it's called. Legend is a woman from over Klamath way faced it down and drove it inside the rock."

"If one woman did that," Rachel said tartly, "why do we need to send for Storm's children?"

"Because the trout said," Heather answered wearily. "That's all I know. Advice given by water."

Poppy, rattling fake pearls in one hand, asked Heather resignedly, "Where are they?"

"South," Heather said. "Somewheres. California. Texas. Lydia called me a year ago on Evan's anniversary. She gave me a number to call if I needed them. Said she changed her name to—oh, what was it? Greensnake. She never said where she was calling from exactly. Number's in my book . . ." She leaned her head back tiredly, closed her eyes, wanting to nap now that she'd fed and warned them. She lifted her head again slowly at the silence, found them all watching her, as still and intent as cats. She shifted. "I suppose—"

"Quit supposing," Rachel said sourly. The phone on its long line was making its way toward her, hand to hand. "Do it."

"Call me Lydia again," Lydia said sweetly. Her hair was green; she wore a short black dress that fit her body like a snakeskin and black heels so high and thin she probably speared a few night crawlers on her way across Heather's lawn. Georgie, hauling bags out, turned to give Lydia a sidelong glance out of glacier-cold eyes. Georgie had hair like a mown lawn, quick-bitten nails, flat, high, craggy cheekbones like her grandfather's, and a gold wedding band on her left hand that flashed like fire as she heaved a suitcase into the porch light. Poppy had driven her old station wagon to pick them up at the airport in Slicum Bay. Joining Heather, she seemed unusually thoughtful. Heather, counting heads anxiously in the dark, said, "Where's—" And then the third head came up, groaning, from between the seats.

Lydia said brightly, "Grace is a little shaken."

Grace hit the grass hands first, crawled her way out of the car. She was skeleton thin, with hair so long and silvery she looked a hundred years old when she stood up, haggard and swaying. "I threw up," she whispered.

"In my car?" Poppy said breathlessly.

"Georgie'll clean it up. I can't travel in anything with wheels. Not even roller skates. It's because I'm so old."

Poppy's agate necklace clattered in her hand. "Oh," she said, and stuck there.

"You can't be more than twenty-five," Heather guessed, calculating wildly.

"Twenty-nine," Georgie said succinctly, and clamped her thin lips together again.

"I mean older than the wheel. Deep in my . . . in my spiritual life."

Lydia hiccuped in the silence. "Oh, I beg," she said. She leaned down from a great height, it seemed, to kiss Heather's cheek. As she straightened,

Heather caught a waft of something scented with oranges. Her head spun a little: Lydia seemed to straighten high as the moon, as long as the Junket River in her black stockings and heels.

They settled in the living room finally, cups of coffee and tea fragrant with that smell of oranges from Lydia's flask. Heather had some herself; a sip or two, and she could swear orange trees rustled at her back, and she could almost see the fire within Georgie's cold, granite face. In his photo, the last taken, Evan seemed to smile a tilted smile. Poppy, who never drank, had a healthy swig in her cup.

"Oyster Rock," Lydia mused, sliding a heel off and swinging it absently from her toe.

"Mask," Poppy said, "they called it back then." She tapped an agate bead to her teeth, frowning. "Whenever then was, that you call back then whenever they were."

"Uh," Grace said with an effort. She held on to her cup with both hands, as if it might leap onto the carpet. A strand of her white hair was soaking in it. "I'll find out."

"Tessa might know more."

"Tessa the one sounds like a sea lion in heat?"

Poppy pushed the agate hard against a tooth. "You might say."

"Uh. She goes back, but not as far."

"As far as—"

"Me. She goes back to when it had a name. I go back to when it didn't."

Grace started to sag then. Lydia reached out deftly, caught her cup before she fell facedown on the couch. Lydia ticked her tongue. "That girl does not travel well."

"She all right?" Heather asked, alarmed.

"Toss a blanket over her," Georgie said shortly. "She'll be back before morning."

Lydia watched Grace a moment. She looked dead, Heather thought, her face and hair the same eerie, silvery white, all her bones showing. Lydia's green head lifted slowly. She seemed to hear something in the distance, though there wasn't much of Junket awake by then. She made a movement that began in her shoulders, rippled down her body to end with a twitch that slid the shoe back on her foot. When she stood up, she seemed taller than ever.

"That place," she said to Heather. "What's its name? Tad's. That still alive?"
"Tad's?" Heather sought Poppy's eyes. "I guess."
"I left something there."
"You—But you haven't been here for seven years!"
"So it's been there seven years. I like a night walk."
"Honey, you can't go in Tad's! You can't go among truckers and drunks with that hair and them shoes. Whatever you left, let it stay left."
"I left a score," Lydia said. She flicked open a gold powder case, smoothed a green brow with one finger, then lifted her lip to examine an eyetooth. "I left a score to settle at Tad's." She snapped the powder case shut. "Coming, Georgie?"
Heather closed her eyes. When she opened them and her mouth, there was only Grace looking like a white shadow on the couch and Poppy wandering around collecting cups. She stared, horrified, at Poppy.
"We got to do—We can't just let—You call Cass, tell him to get down to Tad's and help those girls—"
"No." Poppy shook her head; shell and turquoise clattered with emphasis. "No, ma'am. Those aren't girls, and they don't need our help, and I wouldn't send Cass down there tonight if Tad was singing hymns and selling tickets to heaven. Stop fussing and sit down. Have some more tea."
Heather backed weakly into her rocker, where she could keep an eye on Grace, who looked as if she had bought a ticket and was halfway there. Heather dragged her eyes away from the still face to take a quick look around the room. She said hopefully, "Don't suppose Lydia left her flask..."
Poppy gave her a tablespoon of Lydia's elixir in her tea; she was asleep and dreaming before she finished it.
Grace sat upright on the couch. The house was dark. It wasn't even the Junket house, Heather realized; it was more like the old farmhouse where Storm had been born.
"Shh," Grace said, and held out her hand. She had color in her face; her hair glowed in the dark like pale fire. For some reason she was wearing Heather's old crocheted bedroom slippers. "You can come with me but don't talk. Don't say a word..."
Heather took her hand. Grace led her into the bedroom where she and Evan had slept over fifty years ago. The bed, under its thin chenille spread, glowed like Grace's hair. Then it wasn't a bedspread at all—it was the sea,

foaming pale under the moon. Heather nearly stumbled at a blast of wind. She opened her mouth, but Grace's hand squeezed a warning; she put a finger to her lips. She turned her head. Heather looked in the same direction and nearly jumped out of her skin. The old rock heaved out of the ocean like a whale in their faces, as black against the sea and stars as if it were an empty hole.

Then she knew it wasn't an emptiness. It was something looking for its face. It was a live thing that couldn't be seen—it needed a face to make it real. Then its eyes could open; then its vast mouth could speak. Heather clung like a child to Grace's hand, her mouth open wide. The wind pushed into her so hard she couldn't make a noise if she'd wanted.

Heather, the emptiness said. *Heather.*

She jumped. She opened her eyes, saw Grace rising up on the couch, her hair glowing like St. Elmo's fire, her eyes white as moons. Then her hair turned red. Then blue. Heather, too stunned to move, heard Poppy say, "Guess they finished at Tad's."

It was after one in the morning. Flo Hendrick's son Maury was standing on Heather's lawn talking, while his flashing lights illumined her living room through the open curtains. She couldn't move. Then she heard a strange sound.

Laughter. From Maury Hendrick, who hadn't smiled, Flo said, since his pants fell down in a sack race in the third grade.

Poppy sucked in her breath. Then she grinned a quick, tight grin that vanished as soon as Heather saw it. Maury's car crunched back out over the gravel. Lydia strolled in, carrying a beer bottle.

"Well," she said lightly. "I feel better. Don't you feel better?"

"What happened?" Poppy asked.

"Where's Georgie?" Heather asked.

"Oh, Georgie's still down there helping Tad. Georgie likes tidying things. Remember how she cleaned up the church lot after Grandpa's funeral?"

"What happened?" Poppy asked again. She was so still not a bead trembled; her eyes were wide, her mouth set, the dimples deep in her cheeks. Lydia looked at her, still smiling a little. Something in her eyes made Heather think of deep, deep water, of dark caves hollowed out, grain by grain, by the ancient, ceaseless working of tides.

"A lot of women in Junket suddenly had an urge to drink a beer at Tad's tonight. Funny. There was some trouble over comments made. But as I said, Georgie's helping clean up."

Poppy moved finally, groped for her agates. "Did Tad call Maury in?"

"Nobody was called. It was a private affair. Maury was just cruising Main. He stopped to chat about open containers on public sidewalks. Then he gave me a ride home."

"What'd you say to make him laugh?" Heather demanded. Lydia's smile slanted upward; she turned away restively to Grace, who was sitting motionless on the couch. Heather followed Lydia, still not finished about Tad's, wanting to comb through all the details to get the fret out of her. The wide, moony look in Grace's eyes chilled her.

Lydia stood in front of Grace, gazed down at her silently. Evan, in his sailor suit, looked innocently at them both. Heather wondered suddenly if Evan could have seen them coming, his storm-ridden granddaughters, he would have passed on down the road to peaceable Mary Ecklund and married her instead.

"Grace," Lydia said, so sharply that Heather started. "Where are you?"

"In the dark," Grace whispered. "Watching."

"Watching when? Then? Or now?"

"Shh, Lydia. Whisper."

Lydia softened her voice. "How far back are you?"

"Then. Tide's full. Rock was bigger then. Moon's behind clouds. Seagulls floating on the high tide, little cottony clouds you can barely see. Now—they're all flying. They've all gone. It came out."

Heather's neck crawled. Poppy, walking on eggs, came to stand beside her. Heather clutched at her wrist, got a charm bracelet that clanged in the silence like cowbells. The faint, reckless smile was back in Lydia's eyes.

"What is it?"

Grace was silent a long time. She whispered finally, "I know you." Heather's knees went wobbly. "I know you. I saw you under a full moon ten thousand years ago. You were sucking bones."

Heather sat down abruptly on the floor. For a moment the house wavered between light and shadow; the light from the kitchen seemed to be running away faster and faster. The cuckoo snapped open its door, said the time, but time seemed to be rushing away from her as fast as light. Dark was the only thing not running; it was flowing into the emptiness left by light and time, a great flood of dark, separating Heather from the little, familiar thing that counted off the hours of her life.

Cuckoo, said the clock.

Heather, said the dark.

Cuckoo.

Her eyes opened; light was back in bulbs and tubes where it belonged. "It's two in the morning," she protested to Poppy, who was lifting up the phone receiver. "Who're you waking up?"

Poppy hesitated, receiver to her shoulder, and gave Heather a long look. "I was calling an ambulance."

"I'm all right. I got to go to bed is all."

Lydia was kneeling beside her. Heather groped wearily at her proffered arm. Thin as she was, Lydia pulled Heather to her feet as if she were made of batting.

"Don't be scared, Granny."

"It was eating up everything."

"That's why you called us. We'll handle it, me and Grace and Georgie. But we need you to help."

"I'm too old."

"No. We need you most of all. It's old, too. So's Grace. You get a good night's sleep. Tomorrow you call everyone, tell them to meet us at Oyster Rock at sunset. Georgie, you're back." She smiled brightly at Georgie, who, carrying a couple of empty cans, a flattened cigarette carton, and an old church bulletin, looked as if she had started to tidy up Junket. "Have a good time?"

"Smashing," Georgie said dryly, and did so to a soda can.

"Good. We're about to make another mess."

Between Tessa hobbling on her canes and Lydia wobbling on her spikes, they looked, Heather thought, about as unlikely a gathering as you might meet this side of the Hereafter. They stood on the cliff overlooking the beach and Oyster Rock; they had chosen the Viewpoint Cliff because the sign was so well hidden under a bush that nobody ever saw it. Poppy, wearing stretch jeans and a bubblegum-pink sweater and enough makeup to paint a barn, had driven Heather in the VW. She hovered close to her now, for which Heather was grateful. Georgie had just driven up. She had borrowed Poppy's station wagon earlier and asked directions to the dump. Heather wondered if she had spent the afternoon cleaning it up.

In the sunset, the rock looked oddly dark. The birds had abandoned it; maybe the barnacles and starfish had fled, too. The grass on its crown was turning white. Heather shivered. The sun was sliding into a fogbank. The fog would be drifting across the beach in an hour.

"You all right?" Poppy said anxiously for the hundredth time.

"I'm all right," Heather kept saying, but she wasn't. Her hands felt like gnarled lumps of ice and her heart fluttered quick and hummingbird-light. She could feel the ancient dark crouched out there, just behind where the sun went down, just waiting. It was her face it wanted, her frail old bones it kept trying to flow into. She was weakest, she was easiest, she was closest to the edge of time, she was walking on the tide line. . . .

Maybe I should, she thought, clutching her windbreaker close, staring into the sinking sun. It's about time anyway, with Evan gone and all, and it would save some fuss and bother. . . . Wouldn't get much out of me anyway, I'm so slow; it wouldn't have a chance between naps. . . .

She felt an arm around her, smelled some heady perfume: Lydia, her hair a green cloud, her eyes narrowed, about as dark as eyes could get and not be something other.

"Granny?" she said softly. "You giving up without a fight? After all those blizzards? All the drought and dust storms and poverty you faced down to keep your family safe and cared for?"

"I was a whole lot younger, then. Time ran ahead of me, not behind."

"Granny? If you don't fight this, you'll be the next thing we'll all have to fight. You'll be its face, its eyes, you'll be hungry for us." Heather, stunned, couldn't find spit to swallow, let alone speak. "Am I right, Georgie?"

Georgie picked up a french fry envelope, shook out the last fry to a gull, and wadded the paper. She didn't say anything. Her eyes burned through Heather like cold mountain water. Then she smiled, and Heather thought surprisedly, *There's Storm's face. It's been there all along.*

"Granny'll be all right," she said in her abrupt way. "Granny's fine when she's needed."

The sun had gone. The fog was coming in fast. Waves swarmed around the base of the rock, trying to heave it out of the water or eat it away before morning. But the rock, black as if it were a hole torn through to nothing, just stood there waiting for the rest of night.

Tessa banged on the VW fender with her cane, which must have brought Evan upright in his grave.

"Gather," she commanded in her sea-lion voice, and Poppy snorted back a laugh. Heather poked her, glad somebody could laugh. They circled on the rocky lip of the cliff: Tessa in one of the bulky-knit outfits she wore so constantly that Heather couldn't imagine her even in a nightgown; Dawn chewing gum maniacally, wearing a skirt as short as Lydia's and high-tops with red lips on them; Laura, fragile and calm, wearing her Sunday suit and pearls; Sarah in a denim skirt and a windbreaker, looking like she was trying to remember what was on her grocery list; Rachel, dyspeptic in sensible polyester; Poppy, her hand under Heather's arm; Lydia in red lipstick; Georgie in jeans; and Grace, who looked like she just might live after all, her hair blown wild in the wind and livid as the twilight fog.

Storm's children revealed what they had brought.

Lydia fanned the assortment in her hand and passed around the circle, giving them to everyone but Heather.

"I don't know what this is," Dawn whispered nervously, holding up what looked to be a size J.

"It's a crochet hook."

"But I don't know how."

"It'll come," Lydia said briskly, handing Laura the daintiest. Poppy was looking dubiously at hers. Tessa gave one of her foghorn snorts but said nothing. Lydia surveyed the circle, smiling. "Are we all armed? Granny, you're empty-handed. Georgie, give her your fishing pole."

"I can't cast in this wind," Heather said anxiously. "It's only got one little bitty weight on it. And the water's way over there. And it's too dark to see—"

"Oh, hush, Heather," Tessa growled. "Nobody came here to fish. You know that."

"Granny did," Lydia said sweetly. Her green hair and scarlet lips glowed in the dusk like Grace's hair; so did Georgie's hands, paler than the rest of her, moving like magician's gloves through the air. The sky was misty, bruised purple-black now, starless, moonless. They could still see something of each other—an eye gleam, a gesture—from the lights in the motel parking lot. "Granny's going fishing. It's Georgie's favorite pole, so whatever you catch, don't let go of it. You just keep reeling in. We'll take care of the rest. Ready, Grace?"

Grace held a bone between her hands.

It was some animal, Heather thought uneasily. Cow or sheep shank, some such, big, pearly white as Grace's hair, thick as her wrist. Thick as it was, Grace broke it in two like a twig.

She held both pieces out toward the rock. Her eyes closed; she crooned something like a nursery song. Heather felt her back hairs rise, as if some charged hand had stroked the nape of her neck. The bone dripped glitterings as hard and darkly red as garnet.

Dawn bit down on her crochet hook. Poppy held hers upright like a candle; her other hand gripped Heather as if she thought Heather might take to the air in the sudden wind that pounced over the cliff. Heather heard it howl a moment, like a cat fight, before it hit. It smashed them like a high wave. Heather wanted to clutch at the sparse hair she had left, but Poppy held one arm, and she had the pole in her other hand. She tried to say something to Poppy, but the wind tore her words away and then her breath.

Heather, the dark said, a mad wind crooning in Grace's voice. *Heather,* it said again, a wave now, rolling faster and faster in the path of the wind. *Heather,* it said, sniffing for her like a dog, and she froze on the cliff while it stalked her, knowing she had no true claims to life or time, nothing holding her on earth, even her bones were wearing down, disappearing little by little inside her while she breathed. The circle of shadowy faces couldn't hold her; Poppy's hand couldn't protect her; she was a lone, withered thing, and if this dark didn't get her, the other would soon enough, so what difference was there between them?

"Granny?" Lydia didn't even have to shout. Her voice came as clear and light as if her red neon lips were at Heather's ear. "You can cast anytime, now."

She could feel Poppy's hand again, hear Grace's meaningless singsong. But Poppy's hand felt a thousand miles away; she was just clinging to skin and bone, she could never reach deep enough to hang on to anything that mattered. She couldn't anchor onto breath or thought or time.

"Granny?"

And time was the difference between this dark and death. This thing had all the time in the world.

Heather.

"Granny?"

"Honey, it's just no use—" She heard her own cracked, wavery voice more inside her head than out, with the wind shredding everything she said. "I can't cast against this—"

"Granny Heather, you get that line out there, or I'll let this wind snatch you bald."

Heather unlatched the reel, caught line under her thumb, and flung a hook and a weight that wouldn't have damaged a passing goldfinch into the eye of the dark.

The line unreeled forever. It took on the same eerie glow as Lydia's lips, Georgie's hands, and it stretched taut and kept unwinding as if something had caught it and run with it, then swam, then flew, farther and farther toward the edge of the world. It stopped so fast she toppled back out of Poppy's hold; Poppy grabbed her again, pulled her upright.

What she had caught turned to her.

She felt it as she had felt it looking out of the moon's eye. She went small, deep inside her, a little animal scurrying to find a hiding place. But there was no place; there was no world, even, just her, standing in a motionless, soundless dark with a ghostly fishing pole in her hands, its puny hook swallowed by something vast as fog and night, with the line dangling out of it like a piece of spaghetti. Lightning cracked in the distance; fine sand or dust blew into her face. The wind's voice took on a whine like storms that happened in places with exotic names, where trees snapped like bones and houses flung their rafters into the air. The line tightened again; Heather's arms jerked straight. She felt something fly out of her; the end of her voice, her last breath. She heard Georgie say, "Don't lose my pole, Granny. Grandpa gave it to me."

Evan's old green pole he caught bluegill with, this storm aimed to swallow, along with her and the cliff and most of Crane Harbor. It sucked again; she tottered, feeling her arm sockets giving. Poppy, crochet hook between her teeth, was hanging on with both hands, dragged along with her.

"Heather!" It was Tessa, bellowing like a cargo ship. "Quit fooling around. You've been fishing for seventy years—bring it in!"

She was breathless, her heart bouncing around inside her like a golf ball, smacking her ribs, her side. The line tightened again. This time it would send her flying out of Poppy's hold, over the cliff, and all she could do was hang on, she didn't have the strength to tug against it, she had no more strength, she just didn't—

"Remember, Granny," Lydia said, "not long after Storm was born, when you walked out into the fields with her to give Grandpa his lunch, and halfway back, all the fields lifted off the ground and started blowing straight at you? You couldn't see, you couldn't breathe, you couldn't move against the wind, but you had to get Storm in, you had to find the house, nothing—not wind or dirt or heat—was going to get its hands on Storm. You pushed wind aside to save her, you saw through earth. And then, when you got to the house, the wind shoved against the screen door so hard you couldn't pull it open. You didn't have any more strength, not even for a screen door. You couldn't pull. You couldn't pull against that wind. But you did pull. You pulled. You pulled. You pulled your heart out for Storm. And the door opened and flew away and you were inside with Storm safe."

"I pulled," Heather said, and pulled the door open again, for Storm's children.

It gave so fast Poppy had to catch her. Line snaked through the air, traced a pale, phosphorescent tangle all over the ground. For a second Heather thought she had lost it. Then she saw the end of the line, hung in the air at the cliff edge just above them. She sagged on the ground, her mouth dry as a dust storm, her blood crackling like lightning behind her eyes. She felt the wind change suddenly, as if the world were going backward, and startled, she looked up to see Lydia's blood-bright, reckless smile.

"Georgie?"

Georgie reached behind her to Poppy's station wagon and pulled open the back end. Half the garbage in the Junket dump whirled out, a flood of debris that swooped in the wind and tumbled and soared and snagged, piece by piece, against the thing at the cliff edge. Old milk cartons, bread wrappers, toilet paper rolls, styrofoam containers, orange peels, frozen dinner trays, used Kleenex, coffee grounds, torn envelopes, wadded paper, magazines, melon rinds skimmed over their heads and stuck to the dark, making a mask of garbage over the shape that Heather had hooked. She saw a wide, lipless, garbage mouth move, still chewing at the line, and she closed her eyes. Dimly, she heard Lydia say, "Tessa will now give us a demonstration of the basic chain stitch."

"Dip in your hook," Tessa said grimly. "Twist a loop, catch a strand on the hook and pull it through the loop. Catch a strand. Pull. Catch. Pull."

"Funny," Heather said after a while. Lydia, green hair and lips floating in the dark, knelt down beside her.

"What's funny, Granny?"

"I never knew crocheting was so much like fishing."

"Me, neither."

"You catch, then you pull." She paused. She couldn't see Lydia's eyes, but she guessed at them. "How'd you know about that dust storm? About how the screen door wouldn't open? I never remembered that part. You weren't even born. Your mama was barely two months old."

"She remembered," Lydia said. "She told us."

"Oh." She thought that over and opened her mouth again. Lydia's red floating lips smiled. Might as well ask how she could do that trick, Heather thought, and asked something else instead.

"What's going to happen to it?"

"Georgie'll clean it up."

"She going to put it back inside the rock?"

"I think she has in mind taking it to the dump with the rest of the garbage. It'll take some time to untangle itself and put the pieces back together."

"Will it?"

"What, Granny?"

"Put the pieces back together?"

Lydia patted her hand, showing half a mouth; she was looking at the huge clown face that was loosing bits of garbage as the flashing hooks parted and knotted the dark behind it. She didn't answer. Poppy, at the cliff edge, drawing out a chain of dark from between a frozen orange juice can, an ice-cream container, and a fish head, looked over at Heather.

"You all right, honey?"

"I think so." Beside Poppy, Laura was making a long fine chain, her silver needle flashing like a minnow. Waiting for nine years for her husband to open his eyes gave her a lot of time on her hands, and she could crochet time faster than any of them. Sarah, with a hook as fat as a finger, was making a chain wide enough to hold an anchor. Dawn did a little dance with her high-tops whenever she missed a beat with her hook. Rachel, of all people, broke into a tuneless whistle now and then; Heather didn't know she could even pucker up her lips.

"Nice fishing," Tessa boomed. "Good work, Heather."

"I had help," Heather said. "I had my granddaughters."

Georgie lifted her head, gave Heather one of her burning smiles, like spring wind blowing across a snowbank. Grace had gone to sleep against Georgie's knees, looking, with her hair over her face, like a little ghostly haystack. Heather leaned back against Lydia's arm. She closed her eyes, listened to her heart beat. It wouldn't win any races, but it was steady again, and it would do for a while, until something better came along.

BYNDLEY

THE WIZARD RECK wandered into Byndley almost by accident. He had been told so many ways to get to it that he had nearly missed it entirely. Over a meadow, across a bridge, through a rowan wood, left at a crossroads, right at an old inn that had been shut tight for decades except for the rooks. And so on. By twilight he had followed every direction twice, he thought, and gotten nowhere. He was trudging over thick oak slabs built into a nicely rounded arc above a stream when the lacy willow branches across the road ahead parted to reveal the thatched roofs and chimneys of a village. BYNDLEY, said the sign on the old post leaning toward the water at the end of the bridge. That was all. But the wizard saw the mysterious dark behind the village that flowed on to meet the dusk and he felt his own magic quicken in answer.

"You want to know what?" had been the most common response to the question he asked along his journey. An incredulous snort of laughter usually followed.

How to get back again, how to get elsewhere, how to get *there*....

"But why?" they asked, time and again. "No one goes looking for it. You're lured, you're tricked there, you don't come back, and if you do, it's not to the same world."

I went there, he thought. I came back.

But he never explained, only intimated that he was doing the king's bidding. Then they straightened their spines a bit—the innkeepers, the soldiers, those who had been about the world or heard travelers' tales—

and adjusted their expressions. Nobody said the word aloud; everyone danced around it; they all knew what he meant, though none had ever been there. That, Reck thought, was the strangest thing of all about the realm of Faerie: no one had seen, no one had been, no one said the word. But everyone knew.

Finally somebody said, "Byndley," and then he began to hear that word everywhere.

"Ask over in Byndley; they might know."

"Ask at Byndley. They're always blundering about in magic."

"Try Byndley. It's just that way, half a day at most. Take a left at the crossroads."

And there Byndley was, with its firefly windows just beginning to flicker against the night, and the great oak forest beyond it, the border, he suspected, between here and there, already vanishing out of day into dream.

He stopped at the first tavern he saw and asked for a bed. He wore plain clothes, wool and undyed linen, boots that had walked through better days. He wore his face like his boots, strong and serviceable but nothing that would catch the eye. He didn't want to be recognized, to be distracted by requests for wizardry. The thing he carried in his pack grew heavier by the day. He had to use power now to lift it, and the sooner he relinquished it the better.

"My name is Reck," he told the tavern keeper at the bar as he let the pack slide from his shoulder. "I need a bed for a night or two or maybe—" He stopped, aware of a stentorious commotion as his pack hit the floor. The huge young man standing beside him, half-naked and sweating like a charger, his face flushed as by his own bellows, was rubbing one sandaled foot and snorting. "Did I drop my pack on you?" Reck asked, horrified. "I beg your pardon."

"It's been stepped on by worse," the man admitted with an effort. "What are you carrying in there, stranger? A load of anvils?" He bent before Reck could answer, hauled the pack off the floor and handed it back. Reck, unprepared, sagged for an instant under the weight. The man's dark, innocent eye met his through a drift of black, shaggy hair as Reck balanced his thoughts to bear the sudden weight. The man turned his head, puffed one last time at his foot, then slapped the oak bar with his palm.

"Ale," he demanded. "One for the stranger, too."

"That's kind of you."

"You'll need it," the man said, "against the fleas." He grinned as the tavern keeper's long gray mustaches fluttered in the air like dandelion seed.

"There are no fleas," he protested, "in my establishment. Reck, you said?" He paused, chewing at his mustaches. "Reck. You wouldn't be the wizard from the court at Chalmercy, would you?"

"Do I look like it?" Reck asked with wonder.

"No."

Reck left it at that. The tavern keeper drew ale into two mugs. They were all silent, then, watching the foam subside. Reck, listening to the silence, broke it finally.

"Then what made you ask?"

The young man gave an astonished grunt. The tavern keeper smiled slowly. His fatuous, egg-shaped face, crowned with a coronet of receding hair, achieved a sudden, endearing dignity.

"I know a little magic," he said shyly. "Living so close"—he waved a hand inarticulately toward the wood—"you learn to recognize it. My name is Frayne. On slow nights, I open an odd book or two that came my way and never left. Sometimes I can almost make things happen. This is Tye. The blacksmith, as you might have guessed."

"It wasn't hard," Reck commented. The smith, who had a broad, pleasant face beneath his wild hair, grinned delightedly as though the wizard had produced some marvel.

"My brain's made of iron," he confessed. "Magic bounces off it. Some, though, like Linnea down the road—she can foresee in water and find anything that's lost. And Bettony—" He shook his head, rendered speechless by Bettony.

"Bettony," the tavern keeper echoed reverently. Then he came down to earth as Reck swallowed ale. "There's where you should go to find your bed."

"I'm here," Reck protested.

"Well, you shouldn't be, a wizard such as you are. She's as poor as any of us now, but back a ways, before they started disappearing into the wood for decades on end, her family wore silk and washed in perfumed water and rode white horses twice a year to the king's court at Chalmercy. She'll give you a finer bed than I've got and a tale or two for the asking."

"About the wood?"

The tavern keeper nodded and shrugged at the same time. "Who knows what to believe when talk starts revolving around the wood?" He wiped a drop from the oak with his sleeve, then added tentatively, "You've got your own tale, I would guess. Why else would a great wizard come to spend a night or two or maybe more in Byndley?"

Reck hesitated; the two tried to watch him without looking at him. He had to ask his way, so they would know eventually, he decided; nothing in this tiny village would be a secret for long. "I took something," he said at last, "when I was very young, from a place I should not have entered. Now I want to return the thing I stole, but I don't know how to get back there." He looked at them helplessly "How can you ever find your way back to that place once you have left it?"

The tavern keeper, seeing something in his eyes, drew a slow breath through his mouth. "What's it like?" he pleaded. "Is it that beautiful?"

"Most things only become that beautiful in memory."

"How did you find your way there in the first place?" Tye the blacksmith asked bewilderedly. "Can't you find the same way back?"

Reck hesitated. Frayne refilled his empty mug, pushed it in front of the wizard.

"It'll go no farther," he promised, as earnestly as he had promised a bed without fleas. But Reck, feeling himself once more on the border, with his theft weighing like a grindstone on his shoulders, had nothing left to lose.

"The first time, I was invited in." Again, his eyes filled with memories, so that the faces of the listening men seemed less real than dreams. "I was walking through an oak wood on king's business and with nothing more on my mind than that, when the late afternoon light changed. . . . You know how it does. That moment when you notice how the sunlight you've ignored all day lies on the yellow leaves like beaten gold and how threads of gold drift all around you in the air. Cobweb, you think. But you see gold. That's when I saw her."

"Her," Tye said. His voice caught.

"The Queen of Faerie. Oh, she was beautiful." The wizard raised his mug, drank. He lowered it, watched her walking toward him through the gentle rain of golden, dying leaves. "Her hair . . ." he whispered. "Her eyes . . . She seemed to take her colors from the wood, as she came toward me, gold threads catching in her hair, her eyes the green of living leaves. . . . She spoke to me. I scarcely heard a word she said, only the lovely sound of her voice. I must have told her anything she wanted to know, and said yes to anything she asked. . . . She drew me deep into the wood, so deep that I was lost in it, though I don't remember moving from that enchanted place. . . ."

He drank again. As he lowered the mug, the wood around him faded and he saw the rough-hewn walls around him, the rafters black with smoke, the scarred tables and stools. He smelled stale ale and onions. The two faces, still, expressionless, became human once again, one balding and innocuous, one hairy and foolish, and both avid for more.

Reck drained his mug, set it down. "And that's how I found my way there," he said hollowly, "the first time."

"But what did you steal?" Tye asked breathlessly. "How did you get free? You can't just end it—"

The tavern keeper waved him silent. "Leave him be now; he's paid for his ale and more already." He took Reck's mug and assiduously polished the place on the worn oak where it had stood. "You might come back tomorrow evening. By then the whole village will know what you're looking for, and anyone with advice will drop by to give it to you."

Reck nodded. His shoulder had begun to ache under the weight of the pack despite all his magic. "Thank you," he said tiredly. "If you won't give me a bed here, then I'll take myself to Bettony's."

"You won't be sorry," Frayne said. "Keep going down the road to the end of the village and you'll see the old hall just at the edge of the wood. You can't miss it. Tell Bettony I sent you." He raised a hand as the wizard turned. "Tomorrow, then."

Reck found the hall easily, though the sun had set by then and near the wood an ancient dark spilled out from the silent trees. Silvery dusk lingered over the rest of Byndley. The hall was small, with windows set hither and yon in the walls, and none matching. Its stone walls, patched in places, looked very old. The main door, a huge slab of weathered oak, stood open. As he neared, Reck heard an ax slam cleanly through wood, and then the clatter of broken kindling. He rounded the hall toward the sound and came upon a sturdy young woman steadying another piece on her block.

She let go of the wood on the block and swung the ax to split it neatly in two. Then she straightened, wiped her brow with her apron, and turned with a start to the stranger.

He said quickly, "Frayne sent me."

She was laughing before he finished, at her sweat, her dirty hands, her long hair sliding loosely out of its clasp. "He picked his moment, didn't he?" She balanced the ax blade in the chopping block with a blow, and tossed pieces of kindling into her apron. "You are?"

"My name is Reck. Frayne told me to find a lady called Bettony and ask her for a bed."

"I'm Bettony," she said. Her eyes were as bright and curious as a bird's; in the twilight their color was indeterminate. "Reck," she repeated. "The wizard?"

"Yes."

"Passing through?"

"No."

"Ah, then," she said softly, "you came because of the wood." She turned. "If you can bear carrying anything else, bring some kindling in with you."

Reck, wondering, gathered an armload and followed her.

"I'm my own housekeeper," Bettony said as she piled the kindling on the great, blackened hearth inside the house, and Reck let his pack drop to the flagstones with a noiseless sigh. "Though I have a boy who takes care of the cows." She flicked him a glance. "That heavy, is it? Shouldn't such a skilled wizard be able to lighten his load a little?"

"That's why I came here," Reck said grimly, and she was silent. She lit a taper from a lamp, and stooped to hold it to the kindling. He watched her coax flame out of the wood. Light washed over her face. It looked more young than old, both strong and sweet, very tranquil. Under the teasing flame, he still couldn't see the color of her eyes.

She gave him bread seasoned with rosemary, a deep bowl of savory stew, and wine. While he ate, she sat across from him on a hearth bench and talked about the wood. "My family wandered in and out of it for centuries," she told him. "Their tales became family folklore. Some were written; others just passed from one generation to the next along with the family nose. Even if the tales weren't true, truth would never stand a chance against them."

"Have you ever been—"

"To fairyland and back? No. Nor would I swear, not even on a turnip, that any of my ancestors had. But I've seen the odd thing here and there; I've heard and not quite heard . . . enough that I believe it's there, in that ancient wood, if you can find your way." He nodded, his eyes on the fire, seeing and not quite seeing, and heard her voice again. "You've been there and back."

"Yes," he said softly.

"That weight in your pack. That's what brings you here."

"Yes."

"What—" Then she smiled, waving away the unspoken question. "It's none of my business. I've just been trying to imagine what it must be that you want so badly to give to them."

"Return," he amended.

"Return." She drew a quick breath, her eyes widening, and he saw their color then: a gooseberry green, somehow pale and warm at the same time. "You stole it?"

"A more tactful innkeeper would have assumed that it was given to me," he commented.

"Yes. But if you wanted half-truths I could give you family lore by the bushel. I'm perceptive. Frayne thinks it's a kind of magic. It's not, really. It simply comes of fending for myself."

"Oh, there's some magic in you. I sense it. I think that if we picked apart your family folklore we would unravel many threads of truth in the tangle. That would take time, though. As you so quickly observed, what I carry is becoming unbearably heavy. Even my powers are faltering under it."

"Take it into the wood," she suggested. "Set it down and walk away from it. Don't look back."

"That doesn't work," he sighed. "I've lost count of the number of times and all the places I've walked away from without looking back. It always finds me. I must return it to the place where it will stay." She watched him, silent again, her eyes wide and full of questions. *Is it terrible?* he heard in her reluctant silence. *Is it beautiful? Did you take it out of love or hate? Will you miss it, once you give it back?*

"I stole it," he said abruptly, for keeping secrets from her seemed pointless, "from the Queen of Faerie. It was something she loved; her husband had his sorcerer make it for her. I took it partly to hurt her, because she stole me out of my world and made me love her and she did not love me, and partly because it is very beautiful, and partly so that I could show it to others, as proof that I had been in the realm of Faerie and found my way back to this world. I took it out of anger and jealousy, wounded pride and arrogance. And out of love, most certainly out of love. I wanted to remember that once I had been in that secret, gorgeous country just beyond imagination, and to possess in this drab world a tiny part of that one."

"All that," she said wonderingly.

"I was that young," he sighed. "Such things are so complex then."

"Do you still love her?"

"That young man I was will always love her," he answered, smiling ruefully. "That, I can't return to her."

"But how did you escape their world? And how can you be certain that this time you will be able to find your way out of it again?"

"It wasn't easy," he murmured, remembering. "The king and his greatest sorcerer came after me . . . ." He shrugged away her second question. "One problem at a time. All I know is that I must return. I can't live in my world with what I stole from theirs." He set his plate aside. "If there's any way you can help me—"

"I'll tell you what tales came down to me," she promised. "And I can show you things my ancestors wrote, describing what stream they followed that turned into a path of silver or fairy moonlight, what rose bush they fell asleep under to wake up Elsewhere, what black horse or hare they chased beyond the world they knew. It all sounds like dreams to me, wishes out of a wine cup. But who am I to say? You have been there after all." She rose, lit a pair of tapers, and handed him one. "Come with me. I keep all those old writings in a chest upstairs, along with other odds and ends. Souvenirs of Faerie they're said to be, but none so burdensome as yours."

She told him family folklore, and showed him fragile papers stained with wine, half-coherent descriptions of improbable adventures, and rambling musings about the nature of magic, all infused with a bittersweet longing and loss that Reck felt again in his own heart, as though no time had passed at all in the realm of his memories. The writers had brought tokens back with them, as Reck had. Theirs were dead roses that never crumbled and still retained the faintest smell of summer, dried leaves that in the Otherworld had been buttons and coins of gold, a tarnished ring that once had glowed with silver fire to light the path of Bettony's great-great-grandfather as he stumbled his way from a tavern into fairyland, a rusty key that unlocked a door that had appeared in the oldest oak tree in the wood....

"Such things," Bettony said, half-laughing, half-sighing over her eccentric family. "Maybe, maybe not, they all seem to say. But then again, maybe."

"Yes," Reck said softly. He glanced out a window, seeing through the black of night the faint, haunting shapes of ancient trees. "I'm very grateful that Frayne sent me to you. This must be the place I have been searching for, a part of their great wood that spills into ours and becomes the path between worlds. Thank you for your help. I'll gladly repay you with any kind of magic you might need."

"There's magic in a tale," she replied simply "I'd like to hear the whole of yours when you come back out."

He smiled again, touched. "That's kind of you. Come to Frayne's tavern tomorrow evening and I'll tell you as much as I know so far. That's the debt I owe to Frayne."

She closed the chest and stood up, dusting centuries from her hands. "I wouldn't miss it. Nor will the rest of Byndley," she added lightly. "So be warned."

Reck spent the next day roaming through the great wood, hoping that his heart, if not his eye, would recognize the tree that was a door, the stream that was a silver path into the Otherworld. But at the end of the day the wood was just a wood, and the only place he found his way back to was Byndley. He went to Frayne's tavern, sat down wearily and asked for supper. The pack on the floor at his feet weighed so heavily in his thoughts he scarcely noticed that the comings and goings behind him as he ate his mutton and drank his ale were all comings: feet entered but did not leave. When he turned finally to ask for more ale, he found what looked like an entire village behind him, gazing at him respectfully and waiting.

Even Bettony was there, sitting in a place of honor on a chair beside the fire. She nodded cheerfully to him. So did the blacksmith Tye behind her. He picked the ale Frayne had already poured off the counter; the mug made its way from hand to hand until it reached the wizard.

"Where did we leave off?" Tye asked briskly.

There were protests all around him from villagers clustered in the shadowy corners, sitting on tables as well as benches and stools, and even on the floor. The wizard must begin again; not everyone had heard; they wanted the entire tale, beginning to end, and they would pay to keep the wizard's glass full for as long as he needed.

The innkeeper shook his head. "The tale will pay for itself," he said, and propped himself against the bar to listen.

Reck cleared his throat and began again.

By mid-tale there was not a sound in the place. No one had bothered to replenish the fire; the faces leaning toward Reck were vague, shadowy. As he began to describe what he had stolen, he scarcely heard them breathe. Deep into his tale, he saw very little beyond his own memories, and the rise and fall of ale in his cup that in the frail light seemed the hue of fairy gold.

"I stole what stood on a table beside the queen's bed. To prove that I had been in that bed, and that once I had been among those she loved. Her husband had given it to her, she told me. It was a lovely thing. It was fashioned by the king's sorcerer of a magic far more intricate than I had ever seen, which may have been why he pursued me so relentlessly when I fled with it.

"It was like a tiny living world within a glass globe. The oak wood grew within it. Gold light filled it every morning; trees began to fade to lavender and smoke toward the end of the day. At night—their night, ours, who can say? I was never certain while I was there if time passed at all within the fairy wood—the globe was filled with the tiny countless jewels of constellations in a black that was infinitely deep, yet somehow so beautiful that it seemed the only true color for the sky. In the arms of the queen I watched the night brighten into day within that tiny wood, and then deepen once again into the rich, mysterious dark. She loved to watch it, too. And in spite of her tender laughter and her sweet words, I knew that every time she looked at it, she thought of him, her husband, who had given it to her.

"So I stole it, so that she would look for it and think of me. And because I knew that though she had stolen my heart from me, this was as close as I would ever get to stealing hers."

He heard a small sound, a sigh, in the silent room, a half-coherent word. His vision cleared a little, enough to show him the still, intent faces crowding around him. Even Frayne was motionless behind his bar; no one remembered to ask for ale.

"Show it to us," someone breathed.

"No, go on," Tye pleaded. "I want to hear how he escaped."

"No, show—"

"He can show it later if he chooses. He's been carrying it around all these years; it's not going anywhere else until he ends it. Go on," he appealed to Reck. "How did you get away from them?"

"I don't think I ever did," Reck said hollowly, and again the room was soundless. "Oh, I did what any other wizard would do, pursued by the King of Faerie and his sorcerer. I fought with fire, and with thought; I vanished; I changed my shape; I hid myself in the heart of trees, and under stones. I knew that I only had to toss that little globe in their path, and they would stop chasing me. But I refused to give it up. I wanted it more than reason. Maybe more than life. Eventually the king lost sight of me, confused by all the different shapes of bird and animal and wildflower I had taken. But I could not hide the sorcerer's own magic from him. He never lost sight of the globe, no matter how carefully I disguised it. Once, in hart-shape, I wore it as my own eye; another time I changed it into the mouse dangling from the talons of the falcon I had become. He never failed to see it. . . . Finally, for no matter which way I ran I could not seem to find my way out of that wood, I performed an act of utter desperation.

"I hid myself within the wood within the globe. And then I caused everything—globe, wood, myself—to vanish."

He heard an odd, faint sound, as though in the cellar below a cork had blown out of a keg, or somewhere a globe-sized bubble of ale had popped. He ignored it, standing once again in the tiny wood inside the globe, among the peaceful trees, the endless, ancient light, feeling again his total astonishment.

"It was as though I had been in my own world all along, and I had mistaken all the magic in it for Faerie. . . ." He lifted his glass after a moment, drank, set it down again. "But I could not linger in that illusion. It's not easy to fling yourself across a world when you are both the thrower and the object that is thrown. But I managed. When I stopped the globe's flight and stepped, with great trepidation, out of it and into my own shape, I found myself in the gray, rainy streets of Chalmercy."

He paused, remembering the grayness in his own heart at the sight of the grimy, cold, familiar world. He sighed. "But I had the globe, the world I had stolen out of fairyland. For a long time it comforted me . . . until it began to weigh upon me, and I realized that I had never been forgotten. It was what I had wanted—that the queen should remember me—but she began to grow merciless in her remembering. I had to return this to her or I could never live in any kind of peace again."

He bent then and untied his pack. The tavern was so still it might have been empty. When he lifted the little globe out of the pack, its stars spangled the shadows everywhere within the room, and he heard a sigh from all the throats of the villagers of Byndley at once, as though a wind had gusted through them.

He gazed into the globe with love and rue, seeing the fairy queen again within that enchanted night, and the foolish young man who had given her his heart. After a moment he blinked. He was holding the globe in his palm as lightly as though it were a hen's egg. The strange, terrible heaviness had fallen away from it; in his surprise he almost looked into the open pack to see if the sloughed weight lay at the bottom.

Then he blinked again.

It took no small effort for him to shift his eyes from the world within the globe to the silent villagers of Byndley. Their faces, shadows and stars trembling over them, seemed blurred at first, unrecognizable. Slowly, he began to see them clearly. The wild-haired maker with his powerful face and the enigmatic smile in his dark eyes . . . The tall, silver-haired figure behind the bar, gazing quizzically at Reck out of eyes the color of the tranquil twilight within the globe . . . The woman beside the fire. . . .

Reck swallowed, haunted again, for not a mention of time had troubled that face. It was as beautiful as when he had first seen it, tinted with the fiery colors of the dying wood as she walked toward him that day long before.

She smiled, her green eyes unexpectedly warm.

"Thank you for that look," she said. There was Bettony still in her face, he saw: a glint of humor, a wryness in her smile. The faces around her, timeless and alien in their beauty, held no such human expressions. She held out her hand. Reck, incapable of moving, watched the globe float from his palm to hers under the sorcerer's midnight gaze.

"I always wondered," he told Reck, when the queen's fingers had closed around her globe, "how you managed to escape me."

"And I always wondered," the queen said softly, "why you took this from me. Now I understand."

Reck looked at the king among his mugs, still watching Reck mildly; he seemed to need no explanations. He said, "You have told your tale and been judged. This time you may leave freely. There's the door."

Reck picked up his pack with shaking hands. He paused before he opened the door, said without looking back, "The first time, I only thought I had escaped. I never truly found my way out of the wood."

"I know."

Reck opened the door. He pulled it to behind him, but he did not hear it close or latch. He took a step and then another and then did not stop until he had crossed the bridge.

He stopped then. He did not bother looking back, for he guessed that the bridge and every sign of Byndley on the other side of the stream had vanished. He looked up instead and saw the lovely, mysterious, star-shot night flowing everywhere around him, and the promise, in the faint, distant flush at the edge of the world, of an enchanted dawn.

JACK O'LANTERN

Jenny Newland sat patiently under the tree in her costume, waiting for the painter to summon her. Not far from her, in the sunlight, one of the village girls sneezed lavishly and drew the back of her wrist under her nose. A boy poked her; she demanded aggrievedly, "Well, what do you want me to do? Wipe me nose on me costume?" Jenny shifted her eyes; her clasped fingers tightened; her spine straightened. They were all dressed alike, the half-dozen young people around the tree, in what looked like tablecloths the innocuous pastels of tea cakes.

"Togas?" her father had suggested dubiously at the sight. "And Grecian robes for the young ladies? Pink, though? And pistachio . . . ?" His voice had trailed away; at home, he would have gone off to consult his library. Here, amid the pretty thickets and pastures outside the village of Farnham, he could only watch and wonder.

He had commissioned the renowned painter Joshua Ryme to do a commemorative painting for Sarah's wedding. Naturally, she couldn't wear her bridal gown before the wedding; it was with the seamstress, having five hundred seed pearls attached to it by the frail, undernourished fingers of a dozen orphans who never saw the light of day. Such was the opinion of Sylvester Newland, who claimed the sibling territory midway between Sarah, seventeen, and Jenny, thirteen. It was a lot of leeway, those four years between child and adult, and he roamed obnoxiously in it, scattering his thoughts at will for no other reason than that he was allowed to have them.

"Men must make their way in the world," her mother had said gently when Jenny first complained about Sylvester's rackety ways. "Women must help and encourage them, and provide them with a peaceful haven from their daily struggle to make the world a better place."

Jenny, who had been struggling with a darning needle and wool and one of Sylvester's socks, stabbed herself and breathed incredulously, "For this I have left school?"

"Your governess will see that you receive the proper education to provide you with understanding and sympathy for your husband's work and conversation." Her mother's voice was still mild, but she spoke in that firm, sweet manner that would remain unshaken by all argument, like a great stone rising implacably out of buffeting waves, sea life clinging safely to every corner of it. "Besides, women are not strong, as you will find out soon enough. Their bodies are subject to the powerful forces of their natures." She hesitated; Jenny was silent, having heard rumors of the secret lives of women, and wondering if her mother would go into detail. She did, finally, but in such a delicate fashion that Jenny was left totally bewildered. Women were oysters carrying the pearls of life; their husbands opened them and poured into them the water of life, after which the pearls ... turned into babies?

Later, after one of the pearls of life had finally irritated her inner oyster enough to draw blood, and she found herself on a daybed hugging a hot water bag, she began to realize what her mother had meant about powerful forces of nature. Sarah, tactfully quiet and kind, put a cup of tea on the table beside her.

"Thank you," Jenny said mournfully. "I think the oysters are clamping themselves shut inside me."

Sarah's solemn expression quivered away; she sat on the daybed beside Jenny. "Oh, did you get the oyster speech, too?"

She had grown amazingly stately overnight, it seemed to Jenny, with her lovely gowns and her fair hair coiled and scalloped like cream on an éclair. Sarah's skin was perfect ivory; her own was blotched and dotted with strange eruptions. Her hair, straight as a horse's tail and so heavy it flopped out of all but the toothiest pins, was neither ruddy chestnut nor true black, but some unromantic shade in between.

Reading Jenny's mind, which she did often, Sarah patted her hands.

"Don't fret. You'll grow into yourself. And you have a fine start: your pale gray eyes with that dark hair will become stunning soon enough."

"For what?" Jenny asked intensely, searching her sister's face. The sudden luminousness of her beauty must partially be explained by Mr. Everett Woolidge, who had already spoken to Sarah's father, and was impatiently awaiting Sarah's eighteenth birthday. "Is love only about oysters and the water of life? What exactly was Mama trying to say?"

Sarah's smile had gone; she answered slowly, "I'm not sure yet, myself, though I'm very sure it has nothing to do with oysters."

"When you find out, will you tell me?"

"I promise. I'll take notes as it happens." Still a line tugged at her tranquil brows; she was not seeing Jenny, but the shadow of Mr. Woolidge, doing who knew what to her on her wedding bed. Then she added, reading Jenny's mind again, "There's nothing to fear, Mama says. You just lie still and think of the garden."

"The garden?"

"Something pleasant."

"That's all it took to make Sylvester? She must have been thinking about the plumbing, or boiled cabbage."

Sarah's smile flashed again; she ducked her head, looking guilty for a moment, as though she'd been caught giggling in the schoolroom. "Very likely." She pushed a strand of hair out of Jenny's face. "You should drink your tea; it'll soothe the pain."

Jenny stared up at her, fingers clenched, her whole body clenched, something tight and hot behind her eyes. "I'll miss you," she whispered. "Oh, I will miss you so. Sylvester just talks at me, and Mama—Mama cares only about him and Papa. You are the only one I can laugh with."

"I know." Sarah's voice, too, sounded husky, ragged. "Everett—he is kind and good, and of course ardent. But I've known you all your life. I can say things to you that I could never say to Mama—or even to Everett—" She paused, that faraway look again in her eyes, as though she were trying to see her own future. "I hope he and I will learn to talk to one another . . . Mama would say it's childish of me to want what I think to be in any way important to him; that's something I must grow out of, when I'm married."

"Talk to me," Jenny begged her. "Anytime. About anything."

Sarah nodded, caressing Jenny's hair again. "I'll send for you."

"Why must he take you so far away? Why?"

"It's only a half day on the train. And very pretty, Farnham is. We'll have long rides together, you and I, and walks, and country fairs. You'll see."

And Jenny did: the village where Mr. Woolidge had inherited his country home was charming, full of centuries-old cottages with thick stone walls, and hairy thatched roofs, and tiny windows set, with no order whatsoever, all anyhow in the walls. The artist, Mr. Ryme, had a summer house there as well. Jenny could see it on a distant knoll from where she sat under the chestnut tree. It was of butter-yellow stone with white trim, and the windows were where you expected them to be. But still it looked old, with its dark, crumbling garden wall, and the ancient twisted apple trees inside, and the wooden gate, open for so long it had grown into the earth. The artist's daughter Alexa was under the tree as well, along with four comely village children and Jenny. The village children with their rough voices and unkempt hair would have horrified Mama. Fortunately she had not come, due to undisclosed circumstances that Jenny suspected had to do with oysters and pearls. Sylvester was away at school; Mr. Ryme would add their faces to the painting later. The governess, Miss Lake, had accompanied Jenny, with some staunch idea of keeping up with her lessons. But in the mellow country air, she had relaxed and grown vague. She sat knitting under a willow, light and shadow dappling her thin, freckled face and angular body as the willow leaves swayed around her in the breeze.

The artist had positioned Jenny's father on one side of the little rocky brook winding through the grass. The wedding guests, mostly portrayed by villagers and friends of the painter, were arranged behind him. The wedding party itself would be painted advancing toward him on the other side of the water. A tiny bridge arching above some picturesque stones and green moss would signify the place where the lovers Cupid and Psyche would become man and wife. Papa wore a long tunic that covered all but one arm, over which a swag of purple was discreetly draped. He looked, with his long gold mustache and full beard, more like a druid, Jenny thought, than a Grecian nobleman. He was smiling, enjoying himself, his eyes on Sarah as the artist fussed with the lilies in her hands. She wore an ivory robe; Mr. Woolidge, a very hairy Cupid, wore gold with a purple veil over his head. At the foot of the bridge, the artist's younger daughter, golden-haired and plump, just old enough to know how to stand still, carried a basket of violets, from which she would fling a handful of posies onto the bridge to ornament the couple's path.

Finally, the older children were summoned into position behind the pair. Mr. Ryme, having placed them, stood gazing narrowly at them, one finger rasping over his whiskers. He moved his hand finally and spoke.

"A lantern. We must have a lantern."

"Exactly!" Papa exclaimed, enlightened.

"Why, Father?" the artist's daughter Alexa asked, daring to voice the question in Jenny's head. She thought Mr. Ryme would ignore his daughter, or rebuke her for breaking her pose. But he took the question seriously, gazing at all of the children behind the bridal pair.

"Because Cupid made Psyche promise not to look upon him, even after they married. He came to her only at night. Psyche's sisters told her that she must have married some dreadful monster instead of a man. Such things happened routinely, it seems, in antiquity."

"He's visible enough now," one of the village boys commented diffidently, but inarguably, of Mr. Woolidge.

"Yes, he is," Mr. Ryme answered briskly. "We can't very well leave the groom out of his own wedding portrait, can we? That's why he is wearing that veil. He'll hold it out between himself and his bride, and turn his head so that only those viewing the painting will see his face."

"Oh, brilliant," Papa was heard to murmur across the bridge.

"Thank you. But let me continue with the lantern. One night, Psyche lit a lantern to see exactly what she had taken into her marriage bed. She was overjoyed to find the beautiful face of the son of Venus. But—profoundly moved by his godhood, perhaps—she trembled and spilled a drop of hot oil on him, waking him. In sorrow and anger with her for breaking her promise, he vanished out of her life. The lantern among the wedding party will remind the viewer of the rest of Psyche's story."

"What was the rest, Mr. Ryme?" a village girl demanded.

"She was forced to face her mother-in-law," Alexa answered instead, "who made Psyche complete various impossible tasks, including a trip to the Underworld, before the couple were united again. Isn't that right, Father?"

"Very good, Alexa," Mr. Ryme said, smiling at her. Jenny's eyes widened. She knew the tale as well as anyone, but if she had spoken, Papa would have scolded her for showing off her knowledge. And here was Alexa, with her curly red-gold hair and green eyes, not only lovely, but encouraged to reveal her education. Mr. Ryme held up his hand before anyone else could speak, his eyes, leaf green as his daughter's beneath his dark, shaggy brows, moving over them again.

"Who . . ." he murmured. "Ah. Of course, Jenny must hold it. Why you, Jenny?"

Behind him, Papa, prepared to answer, closed his mouth, composed his expression. Jenny gazed at Mr. Ryme, gathering courage, and answered finally, shyly, "Because I am the bride's sister. And I'm part of Psyche's story, as well, like the lantern."

"Good!" Mr. Ryme exclaimed. His daughter caught Jenny's eyes, smiled, and Jenny felt herself flush richly. The artist shifted her to the forefront of the scene and crooked her arm at her waist. "Pretend this is your lantern," he said, handing her a tin cup that smelled strongly of linseed oil from his paint box. "I'm sure there's something more appropriate in my studio. For now, I just need to sketch you all in position." He gestured to the dozen or so villagers and friends behind Mr. Newland. "Poses, please, everyone. Try to keep still. This won't take as long as you might think. When I've gotten you all down where I want you, we'll have a rest and explore the contents of the picnic baskets Mr. Woolidge and Mr. Newland so thoughtfully provided. I'll work with small groups after we eat; the rest of you can relax unless I need you, but don't vanish. Remember that you are all invited to supper at my cottage at the end of the day."

Jenny spent her breaks under the willow tree, practicing historical dates and French irregular verbs with Miss Lake, who seemed to have been recalled to her duties by the references to the classics. At the end of the day, Jenny was more than ready for the slow walk through the meadows in the long, tranquil dusk to the artist's cottage. There, everyone changed into their proper clothes, and partook of the hot meat pastries, bread and cheese and cold beef, fresh milk, ale, and great fruit-and-cream tarts arrayed on the long tables set up in the artist's garden.

Jenny took a place at the table with Sarah and Mr. Woolidge. Across from them sat Papa and Mr. Ryme, working through laden plates and frothy cups of ale.

"An energetic business, painting," Papa commented approvingly. "I hadn't realized how much wildlife is involved."

"It's always more challenging, working out of doors, and with large groups. It went very well today, I thought."

Jenny looked at the artist, a question hovering inside her. At home, she was expected to eat her meals silently and gracefully, speaking only when asked, and then as simply as possible. But her question wasn't simple; she barely knew how to phrase it. And this was more like a picnic, informal and friendly, everyone talking at once, and half the gathering sitting on the grass.

"Mr. Ryme," she said impulsively, "I have a question."

Her father stared at her with surprise. "Jenny," he chided, "you interrupted Mr. Ryme."

She blushed, mortified. "I'm so sorry—"

"It must be important, then," Mr. Ryme said gently. "What is it?"

"Psyche's sisters—when they told her she must have wedded a monster . . ." Her voice trailed. Papa was blinking at her. Mr. Ryme only nodded encouragingly. "Wouldn't she have known if that were so? Even in the dark, if something less than human were in bed with her—couldn't she tell? Without a lantern?"

She heard Mr. Woolidge cough on his beer, felt Sarah's quick tremor of emotion.

"Jenny," Papa said decisively, "that is a subject more fit for the schoolroom than the dinner table, and hardly suitable even there. I'm surprised you should have such thoughts, let alone express them."

"It is an interesting question, though," Mr. Ryme said quite seriously. "Don't you think? It goes to the heart of the story, which is not about whether Psyche married a monster—and, I think, Jenny is correct in assuming that she would have soon realized it—but about a broken promise. A betrayal of love. Don't you think so, Mr. Newland?"

But his eyes remained on Jenny as he diverted the conversation away from her; they smiled faintly, kindly. Papa began a lengthy answer, citing sources. Jenny felt Sarah's fingers close on her hand.

"I was wondering that, myself," she breathed.

Mr. Woolidge overheard.

"What?" he queried softly. "If you will find a monster in your wedding bed?"

"No, of course not," Sarah said with another tremor—of laughter, or surprise, or fear, Jenny couldn't tell. "What Jenny asked. Why Psyche could not tell, even in the dark, if her husband was not human."

"I assure you, you will find me entirely human," Mr. Woolidge promised. "You will not have to guess."

"I'm sure I won't," Sarah answered faintly.

Mr. Woolidge took a great bite out of his meat pie, his eyes on Sarah as he chewed. Jenny, disregarded, rose and slipped away from her father's critical eyes. She glimpsed Miss Lake watching her from the next table, beginning to gesture, but Jenny pretended not to see. Wandering through the apple trees with a meat pie in her hand, free to explore her own thoughts, she came across the artist's daughter under a tree with one of the village boys.

Jenny stopped uncertainly. Mama would have considered the boy unsuitable company, even for an artist's daughter, and would have instructed Jenny to greet them kindly and politely as she moved away. But she didn't move, and Alexa waved to her.

"Come and sit with us. Will's been telling me country stories."

Jenny glanced around; Miss Lake was safely hidden behind the apple leaves. She edged under the tree and sat, looking curiously at Will. Something about him reminded her of a bird. He was very thin, with flighty golden hair and long, fine bones too near the surface of his skin. His eyes looked golden, like his hair. They seemed secretive, looking back at her, but not showing what they thought. He was perhaps her age, she guessed, though something subtle in his expression made him seem older.

He was chewing an apple from the tree; a napkin with crumbs of bread and cheese on it lay near him on the grass. Politely, he swallowed his bite and waited for Jenny to speak to him first. Jenny glanced questioningly at Alexa, whose own mouth was full.

She said finally, tentatively, "Country tales?"

"It was the lantern, miss." His voice was deep yet soft, with a faint country burr in it, like a bee buzzing in his throat, that was not unpleasant. "It reminded me of Jack."

"Jack?"

"O'Lantern. He carries a light across the marshes at night and teases you into following it, thinking it will lead you to fairyland, or treasure, or just safely across the ground. Then he puts the light out, and there you are, stranded in the dark in the middle of a marsh. Some call it elf fire, or fox fire."

"Or—?" Alexa prompted, with a sudden, teasing smile. The golden eyes slid to her, answering the smile.

"Will," he said. "Will o' the Wisp."

He bit into the apple again; Jenny sat motionless, listening to the crisp, solid crunch, almost tasting the sweet, cool juices. But these apples were half-wild, her eye told her, misshapen and probably wormy; you shouldn't just pick them out of the long grass or off the branch and eat them . . .

"My father painted a picture of us following the marsh fire," Alexa said. "Will held a lantern in the dark; I was with him as his sister. My father called the painting *Jack O'Lantern*."

"What were you doing in the dark?" Jenny asked fuzzily, trying to untangle the real from the story.

"My father told us we were poor children, sent out to cut peat for a fire on a cruel winter's dusk. Dark came too fast; we got lost, and followed the Jack O'Lantern sprite, thinking it was someone who knew the path back."

"And what happened?"

Alexa shrugged slightly. "That's the thing about paintings. They only show you one moment of the tale; you have to guess at the rest of it. Do you want to see it? My father asked me to find a lantern for you in his studio; he won't mind if you come with me."

Jenny saw Miss Lake drifting about with a plate at the far end of the garden, glancing here and there, most likely for her charge. She stopped to speak to Sarah. Jenny swallowed the last of her meat pie.

"Yes," she said quickly. "I'd like that." It sounded wild and romantic, visiting an artist's studio, a place where paint turned into flame, and flame into the magic of fairyland. It was, her mother would have said, no place for a well-brought-up young girl, who might chance upon the disreputable, unsavory things that went on between artists and their models. Jenny couldn't imagine the distinguished Mr. Ryme doing unsavory things in his studio. But perhaps she could catch a glimpse there of what nebulous goings-on her mother was talking about when she said the word.

"You come, too, Will," Alexa added to him. "You don't often get a chance to see it."

"Is there a back door?" Jenny asked, her eye on Miss Lake, and Alexa flung her a mischievous glance.

"There is, indeed. Come this way."

They went around the apple trees, away from the noisy tables, where lanterns and torches, lit against insects and the dark, illumined faces against the shadowy nightfall, making even the villagers look mysterious, unpredictable. Alexa, carrying a candle, led them up a back staircase in the house. Jenny kept slowing to examine paintings hung along the stairs. In the flickering light, they were too vague to be seen: faces that looked not quite human, risings of stone that might have been high craggy peaks, or the ruined towers of an ancient castle.

Will stopped beside one of the small, ambiguous landscapes. "That's Perdu Castle," he said. He sounded surprised. "On the other side of the marshes. There's stories about it, too: that it shifts around and you never find it if you're looking for it, only if you're not."

"Is that true?" Jenny demanded.

"True as elf fire," he answered gravely, looking at her out of his still eyes in a way that was neither familiar nor rude. As though, Jenny thought, he were simply interested in what she might be thinking. He was nicer than Sylvester, she realized suddenly, for all his dirty fingernails and patched trousers.

"When you saw it, were you looking for it?"

"Bit of both," he admitted. "I was pretending not to while I searched for it. But I was surprised when I found it. I wonder if Mr. Ryme knew it was there before he painted it."

"Of course he did," Alexa said with a laugh. "Great heaps of stone don't shift themselves around; it's people who get lost. My father paints romantic visions, but there's nothing romantic about carrying a paint box for miles, or having to swat flies all afternoon while you search. He'd want to know exactly where he was going."

She opened a door at the top of the stairs, lighting more candles and a couple of lamps as Jenny and Will entered. Paintings leaped into light everywhere in the room, sitting on easels, hanging in frames, leaning in unframed stacks against the walls. The studio took up the entire top floor of the house; windows overlooked meadow, marsh, the smudges of distant trees, the village disappearing into night. Richly colored carpets lay underfoot; odd costumes and wraps hung on hooks and coatracks. A peculiar collection of things littered shelves along the walls: seashells, hats, boxes, a scepter, crowns of tinsel and gold leaf, chunks of crystals, shoe buckles, necklaces, swords, pieces of armor, ribbons, a gilded bit and bridle. From among this jumble, Alexa produced a lamp and studied it doubtfully. One end was pointed, the other scrolled into a handle. Gleaming brass with colorful lozenges of enamel decorated the sides. It looked, Jenny thought, like the lamp Aladdin might have rubbed to summon the genie within. Alexa put it back, rummaged farther along the shelves.

Will caught Jenny's eye then, gazing silently at a painting propped against the wall. She joined him, and saw his face in the painting, peering anxiously into a wild darkness dimly lit by the lantern in his hand. Alexa, a lock of red hair blowing out of the threadbare shawl over her head, stood very close to him, pointing toward the faint light across murky ground and windblown grasses. Her face, pinched and worried, seemed to belong more to a ghostly twin of the lovely, confident, easily smiling girl searching for a lamp behind them.

Something flashed above the painting. Jenny raised her eyes to the open window, saw the pale light in the dense twilight beyond the house and gardens. Someone out there, she thought curiously. The light went out, and her breath caught. She stepped around the painting, stuck her head out the window.

"Did you see that?"

"What?" Alexa asked absently.

"That light. Just like the one in the painting..."

She felt Will close beside her, staring out, heard his breath slowly loosed. Behind them, Alexa murmured, "Oh, here it is... A plain clay lantern Psyche might have used; no magic in this one. What are you looking at?"

"Jenny!"

She started, bumped her head on the window frame. Miss Lake stood below, staring up at them. Will drew back quickly; Jenny sighed.

"Yes, Miss Lake?"

"What are you doing up there?"

"I'm—"

"Come down, please; don't make me shout."

"Yes, Miss Lake. I'm helping Alexa. I'll come down in a moment."

"Surely you're not in Mr. Ryme's studio! And was that one of the village boys up there with you?"

Mr. Ryme appeared then, glanced up at Jenny, and said something apparently soothing to Miss Lake, who put a hand to her cheek and gave a faint laugh. Jenny wondered if he'd offered to paint her. They strolled away together. Jenny pushed back out the window, and there it was again, stronger this time in the swiftly gathering dark: a pulse of greeny-pale light that shimmered, wavered, almost went out, pulsed strong again.

"Oh..."

"What is it?" Alexa demanded beside her, then went silent; she didn't even breathe.

Behind them, Will said softly, briefly, "Jack O'Lantern."

"Oh," Jenny said again, sucking air into her lungs, along with twilight, and the scents of marsh and grass. She spun abruptly. "Let's follow it! I want to see it!"

"But, Jenny," Alexa protested, "it's not real. I mean it's real, but it's only—oh, how did my father put it? The spontaneous combustion of decayed vegetation."

"What?"

"Exploding grass."

Jenny stared at her. "That's the most ridiculous thing I've ever heard."

"It is, a bit, when you think about it," Alexa admitted.

"He obviously told you a tale to make you stay out of the marshes." Her eyes went to the window, where the frail elfin light danced in the night. "I have to go," she whispered. "This may be my only chance in life to see real magic before I must become what Mama and Miss Lake and Papa think I should be..."

She started for the door, heard Will say quickly, "She can't go alone."

"Oh, all right," Alexa said. Her cool voice sounded tense, as though even she, her father's bright and rational daughter who could see beneath the paint, had gotten swept up in Jenny's excitement. "Will, take that lantern—"

Will put a candle in an old iron lantern; Jenny was out the door before he finished lighting it. "Hurry!" she pleaded, taking the stairs in an unladylike clatter.

"Wait for us!" Alexa cried. "Jenny! They'll see you!"

That stopped her at the bottom of the stairs. Alexa moved past her toward the apple trees; Will followed, trying to hide the light with his vest. As they snuck through the trees, away from the tables, Jenny heard somebody play a pipe, someone else begin a song. Then Alexa led them through a gap in the wall, over a crumbled litter of stones, and they were out in the warm, restless, redolent dark.

The light still beckoned across the night, now vague, hardly visible, now glowing steadily, marking one certain point in the shifting world. They ran, the lantern Will carried showing them tangled tussocks of grass on a flat ground that swept changelessly around them, except for a silvery murk now and then where water pooled. Jenny, her eyes on the pale fire, felt wind at her back, pushing, tumbling over her, racing ahead. Above them, cloud kept chasing the sliver of moon, could never quite catch it.

"Hurry—" Jenny panted. The light seemed closer now, brilliant, constantly reshaped by the wind. "I think we're almost there—"

"Oh, what is it?" Alexa cried. "What can it be? It can't be—Can it? Be real?"

"Real exploding grass, you mean?" Will wondered. The lantern handle creaked as it bounced in his hold. "Or real magic?"

"Real magic," Alexa gasped, and came down hard with one foot into a pool. Water exploded into a rain of light, streaking the air; she laughed. Jenny, turning, felt warm drops fall, bright as moon tears on her face.

She laughed, too, at the ephemeral magic that wasn't, or was it? Then something happened to the lantern; its light came from a crazy angle on a tussock. She felt her shoulders seized. Something warm came down over her mouth. Lips, she realized dimly, pulling at her mouth, drinking out of her. A taste like grass and apple. She pushed back at it, recognizing the apple, wanting a bigger bite. And in that moment, it was gone, leaving her wanting.

She heard a splash, a thump, a cry from Alexa. Then she saw the light burning in Will's hand, not the lantern, but a strange, silvery glow that his eyes mirrored just before he laughed and vanished.

Jenny stood blinking at Alexa, who was sitting open-mouthed in a pool of water. Her eyes sought Jenny's. Beyond that, neither moved; they could only stare at each other, stunned.

Alexa said finally, a trifle sourly, "Will."

Jenny moved to help her up. Alexa's face changed, then; she laughed suddenly, breathlessly, and so did Jenny, feeling the silvery glow of magic in her heart, well worth the kiss snatched by the passing Will o' the Wisp.

They returned to find the villagers making their farewells to Mr. Ryme. Mr. Woolidge's carriage had drawn up to the gate, come to take Sarah and Jenny, Papa and Miss Lake to his house.

"There you are!" Sarah exclaimed when she saw Jenny. Alexa, staying in the shadows, edged around them quickly toward the house. "Where have you been?"

"Nowhere. Trying to catch a Will o' the Wisp."

Her father chuckled at her foolishness, said pedantically, "Nothing more, my dear, than the spontaneous combustion—"

"Of decayed grass. I know." She added to Mr. Ryme, "You'll have one less face to paint in the wedding party. Will won't be coming back."

"Why not?" he asked, surprised. His painter's eyes took in her expression, maybe the lantern glow in her eyes. He started to speak, stopped, said, "Will—" stopped again. He turned abruptly, calling, "Alexa?"

"She's in the house," Jenny told him. "She slipped in a pool."

"Oh, heavens, child," Miss Lake grumbled. "It's a wonder you didn't lose yourselves out there in the marsh."

"It is, indeed, a wonder," Jenny agreed.

She stepped into the carriage, sat close to Sarah, whose chilly fingers sought her hand and held it tightly, even as she turned toward the sound of Mr. Woolidge's voice raised in some solicitous question.

THE STRANGER

SYL SAW THE STRANGER at ebb tide, standing among the tide pools, half-hidden by great hoary rocks slick with weed and moss and the living sea-things that clung to them. He watched the tide; she watched him as she walked along the shore road that ran between the sea and Liel's sheep pastures. Behind him, the sky turned silken with twilight: rose and mauve and a deep, soft purple, colors she wanted to spin out of the air into thread for tapestries of no more substance than light. Everything in them would be nameless, she decided, her eyes still on the nameless man, like things in dreams. . . . Then the stranger moved.

He pulled something rectangular off his shoulder; his hands flicked across it, opening, pulling, twisting. Odd angles emerged from it, wings, cylinders, strings. He bent his head to it; his hands moved again. A single, deep note broke with a breaking wave, sighed away. A flurry of notes, flute and reed, spun into a gathering wave, and then more strings and a small drum, a single, flat beat, and the wave broke. Syl stopped, swallowing something like a sharp, sweet note in the back of her throat. Then she saw what he was doing to the sky, and the small notes danced along her bones.

Colors moved to his playing, shaped themselves. A cloudy purple wing stretched; an eye peered, whiter than the moon. A dark cloud rolled like tide across the sky; a graceful neck, a black and craggy profile rose out of it like smoke. Gold, a strand of light pulled from beneath the horizon, limned a claw, opening against the black, then plumed into a brilliant cloak of airy feathers. Syl felt the drum beat in the back of her throat.

He is weaving with the sky, she thought. And then the music stopped.

The sky darkened; he was a shadow against it, folding away his secrets, hanging them at his back. Then he blurred, or the night blurred over him. Still she stood motionless, trying to blink away the dark while all the color faded from the sky, and the tide among the broken shells played the only music.

"I saw," she said later to Liel, as she put a bowl of mutton stew in front of him. But she could not say what.

"What, lass?" he asked absently, chewing; his eyes were full of sheep, shearing, skins, wool, lambs to keep, lambs to slaughter. His eyes cleared slowly at her silence; he was seeing her again, his Syl, moving in and out of the firelight, quick, graceful, methodical, laying the bread to be cut on the oak cutting board, the oak-handled knife beside it, and the butter in its yellow crock. She put the back of her hand to her forehead, as she did when she was trying to remember. He waited. Then her hand lifted, her brows lifted, raising brief furrows in her smooth forehead, and she sighed, meeting his eyes.

"I don't exactly know. I was daydreaming, most likely." She sat, spreading her coarse skirt and coarser apron neatly, liking the feel of the rough blue weave and then the rougher cream. He ate another bite.

"Where?"

"Along the shore. I walked to Greta's, to get some black wool from her, since we have so few black, and she has them thick as blackbirds in a field."

"That's where you were, then."

"That's where I was."

They ate a while. The fire whispered, snapped scents and burning stars into the air, whispered again. Liel finished, leaned back in his chair. Syl, musing over the twilight music, lifted her eyes and found his eyes on her. He smiled a little.

"I was just watching you. The way your hands move in the light."

She smiled back, watching the fire pick out threads of brown and gold in his dark hair. He had gray eyes that always told her every thought. His expressions were uncomplicated and familiar: one for sheep, another for thunder, one for watching her weave, another for drinking beer with his brother, another for telling her his dreams, another for untying the ribbons in her hair, and then at her throat, and then at her breast.

She rose, began to clear the table. He watched her a little longer, then got up to open the cottage door and listen to the night as it wrapped itself around the island. He did that every evening, smelling weather in scents of air and earth blowing across from the mainland, listening for unfamiliar noises among the sheep, for warnings in the distant barkings of farm dogs, listening for the tide, which he only heard on the stillest or the stormiest of nights.

"It's quiet," he said at last, and closed the door. She dried the last dish, placed it on the shelf. Then, as she did every night, she stood at her loom, looking at her weaving in the dying firelight, studying the colors and patterns she had chosen. Liel came to stand beside her.

"Pretty," he said, and touched a pearl-gray strand running through a weave of lilac. Then he touched her arm. She turned and followed him to bed.

The next morning, the sea mist swirled across Gamon Kyle's fields, massed itself into a white, winged shape with blue, burning eyes. The fire that came out of its mouth was blue. As the smoke billowed up from Gamon's hayfields, the farmers and fishers came running with buckets, or riding carts from the village full of barrels sloshing half the water out of them before they reached the fields. The animal shaped itself again above their heads. They stared, frozen with wonder at the sight of cloud furling into feather, sky igniting itself. Then the blue poured down again, and they heard the screams inside Gamon's barn.

By the time they got the fire out, most of Gamon's fields were cinder and his barn was a skeleton of charred timber. He stumbled among the ruins carrying salvage: a rake with a burned handle, some harness, a curry comb.

"What was that?" he kept asking hoarsely. "What was that?"

"It was like nothing I've ever seen," Liel told Syl, coming in at midday sweating and streaked with char. She had been at her weaving all morning; the wind had swept smoke and fire in the opposite direction. She stared at him over her loom. Cinders had eaten his shirt to shreds, raised blisters on his skin. He wore an expression she had never seen before. "Enormous," he said, as she coaxed the cloth from his body. "White. White mist. Its fire was blue. Like the sky. Like it had breathed in sky and turned it into flame. And then it turned Gamon's farm into flame."

He winced as she peeled shirt from his shoulders, and she said, not even trying to make sense of fire in the sky, "I'll fetch water. Oh, Liel. Did he lose it all?"

"All but a couple of hens."

"His horses?" she breathed in horror. He nodded, still wide-eyed, stunned with wonder.

"It might have been beautiful," he said absurdly, "if it hadn't been so terrible."

She shook her head mutely at his babbling. "Sit down," she said gently. "Let me take your boots off. Then I'll get water."

"Don't bother with it. I'll go sit in the stream a while. Syl, I wish you could have seen it. Fearful and deadly, but like—a great wave, or a mountain exploding. You hate what it does, but it's like nothing you could ever imagine, nothing—" He swallowed, all the words crowding into his eyes. Syl dropped his smoldering boots outside the door. She looked up at the sky suddenly, trying to connect it with fire. It held a cloud and a couple of blackbirds. She went back inside to help Liel with his trousers.

The next day, Greye Hamil's barn and apple orchards burned; the smell of scorched green apples spread clear across the island. The day after that something clawed furrows a foot deep down the length of the village street, and nine fishing boats moored at the dock turned into charred husks. Dogs were chained up, doors were barred, no one ventured out but Syl, who had come into the village with the shawl she had woven, to leave it at the shop that sold her work. The silence, the deep scars in the street amazed her; so did the shop's barred door.

She tapped on a window until the shopkeeper opened the door and pulled her hastily inside.

"Syl Reed," she said, a heavy woman with a plump rosy face and perpetually startled eyes. "What possessed you?"

"I brought this," Syl said bewilderedly, unfolding the shawl. A butterfly opened its green and peacock blue wings against a filigree of cream wool. The shopkeeper folded her hands under her chin and forgot the fire.

"Oh, Syl, it's lovely, so lovely." Then the terror came back into her eyes. She took the shawl and drew Syl toward the back of the shop. "You can't go home now, not alone."

"I must," Syl said, eluding her fingers. "I left stock simmering on the hearth. What has gotten into this village?"

"It's the things."

"What things?"

"The things—Syl, where have you been the past three days?"

"Weaving," Syl said blankly. "You know how I get when I work." She stopped abruptly, her own eyes widening, as she remembered the unfamiliar expression on Liel's face. "Things. Something terrible, he said. Something beautiful. And then—he kept talking about the sky."

"Cloud," the shopkeeper said. "It forms itself out of cloud."

Syl touched her throat, where a word had stuck. She whispered, "Oh."

"And it burns everything with fire the color of the sky." She paused, sniffing. "Something's burning," she wailed, and Syl wrenched open the door.

The smoke came from the little wood between Liel's pastures and the sea. Running, feeling the heat from the billowing flames, she turned off the road, cut a corner through the trees, and climbed the stone wall into the summer pastures. She stopped then, sobbing for breath, transfixed by what hung in the sky.

Its wings, spanning the length of the field, were teal and purple and bronze. They tapered to an angle along an intricate web of bone, then the pelt or glistening scales parted here and there into a loose, trailing weave through which ovals of blue sky hung. The head, secret and proud like a swan's, rose on a graceful swan's neck of gold. Its claws were gold. Its eyes were huge, lucent, gold moons.

Its shadow spread across the upturned faces of farmers and villagers who had abandoned the fire to wield pitchforks and rakes against it. The sheep had pushed into a noisy, terrified huddle against the field wall. As Syl stared, the great head dipped downward, precisely as a bird's, and caught a black lamb in its mouth. It stretched upward again, higher than seemed possible, tossed the lamb into the air, let it fall free to shatter itself against the ground, then caught it, with a flick of claw, at the last moment. Blood sprayed across the sheep, across the upturned faces.

Syl ran again, scarcely realizing she moved, seeing only Liel among the islanders. She pushed into the crowd, heard his soft grunt of dismay as he saw her. She gripped his arm and heard someone say, "For a price."

She saw the stranger among them.

His eyes were cold and dark as night, his hair as white as spume. He might have come out of the sea; his skin had little more color than mist. His rectangular box of secret music hung from his shoulder, revealing nothing, not a string or a singing reed. "For a price," he repeated to the silent crowd. He had a singer's voice, each word precise and modulated. He was tall and lithe and still, Syl sensed, as a stone. A part of him was that hard, that ancient. He seemed to her scarcely more human than the beautiful, deadly thing in the air above him. "I have seen these monsters invade before. They are ruthless. Your island is tiny. They will destroy it day by day, until by summer's end it will be little more than a charred cinder rising out of the sea. And on that, they will live."

The monster loosed a stream of blood-red silk, red wind, out of its mouth. Trees along the field wall flamed; sheep turned black. The din and the smell became sickening.

Syl, still staring at the stranger, felt something crawl along her bones. She turned her face against Liel, but still she saw, behind her closed eyes, the cloudy wings forming above the sea to the stranger's music.

"What price?" a villager asked frantically: Sim Jame, who owned a tavern there. Mel Grower, with acres of nut trees and an oak wood, echoed him hoarsely, "What price?"

The stranger named it.

There was no sound for a moment, but from the sheep, and the silken fire breaking the bones of trees.

"How can you control them?" Aron Avrel said abruptly, his face white and slick with sweat under his black beard. "Are you mage, or what? Did you follow these monsters or did you bring them? For a price you'll help us. Help us into trouble, then help us out?"

The stranger looked at him, his eyes holding no more expression than stones in a field. "Does it matter?" he asked. "You cannot control them. I have known them all my life."

"Show us," Liel said, his voice grim, exhausted. The stranger looked at him, and then at Syl, standing with her fingers linked around Liel's arm, her long red-gold hair tangled and tumbling around her face from her running, her eyes, golden-green as ripening hazelnuts, wide and stunned with recognition of the stranger's face.

Still his expression did not change. But his eyes did not move away from her as he slid the box off his shoulder. He pushed a lever or a knob, or perhaps he only reshaped air and wood with his fingers. A flute of ebony and gold lay half-cradled in the top of the box, half-extended into air. He bent his head, blew a few soft, breathy notes, and then a clear, wild, tuneless keening that brought tears, hot and stinging with smoke, into Syl's eyes. The sheep stopped their din; the islanders stood motionless. The monster dipped its head dreamily toward the trees. It breathed in fire, or it grazed on fire, pulling strands of flame away from the burning leaves and branches until they stood charred and cold, shaking blackened leaves to the ground. Teal and bronze and flame coiled as the great wings closed around the last of the flames. Colors swirled, began, under the mad, haunting whirlwind of notes, to break apart. Fire turned to light, teal misted into sky. Purple lingered longest, Syl saw, a final streak of smoke or an edge of wing.

The music stopped. The musician lifted his head. The sky was empty. Sun struck his face, traced a line beside his mouth, revealed faint shadows beneath his eyes. It was some time before anyone spoke.

"That much," Aron Avrel said slowly, "we'll have to borrow from the mainland."

The stranger slid the flute back into wood and shadow. "They won't wait for it," he warned them.

"But you'll wait."

"I will."

There was argument, drunken and tumultuous, as the islanders cooled their smoke-dry throats with beer, and ate the bread and cheese and hot peppered lamb Syl set out for them. The stranger was mage, he was monster; they should kill him and steal his box. But no one could play it like he could, and then they'd be left with the monsters, and no telling how many of them there might be. They should send to the mainland for money; they should send to the mainland for help: any help would be cheaper than the stranger. But they knew where they could borrow money, but who knew where to find another mage that fast? Who knew the name of any mage, anywhere, anyway? Money, at least, could be found. Even if they had to borrow it against the price of the entire island. If the monsters didn't turn it into a charred rock, first.

Syl saw them fed, refilled their cups, while Liel and others went to see what could be mended and what must be slaughtered of the sheep. The islanders drifted in and out of the cottage, arguing, and keeping an anxious eye on the sky. Syl wandered among them, fretting over Liel and seeing, now and then, instead of him the white-haired stranger with the burning trees behind him, bending over his flute, or standing at the sea's edge, painting pictures with the sky.

She went to her loom, searched for colors among her dyed wools: that teal, that deep purple. And how could she weave the wings themselves, she wondered, the graceful trailing filigree revealing ovals of sky? She wanted other colors suddenly, colors harder, brighter than wool. Liel made lists on scraps. She found a torn bit of paper and some ink. Salt, Liel had written on the paper. Salve for cow's udder. She turned it over and began to sketch the wings.

Near dawn, they smelled it again: the harsh, acrid smell of burning blown across the island. Liel groaned and dressed. Syl waited until he had gone before she dressed. She went out, saw the red glow on the other side of the village where Sly Granger had his hop fields. She stood a moment, the back of her hand against her brow, and tried to think. Then she didn't think; she just guessed and ran across the pastures to the shore road, and then up it to where she had first seen the stranger.

She found him sitting among the rocks, playing music softly. The tide was high; his back was to her. She watched him for a long time from behind a rock, while he sketched wings and faces, massive bodies that appeared and disappeared in the milky mist above the sea. The sky brightened; the mist turned opal, caught flashes of color he wove into his music. He plucked a string, piped a note; a line of wing appeared, an eye. Cloud separated into bone, scales, teeth. He drew another secret out of the box: thin bands of silver that, struck, sounded like high, sweet bells. The sounds turned into a flock of silver birds that flew into the mist.

The sun rose, burning through the mist. He stopped playing finally and watched the lines of light flash and melt across the waves. Then he turned his head and looked at her.

He did not move or speak, but he drew her across the sand, something alien, marvelous, incomprehensible that chance or wind had blown adrift onto the island. He watched her come, his eyes no longer expressionless, but masking all expression. She said, looking at the bright, empty sky, and then at him, her voice strained with bewilderment, "They're yours. Those monsters. Those beautiful and terrible things. You make them."

"I am them," he said. He folded away the silver bars and then the strings, into the impossibly shallow box. "We are what we make."

She thought about that, holding her hair out of her eyes with one hand against the strong morning wind. "Then you," she said wearily, "are terrible and beautiful, weaving dreams and nightmares with cloud and fire, burning in a breath what small slow things we make through time. And for nothing. For money."

He was silent; again she felt something ancient, wild, inhuman in his stillness. "What," he said finally, "do you make?"

"I dye wool from the sheep you burned. I weave the colors into shawls, blankets, things to wear, to hang."

"For nothing?"

She blinked, at an edge of cold air, of brine. "For money. It's common pay for making things. But I make. I don't unmake. You—" She drew breath slowly, her eyes straying again to the sky. "If I had your colors to make with. If I had the dreams behind your eyes. I would sit here on this beach and weave sea and sky and light until there was nothing left of me but bone to weave with. And then my bones would float away on all the colors of the sea."

There was a flick of expression, a spark off stone, in his eyes. "Colors. They're everywhere."

"For you, maybe. Not for me. I don't know how to make them. You think them into being. You don't have to destroy for that. And you would be paid all the wealth you want."

"I told you," he said evenly, "they are mine. They are what I am. They exist to destroy. They cease to exist when they cannot use their powers. They are made of light and fire. They must use themselves or die. It is what I make."

She was silent then, staring at him. "Then what of you?" she cried abruptly. "What an impossible fire there is in you."

It was as if she struck worn stone, split it through its heart to reveal the secret, jeweled colors, the solid fires of crystals within. And she saw more, as his face struggled against its own expression: the massive burden that had hardened around the secret fire, kept it raw, untouched by time, burning within its secret dark.

He bowed his head. Wordless, he pushed the drumhead back into the box; she saw his hand shake. Then he met her eyes again, his own eyes ancient, haunted, and weary.

"And what light is in you," he said, so softly she barely heard his voice above the tide, "to see me so clearly." He stopped; still held in his gaze she could not move. He was seeing colors now, her colors, her hair, her eyes. He lifted his hand, let a strand of windblown hair brush across his wrist. "Fire," he whispered. "Gold. And your eyes. Amber flecked with green." Her eyes widened; for a moment longer she could not move, she could only watch his hand reach out to her, swift as running tide, then drop, just before he touched her. She could move then. She took a step back, and then another, while he watched.

"I am driven," he said, just before she turned and ran. "I cannot help myself. Nor can I help you."

Liel had come back; she found his ash-streaked clothing on the floor. He was out in the fields, she guessed. Then, with him safe, she stopped thinking. She wove and did not weave, and when she did not weave, she drew, and made watercolors out of her dyes, and painted what she drew, so that when Liel returned at noon, the cottage was full of scraps of paper and linen, covered with wings, faces, eyes.

He said nothing when he saw them. He ate quietly, she nibbled absently, puzzling over how to get the colors brighter, richer, full of fire, full of light. He said finally, finished with his soup, and leaning back in his chair, "Sly lost all his hops. And his house."

She blinked. She saw what surrounded them, then, on chair and loom, hearthstones, floor. She rose quickly, gathered the fragments. She felt him watch her. She said, picking up one last wing, her back to him, "I talked to the stranger."

"Did you?"

"It did no good."

He grunted softly. "No. But you were brave to try." She turned then, met his eyes, saw them wistful, lonely, because she was straying down some dangerous and bewildering path, and he could not see his way to follow.

She went to him; he put his arms around her, as he sat, and dropped his face against her. "It's just the colors," she said helplessly. "They haunt me."

"The colors."

"Is someone going to the mainland?"

"Aron and Gamon and Sim left this morning in Lin Avrel's boat, after we got the fire out. The sooner the better we all decided. There's nothing else we can do. Is there?"

"No."

"Then don't try."

She touched his hair; his hold tightened. She did not answer. He loosed her slowly after a time, looked up at her; her eyes had filled with colors again, the stranger's dreams. He rose, left the house without speaking.

She went back to her weaving.

At mid-afternoon, when the light dazzled through the windows and open door, making the warm shadows even darker, impenetrable, she heard a step on her threshold. She raised her eyes absently, still intent on her weaving. The figure at the door, limned with sunlight, was at once too bright and too dark to recognize.

Then she recognized its stillness.

"I came to see," he said, "what you make."

She stood slowly, feeling her heart hammer in her throat. It was as though she had found the tide at her doorstep, or something wild from the wood wanting in. He did not wait for her to welcome him. He stepped in, glancing around him at all her simple things: the painted crockery, the iron pots, the red vase full of buttercups, a moonshell, a piece of lace, the hanging she had woven to hide the bed. Then he looked at the weave on her loom, of cream and white and pale yellow, with a thread, here and there, of salmon.

"What is it?"

"A blanket," she said. "A wedding gift."

And then he saw the little pile of her sketches.

He looked through them, holding them so carefully not even the papers rustled as he drew one from behind another. In the light that fell from the windows over her loom only his hands were illumined, holding what she had made of his makings. His face was in shadow.

"The colors are too pale," she said finally. Her voice sounded odd, loud and tuneless, in the silence. "I had to use my wool dyes for paint. I don't know any other way."

He looked at her finally; she heard his drawn breath before he spoke.

"Why?" he whispered. "Why do you want them? They burned your sheep, your wood—"

"I don't know," she said helplessly. "Fire burns. Yet we take it into our houses, we live with it. Because we can't live without it. Something in my heart wants them. They drive you to make them. You should understand."

"They don't harm me."

"Oh, yes," she said, her voice shaking. "Oh, yes. They have driven you out of the world. But still you make them because they are so beautiful, so powerful—they set fire to your heart long before they burned anything else. They have charred you, made a dead island of you to live on. And you let them. You let them. You make them out of light and set them free with your music to burn and kill. You never ask yourself why. You make because. Because you can."

He moved abruptly into light, so that she could see his face, white as the moonshell, and she thought of something that had been born in the sea, and died, and left its hollow, brittle ghost behind.

"And would you?" he asked tautly. "If you could?"

Her eyes filled with tears, at the thought of the screaming animals, Liel's shirt frayed to a web with sparks, the charred trees, the barns and boats and houses burned. "No," she whispered. "I could not."

"I can."

She didn't answer. He waited, his eyes burning dark, challenging on her face. She did not speak. He dropped the sketches; they scattered like leaves across the floor. A face, half-bird, half-cloud, stared up at her out of one pale yellow eye. He turned; so did she, dropping down onto the stool at her loom, staring at its soft, pale shades, until she heard him leave.

The next day, Hila Burne's cornfields were swept bare by something, Liel said wearily, red as fire, breathing gold fire, with great amber eyes flecked with green. They saved the house and the barn, he added, as Syl, her eyes wide, burning dry as with smoke, patched the holes in his trousers.

"They're not so beautiful now," she said.

"No." Then he thought, leaning back in his chair, his eyes closed, his feet stretched out toward the cold hearth. "Well. There's always that moment when you first see it. You forget, for just that moment, what it does. All you do is see, and then it's like all the things you thought you'd never see in life. Strange lands, palaces, silver rivers rushing in secret through dark forests, mountains older than the moon. It's part of his magic, I think. That, for that one moment, you forget the past, and each of his makings seems the first one and the most wonderful."

She gazed at him, needle suspended. "I never knew you wanted to see those places."

"I never thought about them until now." He didn't speak again; when she opened her mouth, she heard his slow, exhausted breathing. She put his trousers down then and went quietly to the hearth. She knelt and gathered her sketches off the grate, where they would have been consumed in the morning's fire. She put them on the shelf above her loom.

She woke before dawn and walked to the sea.

She didn't think of Liel finding the bed empty beside him; she didn't think of what the stranger might say or do when he saw her. She stood among the rocks, watching the tide catch each changing hue of dawn, carry it ashore, and spread it out in the sand under her eyes. She heard music. She watched the sun rise; the music seemed to pull the great, hot fiery eye above the world. It pulled her; she drifted, following the beckoning tide. She found him where she had first seen him, standing half-hidden in the shadow of a rock. He did not turn his head; she did not speak, only listened, and watched the sky, to see what he might weave on his vast loom.

His music stopped. He looked at her. He did not speak, but his eyes spoke, making and unmaking her.

She turned her head after a moment, gazed at the tide again. She said softly, "I don't know what you are. Something of you is human, it seems."

"I make trouble, and I am paid, and I leave."

"Yes."

"Nothing more."

"I know."

"I have nothing to do with you."

"No."

"Nothing to do with your small weavings, your painted plates, your paper and dyes, your eyes that see beyond fire into light."

She swallowed. "No."

"This is all I am. All I want."

"Yes."

"To ask me to stop is to ask me to die."

She whispered, "I know."

"It would be like drowning in fire."

"Could you—" She drew breath; her voice trembled. "Could you find another—some other way—"

"How can I know that? This is all I know."

"No one has ever—"

"No one has ever asked. No. No one has ever come to me at dawn to watch me weave with the colors of the rising sun. No. I kill, I burn, I unmake. No one has ever been as inhuman as you."

She felt herself tremble, though the morning wind was gentle. She held herself tightly, felt words, edged, sharp, in her tight, burning throat. "I see what I see. What I can make, I will make. I will never be able to forget you. Because your weavings have come between me and my loom. I will be haunted by your colors until I find ways to make them. You have set fire to my world."

She did not see him again. Two days later, she found, among the rocks, his music open in all its parts, seawater playing the flute and reeds, broken shells playing the small drum. No one came for the money borrowed from the mainland, and on the island, nothing burned except in memory.

THE GORGON IN THE CUPBOARD

Harry could not get the goat to stay still. His model, who was an aspiring actress, offered numerous impractical suggestions as she crouched beside the animal. In fact, she rarely stopped talking. Harry didn't like the look in the goat's eye. It wasn't very big, but it seemed to him arrogant beyond its age, and contemplating mischief.

"Give it something to eat," Moira suggested. "Goats eat anything, don't they? That old leather sack, there."

"That's my lunch," Harry said patiently. "And the less we put into the goat, the less will come out of it. If you get my meaning."

She giggled. She was quite charming, with her triangular elfin face, her large green eyes with lashes so long they seemed to catch air like butterfly wings as they rose and fell. She dealt handily with the goat, who was eyeing Harry's lunch now. It strained against the rope around its neck, occasionally tightening it so that its yellow eyes verged on the protuberant. A bit like hers, Harry thought.

"Try to remain serious," he pleaded. "You're a scapegoat; you've been falsely accused and spurned by the world. Your only friend in the world is that goat."

"I thought you said you were just sketching the outlines today. Putting us in our places. So why do I have to be serious?" The goat, in whose rope her wrists were supposedly entangled, gave an obstinate tug; she loosed one hand and smacked it. "You should have gotten a female. They're sweet-natured. Not like this ruffian." She wrinkled her nose. "Stinks, too, he does. Like—"

"This one was all I could borrow. Please."

They were still for a miraculous moment, both gazing at him. He picked up charcoal, held his breath and drew a line of the goat's flank onto the canvas, then continued the line with her flank and bent knee. She swatted at a fly; the goat bucked; they both seemed to *baa* at once. Harry sighed, wiped sweat out of his eyes. They had been there half the morning, and little enough to show for it. The sun was high and dagger-bright; the tavern yard where he had set his poignant scene was full of sniggering critics. Idlers, he reminded himself, resuming doggedly when the pair settled again. They wouldn't know a brush from a broom straw. Still. He paused to study his efforts. He sighed again. There was something definitely wrong with her foot.

"It's hot," she said plaintively, shaking her heavy hair away from her neck, disturbing the perfect, nunlike veil across her face.

"Ah, don't—"

"And I'm starving. Why can't you paint like Alex McAlister? He lets me sit inside; he dresses me in silks; he lets me talk as much as I want unless he's doing my face. And I get hung every time, too, a good place on the wall where people can see me, not down in a corner where nobody looks."

The goat was hunkered on the ground now, trying to break its neck pulling at the rope peg. Harry glanced despairingly at the merciless source of light, looked again at his mutinous scapegoats, then flung his charcoal down.

"All right. All right."

"You owe me for Thursday, too."

"All right."

"When do you want me to come again?"

He closed his eyes briefly, then fished coins out of his pocket. "I'll send word."

One of the critics leaning against the wall called, "Best pay the goat, too; it might not come back otherwise."

"I might have work," Moira reminded him loftily. Mostly she worked early mornings selling bread in a bakery and took elocution lessons in afternoons when she wasn't prowling the theaters or, Harry suspected, the streets for work.

"That goat won't get any younger neither," another idler commented. Harry gritted his teeth, then snapped his fingers for the boy pitching a knife in a corner of the yard. The boy loosened the goat from the peg, got a good grip on its neck-loop to return it to its owner. He held out his other hand for pay.

"Tomorrow then, sir?" he asked indifferently.

"I'll send word," Harry repeated.

"Don't forget your dinner there, sir."

"You have it. I'm not hungry."

He dropped the charcoal into his pocket, tucked the canvas under one arm and the folded easel under the other, and walked home dejectedly, scarcely seeing the city around him. He was a fair-haired, sweet-faced young man, nicely built despite his awkward ways, with a habitually patient expression and a heart full of ravaging longings and ambitions. He was not talented enough for them, this morning's work told him. He would never be good enough. The girl was right. His paintings, if chosen at all to be hung for important exhibits, always ended up too high, or too close to the floor, or in obscure, badly lit corners. He thought of McAlister's magnificent *Diana*, with the dogs and the deer in it looking so well-behaved they might have been stuffed. And Haversham's *Watchful Shepherd*: the sheep as fat as dandelions and as docile as—as, well, sheep. Why not scapesheep, he wondered despondently, rather than scapegoats? No goat would stand still long enough for mankind to heap their crimes on its head.

Then he saw that which drove every other thought out of his head.

Her.

She was walking with her husband on the other side of the street. He was speaking fervidly, gesturing, as was his wont, probably about something that had seized his imagination. It might have been anything, Harry knew: a poem, the style of an arch, a pattern of embroidery on a woman's sleeve. She listened, her quiet face angled slightly toward him, her eyes downturned, intent, it seemed, on the man's brilliance. He swept fingers through his dark, shaggy hair, his thick mustaches dancing, spit flying now and then in his exuberance. Neither of them saw Harry, who had stopped midstream in the busy street, willing her to look, terrified that she might raise her dark, brooding eyes and see what was in his face. She only raised her long white fingers, gently clasped her husband's flying arm, and tucked it down between them.

Thus they passed, the great Alex McAlister and his wife, Aurora, oblivious to the man turned to stone by the sight of her.

He moved at last, jostled by a pair of boys pursued through the crowd, and then by the irate man at their heels. Harry barely noticed them. Her face hung in his mind, gazing out of canvas at him: McAlister's *Diana*, McAlister's *Cleopatra*, McAlister's *Venus*. That hair, rippling like black fire from skin as white as alabaster, those deep, heavy-lidded eyes that seemed to perceive invisible worlds. That strong, slender column of neck. Those long fingers, impossibly mobile and expressive. That mouth like a bite of sweet fruit. Those full, sultry lips. . . .

I would give my soul to paint you, he told her silently. But even if in some marvelous synchronicity of events that were possible, it would still be impossible. With her gazing at him, he could not have painted a stroke. Again and again she turned him into stone.

Not Aurora, he thought with hopeless longing, but Medusa.

He had tried to speak to her any number of times when he had visited Alex's studio or their enchanting cottage in the country. All he managed, under that still, inhuman gaze, were insipid commonplaces. The weather. The wildflowers blooming in the garden. The stunning success of McAlister's latest painting. He coughed on crumbs, spilled tea on his cuff. Her voice was very low; he bent to hear it and stepped on her hem with his muddy boot sole, so that whatever she had begun to say was overwhelmed by his apologies. Invariably, routed by his own gracelessness, he would turn abruptly away to study a vase that McAlister had glazed himself, or a frame he was making. McAlister never seemed to notice his hopeless passion, the longing of the most insignificant moth for fire. He would clap Harry's shoulder vigorously, spilling his tea again, and then fix him in an enthusiastic torrent of words, trying to elicit Harry's opinion of some project or profundity, while the only thought in Harry's head was of the woman sitting so silently beyond them she might have been in another world entirely.

He walked down a quiet side street shaded by stately elms and opened the gate in front of the comfortable house he had inherited from his parents. Looking despondently upon his nicely blooming hollyhocks, he wondered what to do next.

If only I could create a masterwork, he thought. An idea no one has thought of yet, that would attract the attention of the city, bring me acclaim. Make me one of the circle of the great.... Now I'm only a novice, a squire, something more than apprentice yet less than master. Harry Waterman, dabbler at the mystery of art. If only I could pass through the closed doors to the inner sanctum. Surely She would notice me then....

He went across the garden, up the steps to his door, and stopped again, hand on the latch, as he mused over an appropriate subject for a masterpiece. The goat, while original and artistically challenging, held no dignity; it would not rivet crowds with its power and mystery. At most, viewers might pity it and its ambiguous female counterpart, and then pass on. More likely they would pity the artist, who had stood in a sweltering tavern yard painting a goat.

Aurora's face passed again through his thoughts; his hand opened and closed convulsively on the door latch. Something worthy of those eyes he must paint. Something that would bring expression into them: wonder, admiration, curiosity....

What?

Whatever it was, he would dedicate his masterpiece to Her.

The door pulled abruptly out of his hold. Mrs. Grommet, his placid housekeeper, held a hand to her ample bosom as she stared at him. "Oh, it's you, Mr. Waterman. I couldn't imagine who was making that racket with the door latch." She shifted aside, opened the door wide for him to enter.

"Sorry, Mrs. Grommet," he murmured. "Throes of creation."

"Of course, Mr. Waterman. I didn't expect you back so soon. Have you had your lunch, sir?"

"No. Just bring me tea in my studio, please. I expect to be in the throes for the rest of the afternoon."

"Yes, sir."

In the highest floor of the house, he had knocked down walls, enlarged windows to give him space and light, views from a city park on one side, the broad, busy river on the other. Mrs. Grommet came panting up with a great silver tray. He slumped in an easy chair, sipped tea as he flipped through his sketchbooks for inspiration. Faces, dogs, flowers, birds, hills, rocks, pieces of armor, horses, folds of heavy tapestry, drifting silk, hands, feet, eyes... nothing coherent, nothing whole, nothing containing the lightning bolt of inspiration he craved.

He read some poetry; words did not compel an image. He paced for a while, his mind a blank canvas. He beseeched his Muse. Anybody's Muse. Inspiration failed to turn her lovely face, her kindly attention, toward him. He wandered to his cupboards, pulled out old, unfinished canvases, studied the stilted figures, the fuzzy landscapes for something that he might redeem to greatness.

One caught at memory: a head without a mouth. He placed it on the easel, stood studying it. The head, when completed, would have belonged to Persephone at the moment she realized that, having eaten of the fruits of the Underworld, she was doomed to spend half her life in that gloomy place. The young model he had chosen for it had vanished before he could finish it. Harry gazed at her, struck by her beauty, which had inspired his normally clumsy brushwork. The almond-shaped eyes of such pale gray they seemed the color of sun-kissed ice, the white-gold hair, the apricot skin. A true mingling of spring and winter, his model, who had disappeared so completely she might have been carried away into the netherworld herself.

He tried to remember her name. May? Jenny? She had gotten herself into trouble, he suspected. Harry had noticed a certain heaviness in her walk, the frigidity of terror in her expression. Moved, he had offered, in his nebulous, hesitant way, to help. But she had fled. Or died, perhaps, he was forced to consider. In childbirth, or trying to get rid of the child, who could know? He had tried to find her so that he could finish the painting. But no one seemed to know anything at all about her.

He wondered if it might be worth finishing. Her eyes, gazing straight out at the viewer, compelled attention. Idly, he traced a mouth with his forefinger, rifling through all the likely mouths he might borrow to finish it. There was Beresford's cousin Jane... But no, even at her young age, her lips were too thin to suggest the hunger that had caused Persephone to eat forbidden fruit.... Or was that a different tale?

He recognized the invisible mouth his finger had outlined, and swallowed.

Some passing Muse, a mischievous sprite, tempted him to reach for crimson paint. The lips that haunted him burned like fire in memory . . . but darker than fire, darker than rose, darker than blood. He toyed guiltily with all those colors on his palette. Only paint, he told himself. Only memory. The color of wine, they were, deep, shadowy burgundy, with all the silken moistness of the rose petal.

Vaguely he heard Mrs. Grommet knock, inquire about his supper. Vaguely he made some noise. She went away. The room darkened; he lit lamps, candles. Mrs. Grommet did not return; the streets grew even quieter; the river faded into night.

He blinked, coming out of his obsessive trance. That full, provocative splendor of a mouth was startling beneath the gentle, frightened eyes of his Persephone. But the likeness transfixed him. Aurora's mouth it was; he had succeeded beyond all dreams in shifting it from memory into paint. He could not use it. Of course he could not. Everyone would recognize it, even on some other woman's face. Which he would need to go out and find, if he wanted to finish this Persephone. Maybe not his masterwork, but far easier to manage than the goat; she would do until inspiration struck.

He lingered, contemplating that silent, untouchable mouth. He could not bring himself to wipe it away yet. He would go down and eat his cold supper, deal more ruthlessly with the mouth after he had found a replacement for it. It did not, after all, belong to him; it belonged to the wife of his dear friend and mentor. . . . He tore his eyes from it, lifted the canvas from the easel, and positioned it carefully back in the cupboard, where it could dry and be forgotten at the same time.

He closed the door and the lips spoke.

"Harry!" Its voice was sweet and raucous and completely unfamiliar. "You're not going to leave me here in the dark, are you? After calling me all afternoon? Harry?"

He flung himself against the door, hearing his heart pound like something frantic trying to get out of him, or trying to get in. He tried to speak; his voice wouldn't come, only silent bleats of air, like an astonished sheep.

"Harry?"

"Who—" he finally managed to gasp. "Who—"

"Open the door."

"N."

"You know I'm in here. You can't just keep me shut up in here."

"N."

"Oh Harry, don't be so unfriendly. I won't bite. And even if I did—" The voice trilled an uncouth snigger, "you'd like it, from this mouth."

Harry, galvanized with sudden fury, clutched at the cupboard latch, barely refraining from wrenching it open. "How dare you!" he demanded, feeling as though the contents of his inmost heart had been rifled by vulgar, soiled hands. "Who are you?"

"That's it," the voice cooed. "Now lift the latch, open the door. You can do it."

"If you force me to come in, I'll—I'll wipe away your mouth with turpentine."

"Tut, Harry. How crude. Just when I'm ready to give you what you want most."

"What I want—"

"Inspiration, Harry. You've been wishing for me ever since you gave up on the goat and gave me a chance to get a word in edgewise."

"You're a mouth—" He was breathing strangely again, taking in too much air. "How can you possibly know about the goat?"

"You called me."

"I did not."

"You invoked me," the voice insisted. "I am the voice of your despair. Your desire. Why do you think I'm coming out of these lips?"

Harry was silent, suddenly breathless. A flash went through him, not unlike the uncomfortable premonition of inspiration. He was going to open the door. Pushed against it with all his strength, his hands locked around the latch, he was going to open. . . . "Who are you?" he pleaded hoarsely. "Are you some sort of insane Muse?"

"Guess again," the voice said coolly. "You looked upon your Beloved and thought of me. I want you to paint me. I am your masterwork."

"My masterwork."

"Paint me, Harry. And all you wish for will be yours."

"All I wish. . . ."

"Open the door," the voice repeated patiently. "Don't be afraid. You have already seen my face."

His mouth opened; nothing came out. The vision stunned him, turned him into stone: the painting that would rivet the entire art world, reveal at last the depths and heights of his genius. The snake-haired daughter of the gods whose beauty threatened, commanded, whose eyes reflected inexpressible, inhuman visions.

He whispered, "Medusa."

"Me," she said. "Open the door."

He opened it.

Down by the river, Jo huddled with the rest of the refuse, all squeezed under a butcher's awning trying to get out of the sudden squall. In the country, where she had walked from, the roads turned liquid in the rain; carriages, wagons, horses, herds of sheep and cows churned them into thick, oozing welts and hillocks of mud deep enough to swallow your boots if you weren't careful. Here the cobbles, though hard enough, offered some protection. At least she was off her aching feet. At least until the butcher saw what took up space from customers looking in his windows and drove them off. Jo had been walking that day since dawn to finish her journey to the city. It was noon now, she guessed, though hard to tell. The gray sky hadn't changed its morose expression by so much as a shift of light since sunrise.

Someone new pushed into the little group cowering under the awning. Another drenched body, nearly faceless under the rags wrapped around its head, sat leaning against Jo's shoulder, worn shoes out in the rain. It wore skirts; other than that it seemed scarcely human, just one more sodden, miserable, breathing thing trying to find some protection from life.

They all sat silently for a bit, listening to the rain pounding on the awning, watching the little figures along the tide's edge, gray and shapeless as mud in their rags, darting like birds from one poor crumb of treasure the river left behind to the next. Bits of coal they stuffed into their rags to sell, splinters of wood, the odd nail or frayed piece of rope.

The bundle beside Jo murmured, "At least they're used to being wet, aren't they? River or rain, it's all one to them."

Her voice was unexpectedly young. Jo turned, maneuvering one shoulder out from beneath a sodden back. She saw a freckled girl's face between wet cloth wrapped down to her eyebrows, up to her lower lip. One eye, as blue as violets, looked resigned, calm. The other eye was swollen shut and ringed by all the colors of the rainbow.

Jo, her own face frozen for so long it hardly remembered how to move, felt something odd stirring in her. Vaguely she remembered it. Pity or some such, for all the good it did.

She said, "Whoever gave you that must love you something fierce."

"Oh, yes," the girl said. "He'll love me to death one of these days. If he finds me again."

There was a snort from the figure on the other side of Jo. This one sounded older, hoarse and wheezy with illness. Still she cackled, "I'd one like that. I used to collect my teeth in a bag after he knocked them out. I was so sorry to lose them, I couldn't bear to give them up. I was that young, then. Never smart enough to run away, even when I was young enough to think there might be a place to run to."

"There's not," Jo said shortly. "I ran back home to the country. And now I'm here again."

"What will you do?" the girl asked.

Jo shrugged. "Whatever I can."

"What have you done?"

"Mill work in the country. I had to stop doing that when my mother died and there was no one else to—to—"

"Care for the baby?" the old woman guessed shrewdly.

Jo felt her face grow cold again, less expression on it than on a brick. "Yes. Well, it's dead now, so it doesn't matter."

The girl sucked in her breath. "Cruel," she whispered.

"After that I got work at one of the big houses. Laundry and fires and such. But that didn't last."

"Did you get your references, though?"

"No. Turned out without."

"For what? Stealing?"

"No." Jo leaned her head back against the wall, watched rain running like a fountain over the edge of the swollen awning. "I wasn't that smart."

The old woman gave her crow-cackle again. "Out of the frying pan—"

Jo nodded. "Into the fire. It would have been, if I hadn't run away. If I'd stayed, I'd have had another mouth to feed when they turned me out. So I came back here."

Another voice came to life, a man's this time. "To what?" he asked heavily. "Nothing ever changes. City, country, it's all the same. You're in the mill or on the streets from dark to dark, just to get your pittance to survive one more day. And some days you can't even get that." He paused; Jo felt his racking cough shudder through them all, piled on top of one another as they were. The old woman patted his arm, whispered something. Then she turned to Jo, when he had quieted.

"He lost his wife, not long ago. Twenty-two years together and not a voice raised. Some have that."

"Twenty-two years," the man echoed. "She had her corner at the foot of the Barrow Bridge. She sang like she didn't know any better. She made you believe it, too—that you didn't know anything better than her singing, you'd never know anything better. She stopped boats with her voice; fish jumped out of the water to hear. But then she left me alone with my old fiddle and my old bones, both of us creaking and groaning without her." He patted the lump under his threadbare cloak as though it were a child. "Especially in this rain."

"Well, I know what I'm going to do when it quits," the girl said briskly. "I'm going to get myself arrested. He'll never get his hands on me in there. And it's dry and they feed you, at least for a few days before they let you out again."

"I got in for three months once," a young voice interposed from the far edge of the awning.

"Three months!" the girl exclaimed, her bruised eye trying to flutter open. "What do you have to do for that?"

"I couldn't get myself arrested for walking the streets, no matter how I tried, and I was losing my teeth and my looks to a great lout who drank all my money away by day and flung me around at night. I was so sick and tired of my life that one morning when I saw the Lord Mayor of the city in a parade of fine horses and soldiers and dressed-up lords and ladies, I took off my shoe and threw it at his head." The old woman crowed richly at the thought. "I let them catch me, and for three months I had a bed every night, clean clothes, and food every day. By the time I got out, my lout had moved on to some other girl and I was free."

"They don't make jails nowadays the way they used to," the fiddler said. "They never used to spoil you with food or a bed."

Jo felt the girl sigh noiselessly. "I'd do three months," she murmured, "if I knew where to find a Lord Mayor."

Jo's eyes slid to her vivid, wistful face. "What will you do," she asked slowly, "for your few days?"

"I've heard they take you off the streets if you break something. A window, or a streetlamp. I thought I'd try that."

Jo was silent, pulling a tattered shawl around her. Jo had made it for her mother, years earlier, when her father had been alive to tend to his sheep and his cows, make cheese, shear wool for them to spin into thread. When she'd gone back, her mother had given the shawl to her to wrap the baby in. The sheep and cows were long gone to pay debts after her father died. Her mother's hands had grown huge and red from taking in laundry. Alf, they called the baby, after her father. Alfred Fletcher Byrd. Poor poppet, she thought dispassionately. Not strong enough for any one of those names, let alone three.

The man who was its father showed his face in her thoughts. She shoved him out again, ruthlessly, barred that entry. She'd lost a good place in the city because of him, in a rich, quiet, well-run house. A guest, a friend of the family, who had a family of his own somewhere. He'd found her early one morning making up a fire in the empty library.... The only time she'd ever seen him, and it was enough to change her life. So she'd run out of the city, all the way back home to her mother. And all she had left of any of that time was an old purple shawl.

That was then, she thought coldly. This is now.

Now, the rain was letting up a little. The young girl shifted, leaning out to test it with her hand. Jo moved, too, felt the coin or two she had left sliding around in her shoe. Enough for a loaf and a bed in some crowded, noisy, dangerous lodging house run by thieves. Might as well spend it there, before they found a way to steal it.

Or she could break a window, if she got desperate enough.

A door banged. There was the butcher, a great florid man with blood on his hands and a voice like a bulldog, growling at them to take their carcasses elsewhere or he'd grind them into sausages.

The girl wrapped her face close again, hiding her telltale eye. The fiddler coughed himself back into the rain, his instrument carefully cradled beneath his cloak. The old woman, wheezing dreadfully, pulled herself up with Jo's help. Jo picked up her covered basket for her. Flowers, she thought at first, then caught a pungent whiff of it. Whatever it was she sold, it wasn't violets. The woman winked at her and slid the basket over her arm. She trailed off after the rest of the bedraggled flock scattering into the rain.

Jo saw a lump of masonry, or maybe a broken cobblestone, half the size of her fist near the wall where the old woman had been sitting. She picked it up, slipped it into her pocket in case she needed it later.

You never knew.

Harry stood in the enchanted garden of the McAlisters' cottage in the country. Only a few miles from the city, it might have existed in a different time and world: the realm of poetry, where the fall of light and a rosebud heavy with rain from a passing storm symbolized something else entirely. The rain had stopped in the early afternoon. Bright sun had warmed the garden quickly, filled its humid, sparkling air with the smells of grass and wild thyme, the crushed-strawberry scent of the rambling roses climbing up either side of the cottage door. The cottage, an oddly shaped affair with no symmetry whatsoever, had all its scattered, mismatched windows open to the air. There was no garden fence, only a distant, rambling stone wall marking the property. The cottage stood on a grassy knoll; in nearby fields the long grass was lush with wildflowers. Farther away, brindled cows and fluffy clouds of sheep pastured within rambling field walls. Farther yet, in a fold of green, the ancient village, a bucolic garden of stone, grew along the river. On the next knoll over, John Grainger was battling the winds, trying to paint the scene. Occasionally, as a puff of exuberant air tried to make off with Grainger's canvas, Harry could hear his energetic swearing.

Harry had come up for the day to look for a face for his Medusa among the McAlisters' visitors. Painters, their wives and families, models, friends who encouraged and bought, and who brought friends who bought, wandered around the gardens, chatting, drinking wine and tea, sketching, painting, or watching McAlister paint.

McAlister was painting his wife. Or rather, he was painting her windblown sleeve. She stood patiently against the backdrop of climbing red roses, all of which, Harry noticed, were the exact shade of her mouth. He tried not to think of that. Thinking of her mouth made him think of the monstrous creation in his cupboard. In the sweet light of day, there in the country, he was willing to attribute his Gorgon to the morbid churning of his frustrated romantic urges. But she had inspired him, no doubt about that. Here he was in McAlister's garden, looking at every passing female, even the young girl from the kitchen who kept the teapot filled for his Medusa.

McAlister was unusually reticent about his own subject matter. Whatever figure from myth or romance he was portraying, he needed her windblown. He had captured the graceful curves of his wife's wristbone, her long, pliant fingers. The flow of her silky sleeve in the contrary wind proved challenging, but he persevered, carrying on three discussions at once with his onlookers as he painted. Aurora, her brooding eyes fixed on some distant horizon, scarcely seemed to breathe; she might have been a piece of garden statuary.

Harry drifted, trying not to watch.

He sat down finally next to John Grainger's mistress, Nan Stewart. She had modeled many times for John's drawings and paintings, as well as for other artists who needed her frail, ethereal beauty for their visions. Grainger had discovered her sitting in the cheaper seats of a theater one evening. A well-brought-up young girl despite her class, she refused to speak to an artist. Undaunted, he found out who she was and implored her mother's permission to let her model for him. Her mother, a fussy lump of a bed mattress, as Grainger described her, accompanied Nan a few times, until she realized that the girl could make as much in an hour modeling for artists as she could sewing for a week in a dressmaker's shop. Eventually Nan came to live with the brilliant, volatile Grainger, which explained, Harry thought, her pallor and her melancholy eyes.

She had fine red-gold hair and arresting green eyes. With marriage in view at one point in their relationship, Grainger had hired someone to teach her to move and speak properly. She smiled at Harry dutifully as he filled the empty chair beside her.

"More tea?" he asked.

A vigorous, incoherent shouting from the knoll beyond made them both glance up. Grainger, hands on his easel, seemed to be wrestling with the wind.

Nan shook her head. She had a bound sketchbook on her lap, as well as a pencil or two. Grainger encouraged her to draw. She had talent, he declared to the world, and he was right, from what Harry had seen. But that day her sketchbook was shut.

"Not inspired?" he ventured.

"Not today." She turned her attention from the painter on the knoll finally. "How are you, Harry?"

"Flourishing."

"Are you painting?"

"I have a subject in mind. I'm prowling about for a face."

"What subject?"

"It's a secret," he said lightly. "I'm not sure I can pull it off. I don't want to embarrass myself among you artists."

Her smile touched her eyes finally. "You're a sweet man, Harry. I'm still such a novice myself."

"John praises your work to the skies. He thinks very highly—"

"I know." Her face was suddenly angled away. "I know. I only wish he still thought so highly of me."

"He does!" Harry said, shocked. "He's loved you for years. You live together, you work together, you are twin souls—"

"Yes." She looked at him again, her expression a polite mask. "Yes."

He was silent, wondering what was troubling her. His eyes strayed to the group beside the rose vines. Children ran out of the cottage door; he recognized Andrew Peel's gray-eyed little beauty, and her baby brother trundling unsteadily after. Nan sighed absently, her eyes on the children. Harry's own eyes strayed. Across the garden, the statue came to life; the dark, unfathomable eyes seemed to gaze straight at him.

He started, his cup clattering, feeling that regard like a bolt from the blue, striking silently, deeply. He became aware of Nan's eyes on him, too, in wide, unblinking scrutiny. Then she set her cup down on a table; it, too, rattled sharply in its saucer.

"She's pregnant, you know," Nan said. Harry felt as though he had missed a step, plunged into sudden space. He started again, this time not so noisily. Nan added, "So am I."

He stared at her. "That's wonderful," he exclaimed finally, leaning to put his cup on the grass. He caught her hands. That's all it was then: her inner turmoil, her natural uncertainties. "Wonderful," he repeated.

"Is it?"

"Of course! You'll marry now, won't you?"

She gave him an incredulous stare. Then she loosed her hands, answered tonelessly, "Yes, quite soon. Next week, perhaps, and then we'll go away for a bit to the southern coasts to paint."

"I couldn't be happier," Harry told her earnestly. "We've all been expecting this for—"

"For years," she finished. "Yes." She hesitated; he waited, puzzled without knowing why. Something about the event, he supposed, made women anxious, prone to fear disasters or imagine things that were not true.

Grainger's voice, sonorous and vibrant, spilled over the group. He appeared tramping up the knoll, his hat gone, his canvas in one hand, easel in the other, paints in the pockets of his voluminous, stained jacket. He blew a kiss to Nan, leaving a daub of blue on his bushy, autumn-gold mustaches. Then he turned to see how McAlister's sleeve was coming Above his broad back, Harry saw the statue's eyes come alive again; her cheeks had flushed, in the wayward wind, a delicate shade of rose. Ever the consummate professional, she did not move, while Grainger, lingering in the group, expounded with witty astonishment how like a wing that sleeve seemed, straining for its freedom on the wind.

Harry turned back to Nan, breath indrawn for some pleasantry.

Her chair was empty. He looked around bewilderedly. She had flown herself, it seemed, but why and on what wayward wind, he could not imagine.

Jo walked the darkening streets, fingering the broken cobble in her pocket. The day had been dryer than the previous one; that was as much as she could say for it. Sun seemed to linger forever as she trudged through the noisy, stinking streets. She asked everyone for work, even the butcher who had driven her out from under his awning, a shapeless, faceless, unrecognizable bundle he didn't remember in the light. But he only laughed and offered the usual, smacking with the flat of his hand the quivering haunch of meat he was slicing into steaks.

"Come back when you get desperate," he called after her, to the amusement of his customers. "Show me how fine you can grind it."

She got much the same at inns and alehouses. When she stopped at crossings to rest her feet and beg for a coin or two, she got threats from sweepers' brooms, screeches from ancient heaps of rags whose territory she had invaded, shoves from lean, hollow-cheeked, cat-eyed girls with missing teeth who told her they'd cut off her hair with a rusty knife if they saw her twice on their street.

Toward late afternoon she was too exhausted to feel hungry. She had money for one more night's lodging, or money for food. Not both. After that—she didn't think about it. That would be tomorrow, this was not. Now she had her two coppers, her two choices. And she had the stone in her pocket. She drifted, waiting for night.

When the streetlamps were lit, she made up her mind. Just in that moment. She was sitting in the dark, finally safe because nobody could see her nursing her blistered, aching soles. Nobody threatened, yelled, or made lewd suggestions; for a few precious moments she might have been invisible.

And then the gas lamps went on, showing the world where she was again. Caught in the light, she didn't even think. She was on her feet in a breath, hand in her pocket; in the next she had hurled the broken stone furiously at the light. She was startled to hear the satisfying shatter of glass. Someone shouted; the flare, still burning, illumined a couple of uniformed figures to which, she decided with relief, she would yield herself for her transgression.

There was a sudden confusion around her: ragged people rushing into the light, all calling out as they surrounded the uniforms. Jo, pushing against them, couldn't get past to reveal herself to the law.

"I did it," a woman shrieked.

"No, it was me broke the lamp," somebody else shouted. The crowd lurched; voices rose higher. "Give over, you great cow—it was me!"

"I did it!" Jo shouted indignantly. "It wasn't them at all!"

The crowd heaved against her, picked her off her feet. Then it dropped her a moment later, as it broke apart. She lost her balance, sat on the curb staring as the uniforms escorted the wrong woman entirely out of the light. She went along eagerly enough, Jo noted sourly. She pulled herself up finally, still smarting over the injustice of it all.

Then she realized that her purple shawl was gone.

She felt her throat swell and burn, for the first time in forever. Even when her mother had died she hadn't cried. Not even when the baby had died. She had taken the shawl off her mother, and then off the baby. It was all she had left to remember them by. Now that was gone. And she was blinded, tears swelling behind her eyes, because the tattered shawl had borne the burden, within its braided threads, of her memories.

Now she was left holding them all herself.

She limped to find some private shred of shadow, refusing to let tears fall. All the shadows seemed occupied; snores and mutterings warned her before she could sit. She wandered on and on through the quieting streets, unable to stop the memories swirling in her head. Her innocent young self, cleaning the ashes out of the fireplace in the fine, peaceful library. The handsome stranger with the light, easy voice, asking her name. Asking about her. Listening to her, while he touched her cuff button with his finger. Shifted a loose strand of her hair off her face. Touched her as no one had, ever before. Then gone, nowhere, not to be seen, he might have been a dream. And she, beginning to wake at nights, feeling the panic gnawing at her until she could bear it no longer, and upped and ran.

But there was something else. A street name dredged it up as she walked. Or the night smell of a great tree in a line of them along the street. She had run from someone else. Oh, she remembered. Him. The young painter. He had a gentle voice, too, but he only touched her to turn her head, or put her loose hair where he wanted it. He paid well, too, for the random hour or two she could spare him. It was his money she saved to run with, when she knew she could no longer stay. When her skirts grew tight. When the other girls began to whisper, and the housekeeper's eyes drew up tight in her head like a snail's eyes at the sight of Jo.

What was his name?

She walked under the great, dark boughs that shielded her from the streetlights. She could sleep under them she thought. Curl up in their roots like an animal; no one would see her until dawn. The street was very quiet; a sedate carriage or a cab went by now and then, but she heard no voices.

He lived on a street like this; she remembered the trees. She'd walk there from the great house, his housekeeper would let her in, and she would climb the stairs to his—his what was it? His studio. He painted her with that strange fruit in her hand, with all the rows of little seeds in it like baby teeth.

He told her stories.

You are in the Underworld, he said. You have been stolen from your loving mother's house by the King of Hades. You must not eat or drink anything he offers you; if you refuse, he will have no power over you, and he must set you free. But, you grow hungry, so hungry, as you wait. . . .

"So hungry," she whispered.

You eat only a few tiny seeds from this fruit thinking such small things would do no harm. But harm you have done, for now he can claim you as his wife and keep you, during the darkest months of the year, in his desolate and lonely realm. . . .

What was her name?

Her eyes were closing. Her bones ached; her feet seemed no longer recognizable. Not feet any longer, just pain. Pain she walked on, and dark her only friend. . . . She didn't choose; she simply fell, driven to her knees in the damp ground beneath a tree. She crawled close to it, settled herself among its roots, her head reeling, it felt like, about to bounce off her shoulders and roll away without her.

What was its name?

She closed her eyes and saw it: that bright, glowing fruit, those sweet, innocent seeds. . . .

Pomegranate.

Would he want to finish his painting? she wondered.

But there was someone guarding her passage out of the Underworld. Someone stood at the gates she must pass through, protecting the serene upper realms from the likes of her. Someone whose word was law on the border between two worlds. . . .

What was her name?

Her eyes. Jo could not remember her eyes, only felt them watching as she fled into the ancient, timeless dark. Only her bun, the light, glossy brown of a well-baked dinner roll, and her chins and the watch pinned to her bosom, at one corner of her apron.

What would her eyes say when she saw Jo?

She remembered as she felt the strong arms seize her, pull her off the earth into the nether realms of sleep.

Mrs. Grommet.

Harry, having returned from the country without his Medusa, avoided his studio. He did not want to open the cupboard door again. He couldn't decide which might be worse: his painting talking to him or his painting not talking to him. Was expecting a painting to speak to him worse than having it speak to him? Suppose he opened the cupboard door with expectations, and nothing happened? He would be forced to conclusions that, in the cheery light of day, he did not want to think about.

So he left the house at midmorning and dropped in at a gallery where a new painting by Thomas Buck was hung. The gallery, recently opened, had acquired pieces indiscriminately in its desire to become fashionable. It aimed, it declared affably, to encourage the novice as well as to celebrate the artist. Tommy Buck's work showed promise. It had been showing promise for years. Harry, studying the new painting called *Knight Errant*, was gratified to see that Buck still could not draw to save his life. The horse was absurdly proportioned; its wide, oblong back could have been set for a dinner party of six. And the knight's hands, conveniently hidden within bulky gauntlets, gripped the reins awkwardly, as though he were playing tug-of-war. The young woman tied to a tree, toward whom the knight rode, seemed to be chatting amiably with the dragon who menaced her.

I could do better than that, Harry thought.

He felt the urge, remembered the anomaly in the cupboard, and was relieved when some friends hailed him. They carried him away eventually to dine, and from there to another friend's studio where they drank wine and watched the painter struggle with his Venus, a comely enough young woman with something oddly bland about her beauty. She bantered well, though, and stayed to entertain them over a cold supper of beef and salad. Harry got home late, pleasantly tipsy, and, inspired, went immediately up to his studio to view his work within the context of his friend's.

The Gorgon spoke when he opened the cupboard, causing him to reel back with a startled cry: he had actually forgotten her.

"Hello, Harry."

"Hlmph," he choked.

"Have you found me yet?"

He tugged at his collar, tempted to slam the cupboard shut and go to bed. But he answered, venturing closer, "No. Not yet."

"Did you even look for me?"

"Of course I did! I looked for you in every female face I passed. I didn't see you anywhere." Except, he thought, in McAlister's garden, where Her eyes had immobilized him once again. "You aren't easy to find," he added, speaking now into the shadows. "You're a very complex matter."

"Yes, I am, aren't I?" she murmured complacently. "Harry, why don't you let me out?"

"I can't. What if someone sees?"

"Well, I don't intend to pass the time of day with Mrs. Grommet, if that's what worries you."

"No, but—"

"Hang a cloth over my face or something. Pretend I'm a parrot."

"I don't think so," he sighed, sitting down on the floor because he had been standing much of the day. A lamp on the wall above his head spilled some light into the open cupboard; he could see the edge of the canvas, but not the moving mouth. Less afraid now, lulled by wine and company, he asked her curiously, "Where do you think I should look for you?"

"Oh, anywhere. You'll know me when you see me."

"But to see you is to be—"

"Yes," she said, laughing a little. "You'll recognize your model when she turns you, for just a tiny human moment, into stone."

"Only One can do that," he said softly.

"Maybe. You just keep looking."

"But for what? Are you—were you, I mean, really that terrible? Or that beautiful? Which should I be searching for?"

"Oh, we were hideous," she answered cheerfully, "me and my two Gorgon sisters. Stheno and Euryale, they were called. Even in the Underworld, our looks could kill."

"Stheno?"

"Nobody remembers them, because nothing much ever happened to them. They didn't even die, being immortal. Do you think anyone would remember me if that obnoxious boy hadn't figured out a way to chop my head off without looking at me?"

Harry dredged a name out of the mists of youthful education. "Perseus, was it?"

"He had help, you know. He couldn't have been that clever without divine intervention. Long on brawn, short on brains, you know that type of hero."

"That's not what I was taught."

"He forced our guardian sisters, the gray-haired Graie, to help him, you must have heard. He stole their only eye and their tooth."

"They had one eye?" Harry said fuzzily.

"They passed it back and forth. And the tooth. Among the three of them." She gave an unlovely cackle. "What a sight that was, watching them eat. Or squabble over that eyeball. That's what they were doing when they didn't see that brat of a boy coming. He grabbed their goods and forced them to give him magic armor and a mirror to see me in, so he wouldn't have to meet my eyes. Then he lopped my head off and used me to kill his enemies. Even dead, I had an effect on people."

"He doesn't sound so very stupid."

"He had help," she repeated with a touch of asperity. "Anyway, it was loathsome, gray-haired old biddies who armed him to fight me. Not lissome, rosy-fingered maidens. You remember that when you paint me."

"I will." He added, brooding over the matter, "If I can find you."

"Oh, you will," she said more cheerfully. "Never fret. I do wish you would take me out of here and let me watch, though."

"No."

"I could advise you."

"You'd scare my model."

"I wouldn't talk, I promise you! And if I forget, just cover me up. Please, Harry? After all, I have inspired you. You could do me a favor. It's awfully dark in here."

"Well."

"Please? Harry?"

"Well." He got to his feet again, dusted off his trousers, yawning now and forgetting why he had come up. "I'll think about it. Good night."

"Good night, Harry."

He closed the cupboard door and went to bed.

The next morning, his ambition inflamed by what the gallery seemed to think worth hanging, he ate his breakfast hastily and early. He would not come home without his Medusa, he was determined, even if he had to search the ravaged streets and slums for her. No, he told Mrs. Grommet, she should not expect him home before evening, if then. He would go as far as he must to find his inspiration, even as far, he admitted in his inmost heart, as the country, to see if he might find that unexpected face in Aurora's shadow.

He got as far as the street. He paused to latch the garden gate behind him and was turned to stone.

A woman appeared out of nowhere, it seemed. She murmured something to him; he hardly knew what. He looked at her and time stopped. The normal street noises of passing carriages, birds, doors opening, voices calling simply vanished. He heard the faint hum of his own blood in his ears and recognized it as a constant, unchanging sound out of antiquity. The sound heard when all else is silent; nothing moves.

Her face was all bone and shadow, full of stark paradoxes: young yet ancient with experience, beautiful yet terrifying with knowledge, living yet somehow alive no longer. Whatever those great, wide-set eyes had seen had left a haunting starkness in them that riveted him where he stood. She spoke again. She might have been speaking Etruscan, for all the words made sense to Harry. Her mouth held the same contradictions: it was lovely, its grim line warned of horror, it hungered, it would never eat again.

Sound washed over him again: a delivery wagon, a yowling cat, a young housemaid chasing after it down the street. He heard his stammering voice. "Where—where did you come from?"

She gestured. Out of a tree, out of the sky, her hand said. She was very poorly dressed, he realized: her thin, tight jacket torn at both elbows, the hem of her skirt awash with dried mud, her shoes worn down and beginning to split. She spoke again, very slowly, as if to a young child, or a man whose wits had badly strayed.

"I wondered if you had some work for me, sir. If maybe you could use me for your paintings. Anything will do. Any amount of time—"

One of his hands closed convulsively above her elbow; his other hand pulled the gate open.

"Oh, yes," he said unsteadily. "Oh, yes. Miss. Whoever you—"

"Jo, sir."

"Jo. Come in." He swept her down the walk, threw the door wide, and shouted, "Mrs. Grommet! Mrs. Grommet! We need you!"

***

"You have lice," Mrs. Grommet said.

Jo, hearing her within a cascade of lukewarm water, thought her voice sounded simply matter-of-fact. The kitchen maid stopped pouring water, began to pass a hard, lumpy bar of soap over Jo's wet hair. It took time to work up a lather.

"I'm not surprised," Jo murmured. She knelt in her tattered chemise beside a huge tub, allowing Mrs. Grommet the sight of her cracked, filthy feet. She could only hope that whatever vision had possessed Mr. Waterman to let her in the house would not be washed down the drain. But, she told herself coldly, if that happens then I will be no worse than I was before, and at least I will be clean.

"Go on, girl," the housekeeper said. "Give it a good scrub. Pretend you're doing the front steps."

"There's such a lot of it," the maid ventured. Jo closed her eyes, felt the blunt, vigorous fingers work away at her until she imagined herself underwater, floating in some river god's grip, being flailed back and forth like water weed.

"Rinse now," Mrs. Grommet ordered, and the water flowed again, copious and mercilessly cold. "There," the housekeeper said at last with satisfaction. "That should do it."

Freed, Jo straightened. The maid tossed a towel over her head and began to pummel her again.

"Go and boil some water," Mrs. Grommet told her. She added to Jo when the girl had gone, "Sometimes they work and sometimes they don't, these new hot water pipes. He didn't recognize you, did he?"

Jo swallowed. Mrs. Grommet's eyes, green as unripe tomatoes, said very little beyond her words. She knows, Jo thought. She knows why I ran away. But what Mrs. Grommet felt about that, Jo could only guess. Anyone else in the housekeeper's position would have made her sentiments about this immoral, unwashed bit of dredge crossing her employer's threshold very plain, very soon.

"No," Jo said simply. "He doesn't. He saw my face and wants to paint it. That's all. I don't know if he'll feel the same when he sees it again. If not, I'll go."

Mrs. Grommet did not comment on that. "I'll see what I can find for you to wear while you wash."

"Mrs. Grommet—" Her voice faltered; the housekeeper, hand on the doorknob, waited expressionlessly. "I know my clothes are a disgrace, but they're all I've got, if I go. Please—"

"Don't worry, girl," Mrs. Grommet said briskly, "I won't turn you out naked into the street, whatever becomes of you."

An hour later, Jo sat at the kitchen fireplace, letting her hair dry while she ate some cold beef and bread. She was dressed in a dark, shapeless gown that had made its way, some time in the distant past, to Harry's costume closet. Made to fit tight at wrists and neck and beneath the bosom, it hung on Jo like a sack. The kitchen maid, chopping onions for a pie, could not stop staring at her. Jo, too weary to eat much, didn't wonder at her staring, until the cook, a great mound of a woman with cheeks the color of raw beef, who was rolling out pastry, made as though to swat the maid with a floury hand.

"Leave her be, then," she grunted.

"I'm sorry, miss," the girl murmured to Jo. "I can't help it. It's your hair."

Jo glanced sideways at it, as it fell around her face. It did look unfamiliar clean, but other than that it was just her hair.

"What's the matter with it? Have I got the mange, too?"

"No," the maid whispered, flicking her eyes to it again. "It's so beautiful, all long and gold and curly."

Jo blinked, at a loss. Her eyes rose helplessly, sought Mrs. Grommet's.

The housekeeper, sipping tea at the table and still inscrutable, gave a brief nod. "Oh, yes. He'll like that."

Jo, suddenly terrified, stood abruptly, her meal scattering out of her fingers into the fire. "I have to go, then," she heard herself babble. "I have to go. Where are my shoes? I had a couple of coppers in my shoes—"

Mrs. Grommet gazed at her wordlessly. Her eyes came alive suddenly, as she pushed herself to her feet. "There now, Jo," she said faintly, rounding the table to Jo's side. "Mr. Waterman's not like that. You know that. There's no need to run away from him again." She put her hand on Jo's arm and pointed to a grubby little pile near the hearth. "There's your shoes and clothes. The coins are in there, just as I found them. If you need them, you'll have them."

"Why," Jo asked her wildly, "are you treating me this way?"

"What way?" Mrs. Grommet asked, astonished.

It took Jo a moment to remember the word. "Kind." Spoken, it seemed to surprise them both. "Why are you being kind to me? You know—you—"

Mrs. Grommet's eyes went distant again. But she kept her hand on Jo's arm, patted it a little. "Stay a bit," she said finally, eluding the question. "Mr. Waterman will think we drove you away if you leave now. He'll only go looking for you."

"But I don't understand—"

"Well, you might ask him what he has in mind. You might stay long enough to listen to him. Whatever it is, I'm sure it's nothing more than a painting."

Jo, still trembling, sat down at the hearth again. She heard whispering; after a moment, the little maid brought her a cup of tea. She sipped it wordlessly, the kitchen silent behind her but for the thump of the rolling pin. When she knew she could stand again, she knew it was time. She rose, set the cup on the table. Mrs. Grommet looked at her.

"I'll take you up," she said briefly. Jo nodded gratefully, too light-headed to speak.

She passed familiar hallways, paintings, patterns of wallpaper, carpets that seemed more real in memory. It was, she thought dazedly, like being in two places at once; she was uncertain, from one step to the next, if she were moving backward or forward in time. They went up the second flight of steeper stairs into the top of the house. There, as Mrs. Grommet opened the door, Jo saw another memory that was real: the long rows of windows overlooking the street, the park across from them, and on the other side of the house, the river. She could see the tree under which she had wakened in the other world at dawn. She smelled oils and pungent turpentine, saw the untidy shelves of books and sketches, the oddments everywhere—peacock feathers, beads, baskets, seashells, tapestries, rich shawls of taffeta, goblets, moth-eaten furs.

She saw Harry. He stood across the room, watching her silently as she entered. She had never seen anyone look at her like that before, as though she were something not quite human, a piece of dream, maybe, that he had to step into to see her properly.

He said absently, "Thank you, Mrs. Grommet."

"Yes, sir." She lingered. "Will you need—"

"Nothing. Thank you."

She closed the door behind her. Harry crossed the room, came close to Jo. Still in his dream, she saw, he reached out, touched her hair with one finger. She felt herself stiffen. He drew back hastily. She saw his eyes again, anxious now, tentative, fascinated. Like some mooncalf boy in love for the first time, she realized, and not even sure with what.

"Will you let me paint you?" he asked huskily.

"Of course," she answered, so amazed she forgot her terrors.

"I see you—I see you as a very ancient power, a goddess, almost, who is herself mortal, but who can kill with a look. To see her is to die. But not to see her is to live without living. I see you, in all her terrible, devastating beauty, as Medusa."

"Yes, Mr. Waterman," she said, completely mystified, and thought with wonder: he doesn't recognize me at all.

Much later that day, almost into the next, Harry sat on the floor beside the open cupboard door, babbling to the Gorgon.

"The lines of her face are stunning. They transfixed me the moment I saw them. They seem shaped—sculpted—by primal forces, like stone, yet very much alive. They are beauty, they are death, they are youth, they are ancient beyond belief. And her eyes. Medusa's eyes. They gaze at you from another world, the Underworld perhaps; they are portals to that grim world. Of the palest gray, nearly colorless, like the mist between life and death—" He heard a vague noise from within the cupboard, almost as if the Gorgon had sneezed. "I beg your pardon. Did you speak?"

"No," she said faintly.

"And her hair. I've never seen anything like it. White gold, rippling down from her face to her knees. Again that suggestion of youth and antiquity, knowledge gained too early from unearthly places—"

"Harry."

"Her mouth—there again—"

"Harry."

"Yes, what is it?"

"I think you should let me see her."

"Her mouth is like—"

"I promise, by Perseus's shield that bore my reflection and killed me, that I won't speak a word in her presence."

"Again, it contradicts itself—it should be mobile, plump, alluring, the delicate pink of freshwater pearls—"

"You can put me in a dark corner where she won't notice me."

"But it has long forgotten how to smile; its line is inflexible and determined—"

"Harry. It's me you're painting. I haven't seen myself in thousands of years. Have a heart. Let me see what humans think of me these days. I'm not used to being associated with beauty."

Harry was silent. He thought he perceived the faintest undertone in the Gorgon's plea, as though she were laughing at him. But her words argued otherwise. And it did seem an appropriate request. She had, after all, inspired him; how could he deny her his vision of herself?

"You'll forget," he said guardedly, "and say something impulsive and frighten her away."

"I won't. I have sworn."

"I'll think about—"

"Harry. Stop thinking about it. Just do it. Or I'll yell my head off here in the cupboard like one of Bluebeard's wives."

Harry blinked. "You could have done that—"

"Today, while she was here. Yes. But I didn't, did I? I am capable of controlling myself. I won't say a word in her presence, no matter how—"

"How?"

"No matter what."

"Do I amuse you?" Harry demanded indignantly.

"No, no," the Gorgon said soothingly. "No. I'm just incredibly old, Harry, and my sense of humor is warped. I'm very ignorant of the modern world, and it would do me good to see even a tiny corner of it."

Harry sighed, mollified. "All right. Tomorrow morning, before she comes."

"Thank you, Harry."

He got up early to hang the Gorgon above some high bookshelves, among other old sketches and watercolors scattered along the wall. The contradictions in the face startled him anew: the frightened eyes, the pale, anxious brows, the lush, voluptuous, wine-red mouth. His eyes lingered on that mouth as he descended the ladder. He would make a trip to the country soon, he decided. She was down there with Alex nearly every weekend. The mouth seemed to crook in a faint smile; his foot froze on the bottom rung.

"No," he said sharply. "You must be absolutely still."

The mouth composed itself. The eyes gazed unseeingly across the room. He had placed the painting where most often his model would have her back to it. She would only glimpse it as she faced the door to leave. And few people looked that high without reason, Harry had learned to his chagrin when his work had been hung near the ceiling in exhibits. She would never notice the peculiar face with its mismatched features unless she looked for it.

He spent a few days sketching Jo, learning every nuance of her face, experimenting with various positions, draperies. He decided, in the end, simply to paint her face at the instant she saw herself reflected in the young hero's shield. The Medusa turning her baleful gaze upon herself and realizing in that instant that she had slain herself. The shield would frame her within the canvas. The pale, rippling beauty of the model's hair would transform itself easily into gorgeous, dangerous snakes. Jo's stark-white skin, drained of life-force it seemed, hollowed and shadowed with weariness and strain, hinted of the Medusa's otherworldly origins. He positioned black silk in graceful folds about her neck to emphasize the shadows. That would be her only costume. That and the snakes in her hair, which might suggest, in their golden brilliance, the final light of the sun upon her dying and deadly face.

So lost he was in the excitement of inspiration that he scarcely remembered to speak to his model. She came in the mornings, murmured, "Good morning, Mr. Waterman," and sat in her chair beside his easel. He arranged the silk about her throat, giving her a greeting or a pleasantry. Then she became so still she hardly seemed to breathe. He worked, utterly absorbed, until the light began to fade. Then, her pallor deep by then, her humanity began to intrude upon him. She is tired, he would realize. She must be hungry. I am.

He would put his palette down and open the door. "Mrs. Grommet," he would call down the stairs. Then he would study the day's work until the housekeeper hove into view, bearing a tea tray and Jo's wages for the day. Jo would follow her down. Mrs. Grommet would feed her in the kitchen, for Harry was reluctant to glimpse, at this sensitive stage, his Medusa with her cheeks full of mutton.

The Gorgon above their heads watched all this silently, refraining from comment.

She hardly saw Jo, Harry knew, except when she rose to leave. Then the wan, beautiful face would be visible to the painting above her head. Jo never looked that high; she seemed oddly incurious about the studio. Other models had prowled around peering at his canvases, opening books, trying on bits of finery, fingering this and that. But Jo just came and left, as though, Harry thought, she truly vanished into another world and was not much interested in his.

The Gorgon finally asked one evening, after Jo had followed Mrs. Grommet downstairs, "Where does she go?"

"What?" Harry asked through a bite of sandwich.

"Your model. Where does she sleep at night?"

"How should I know?" He was sitting in a soft stuffed chair, weary from standing all day, and devouring sandwiches and cakes, he suspected, like a well-brought-up vulture. He could see the Gorgon's face from that position if he wanted. Her voice startled him; she hadn't said much for days.

"Aren't you pleased with me, Harry?"

"For being so quiet? Oh, yes, I'm very grateful." He swallowed another mouthful of hot, sweet tea, and looked up at her. "What do you think of her?"

"Oh, a great deal," the painting answered vaguely, and gave a sudden, crude snort of a laugh. "She's far too beautiful for the likes of me, of course. But I see your point in her."

"Do you?"

"Beauty that can kill. But Harry, she's bone-thin and she's not much use to you dead. She might sleep in an alley for all you know. Anything could happen to her, and you'd never know what."

Harry was silent, blinking. He took another scalding sip. "I hadn't thought of that."

"Well, think of it. What would you do if tomorrow she didn't appear?"

The thought brought him out of his chair to pace a little, suddenly edgy. "Surely I pay her enough for decent lodgings. Don't I?"

"How much is enough?"

"I don't—"

"And suppose she has others dependent on her? Who need every coin she brings to them?"

"Well, maybe—" He paused, still tramping across the room; then he dropped into his chair again. "I'll ask Mrs. Grommet."

"You could ask your model."

Harry rolled his head to gaze up at the painting. "How?" he pleaded. "She is my Medusa. She exists only in this little world, only to be painted. I dare not make her real. She might lose all her power, become just another woman in my eyes."

The Medusa snorted again, this time without amusement. "She'd still be there for you to paint her. Your brush knows how to lie. If she vanishes into the streets out there, where will you go to look for her? You might at least ask her that."

Harry tried, at least three times, the next morning, before he got a question out. His model, whose name he kept forgetting, sat silently gazing as he had requested, at the back of his easel. What she saw, he could not begin to guess. Her wide, eerily pale eyes seemed to glimpse enormities in his peaceful studio. Until now, he had absently confused her expression with the Gorgon seeing herself for the first time and the last. Now he wondered, despite his better judgment, what those eyes had truly seen to make them so stricken.

He cleared his throat yet again. Her eyelids trembled, startled, at the sound of his voice. "Tell me, er—Jo?"

"Yes, sir?"

"Do you have a decent place to stay at night? I mean, I do pay you enough for that, don't I?"

She kept her face very still, answered simply, "Yes, Mr. Waterman. I go to a lodging house on Carvery Street."

"Alone?"

Her eyes flicked up, widening; he caught the full force of the Gorgon's stare. "Sir?"

"I mean—I only meant—do you have other people to care for? Others dependent on you?"

"Oh." The fierce gaze lowered once again to the middle distance. "No, sir. They're dead."

"Oh," he said inanely. He painted in silence a while, aware, though he told himself he imagined it, of eyes boring into his head from above the bookshelves. He glanced up finally, was appalled to see the full red lips moving wildly in a grotesque parody of speech.

He cleared his throat again hastily. "Do you get enough to eat? I mean, you're very thin."

"I'm eating better now," she answered.

The question sent a faint, unwelcome patina of color into her white face that at first alarmed him. Then he thought, Why not? Medusa, seeing her own beauty for the first time, may well flush with pleasure and astonishment before she turns herself into stone.

"Do you know," he asked aimlessly, trying to make conversation, "the story of Medusa?"

"Something of it," she said hesitantly. "Some sort of monster who turned people into stone?"

"Yes."

"Ugly, wasn't she?"

"Hideous," he answered, "by all accounts."

He heard her take a breath or two then, as if to speak. Then she grew still again, so still that he wondered if he had somehow turned her into stone.

He let his model rest a day or two later and spent a tranquil afternoon in the country, watching others work. Arthur Millidge was there, putting a honeysuckle background to what would be his *Nymph Dying for Love of a Shepherd*. He kept knocking his easel over swatting at bees. John Grainger was there as well, to Harry's surprise, back on his windy knoll painting the distant village. McAlister had finished his wife's windblown sleeve; now he was engrossed in her bare feet and ankles, around which green silk swirled and eddied. Harry, after his first glimpse of those long marble toes and exquisite anklebones, took the first chair he found and tried not to think about them.

Arthur Millidge's wife, Holly, handed him a cup of tea and sat down beside him. She was a pretty, good-natured, giddy-headed thing, who could pull out an arrow and hit an astute social bull's-eye just when she seemed at her most frivolous. She was watching her suffering husband with a great deal of amusement.

"Oh, poor Arthur," she cried, when he batted at a wasp with his brush and actually hit it; it stuck, struggling, to the yellow-daubed bristles. "At least it's the right color."

Her husband smiled at her wanly.

"I thought," Harry said blankly, "that Grainger and Nan would still be at the south coast."

"Oh, no," Holly answered briskly. "They only spent a few days there."

"But they are—they did get married?"

"So it seems. She's wearing a ring."

"Is she here?"

"No, poor thing, the traveling exhausted her in her condition, so she let John come alone."

Harry's eyes crept back to Aurora. Her condition, as well, he remembered; he could not, for a prolonged moment, stop studying her. The flowing, voluminous silk hid everything. Her face seemed a trifle plumper, but then he had been gazing at his emaciated model for days, he reminded himself. Aurora's face seemed exquisitely serene, he realized, ivory, full and tranquil, like a midsummer moon.

"The condition suits Aurora," Holly said, reading Harry's thoughts in her uncanny way. "I think poor Nan will have a great deal of difficulty with it. She's frail anyway and suffers from imagination."

Harry pulled his eyes away from McAlister's wife, dipped his hand into a bowl full of cherries. "Which of us doesn't?" he asked lightly.

"I'm sure I don't." Holly laughed and helped herself to a cherry or two from Harry's hand. "I heard you're painting something mysterious, Harry. Tommy Buck said that he and some friends came to visit you, and you refused to let them into your studio."

"They frightened my model," Harry said, remembering the shouts, Mrs. Grommet's flurried protest, the stampede up the stairs. "I thought she might faint, she was trembling so badly."

Holly maneuvered a cherry pit daintily from lips to palm and tipped it into the grass. "But who is she? Someone we know?"

"No. I found her in the street."

"How exciting! And what are you making of her?"

"Oh, I'm experimenting with this and that," he answered airily. "Nothing much, yet."

"She must be very pretty."

"In a wild kind of way. She's very shy. Not used to company."

"Everyone," Holly sighed, "is full of secrets. Alex won't tell what he's working on, either. You should bring her here, Harry."

"I should?"

"It might calm her, knowing others like her who model. Besides, if you decide you can't make anything of her, someone else might, and then she wouldn't have to go back into the streets."

"True," he said absently, flinging a cherry pit at a bee buzzing in the honeysuckle. "Oh, sorry, Arthur. I was aiming for the bee."

"Don't try to be helpful, Waterman."

"I won't, then."

"Will you bring her, Harry?"

"I might," he answered vaguely and changed the subject. "What do you think McAlister is making out of his wife?"

"Oh, who knows?" Holly said, waving midges away from her face. "Blind Justice? Aphrodite? Maybe even he doesn't know. The point is to keep her here, don't you think?"

"Here?" Harry repeated, mystified. Holly turned her head, regarded him blithely a moment, chin on her fist. Abruptly she laughed and got to her feet.

"Oh, Harry. You are so unbearably sweet. Arthur, come into the shade with us and have something to drink before you melt in all that light. I'm trying to worm secrets out of Harry."

"Harry has secrets?" John Grainger's deep, vigorous voice intoned incredulously behind them. "*Mirabile dictu!*" He dropped into a chair, dipped into the cherries with cerulean-blue fingertips, and demanded of the hapless Harry, "Tell all."

Jo sat in Harry's kitchen, eating her supper after he had returned from the country and began to paint her again. At his request, she had given Mrs. Grommet explicit instructions about where to find her if Harry needed her. Mrs. Grommet dutifully wrote the address down. Then, to Jo's surprise, she poured herself a cup of tea and pulled out a chair at the end of the table near Jo, where she sat close to the fire.

Mrs. Grommet said, "I know Mrs. Atkins, the woman who owns the lodging house on Carvery Street. She's a good, honest woman. Or at least she was when we worked together, in a great house over on Bellingham Road."

Jo's eyes slid uncertainly to her face. She managed an answer, after a moment. "She seems kind."

"She married unexpectedly. Lucky for her, her husband had saved a little money. And had a very loving heart. Married they were for thirty years before he died, and never a word passed his lips that their child wasn't his."

Jo coughed on a bit of pickled beet. The kitchen maid was on the far side of the kitchen, banging pots noisily in weltering dishwater. The cook was in the pantry counting spoons, which was her way of saying resting her feet and having a nip. Mrs. Grommet's green eyes opened meaningfully upon Jo, then lowered again. She sipped tea, half-turned at a splash from the sink.

"Go easy, girl! You're washing pots, not the flagstones."

Jo put two and two together, cleared her throat. Still, words came out with difficulty. "That's why—" She drew a breath, met the housekeeper's eyes. "That's why you're kind to me."

"Things happen," Mrs. Grommet said, the corners of her mouth puckering a moment. "They're not always our fault."

"No." She lifted her cup. It trembled badly; she put it down again quickly before she spilled. She folded her hands tightly, said to them, "It takes a special heart to see it that way, though."

Mrs. Grommet patted her hands. "I saw how you were with Mr. Waterman the first time you came here. So quiet and nicely behaved. Some of his models—well, the less said. Not that he was that way, at least not under his own roof. But I hear the young men talking about the girls they paint, about which would only pose and go, and which might stay around after for their bit of fun." She became aware of the maid handling the pots as gently as possible, and raised her voice again. "Finish up there, Lizzie, then go and see if Cook needs help in the pantry."

"Yes, Mrs. Grommet."

Jo said very softly, "You were friends, then, you and Mrs. Atkins, when you worked on Bellingham Road."

"Mary. Mary Plum she was, then. We started there very young, you see, and during the same summer. We were there together for five years. What happened to her seemed so unfair to me. It was one of the young friends of the family—"

"Yes," Jo whispered.

"Nothing to him, of course. He told her he loved her and would care for her. He couldn't even remember her name or her face, next time he came. He looked straight at her, she said, when she was serving dinner, and didn't even see her. She was at the point then when she had to leave. She had no choice. But then Martin—Mr. Atkins—found her weeping under the privet hedge when he went to trim it. He was a gardener there, then, and very well thought of. He'd saved all his money for years for an investment, he said. He asked Mary to be his investment." She paused, watching Jo's struggling face. "I've never seen you smile before."

"I've nearly forgotten how. Did he really put it like that?"

"She was a pretty thing," Mrs. Grommet said reminiscently. "He said he'd had his eye on her, but never thought he'd have a chance. Well, chance came, wearing an unexpected face, and he was brave enough to take it. She had a daughter who looked just like her. After some years, he'd worked so hard that—" She stopped abruptly. "Oh, dear."

The tears came out of nowhere Jo could name, hot, fierce, and seemingly unstoppable. She put her hands over her mouth, turned her back quickly to face the fire again. She heard Mrs. Grommet say something sharply to Lizzie; all sounds faded in the kitchen. Jo felt a tea towel pushed into her hand.

She buried her face in it, seeing, feeling, smelling all at once, as though memory, locked so carefully away, had crashed and blundered out of its door. His warm, slight weight in her arms, the smell of milk in his hair, his wide, round eyes catching at hers.

"Poor Alf," she whispered into the towel. "Oh, poor Alf. Poor little poppet. Oh, Mrs. Grommet, I did love him despite everything—"

"Now, then."

"He was just too frail to go on."

"There now." Mrs. Grommet patted her shoulder.

"I'm sorry."

"It's all right; Lizzie's gone. You have a good cry."

"I haven't—I forgot to cry, when—when—" Her voice wailed away from her, incoherent. She shook hair over her face and eyes like a shroud, trying to hide in it while tears came noisily, messily, barely restrained under the wad of tea towel. "Poor mite, he was all my heart. I think we must have gotten buried together, and I have been just a ghost ever since. No wonder Mr. Waterman sees me as that stone-eyed monster—"

"What?"

She drew a raw, ragged breath that was half sob. "Some—Medusa—who turns people into stone with her eyes. That's what he sees when he looks at me." Then she felt an odd bubble in her chest; loosed, it sounded strangely like a laugh. "I'd terrify anyone with these eyes now—"

"Let me see," Mrs. Grommet said faintly. Jo lifted her face from the towel, pulled wet strands of hair from her cheeks. Her throat ached again at the housekeeper's expression. But it was not grief so much as relief that she could still cry, she could still laugh. Which she found herself doing again amid her tears, in a damp, inelegant snort. "Look what I've done to you. You're stunned. . . ."

"You do look a bit fiery around the eyes," Mrs. Grommet admitted. "But no wonder Mr. Waterman doesn't remember you, with all that happened to you since."

"I was a maid when he began his first painting. Now, I'm Medusa." She sat again, drew a shuddering breath as she mopped her eyes.

"Maybe. But you look all the younger now for those tears." She refilled their cups. "Not that you're much more than a girl. But you just seemed . . . like you'd seen a Medusa, yourself. And lived to tell about it."

Jo wrapped her fingers around the cup, managed to raise it without spilling. "Mrs. Grommet, you've been so good to me," she said huskily. "I don't know how to thank you."

"Well. You reminded me so of Mary, when you disappeared like that. I couldn't see that you could have found any way to help yourself, except maybe into the river. Mr. Waterman looked for you when you left. He fretted about you. And not only for his painting. He wanted to help."

"I know." She got a sip past the sudden burn in her throat. "I was too frightened to think then. And now, I don't care if he never recognizes that terrified waif. I don't want him feeling sorry for me. I'm glad he doesn't know me."

"I did," Mrs. Grommet said, "the moment I saw you. I don't see how he can't. Being a painter as he is. Faces are his business."

"He doesn't see me. He sees the woman he wants to see. And I hope—" She touched her swollen eyes lightly. "I hope she's still there, in spite of my tears."

"Now he's got you thinking that way," Mrs. Grommet said roundly. "As if you're not yourself."

"But I never am, when he paints me. I am always the woman he has in mind. I think that's why he doesn't like to talk to me. He only wants to know the woman in his head. The dream he has of me. If I told him too much about"—she swallowed, continued steadily—"about Alf, about the streets, the mill, about my mother's hands all cracked from taking in laundry, about the purple shawl, the dream would be gone. All he'd have left is me."

Harry was gazing at his Medusa, a ham sandwich forgotten in one hand. With the other hand he was pointing out to the Medusa overhead various examples of his brilliance or his clumsiness, which seemed, judging by the Gorgon's expression, to be running about neck and neck that day.

"Look there. Putting that fleck of pure white just so, I've captured perfectly the suggestion of ice in her gray eyes. Do you see it? Of course the delicate line of the inner eye is a bit blurry, there; I'll have to rework it." Raptly, he took a bite of sandwich. "And there . . . ," he said with his mouth full, overcome. "You see what I did?"

"Harry. You still don't know anything about this woman."

"I told her to give Mrs. Grommet her address. You made a good point about that. Now, her hair. I shall have to go to the zoological gardens, observe some snakes." He paused, chewing, added regretfully, "I should have brought a few back with me from the country. I didn't think of it. Perhaps because I don't see the point of them. They just begin and go on and keep going on the same way they began, and then they end without any reason whatsoever." He paused again.

"Don't say it," the Gorgon pleaded.

Harry glanced at her, took another bite. "All right, I won't. But it is a bit like life, isn't it?"

"Harry!"

He smiled. "I'd give a lot to see your snakes, though. What color were they?"

"Ugly."

"No color is ugly."

"Maybe," the Medusa sighed, "but you must remember that I was hideous. I never looked at myself, of course, and my snakes were usually twined around my head. But now and then a loop or a head would lose its direction and slide near my eyes. They were fairly drab: brown, black, gray, without any interesting patterns. Big, they were, though. Thick as your wrists."

"Really? What did they eat?"

"Air, I suppose. Thoughts. They were my hair, Harry; they weren't meant to exist like ordinary creatures. Your hair feeds on you."

"I'll make hers like treasure," Harry said, studying the magnificent, haunting eyes again, the dangerous, irresistible mouth. "Gold, white gold, silver, buttercup, lemon. A shining, glittering swarm of colors. Tomorrow morning, I'll go—"

"She's coming tomorrow."

"I'll paint her in the morning then and visit the snakes in the afternoon."

"You could," the Gorgon suggested, "take her with you. You might get a better perspective on the snakes as hair if you see them both together."

Harry grunted, struck. "Possibly . . ." Then he blinked. "No. What am I saying? I can't possibly watch this devastatingly powerful creature wandering around looking at snakes in the zoological garden. Something would happen."

"Like what?"

"She'd step in a puddle, get a paper stuck to her shoe, some such. She'd mispronounce the names of things, she'd want tea and a bun, or peanuts for the bears—"

"I can't see that frozen-eyed woman tossing peanuts to the bears. But what you're saying, Harry, is that she would be in danger of turning human."

"Exactly," Harry said adamantly. "I don't want her human, I want her Gorgon—"

"I bet she'd be a charming human."

Harry opened his mouth. As though one of the Medusa's snakes had streaked down quick as thought and bit him, he glimpsed the potential charms in those eyes, warming in a smile, that hair, piled carelessly on her head, tendrils about her face playing in a breeze. He clenched his fists, pushed them in front of his eyes. "No," he said fiercely. "No, no, and no. This is my masterwork, and nothing—" He lowered his hands as suddenly. "What on earth is that hubbub downstairs?"

There seemed to be a good deal of shouting and thumping coming up the stairwell. Mrs. Grommet's voice joined it and it resolved itself easily then, into any number of friends in every stage of revelry pushing their way upstairs to join Harry.

He threw open the door, heard their chanting as they ascended. "Where is she, Harry? We must see her. We want to see your painting, foul as it may be. We have come to kneel at the feet of your Muse, Harry!"

Harry had just enough time to remove the painting from the easel and slide it carefully into the cupboard. Where, he hoped fervently, it would not also acquire a voice. He opened his study door, stepped into the landing. Half a dozen friends, a couple of them painters, one planning a gallery, others budding poets or philosophers, or whatever was fashionable this week, reeled into one another at the sight of him. Then, they rushed the second flight of stairs. Harry glimpsed Mrs. Grommet below, flinging her hands in the air, turning hastily back to the kitchen.

"Don't you dare lock your door this time," the honey-haired, sloe-eyed Tommy Buck called. "We'll sit on your stairs and hold them hostage until you reveal her. We'll—"

"She's not here," Harry said, with great relief. "She left an hour ago."

"Then let's see your painting."

"No. It's too dreadful." He turned adroitly as they reached the landing,

The Gorgon in the Cupboard

and locked the door behind him. "You'll laugh, and I'll be forced to become a bricklayer."

"She's in there." Tommy Buck paused to hiccup loudly, then banged upon the door. "You've hidden her."

"I have not. She's a shy, sensitive woman and you lot would cause her to turn into a deer and flee."

"Prove it."

"Prove what?"

"Prove she's not there."

"All right, I will. But I don't want you all rummaging about my studio and tossing my bad paintings out the window. You can look in and see, Tommy. The rest of you go downstairs and wait."

"No," said one of the poets, a burly young man who looked like he might have flung bricks around in an earlier life. "Open up, Harry boy. Show us all."

"No. I shall defend all with my life."

"What's that in your hand?" Tommy asked, swaying as he squinted at it. Harry looked. "My ham sandwich."

"Ham. He has ham in there," someone said wistfully. "I'm hungry."

"Here," Harry said, tossing him the remains.

"I saw it first," Tommy said indignantly. "I'm hungrier." He paused, still swaying lithely, like a reed in a breeze. "I've got an idea."

"He has an idea."

"I'd rather have a sandwich."

"Silence! I will speak! My idea is this. We all leave—" He waved his arms, fending off protests. "Listen. If we all go out to dinner, and Harry goes out to dinner with us, and then goes wherever we happen to go after that, it will prove that he hasn't got a model locked up in his studio. Won't it?"

"He could get the Grommet to unlock her," someone muttered.

"I won't speak to her," Harry promised. "And—" he dangled it. "I have the only key."

Tommy made a snatch at it. Harry tucked it out of reach. "She really has gone home," he told them. "And I think Tommy has an excellent idea. Maybe, if we hurry out, we'll catch a glimpse of her on the street."

They were quiet, staring at him, faces motionless in the stair lights.

Then, as one, they turned, clattered furiously back down the stairs.

185

Harry followed more slowly, brushing crumbs off his shirt and rolling down his sleeves. He heard the street door fly open, voices flow down the hall and out. Someone called his name, then the sounds faded. He didn't hear the door close. He wondered if Mrs. Grommet had taken refuge in a closet until the barbarian horde had gone.

He reached the hall and nearly bumped into his Medusa, coming quickly out of the kitchen with Mrs. Grommet at her heels.

"Jo—" he exclaimed, startled.

She pulled up sharply, staring at him, just as surprised.

"Mr. Waterman," she breathed. "I thought you had left with them."

He was silent, studying her. Something was awry with her face. It seemed streaked, flushed in odd places; her cold, magnificent eyes looked puffy and reddened, oddly vulnerable. He caught his breath, appalled.

"What have you done?"

"Sorry, Mr. Waterman," she said tremulously, brushing at her eyes. "It'll be gone by morning."

"But—" Something else was happening to her face as he stared. Lines shifted. Memory imposed itself, rearranging a curve here, a hollow there. He swallowed, feeling as though the world he knew had vanished for an eye blink, and then returned, subtly, irrevocably altered.

"Jo," he said, feeling his heart beat. "Jo Byrd."

She said simply, "Yes."

She returned the next morning as she promised, though not without misgivings. She looked for the same apprehension in the artist's eyes, searching for his Medusa in her face while he arranged the black silk around her neck, to draw out her pallor as he said. She wasn't certain about the pallor. The face in the tiny mirror above her washstand had been more colorful than usual. Nor was she at all certain what Mr. Waterman was thinking. He was very quiet, murmuring instructions now and then. She would have described his expression as peculiar, if he had asked. He looked like someone who had swallowed a butterfly, she thought: a mixed blessing, no matter how you turned it.

She said finally, hesitantly, "Mr. Waterman. If you can't see your Medusa now for seeing me, I'll understand."

He gave his head a quick little shake, met her eyes. "As the Gor—as someone pointed out, I tell lies with my brush. Let's see how well I can do it."

"But—"

"We'll give it a try," he insisted calmly. "Shall we?"

"If you say so, sir." She subsided, prepared herself to sit as silently as usual. But, strangely, now he seemed in a mood to talk. "I am," he said, touching white into the black around the Medusa's throat, "incredibly embarrassed that I didn't recognize you."

"I've gotten older."

"By how much? A year? I'm a painter! I've been staring at you daily. Not to mention—" His lips tightened; whatever it was, he didn't mention it.

"Yes, sir."

He looked at her again, instead of the silk. "I can't imagine what you've gone through. Or, rather, I can only try to imagine it. The child . . . it must have died?"

Her voice caught, but she had no tears left for that, it seemed. "Yes. He was never strong."

"Where did you go, when you vanished in the middle of my painting?"

"I went home to my mother's, in the country."

"I looked for you."

"I know. Mrs. Grommet told me."

His mouth crooked ruefully. "So she recognized you."

"The way I see it," Jo explained, "Mrs. Grommet was protecting your household. She has to know what she opens your door to. You remember what I looked like, then."

"Yes."

"She had to make decisions in her own mind about me. You were only seeing your painting. She was seeing a hungry, filthy wreck of a girl and trying to judge all in a moment whether I would steal the silver, eat with a fork or my fingers, go mad and break all the crockery. She was looking for reasons not to be afraid to let me through the door. You just saw your dream and let me walk right in."

He ran his hand through his hair, nearly tangling the brush in it. "Makes me sound like a fool."

She thought about that, shrugged. "I don't know. How do you like your painting?"

He looked at it, his eyes going depthless, still, like water reflecting an empty sky. They were, she realized suddenly, the exact blue of the dragonflies in the stream behind her parents' cottage. She'd lie and watch them dart and light, little dancing arrows as blue as larkspur.

Mr. Waterman blinked; so did she. They both drew back a little from what they'd been examining. She recognized that expression on his face; it was how he had been looking at her until now.

"I think—" he said, still gazing at his painting, and stammering a little, "I think—I wasn't a fool, after all. I think it's at least better than anything I've done so far. Jo. . . ." He turned to her abruptly. "I have such amazing visions of your hair. Are you afraid of snakes?"

"No more or less than anything else that might bite me. But, sir," she amended warily, "surely you're not going to put them in my hair? I don't think I want to wear them."

"No, no." His thoughts veered abruptly. "I have to fix that eye before I go on. Look at me. Don't blink." He added, after a moment or two, "You can talk."

"About what?"

"Anything that won't make you cry." She felt her eyes flush at the thought; he looked stricken. "I'm sorry, Jo."

"It's just—somehow I never got around to crying before."

"Tell me something, anything you remember, that once made you happy. If there was anything," he added carefully.

"Well." The tide retreated; she gazed, dry-eyed, at her past. "When my father was alive, he kept a small flock of sheep for wool. I liked to look at them, all plump and white in their green field, watch the lambs leap for no reason except that they were alive. He'd shear them and we'd spin the wool into yarn to sell. Sometimes we'd look for madder root to dye it purple."

"We?" he asked, busy at the corner of her eye, from what she could see. "Sister?"

"My mother. I didn't have sisters. I had a little brother for a couple of years once, but he died."

"Oh. But you chose not to stay with your mother? To come back here instead?"

"She died, too."

"Oh. I'm sorry."

"Yes," she said softly, but without tears. "So was I. So I came back here. And you rescued me."

He looked at her, oddly surprised. "I did?"

"You did," she said huskily. "I couldn't find work, I was exhausted, I had two coppers to my name. I found my way to your street just muddling around in the dark, and then I remembered you. I slept under a tree, that night before I came to your door. I didn't have any hope, but I didn't have anything left to do. I even—I even tried to get myself arrested for breaking a streetlamp, to have a place to sleep."

He was watching her, brush suspended. "When you do that—"

"What, sir?"

"Even when you only think about smiling, you change the shape of your eye. Medusa does not smile." He stopped abruptly, cast an odd glance above her head, and amended, "At least we have no recorded evidence that she smiled."

"You asked me to think about something happy."

"You didn't smile, then. It was irony, not happiness, that made you smile."

She mulled that over. "You mean trying to get into jail for a bed?"

"Yes. What happened? Did you miss the streetlamp?"

"No. I hit it dead-on. But a dozen others stepped up on the spot and swore it was them that threw the stone. Someone else got my bed. So I wandered on—"

"And," he said softly, his brush moving again, "you found me."

"You found me," she whispered.

"No tears. Medusa does not cry."

She composed her face again, summoned the icy, gorgeous monster to look out of her eyes. "She does not cry."

"But," he said after a while, "she might perhaps like to come with me this afternoon to look at snakes. No blinking."

"No blinking."

"But snakes?"

"Looking at snakes," she said, suddenly aware of his own fair, tidy hair, on a nicely rounded head, his young face with its sweet, determined expression, "would make Medusa happy."

....

Harry stood on the ladder in his studio, detaching the Gorgon from her nail. He had gotten in late. After spending a few hours among the reptiles and other assorted creatures, he had walked Jo to her lodging house on Carvery Street. Then he had wandered aimlessly, oddly light-headed, dropping in at studios here and there to let his friends tease him about his imaginary model, his hopeless daub of a painting so dreadful he was forced to keep it hidden behind locked doors. He laughed with them; his thoughts kept straying back to his studio, sometimes to the reptiles, none of which had done justice to his Medusa's hair.

But my brush can lie, he told himself. He had insisted on buying Jo peanuts in the zoological garden. But instead of throwing them to the animals, she had simply given them to a wiry, dirty-faced boy who had somehow wriggled his way in and was begging near the lions' den.

His elbow hit a book on top of the shelves as he maneuvered the painting down and under his arm. The book dropped with a thud that probably woke the house. He breathed a curse, trying to be as quiet as possible. The ladder rungs creaked ominously.

The Gorgon, who had been blessedly silent until then, said sharply, her mouth somewhere under his armpit, "Harry, you're not putting me back into the cupboard."

"Shh—"

"Don't shush me. Just because you don't need me anymore."

"What do you mean I don't need you?"

"I saw the way you looked at her."

"I was not aware that I looked at her in any particular way."

"Ha!"

"Shhh," Harry pleaded. "Mrs. Grommet will think I'm up here entertaining lewd company."

"Thank you," the Gorgon said frostily. But once started, she could never be silent for long, Harry knew. He felt the floor beneath his foot at last, and her curiosity got the better. "Then what are you going to do with me?"

"I just want to look at you."

He positioned a wooden chair beside the easel, propped the painting on it. Then he drew the black silk off the new Medusa. Side by side, Jo past and Jo present, he studied them: the young, terrified girl; the haunted, desperate woman. A year in the life. . . . "What a life," he breathed, moved at the thought of it.

The Gorgon spoke, startling him again. "What are you looking for?"

"I wanted to see why it was I didn't recognize her. I understand a little better now. That hair—I should have known it anywhere. But the expressions are completely different. And the skin tone. . . . She was at least being fed when she came to me the first time." His voice trailed away as he studied them: Persephone who had innocently eaten a few seeds and transformed herself into the doomed Medusa. He asked, suddenly curious himself, "Where do you live? I mean, where were you before you took up residence in my painting?"

"Oh, here and there," she answered vaguely.

"No, really."

"Why? Are you thinking of ways to get rid of your noisy, uncouth Gorgon?"

He thought about that, touched the Medusa on the easel. "Who inspired this out of me? No. Stay as long as you like. Stay forever. I'll introduce you to my friends. None of them have paintings that speak. They'll all be jealous of me."

"You invited me," she reminded him.

"I did."

"I go where I'm invited. Where I am invoked. When I hear my name in someone's heart, or in a painting or a poem, I exist there. The young thug Perseus cut my head off. But he didn't rid the world of me. I've stayed alive these thousands of years because I haven't been forgotten. Every time my name is invoked and my power is remembered anew, then I live again, I am empowered."

"Yes," Harry said softly, watching those full, alluring lips move, take their varying shapes on canvas in ways that he could never seem to move them in life. "I understand."

"You understand what, Harry?" the Gorgon asked so gently that he knew, beneath her raucous ways, she understood a great deal more than he had realized.

"I understand that I must go to the country again soon."

"Good idea. Take Jo with you."

"Should I? Really? She might be uncomfortable. And Grainger will try to seduce her away from me. He tries to steal everyone's models."

"That will happen sooner or later in any case, unless you are planning to cast her back into the streets once you've finished with her."

"No. I don't want to do that. I hadn't really thought ahead. About sharing her. Or painting her as someone else. Until now she was just my inspiration." He paced a step or two, stopped again in front of the paintings. Jo then. Jo now. "She's changed again," he realized. "There's yet another face. I wonder if that one will inspire another painting."

"Something," the Medusa murmured.

"Something," Harry agreed absently. "But you're right. I certainly can't put her back on the streets just so that she stays my secret. If she can get other work, she should. If I decide I don't—"

"Harry," the Gorgon interrupted. "One thing at a time. Why don't you just ask her if she'd like to come to the country with you and be introduced to other painters? She'll either say yes or she'll say no. In either case, you can take it from there."

Harry smiled. "That seems too simple."

"And find her something nice to wear. She looks like a bedpost in that old dress. Went out of style forty years ago, at least. I may not have a clue about what to do with my hair, but I always did have an eye for fashion. Though of course, things were incredibly boring in my day, comparatively speaking. Especially the shoes! You wouldn't believe—"

"Good night," Harry said, yawning, and draped the black silk over her. "See you in the morning."

Jo sat in the McAlisters' garden, sipping tea. She felt very strange, as though she had wandered into a painting of a bright, sunny world strewn with windblown petals, where everyone laughed easily, plump children ran in and out of the ancient cottage, and a woman, still as a statue at the other side of the garden, was being painted into yet another painting. Some guests had gathered, Harry among them, to watch Alex McAlister work. Jo heard the harsh, eager voice of the painter, talking about mosaics in some foreign country, while he spun a dark, rippling thundercloud of his wife's hair with his brush. Aurora McAlister, a windblown Venus, it looked like, her head bowed slightly under long, heavy hair, seemed to be absorbed in her own thoughts; her husband and guests might have been speaking the language of another world.

Someone rustled into the wicker chair next to Jo. She looked up. People had wandered up to her and spoken and wandered off again all afternoon; she was struggling hopelessly with all the names.

"Holly," this one said helpfully, "Holly Millidge." She was a pretty, frothy young woman with very shrewd eyes. She waved a plate of little sandwiches under Jo's nose; Jo took one hesitantly. "They're all right. Just cucumber, nothing nasty." She set the plate back on the table. "So you're Harry's secret model. We've all been wondering."

"I didn't know I was a secret," Jo said, surprised.

"I can see why."

"Why what?"

"Why he tried to keep you secret. Tommy Buck said he'd been twice to Harry's studio trying to see you, and Harry locked the door on him."

Jo remembered the clamoring voices, the thunder up the stairs. "Why," she asked warily, "did he want to see me that badly?"

"To see if he should paint you, of course." Holly was silent a little, still smiling, studying Jo. "They're noisy, that lot. But they're good-hearted. You don't have to be afraid of them."

"I'm used to being afraid," Jo said helplessly. "I'm not used to this."

"It's not entirely what you think," Holly said obscurely, and laughed at herself. "What am I trying to say? You're not seeing what you think you see."

"Painters don't, do they?"

"Not always, no." She bit into a strawberry, watching the scene on the other side of the garden. "They'd see how pretty you are and how wonderful and mysterious the expression is in your eyes. But they wouldn't have any idea how that expression got there. Or the expression, for instance, in Aurora's eyes."

Jo looked at the still, dreaming face. "She's very beautiful."

"She is." Holly bit into another strawberry. "Her father worked in the stables at an inn on Crowdy Street. Aurora was cleaning rooms for the establishment when Alex met her. Barefoot, with her hair full of lice—"

A sudden bubble of laughter escaped Jo; she put her hands over her mouth. "Her, too?"

"And whatever her name was then, it was most certainly not Aurora. Most of us have a skewed past. As well as a skewed present." She gave a sigh, leaned back in her chair. "Except for me; I have no secrets. No interesting ones, at any rate. When they put me in their paintings, I'm the one carrying the heartless bride's train, or one of the shocked guests who finds the thwarted lover's body in the fishpond."

Jo, feeling less estranged from her surroundings, took another glance around the garden. Seen that way, if the goddess had been a chambermaid, then everyone might be anyone, and no telling what anybody knew or didn't know about life. Except for Harry, she thought. And then she glimpsed the expression on his face and had to amend even that notion.

Nothing, apparently, was plain as day, not even Harry. While the other guests were laughing and chatting, Alex's voice running cheerfully over them all, Harry was standing very quietly among them, his eyes on the tall, dark goddess. Jo drew a breath, feeling an odd little hollow where her certainty had been.

"Harry," she said, hardly realizing she'd spoken aloud.

Holly nodded. "Oh, yes, Harry. And John Grainger, and half the painters in the McAlister constellation, including one or two of the women. Dreamers, all of them, in love with what they think they see instead of what they see."

"John Grainger. The one with the wild hair and rumbly voice and the black, black eyes?"

"Yes, that's him."

"He talked to me earlier."

"Everyone talked to you earlier," Holly said lightly. "I was watching. They're making their plans for you, don't you fret."

"I didn't like him," Jo said. "He has a way of putting his hand on you as though it's supposed to mean something to you. It made me uncomfortable."

Holly laughed. "Then he'll have to watch his manners with you. He's a fine painter, though, and very generous; if you let him paint you, you'll be noticed. Others will find you, if you want." She lifted her bright face to greet a lovely, red-haired woman with somber green eyes. "Nan! Have you met Harry's painting yet? Jo Byrd. Nan Grainger."

"Jo Byrd. Why do I know that name?" Nan eased herself into a chair, gazing at Jo. "Harry must have talked about you. But that was some time ago. Oh!" She gave a little start, her pale skin flushing slightly. "I remember now."

"I ran away."

"Yes. In the middle of his Persephone. He was bereft."

"Yes, well," Jo said, her mouth quirked, for everyone seemed to know everything anyway. "So was I."

Nan was silent, gazing at her without smiling. *What have I said?* Jo wondered, and then saw what lay beneath Nan's hands clasped gently over her belly.

Holly interrupted Nan's silence adroitly, with some droll story about her husband. Jo sighed noiselessly, her eyes going back to the group around the goddess. John Grainger stood closest to Aurora, she saw. They did not look at one another. But now and then the trailing green silk around her bare feet, raised by a teasing wind, flowed toward him to touch his shoe. He would glance down at that flickering green touching him, and his laugh would ring across the garden.

Secrets, she thought. *If you look at this one way, there's a group of cheerful people standing together on a sunny afternoon in a garden. That's one painting. If you look at them with a different eye, there's the story within the painting.* . . . She looked at Harry again, wanting the uncomplicated friend she thought she knew, who got excited over the golden snakes in the reptile house, and who made her go shopping with Mrs. Grommet for a dress, he said, that didn't look as if his grandmother had slept in it.

Unexpectedly, as though he'd felt her thoughts flow in his direction, against the wind, he was looking back at her.

"What beautiful hair you have," Nan said, watching the white-gold ripple over Jo's shoulders. "I'd love to paint it." Her green eyes were gathering warmth, despite the silk fluttering over her husband's shoe, despite her fears and private sorrows; for a moment she was just a woman smiling in the light. "Jo, have you ever tried to draw? You might try it sometime. I forget myself when I do; it makes me very tranquil."

I might try it, Jo thought, *after I lose this feeling that I've just fallen off the moon.*

But she didn't say that, she said something else, and then there was another cup of tea in her hand, and a willowy young man with wayward locks the color of honeycomb kneeling in the grass at her feet, who introduced himself as Tommy Buck. . . .

Harry watched Tommy kneel beside Jo's chair. Their two faces seemed to reflect one another's wild beauty, and he thought dispassionately: I would like to paint them both together. Then, he felt a sharp flash of annoyance at Tommy, who could barely paint his feet, dreaming of capturing that barely human face of Jo's with his brush.

His attention drifted. He watched the green silk touch Grainger's shoe, withdraw, flutter toward him again. Seemingly oblivious, Aurora watched the distant horizon; seemingly oblivious, her husband orated in his hoarse, exuberant crow's voice about the architectural history of the arch. Harry thought about Aurora's long, graceful hands, about her mouth. So silent, it looked now; he had gotten used to it speaking. He wondered if he could ever make this mouth speak.

And then she moved. The little group was breaking up around McAlister. "Too sober," he proclaimed them all. "Much too sober." Lightly he touched his wife, to draw her with him toward the cottage. As lightly, she slipped from his fingers, stayed behind to find her shoes under the rose vines. Grainger glanced at his wife across the garden, then at Aurora, then at his wife again. In that moment of his indecision, Aurora put her hand out to steady herself on Harry's arm as she put on her shoes.

"She's lovely, Harry," he heard her say through the blood drumming in his ears. "I like her. Where did you find her?"

"In the street," he stammered. "Both times. She—she has been through hard times."

"I know." She straightened, shod, but didn't drop her hand. Behind her, Grainger drifted away. Her voice, deep and slow and sweet, riveted Harry. "I know those times. I hear them in her speech, I see them in her eyes. I know those streets."

"Surely not—"

She smiled very faintly. "Harry, I grew up helping my father shovel out the stables until I was old enough to clean up after humans. Didn't you know that? I thought everybody did."

"But the way you speak," Harry said bewilderedly. "Your poise and manners—"

"A retired governess. Alex hired her to teach me. Beyond that I have my own good sense and some skills that Alex finds interesting. He likes my company."

"He adores you."

"He thinks he does. He adores the woman he paints. Not the Livvie that I am."

"Livvie?"

Her mouth crooked wryly; he saw her rare, brief smile. "Olive. That's my real name. Livvie, they called me until I was seventeen and Alex looked at me and saw painting after painting. . . . He said I was the dawn of his inspiration. So Olive became Aurora."

"Why," he asked her, his voice finally steady, "are you telling me this?"

"Because I've often thought I'd like to talk to you. That I might like having you as a friend, to tell things to. But for the longest time you could only see me the way Alex sees me. But then I saw how you looked at Jo today, knowing all you know about her. So I thought maybe, if I explained a thing or two to you, you might look at me as a friend."

She waited, the dark-eyed goddess who had pitched horseshit out of stables and whose name was Livvie. Mute with wonder, he could only stare at her. Then his face spoke, breaking into a rueful smile.

"I hope you can forgive my foolishness," he said softly. "It can't have been very helpful."

"I do get lonely," she confessed, "on my pedestal. Come, let's have some tea with Jo, and rescue her from Tommy Buck. He's not good enough for her."

"Will you come some day and see if I'm good enough to paint her? I would value your opinion very much."

"Yes, I will," she promised and tucked her long sylph's hand into the crook of his arm, making him reel dizzily for a step. He found his balance somewhere in Jo's eyes as she watched them come to her.

Much later, he reeled back into his studio, stupefied with impressions. Jo had promised, sometime before he left her at her door, to sit for the unfinished Persephone as well. So he would see her daily until—until he dreamed up something else. Or maybe, he thought, he would do what Odysseus's Penelope had done to get what she wanted: weave by day, unweave by night. He pulled the black silk off Persephone's head, saw the lovely, wine-red mouth and smiled, remembering the real one speaking, smiling its faint sphinx's smile, saying things he never dreamed would come out of it. But he no longer needed to dream, and he did not want Jo to see that mouth on her own face and wonder.

He was wiping it away carefully with cloth and turpentine when he remembered the Gorgon.

Horrified, he dropped the cloth. He had erased her entirely, without even thinking. What she must be trying to say, he could not imagine. And then he realized that the voluble Gorgon, who had talked her way out of his cupboard and into his life, had said not a word, nothing at all, to rescue herself.

Perhaps, he thought, she had nothing left to say. Perhaps she had already gone....

He picked up the cloth, gazing at the clean, empty bit of canvas where Persephone's mouth would finally appear. He heard the Gorgon's voice in his head, having the last word as usual.

If you need me, Harry, you know how to find me.

He left them side by side, his unfinished faces, and went to bed, where he would have finished them, except that he could not keep Persephone from smiling in his dreams.

MER

THE WITCH HAD HITCHED A RIDE in some gorse plants that Lord Beale of County Cork, homesick for them, had shipped to himself in far Port Dido around the turn of the century, after he founded the town. The witch, napping amid the thorny prickles through the months of the sea journey to the Pacific Northwest, had lost track of her name when the vessel finally docked and she woke. Something to do with battles? Graculus or suchlike? Something about ravens? Never mind, it wouldn't be the first name she had mislaid. Leaving the gorse, she caught sight of letters on the door sign of a small, sturdy building overlooking the dock. HARBORMASTER, they said. PORT DIDO.

Dido, she thought. That might do.

A cormorant nesting in a tree greeted her with a gentle, woeful croak. She grunted back at it, then climbed gratefully into the heart of its nesting tree, a sturdy spruce, and, still feeling the slightest bit seasick, she went back to sleep for a time.

When she finally emerged, the birds had gone, the tree had died of their guano, and there was considerably more of Port Dido than there had been before.

She half-saw, half-sensed that. She could see in the dark; she could understand the gist of the language of leaves. She could hear laughter within the tavern on an island up the estuary a mile away, and she understood the gist of that as well. Most around her were asleep, lulled by the distant roar of tide at the mouth of the bay. But not everyone.

Spring, she thought, smelling it. And then she saw the face of the moon.

It was full and luminous, a great wide eye above the high forests and the silent waters of the estuary. It was staring straight at her. So, she realized suddenly, was someone—something?—else.

A goddess, she thought, startled, and she heard herself bleat like one of the dark, snake-necked birds she had last spoken to. She was still invisible to humans, but beyond that, boundaries got nebulous. This goddess she recognized as one that took her power from the moon, but she had no idea what name that power claimed in this ancient place.

Nor, she remembered, did she know her own.

"I need a body," the goddess said inside the witch's head. "It's that time of the century. The one I have now is tired and needs a break." Her sacred voice sounded taut, restless, barely constrained; the witch felt her own bones smolder and shine, becoming illuminated with the intense, radiant scrutiny. "You recognized me. You know me—"

"I did once," the witch agreed, "but in a place very far away, and by a different name. Which," she sighed, "I have completely forgotten, along with my own."

"Perfect," the goddess said briskly. "Listen. Do you hear me?"

The witch did indeed: the roaring, growling turmoil along the edges of the earth, the rear and smack, the long, long roll, the break and thunder, the slow hiss, the whisper and pop of clams dancing in the tidal foam.

"Yes, Mistress," she said. She was fearless, adventurous—why else was she there?—and she had, as yet, no other place in the vast new world. Why not this?

"It's only for a hundred years," the goddess assured her. "And then you'll find someone to take your place. You will be feared, loved, cursed, praised, studied; you will be the flow of life; you will be bitter death; you will serve the moon, the sea, and all those your foamy fingertips can reach. Oh, and you will be worshipped. They're an odd lot, the worshippers, but very dedicated. You will be visible to them only once, near morning: the new face of my power." The goddess's voice was getting fainter, or the tide was getting louder, roiling into the witch's heart, into her blood. Her foamy fingers seemed everywhere, all around and very far away, following the path of the moonlight down the long pull of water. "Look this borrowed body up," she heard, "when you're yourself again. It'll be around."

She had no time to answer, learning names, shapes for everything she touched: every scale, worm, new thin shell, tiny unblinking eye, every floating strand of grass, transparent thread of jelly, everything new, just being born, all at once it seemed and already as moonstruck as she.

In the darkest hours she had reached the far edges of her realm, exploring every winding channel, every narrowing stream, every churning edge where the tide sculpted the world to its shape.

That's when she saw their fires and heard her name.

She appeared to them in the goddess's shape: a being made of spindrift, eyes of iridescent purple-black nacre, hair white and wild as spume, a voice like the most tender lilt and break of foam. She greeted them. The figures around the fires, all human, all women, all went as still as the great trees above them, boughs lifted as though to receive the descending moon.

Then they leaped to their bare feet, laughing, clapping, calling to the goddess, the same word again and again, which, the witch/goddess realized sometime later, as she busily withdrew herself across the mudflats and back into the sea, must have been her name. Her final coherent thought for a century was that, once again, she had forgotten it.

A hundred years later, give or take the time the moon took returning to the full, the witch, exhausted and desperate for a change of shape, poured all the powers of the tidal goddess into the first likely body that gave permission. The body, half-human and half-local spirits, seemed surprised at the forces, but on the whole quite curious, and responded with alacrity to her changed state.

The witch, herself again, crept with great relief into the heart of a wooden female shape nearby and went back to sleep.

Jake Harrow and Scott Cowell were trying to load the seven-foot wooden mermaid with her scallop-shell bra and her long blue tail with the cormorant perched in its curve off one end of the Port Dido bridge into the back of Markham Cowell's pickup truck when all hell broke loose.

It was after midnight and the town was asleep. Then it was dawn, or some lurid, colorless version of light, by which the two young men could suddenly see one another's pallid, surprised faces beneath the mermaid's cheery red smile. In the same nanosecond the bell in the tower at Our Lady of the Cormorants pealed like someone had whacked it with a tire iron, and a cannon blew off next to them. They leaped. The mermaid slid out of their hands and toppled toward the back of the pickup, which is what they had wanted her to do in the first place. But the pickup was no longer there, Markham having stomped the accelerator at the sound of the blast, sending the truck careening halfway across the bridge.

The mermaid fell on her back and slid down the embankment into the bay.

For one stark moment, by the light of the streetlamp in the middle of the bridge, they saw her smile under the shallow wash of the tide. Then she sank a little deeper into darker water. Markham and Jake stared at where she had been, and then at each other. Lights were flicking on all around them in houses on the cliffs and along the water, in the Marine Institute's dorms, in the harbor where those who lived on their boats were scrambling onto the docks. There was a squeal of tires, a rattle of muffler as Markham backed wildly; Jake and Scott leaped to meet the truck, flung themselves inside.

"What the hell—" Markham breathed, shifting gears.

"Go," Jake said tersely.

"Where's the mer—"

"Go!"

They ventured back near dawn, on the off chance that the mermaid herself hadn't gone anywhere, and they might winch her out of the water before anyone else noticed her. But the slowly awakening sky revealed nothing, except that, where mermaid had been, there was now none. Most, Jake guessed, were so used to seeing her they didn't much notice her anyway, there or not. They would notice, maybe even remember, the three standing where she usually stood, looking down the bank for something in the water.

"Must have sunk like a stone," Markham murmured bemusedly.

"Most logs don't," Scott argued. "They float."

"Then she floated away."

"Let's take a walk on the docks," Jake suggested. "Look for her there. The bridge is going up, and people idling here are going to notice our faces instead of hers."

Fishing boats on the landward side of the harbor were heading out to sea. Two slabs of tarmac rose to sandwich air so they could get by, and traffic had begun to line up along the road. The three crossed between idling cars to where they had left the truck behind Sylvia's Bait and Tackle. When the bridge folded itself down again, they drove across, and turned onto Port Dido's single busiest street, where you could rent crab rings, buy groceries, find a beer and a barstool, or, at the far end of it, an education in marine biology. From there they took a side street, passed the fish-processing plant, several ancient restaurants, and the Landlubber, Port Dido's only motel. The street ended in the parking lot beside the harbor.

The three walked down a ramp and separated on the docks to search between trawlers, sailboats, cruisers, motorboats, and scows for the mermaid that might have gotten washed between them and wedged there by the tide. Everyone Jake passed, crabbers with their rings in the water, boat people gathered for coffee on one another's decks, talked about the same thing: the ferocious flash of light, the wild jangle of church bell like a call to judgment, the instantaneous detonation of thunder. Hell, he thought, even the harbor seals clustered on their favorite dock were probably barking it over.

Nobody mentioned the missing mermaid.

Yet.

She finally surfaced in the Foghorn Café where the three slid wearily into a booth for breakfast. The Foghorn cook, driving early to work, had marked the mermaid among the missing after that tumultuous night. Word spread quickly among the staff and passed to the diners along with every breakfast order. From what Jake could catch of the excited gabble, nobody was certain of anything, though nobody could get enough of it. The lightning, as sudden and vivid as a dead eye opening, the horrendous blast, the scarred, blackened bell tower, the vanished mermaid were puzzled over separately and together; nothing seemed to fit.

"That tall ship that comes to visit every year—the *Lady Ysabelle*—did she sail in last night? Maybe somebody shot off her cannon and hit the Cormorants' bell? Maybe it took out the mermaid along the way?" Jake, who had his back to her, recognized the lilting ebb and wash of Carey O'Farrell, who owned Sea Treasures, in which tourists could buy wind chimes made of jingle shells, local art and jewelry, and Port Dido tea towels.

"The *Lady Ysabelle*'s not due until late summer," Parker Yeong, one of the Institute's professors, reminded her. "Besides, they only fire off gunpowder in their fake battles, not real cannonballs. I like your theory, though," he added cheerfully. "It's better than the single-bolt-of-lightning theory. That might explain the bell tower, but not the missing mermaid; she wouldn't have been in its trajectory."

"Yes, and what have those Cormorants been up to?" Emma Cadogan demanded darkly from the table on the other side of Carey. Her portentous, fluting voice caused Shirley Watson, of Watson Fishing and Whale Watching Excursions, to stiffen on her stool at the counter. "I always knew they were an evil bird. Blasphemous to think that the Mother of God would consort with cormorants."

Shirley spun on the stool, her whacked-out, sideways grin flashing her gold eyetooth. "So the Lord flung a lightning bolt, missed the birds, but got the church tower instead?"

Markham loosed a snort of laughter over his coffee. Scott, red-eyed, rattled, punched his brother's arm, but it was too late. Emma, loftily ignoring Shirley, trained her sights at the three young men in the booth. She was a massive, formidable woman who spent her hours at the Port Dido Visitors' Center, telling tourists where to go and showing them the quickest way to get there.

"What do you boys know about all this?" she asked, riveting them in an instant, like that snake-haired Greek with the snarky eyes who lingered in Jake's memory long after her name. "You must have been out late last night after graduation."

Jake heard Markham's breath again, freed from the stone he had almost become. "Graduated three years ago, ma'am," he said with a genuine edge of indignation. "Last thing on my mind back then would have been a woman made of wood with a fish tail instead of legs."

Emma's eyes didn't flicker, Jake saw; she might have pursued the matter for no other reason than to listen to her own voice. But Sally Goshen edged between table and booth wielding a tray full of breakfasts.

"Did you all hear what happened last night?" she asked them breathlessly. "I just heard—I started my shift late. I was home all the way over in Greengage when that bolt woke me and my son Jeremy and the dogs. Louise in the kitchen said her boyfriend was out with the Coast Guard late last night in a cutter, and they saw the entire bay bright as day when the lightning flashed. He knew it got the Cormorants because they're the only church in the county with a real bell in the tower."

Dr. Yeong swiveled from his breakfast burrito to look at her. "Did he know anything about the mermaid?"

"What? No." She stared at him, giving Jake Markham's mile-high stack with bacon and extra butter. "He didn't say. Somebody found a mermaid?"

"No," Carey explained. "The mermaid on the bridge? She went missing last night."

"You're kidding!"

"Vanished," Markham said, gazing raptly at Sally's face, with its skin like a ripe, golden, finely freckled apricot. Scott joggled his elbow; he looked vaguely around, then focused on his plate. "Heck's this?"

"My Greek omelet," Jake said. "Spinach and feta and capers."

"Capers." Markham speared one on a fork prong. "Looks like bait to me."

"Oop—sorry," Sally said, putting Scott's salmon scramble in front of Markham instead. "Oh, yeah, that mermaid. Well? What happened to her?"

Jake shook his head, drawing in a deep breath of syrup and melting butter as he passed the pancakes to Markham, who handed his brother the scramble. "We have absolutely no idea."

They parted company after breakfast, Markham to work catching and baiting fish with huge hooks to catch the cormorants who swallowed the fish, Scott to the community college over in Myrtlewood to study Spanish and welding, and Jake to the South Coast Culinary Institute to learn the difference between hollandaise, béarnaise, and mayonnaise, and which belonged on what.

The witch opened her eyes and found herself floating on her back with a cormorant sitting on her front holding its wings out to dry.

Her whole being, whatever it was at the moment, protested the wakening. It was far too soon after a hundred restless years; she needed most of a year to sleep, not half a night—and why was she back in the tide?

The bird opened its long beak soundlessly, seeming to sense the witch's ire at the world through its great, flat feet. Then it levitated with a powerful, graceful thrust of its wings. The witch caught its eyes, its vision; for a dizzying moment, she looked down at herself, the wooden mermaid in the water, with her scallop shells and her bright yellow hair curved along her cheek and one side of her smile, her long tail curved upward, fin spread like a fan, the arc broad enough to hold something, the cormorant maybe, that might have perched there.

Oh, why not, the witch thought with exasperation. At least human, I could have a bed.

She guided the wood figure carefully away from fishing boats in the bay, from boat ramps and docks crowded with crabbers. Passing gulls took note of the mermaid's glowering eyes and changed their minds about landing there. After a century, the witch knew the waters—estuary, harbor and bay, every stone, barnacle, and bit of wrack—like she knew her own mind. She brought the stiff, heavy statue easily and unobtrusively to the sandy shore inside a half-hidden cove. There she let her powers flow everywhere into the wood, just as she had for the last century. Eyes blinked, hair shifted in the wash of water, the tree heart thumped, sap moved along its secret ways. The witch swallowed, spoke, making a hollow blat at first. When she tried to stand, she remembered what she had forgotten. Fin morphed into feet bigger than any she had ever had. She stumbled over them at first, and nearly bumped her head on the rocky ceiling. She touched her hair, examined her toenails, gazed with bemusement at the two scallop shells on her chest, no longer wood but real, and at the short, wetly gleaming, scale-patterned blue skirt that barely reached halfway down her thighs. She possessed nothing else: no shoes, no money, not even, she realized irritably, a name.

"Maybe," she said aloud, then, remembering, and her smile appeared, a living thing as responsive to her thoughts as language. "Maybe in this body I'm Dido."

She vanished for a while to climb up the cliff above the cave, a simple matter for her great, splayed feet and her long, hard arms; then she walked a back road down into Port Dido.

She let her oddly tall, ungainly but comely shape appear gradually on the sidewalks: a barefoot, very tired, very hungry young woman wearing only seashells and fish scales. People had changed, she noted with interest, during the hundred years she'd been in the water. Like the mermaid, they exposed anything at all of themselves, and much of what they exposed had colorful artwork on it, as though they kept their histories in living canvases on their skin. They let their hair do whatever it wanted; they put extraordinary things on their feet. Even so, some still gave her startled glances. Others grinned at her, or extended a thumb, which meant something, she guessed: maybe it warded away witches.

She was dawdling outside a cluster of shop windows in a little square, intrigued equally by the clothes in one, the bottles of wine in another, the little tarts and buns in a third. Her mouth watered; her chilly fingers and feet tried to warm each other. Money, she remembered distantly, was the difference between having nothing and having something. At least it was for mortals, but not necessarily for witches inhabiting the shape of a wooden mermaid turned temporarily human. She was debating in the mermaid's head the merits of pickpocketing, begging, scaring the change out of the next passerby, or enchanting a few dried leaves into coins, when a shop door flew open.

"There you are! I've been keeping an eye out." The witch, surprised by the young, brown, dark-browed face peering out, recognized under the thick curly hair and the flawless skin of someone not long in the world the force that had been the tidal goddess's previous body. She was part cormorant, the witch sensed, and part human, with some very old regional powers tossed into the mix. Like the witch herself, she'd been around a long time, and had many connections, not all of them innocent or unambiguous. "Come out of the cold. Port Dido blows in a fogbank every afternoon and calls it spring. I'm Portia. Did you remember your name?"

"Not yet," the witch answered, crossing the threshold. "But I've decided the mermaid is Dido. It's easy to remember." She smelled all good things then: meat, fruit, chocolate, fungi, grains, spices, and her knees shook. She sat suddenly; a chair caught her midway down.

"You poor thing."

"Something woke me before I had even begun to dream. I'm not sure what it was, but I found myself in this—this—"

"Yes." A dimple deepened in one firm cheek; in her smile a bit of ancient mischief sparked. "You did. I can give you a place to sleep for a hundred nights. Or I can give you dinner, a bed for the night, and a job in the morning. Not too early," she added quickly. "Pub hours. Your choice. Here. Eat this."

The witch, biting into strawberries, thick, heavy cream, dark chocolate, and golden pastry that crumbled and floated in air, decided in that moment, that mouthful, to stay awake and human for a while. There were benefits.

"But what do you get out of it?" she wondered. Even the most noble of witches had her own best interests at heart.

Portia dropped the lid over an eye dark as the backside of the moon. "You'll see."

By the week's end, opinion seemed pretty evenly divided between blaming the mermaid's disappearance on the congregation of Our Lady of the Cormorants, whose passion for the demonic bird must have led them into unimaginable wickedness, or the Port Dido High School's graduating class, which was known for its pranks, or any of the rich tourists who might have driven off with the mermaid as a souvenir of the quaint little town where they had hired a boat for a day to haul salmon and tuna out of the sea. A reward donated by the Chamber of Commerce was posted for information leading to her whereabouts. Merchants set out donation jars to add to the reward. The local paper published a photo of the missing mermaid, the history of her life on the bridge welcoming visitors, and a plea from the chainsaw artist who had created her to return his masterwork, no questions asked.

Jake's girlfriend, Blaine, pretty much said the same thing, wailing into his cellphone as he sat with Markham and Scott in a shadowy corner of the Trickle Down Brewery and Pub, "Jake, how could you lose a seven-foot mermaid? You have to find her. I promised Haley! I promised her! That's the focal point of the whole color scheme of her wedding. My best friend is getting married and I want her day to be perfect. I don't care where she went, you have to get her back by Saturday."

"I know, baby," Jake said softly. "I will. Ah—where are you?"

"Here at Haley's with the girls, making the wedding favors. Oh, don't worry, nobody's here who doesn't know you're involved. Everything—the favors, the cake, our heels and dresses, the bouquets, the corsages and decorations—they're all her colors! Red and that dark, gleaming blue with yellow trim for her hair. Nothing will make any sense without her. You were just supposed to borrow her for a few days then put her back, not drop her into the bay."

"It just happened," he answered helplessly.

"I know, I know: the lightning whacking the church bell, the thunderclap—I understand that. But why did it have to happen to Haley?"

"We still have until Saturday. We'll find her."

"What can I get you guys?" the waitress asked.

Blaine's voice grew small and far away as Jake stared. She wasn't covered in blue scales; she had two legs under a short black skirt and black tights. But that red mouth, that generous smile, the curve of golden hair along one side of the smile, all that and the fact that she was taller than anyone in the room made his thoughts tangle to an abrupt halt, like an engine seizing up. He ended the call absently, forgetting Blaine. Beside him, Markham and Scott were absolutely still.

"Guys?" She twiddled the pencil between her fingers against the order pad. "Drinks?"

"You—" Jake breathed. "You."

"Oh, for—" She gazed at them with pity, one hand on her hip, and shook her head. "No. I am not the Port Dido mermaid come to life. What is it with everyone? I was the chainsaw sculptor's model. That's all."

"Lived here all my life," Markham managed. "Never saw you before."

"I've never lived here before." She raised the pencil. "Let's try again. What can I get you?"

She took their orders. They watched her return to the bar; then their heads swiveled slowly; their eyes met.

"No," Jake said flatly, to his own and everyone else's unspoken suggestions.

"But the timing—it's got to be more than coincidence," Markham said weakly.

"So? What?" Scott demanded. "So she really was a wooden mermaid a couple of days ago and the fall into the water turned her human?" He batted the back of his brother's head lightly. "Get real."

They were silent, watching her again. Markham mused, "She could come to the wedding anyway. Couldn't she? Don't suppose Haley would—"

"No. I don't suppose Haley would accept a human substitute dressed up as the Port Dido mermaid. Especially not one who looks like that." Jake drew a sudden breath. "Did I really hang up on Blaine? I'd better call her back."

The mermaid returned with their drinks. Their expressions transformed her enchanting smile into a broad grin. "Don't worry," she said briskly. "You'll get used to me."

On Sunday, the witch went to church.

Our Lady of the Cormorants was a modest chapel framed by a stand of old fir trees, its altar windows overlooking the blue-green estuary. Though its bell tower, tall and rounded like a tree trunk, had been scorched by the lightning, the bell still called the congregation to gather with a sweet, mellow toll. The congregation, the witch who called herself Dido noted, seemed to be all women. In fact, they were all witches with some level of power, though not all of them knew it. They simply felt comfortable, the witch guessed, among the eccentrically skewed worshippers dedicated to the smiling statue generically clothed in a long white robe and a blue mantle, her open hands outstretched over the dark pair of wiry-necked, long-billed, waddle-footed birds gazing up at her.

Seated on a pew smelling of cedar and candle wax, the witch napped through most of the service, waking only when the pastor, Reverend Becky, unsheathed an edge in her gentle, soothing voice.

"It's that time again, Ladies. Those of you with cormorant heritage will need to find and waken those powers to protect the nestlings from predators. Especially from Niall Parker at Davy Jones' Liquor Locker, who harpoons nests at night when he's drunk, and Markham Cowell, who gets paid to stuff freshly dead fish with hooks and run them fast underwater to attract the parent birds. Those who can will circle the nestling trees and grounds with your darkest powers so that humans can't pass among them. Those with other powers: get creative. Invent noises to scare the predators, swamp their boats if you catch them shooting the birds from the water, put whatever charms and distractions you dream up in places where they'll do the most good. Keep eyes and ears open for trouble, and stop it if you can before it starts. We are the faithful of Our Lady of the Cormorants. It is our belief that we are all—even idiots like Niall and Markham—part of Holy Mother Nature, that we all belong to this earth, that cormorants are of an ancient and wild power that should be protected, and that the sea will provide for us all, human and bird, if we take care of one another and the sea. Amen, Ladies."

"Amen."

"Please stand for the closing hymn."

The witch yawned a great yawn, sent her body sprawling along the suddenly empty pew and went back to sleep.

She woke up in a tree.

It was night. She was surrounded by dreams of a fishy, feathery, egg-nesty kind, fraught with swift flights over water, sudden, deep dives, the struggles to stretch and shape a long throat and neck around the body struggling equally to wriggle out of them. She had to shield her human nose from the acrid smell of guano on the tree limbs, which seemed to cover them like perpetual moonlight. Parents, half-waking in their twiggy nests, made little blats and moans around her, disturbed without knowing why. The witch woke up a bit more, spread her rangy self more comfortably along the boughs, and got around finally to wondering why she was up a tree.

She heard voices.

The patch of forest, between the shops at one end of the street and the Institute at the other, overlooked the bay and a small beach over which the low tide gently sighed and slid, sounding like a contented dreamer. The only lights were distant: from the dorms, from vessels in the marina, from the occasional streetlamp. The half-dozen men gathering under the nesting tree had no reason to be quiet; the wakening parents above, some nervously croaking, weren't going anywhere. The men, the witch observed dourly, weren't much more articulate.

"Whaugh, this place stinks. Who's got the bottle?"

"Here."

"That one there, Niall. That big nest, higher up. Harpoon that one and it'll pull the others down along the way."

The witch heard a gulp, a spit, a sudden, sharp laugh. "Last time you'll snarf our fish, you up there. Look at them. All they do is eat and breed, make more mouths to take the fish out of ours. Do it, Niall."

A light went on; it searched the tree, falling short of where the witch sat. She could see a reddened, raspy face or two, the hands of the harpooner adjusting his line, raising the long weapon with its sharp, glinting dart, taking aim.

Get out, Portia's voice in the witch's brain said very clearly. *Fast. Now.*

There was a grunt, a whip of line, and a strangely solid thud. The witch, balanced precariously on the very tip of the tree, once again invisible, heard branches cracking, something heavy careening through them, men shouting in warning, the bottle breaking.

The thing finished its fall with a massive thud in the middle of the road.

There was utter silence. The witch, all her senses galvanized, powers she had forgotten she possessed, crouched, alert, waiting to attack, finally heard a dry swallow below.

"Damn, Niall. You harpooned the Port Dido mermaid."

Jake, driving back from his culinary classes at the end of the day, thinking of nothing more complex than a cold one at the brewpub, saw the mermaid at her post on the bridge giving him her familiar, welcoming smile. He was so used to seeing her, he barely noticed her, for as long as a couple of seconds. Then he swore, slammed on the brakes, and backed up without thinking once, let alone twice, and causing the car behind him to swerve onto the embankment.

Jake ignored the furious horn while he stared. The mermaid seemed her usual cheerful self, except for the large, oddly metallic fish scale in her tail near where human knees might have been. Jake squinted. The oversized fish scale looked weirdly like the bottom of a beer can, sliced off and nailed or glued into place to hide some—what?

Something fishy.

A face loomed into his open window, grey-browed, time-furrowed, and as annoyed with him as she had been all during second grade.

"Jake Harrow, you nearly ran me into the harbor!"

"Sorry, Ms. Priestly."

"Well, are you planning to move anytime soon? People are piling up behind us."

"Yes, Ms. Priestly. Sorry."

Something else he realized as he parked at the Trickle Down: something else was wrong with the mermaid. But what? The short, slender, dark-haired waitress who greeted him as he joined the Cowell brothers looked absolutely nothing like the mermaid they had seen there before. That fact he thought about briefly, then decided never, ever, to think about it again.

The expression on Markham's face, usually stolid and already set in its ways until now, told Jake exactly what he wanted to know.

"You put her back," he breathed, after the waitress had delivered his beer.

"We did. Late last night. I was with Niall and some of the fishers—they were nest-rustling—" He paused, drank, then stared, wide-eyed and stunned, into his glass. Jake wondered if he had forgotten how to blink.

"Well, where did you find her?"

Markham drank again. "Up a tree." Jake stared at him, then at Scott, who shook his head slightly.

"No, I wasn't there to see it, but I wish I'd been."

"Me, too," Jake said fervently. "How'd she get up—"

"Ask him how she got down," Scott said, and answered for his brother. "Niall brought her down with a harpoon."

"He—what—what the hell, Markham?"

"We didn't know she was up there! Who would have guessed a mermaid up a tree? We were aiming for the cormorants' nests. But down she came instead, nearly fell on our heads." He paused to gulp beer. "But that's not the weirdest thing. The weirdest thing was that he shot up, she came down—all seven feet of her, and you know how heavy—but nothing else did. Not a bird, not an egg, not a feather, not a twig. Nothing. Birds all sat there and watched while Niall pulled out his harpoon, which should have just bounced off her—unless of course she'd been a real mermaid, and then—" He blinked finally, and shook his head, looking rattled. "And anyway, Adam Paring found some cutters in his tackle box and made a patch out of a beer can to hide the damage on her scales."

"But how did—who—? What, she climbed into the tree herself? A sneaker wave floated her up and left her there without drowning the nests?"

"You know what I know, and that's all I know," Markham said heavily. "Except that I need another beer."

"Well, that explains the beer can in her tail."

"You noticed that?"

"Well, yeah. It's not exactly subtle. Other than that, though, she seems...." His voice trailed. He examined his first glimpse of her, felt the lack again, nothing where there should be . . . what?

"Her cormorant is gone," Scott said, and Jake nodded, relieved.

"Yes. That's it. That's what I was missing."

"Way things are happening, maybe it flew away when she slid into the water," Markham said, and reached for Jake's beer. "And maybe it picked her up later and dropped her in the tree. I don't know. You can't think about it too much. Things start happening in your head. Weird thing is—"

"What's weirder? What could be?"

"You know how the cormorant stood in the curve of her tail? And now it's gone. But there's no sign it had ever been there. No paint missing where its big, flat feet should have been. No bare patches in the tail. Just blue scales. So." He paused to drain Jake's glass. "Maybe it really did fly away." He looked around the pub. "And now we've got the mermaid back, but where's the waitress we thought was her?"

"I am so not thinking about that," Jake groaned. "I'd better call Blaine—"

"No," the brothers said together.

"Don't worry. I'm not going anywhere near that mermaid again. If the bride wants something blue and yellow and red I'll dye my hair and paint myself." He was silent then, musing over maybes, and what-ifs, and teasing the improbable out of the impossible. What did a lightning bolt, a church bell, a mermaid have in common? A cormorant, of course. A beer appeared in front of him like a lifeline, pulling him back out of his thoughts. "Promise me," he pleaded.

"What?" the brothers asked.

"If you ever figure all this out, don't tell me. I will never want to know."

"You might have warned me," the witch said grumpily.

"You were sleeping so soundly I didn't want to wake you," Portia said sweetly. They were back in her shop, inhaling tea and laying waste to a tray of sweet and savory tarts. The witch, who had forgotten what she looked like, even if she could remember where she had left her original self, had cobbled a body out of forgotten reflections she had coaxed from a mirror in a thrift shop.

"That harpoon might have killed me."

"Nope. I was guiding it all the way up, and the mermaid all the way down. I had everything under control, even the birds; it helps to speak their language. Reverend Becky told us to be creative against the predators." There was a look in her dark eyes, where antiquities lurked, that made the witch instantly suspicious.

"Now what?"

"Just a thought." Portia straightened a nicely painted index finger, licked chocolate off of it.

The witch felt a yawn ballooning in her, tried to hide it, then gave up and let it happen.

She said, tiredly, "I don't want to hear it."

"Well, I won't say anything if you don't want me to. But it would be a place to sleep for as long as you want. After all, they've got that mermaid attached to an antique ship's anchor now, and she's not going anywhere. They can't seem to find her missing cormorant."

"I suppose you haven't a clue."

Portia gave her a smile, lovely, carefree, inviting, not unlike the mermaid's. The witch stifled another yawn, felt herself drifting again on a slow ebb toward dreams.

"Well," she said. "Maybe. But promise me: no more surprises. I just want a long and very peaceful nap."

"You got it."

The wooden cormorant was back on its roost in the curve of the mermaid's tail sometime before dawn, where it remained undisturbed for months until it finally woke again and flew away.

WEIRD

"WHAT'S THE WEIRDEST THING that ever happened to you?" he asked.

"Weird," she repeated. "You mean like weird funny? Weird spooky?"

"Just weird." He brushed the crook of her elbow, the little hollow there, with one finger, lightly. "As in: for which there is no other word."

She thought. "You mean like the time I got swept up into an alien spaceship and examined by doctors who looked like talking iguanas wearing surgery gowns?"

He shook his head. "No. That's just silly. True weird."

"Well." She paused, lips parted, eyes dazzled by light, feeling his warm lips burrow into the hollow, leave a kiss that lingered there, an echo, a memory. "That would have to be what happened at my cousin Delaney's wedding when the shoe landed in the wedding cake."

He lay back, one hand under his head, the other touching, just barely with the tips of his fingers, the underside of her wrist. "Did it happen to you?"

"Not really. Except it being my shoe that landed in the cake. But it wasn't personal."

"That doesn't count."

She thought again. They were lying on every bath towel they could find. The bathroom floor was white and green tile, hard and cold but generously wide. They had piled hand towels under their heads, and used the bath sheets for blankets. The pretty gold wire wastebasket was filled with fruit, both fresh and dried, some Italian salami, packets of water crackers and digestive biscuits, a little jar of Kalamata olives, another of gourmet mustard, individually wrapped wedges of mushroom Brie, a bar of hazelnut chocolate, and a small vacuum pack of smoked, peppered salmon, along with the considerable length of purple ribbon that had been wrapped around the gift tray. The tray itself, a very nice bamboo hors d'oeuvres board, had gone out the window just before she slammed it shut and locked it.

They had water; they had plumbing; they were a little short on utensils, but, as he pointed out, they could use toothbrush handles, and the little files that slid in and out of nail clippers.

She remembered something suddenly. "Oh. My grandfather Pippin's funeral."

"Pippin?"

"Yeah. Like the apple. He was ninety-two. He wore leather bedroom slippers for twenty years because he kept his money in his shoes."

"Again," he said patiently, "is this about you?"

"No," she said. "But it is weird. The slippers seemed to have melted into his feet. In later years, they guessed, he showered in them. I won't even mention what state his toenails were in. They were sort of woven together—"

"You're making this up!"

She gave a little, liquid chuckle, like a pipe's gurgle. "Just the toenail part. Sorry. I got carried away. But the weird thing was, after they got him safely underground and came back to his house to clean it out, they found those slippers, a little worse for the wear, you know, bits of dirt and grass on them, right beside his bed, as if they had walked there after the funeral."

"You are so inventing this," he groaned. "And it's not even very good. Concentrate. The weirdest thing that happened to you. Not your cousin or heaven help us your demented grandfather or your pet tortoise—" The howling started; he had to raise his voice a little, close as they were, to be heard over it. "You do know what weird means."

"Fate."

"What?"

She turned her head, shouted into his ear. "Fate. It's one of the earliest meanings. I learned that when—" The menacing, furious, strangely desperate racket ceased as abruptly as it had begun; her own yelling softened into laughter. "Sorry. Anyway. Speaking of which—"

"Of what?"

"*Macbeth*. The three weird sisters. I did meet a witch once—a real one."

He sat up indignantly, sending hand towels rolling. Leaning on one arm, looking down at her, he demanded, "Are you making this up, too?"

"No. This is true." She paused, admiring the honey-amber glow of his skin; she held the back of her wrist against his breast, her ivory on his rich warmth. "Come back down. I'll tell you. And, yes, it happened to me."

She waited while he piled the hand towels again for his head, sank back down beside her. Then they both had to wait during the thundering clatter, like some gigantic backhoe scooping up a hundred old-fashioned metal garbage cans into its vast maw and dropping them from a great height onto a street jammed with empty cars, trucks, buses. She could feel the floor vibrate slightly under the appalling din. Her own voice sounded small, diminished, in the silence that followed.

"Her name was Jehane. She had long, wild, curly red hair and the most lovely, wicked smile, even though she had lost one eyetooth, maybe during an initiation ceremony or something." She felt him shift, but he didn't question the tale, not yet. "She told me she lived in an RV with a cat, a raven, and a snake, all with bizarre names. I mean, who would name a cat Tisiphone?"

"You," he said. "Where are you in this?"

"I met her in a bar where my crazy boyfriend at the time played bass in a band. Concert bass, not electric. She was drinking a mojito and writing a spell on a napkin when I came up and accidently knocked her glass over onto the napkin. Well, I thought it was an accident. But when I apologized, she said, 'There are no accidents.' She had an odd accent. Portuguese, maybe, or something Balkan. Ancient Irish? Anyway, I bought her another drink and she invited me to sit beside her. No. It was more like a command than an invitation. She told me that my boyfriend played the bass very well, and that he would dump me before the year ended for a singer-songwriter who wore only black."

"Did you still pay for her drink?"

"The witch offered to sell me a spell to keep him from leaving. She smiled her charming smile, which was itself a spell, and we both laughed.

I didn't think about it again until he did leave me, a few weeks later, for a little whey-faced musician with a skinny voice who wrote morose songs on her acoustic guitar. I remembered then that there was no way for the witch to have known the bass player was my boyfriend, when she said what she said. No explicable way, I mean. Except that she was a witch."

"Is that as weird as it gets?"

She shook her head. "Not even close."

Someone or something pounded ferociously on the bathroom door. The door rattled and shook; the glass holding the toothbrushes clattered into the sink; her bathrobe fell off the hook on the door. The banging, fierce and energetic, was accompanied by deep, barking shouts in an unfamiliar language. Their hands shifted under the towels, seeking each other; their eyes locked. One final, exasperated pound was accompanied by a more familiar word, "Shit!"

They waited; the silence held.

He said finally, "Go on."

She drew a breath. "Well. The real weirdness started that first night. The bartender mopped up the puddle I made and threw the mojito-soaked spell away. I was about to stop him, but the witch said before I could speak, 'Don't bother. The spell hasn't gone anywhere.' Like she read my mind."

"Then why was she writing it down?"

"I asked her that. Someone at the bar had requested it, then left after paying for it and hadn't returned. I asked her what the spell had been for. She only told me, 'Spells are alive. Spoken about, they find carriers and travel like rumor until they reach the one who craves that particular spell and will pay for it. The spell will be turned into words, and therein lies its terrible and wonderful power.' Really. That's what she said. 'Therein.' Then the band took a break and my boyfriend came to the bar. I introduced them."

She paused. He said, "Go on."

"I still wonder why she bothered to wait through his affair with the singer-songwriter. I mean, she knew it would happen, so why didn't she cast a spell over the girl and make her lose interest in him?"

She heard him take a breath, hesitate. "You mean—"

"Yes. I mean. Far as I know, they're still together. The witch and my bass player."

He laughed a little, softly. "I didn't expect that. But the unexpected isn't necessarily weird. Complications and ironies in relationships happen to everyone."

She raised her head to look into his eyes. "Do they happen to you?"

His eyes flickered. But it could have been the lights going out, not in a normal blink into darkness, but vanishing more slowly, accompanied by a long, deep, growling, indrawn breath that seemed to suck the light into itself, swallow it whole.

She stared back at the absolute black. She couldn't even see the faint glow of city lights behind the window curtain; the entire planet had disappeared. Then the light came back in a stunning sheet, as though a gigantic eyelid had lifted to reveal the white of a monster's eye.

She blinked until she could see his face again behind the prickling dazzle of aftershocks across her vision.

"Parts of your witch story were weird," he admitted. A star gleamed in his nostril, went out; another flared and faded under his eye. "But as a whole, commonplace. Not truly weird."

She heaved a sigh. "True weird." She was silent, digging deep into memory. He got up after a time, rummaged through the wastebasket and pulled out the mushroom Brie. He rinsed the soap dish, a pretentious little rectangle with curved edges. He dried it, unwrapped the Brie and laid it on the dish. Then he found the fingernail clippers in his bathroom bag, rinsed and dried the little nail file tucked under the upper blade. She watched while he cut the pale, oozing cheese into chunks, wiping the file with a tissue when it got too sticky. He sat beside her on the towels, set the dish between them.

"True weird," he said inflexibly. "Try again."

She chose a piece from the soap dish, ate it dreamily, licked her fingers when it was gone. She settled back again. "This was when I was very young," she said slowly.

"How young?"

"I knew how to read a few words; I might have started school. Maybe not. Young enough that everything was new. I had no concept of history, and of course my past was very short. I used to sit and try very hard to remember where I had been before I became myself. I thought there must be some kind of before, before—you know. I didn't understand why I couldn't remember very far back. It was before I learned that there was nothing of me before I began. It was very strange."

"But not weird," he said, swallowing Brie.

"No," she said softly. "Not. Anyway, I was living overseas then. I had no idea what weird meant. Everything was, or nothing was. I had no context."

He nodded, hooked a bite of cheese on the tiny curved tip of the file and fed it to her. He watched the movements of her full lips, her throat as she swallowed. "Go on," he said.

"We lived in a small town, in a house so old that parts of the floor were slabs of stone. Milk was delivered in glass bottles, with the cream floating on top, so you had to shake it before you used it. A man drove a horse-drawn wagon down our street once a week. He had a strange, piercing cry, more like a bird than a person. He was called the Rag-and-Bone man. That's what he shouted, I was told. People gave him their garbage. His horse was slow and placid. I didn't know then, but now I know that I was seeing something out of a distant past that would one day ride out of the world and only exist in memory." She paused, reminiscing. "But that's not the weirdness, because nobody back then would have called it that."

"No," he said, though he sounded, she thought, not entirely certain. She smiled, a quick, private smile of satisfaction while he speared another piece of Brie.

"One day I decided I wanted to ride with him on his wagon, see where he went. I filled a paper bag with odd things I found around the house that I thought nobody would miss: a chipped coffee mug, a doll missing one arm and most of her hair, a mangy teddy bear with the stuffing coming out of its seams, an old pipe of my father's that had been lying on a windowsill for months, a pair of bedroom slippers my mother never wore—things like that. And since I thought he wouldn't accept the bag without them, I put a rag and a bone on top of the bag. The rag was a skirt with a torn pocket that didn't fit me anymore. The bone was something I'd found in the garden, a little hollow thing that had belonged to some bird or animal. I kept it because I liked the sound it made when I blew into it. I waited with my bag on the sidewalk until I saw the wagon coming. Then I walked into the middle of the street in front of the horse.

"It didn't stop until it was almost on top of me. The Rag-and-Bone man was making his bird cries, high and harsh and eerie, in the quiet street. He might have been telling me to move, but I never understood anything he said. The horse—"

There was an immense thump over their heads, as though a gigantic fist had punched the roof of the building. They both jumped. The walls shuddered around them; the floor seemed to undulate. They clung to it, as to a raft on a violent sea. In the room beyond the door something hit the floor and shattered.

They waited, silent, motionless. Nothing more happened. She cleared her throat finally; he eased upright again, reaching for the Brie.

"The horse loomed over me. It seemed nothing like the slow, placid animal I expected. It was massive; it exuded darkness. Its nostrils were huge, its eyes unrelentingly black. I stood transfixed under it, holding the paper bag in my arms, unable to speak or look away from its shadowy gaze. From very far away, from another world, I heard the Rag-and-Bone man's voice. The horse moved its head finally. I felt its nostrils whuff at my hair. Then it lowered its great head to the bag in my arms and whuffed at that.

"It opened its great, blocky teeth, picked the bone out of the bag and ate it. I heard it crunch. The Rag-and-Bone man gave a sharp cry. My legs refused to hold me; I toppled down in the middle of the street under the horse's nose. It shouted, then, a great, fierce blare that I swear blew the hair back from my face.

"Then it somehow slipped its traces and leaped over me. I smelled it, felt its bulk, its enormous hooves clearing my head. The Rag-and-Bone man jumped into the street. For a moment I heard hooves galloping down the cobblestones. The Rag-and-Bone man ran after them. I turned, scared and astonished, just as I realized that the sound of the hooves had stopped. I saw a barefoot boy with wild black hair turn a corner with the Rag-and-Bone man running after him, and bending now and then, as he ran, to try to catch the boy's shadow.

"They both disappeared around the corner. I scrambled to my feet, hurled the bag onto the hillock of trash in the wagon, then I ran as fast as I could back into the house and hid in the coat closet for the rest of the afternoon. When I finally peeked outside at twilight, the wagon was gone. I never saw the Rag-and-Bone man again." She looked at the soap dish, then at him, as he sat propped on one hand, motionless, gazing at her. She said reproachfully, "You finished the Brie."

He swallowed. "Did I?"

"Was that weird or what?"

He shook his head slowly, still holding her eyes. She felt the floor lurch again, or maybe it was her thoughts skittering over something that had suddenly loomed out of nowhere.

"Do you know," he began. His voice had gone somewhere; it was thin, hollow, like the note blown out of a bone. "What's even weirder?"

She tried to speak, could only shake her head in a no that turned by imperceptible degrees into a nod.

"You left your skirt with him. Your doll. Your bear. You left him things of yours to recognize you."

"It was you," she whispered, recognizing his dark hair, his black, black eyes.

"It was you. In trouble and hiding in a closet then. Now you're in—"

Their heads turned toward the bathroom door, as though they could see through it to the raging menace beyond. She began to laugh softly, weakly, until her laughter brought tears; she brushed at them as they fell, and then he did, his hand warm, very gentle. When she finally stopped, he moved the soap dish aside and lay back, shoulder touching hers, his hand finding hers.

"Is that," she said shakily, "what on earth all this fuss is about? It's your turn, now, you know. Was that the weirdest thing that ever happened to you?"

"Not even close," he said, and waited until the ancient cry filling the room, wanting, seeking the least scrap, the smallest bone of their lives, reverberated through the plumbing pipes, rattled the screws and hinges, and finally ebbed back into silence.

HUNTER'S MOON

They were lost. There was no other word for it. Dawn, trudging glumly through the interminable trees, tried to think of a word that wasn't so definite, that might have an out. Ewan had been quiet for some time. He had stopped kicking over rocks to find creepy-crawlies and shaking hard little apples out of gnarly branches onto his head and yelling at her to comelookathis! Now he just walked, his head ducked between his shoulders, both hands stuffed into his pockets. He was trying not to reach for her hand, Dawn knew, trying not to admit he was afraid.

Lost. Misplaced. Missing. Gone astray. They were in that peculiar place where lost things went, the one people meant when they said, "Where in the world did I put that?" She was stuck with her baby brother in that world. It was gray with twilight, hilly and full of trees, and they seemed to be the only people in it. The leaves had begun to fall. Ewan had stopped doing that, too: shuffling through piles of them, throwing up crackling clouds of red and gold and brown. Dawn huffed a sigh, knowing that he expected her to rescue them. She hadn't wanted to take him with her in the first place. She had followed him aimlessly through the afternoon while he ran from one excitement to the next, splashing across streams and chasing squirrels. Now he was tired and dirty and hungry, and it was up to her to find their way home.

Trouble was, home wasn't even home. Here in these strange mountains, which weren't green, but high, rounded mounds of orange and yellow and silver, where rutted dirt roads ran everywhere and never seemed to get anywhere, and nobody seemed to use them anyway, she didn't know how to explain where Uncle Ridley's cabin was even if they did stumble across anyone to ask. It wasn't like this in the city. In the city there were street signs and phones and people everywhere. And lights everywhere, too: in the city not even night was dark.

A bramble came out of nowhere, hooked her jeans. She pulled free irritably. Something fell on her head, a sharp little thump, as though a tree had thrown a pebble at her.

"Ow!" She rubbed her head violently. Ewan looked at her and then at the ground. He took one hand out of his pocket and picked a small round thing out of the leaves.

"It's a nut." He looked up at her hopefully. "I'm starving."

She took it hastily. "Don't you dare."

"Why not? Eating nuts never hurt me."

"That's because you never ate the poisoned ones."

She threw it as hard as she could into some bushes. The bushes shook suddenly, flurried and thrumming with some kind of bizarre inner life. Dawn froze. A bird shot up out of the leaves, battering at the air with stubby wings. It was large and gray, with long, ungainly legs. It fell back to the ground and stalked nervously away, the weirdest bird that Dawn had ever seen.

"What is that?" Ewan whispered. He was tugging at her sweater, trying to crawl under it to hide.

"I don't know." Then she knew: she had seen that same bird on one of Uncle Ridley's bottles. "It's a turkey," she said, wonderingly. "Wild turkey."

"Where's its tail?" Ewan asked suspiciously; he was still young enough to color paper turkeys at school for window decorations at Thanksgiving.

"I guess the Pilgrims ate all the ones with tails." She twitched away from him. "Stop pulling at me. You're such a baby."

He let go of her, shoved his hands back into his pockets, walking beside her again in dignified silence. She sighed again, noiselessly. She was older by six years. She had held him on her lap and fed him, and helped him learn to read, and reamed into bullies with her backpack when they had him cornered in the schoolyard. But now that she had grown up, he still kept following her, wanting to be with her, though even he could see that she was too old, she didn't want her baby brother hanging around her reminding her that once she too had been small, noisy, helpless, and boring. She kicked idly at a fallen log; bark crumbled and fell. She had wanted a walk in the woods to get out of the cabin, away from Uncle Ridley's endless fish stories and her father trying to tie those little feathery things with hooks that looked like anything but flies. But she couldn't just be by herself, walking down a road to see where it went. Ewan had to come with her, filling the afternoon with his chattering, and leading them both astray.

"I'm so hungry," Ewan muttered, the first words he had spoken in some time. "I could eat Bambi."

"Bambi" was what their mother said their father had come to the mountains to hunt with his brother, who had run away from civilization to grow a bush on his chin and live like a wild man. Uncle Ridley had racks of guns on his cabin walls, and a stuffed moose head he had shot "up north." Painted wooden ducks swam across the stone mantelpiece above his fireplace. The room Ewan and their father shared was cluttered with tackle boxes, fishing poles, feathered hooks, reels, knives, handmade bows and arrows. Dawn slept on the couch in the front room underneath the weary, distant stare of the moose. Once, when she had watched the fire burn down late at night, an exploding ember had sparked a reflection of flame in the deep eyes, as though the animal had suddenly remembered life before Uncle Ridley had crossed his path.

A root tripped her; she came down hard on a step, caught her balance.

She stopped a moment, looking desperately around for something familiar. There was a farmhouse on the slope of the next hill, a tiny white cube at the edge of a stamp-sized green field. Bright trees at the edges of the field were blurring together, their colors fading in the dusk. The world was beginning to disappear. Dawn's nose was cold; so were her hands. She wore only jeans and her pale blue beaded sweater. The jeans were too tight to slide her fingers into her pockets, and her mother had been right about the sweater. Ridiculous, she had said, in the country, where there was no one to see her in it, and useless against the autumn chill.

"I think we're close," she told Ewan, who was old enough to know when she was lying, but sometimes young enough to believe her anyway.

"It's getting dark."

"Your point being?"

"Things come out in the dark, don't they? In the forests? Things with teeth? They get hungry, too."

"Only in movies," she answered recklessly. "If you see it in a movie, it isn't real."

He wasn't young enough to buy that. "What about elephants?" he demanded. "Elephants are real."

"How do you know?"

"And orcas—I saw one in the aquarium. And bats—"

"Oh, stop arguing," she snapped crossly. "Nothing in these woods is going to come out in the dark and eat you, so—"

He grabbed for her at the same time she grabbed for him at the sudden, high-pitched scream of terror that came from the depth of the wood. They clung together a moment, babbling.

"What was that?"

"Somebody's getting eaten. I told you they come out now, I told you—"

"Who comes out?"

"Werewolves and vampires and witches—" Ewan dived against her with a gasp as something big crunched across the leaves toward them. Dawn, her hands icy, hugged him close and searched wildly around her for witches.

Someone said, "Owl."

She couldn't see him. She spun, dragging Ewan with her. A tree must have spoken. Or that bush with all the little berries on it. She turned again frantically. Maybe he was up a tree—

No. He was just there, standing at the edge of shadow under an immense tree with a tangle of branches and one leaf left to fall. He seemed to hover under the safety of the tree like the deer they had seen earlier: curious but wary, motionless, tensed to run, their alien eyes wide, liquid dark. So were his, under a lank flop of hair like the blazing end of a match. He didn't say anything else. He just looked at them until Dawn, staring back, remembered that he was the only human they had seen all afternoon and he might vanish like the deer if she startled him.

"Who," she said, her breath still ragged. "I thought owls said who."

"Screech owl," he answered and seemed to think that explained matters.

His voice was gentle, unexpectedly deep, though he didn't look too much older than she.

Ewan was peeking out from under Dawn's elbow, sizing up the stranger. He pulled back from her a little, recovering dignity.

"We're lost," he admitted, now that they had been found. "We walked up a road after lunch, and then we saw some deer in the trees, and we tried to get closer to them but they ran, and we followed, and then we saw a stream with some rocks that you could walk across, and then after we crossed it, there were giant mushrooms everywhere, pink and gray and yellow, and that's where we saw the black-and-white squirrel."

The stranger's face changed in a way that fascinated Dawn. Its stillness remained, but something shifted beneath the surface to smile. His thoughts, maybe. Or his bones.

He let fall another word. "Skunk."

"I told you so," Dawn breathed.

"And then we followed—"

"My name is Dawn Chase," she interrupted Ewan, who was working his way through the entire afternoon. "This is my brother Ewan. We're staying with our uncle Ridley."

The young man's face went through another mysterious transformation. This time it seemed as though he had flowed away from himself, disappeared, leaving only a mask of himself behind. "Ridley Chase."

"You know him?"

He nodded. He took a step or two out of the trees and pointed. Dawn saw nothing but more trees, and a great gathering of shadows spilling down from the sky, riding across the world. She clasped her hands tightly.

"Please. I don't know where I am, or where I'm going. I never knew how dark a night could get until I came here. Can you take us back?"

He didn't answer, just turned and started walking. Dawn gazed after him uncertainly. Then she felt Ewan's damp, dirty hand grip hers, tug her forward, and she followed.

The moon rose just when it got so dark that the bright hair always just ahead of them seemed about to disappear. Dawn stopped, stunned. It was a storybook moon, immense, orange as a pumpkin, the face on it as clear as if it had been carved out of crystal. Surely it couldn't be the same little white thumbnail moon that she noticed now and then floating above the city, along with three stars and a dozen flashing airplane lights. This moon loomed over the planet like it had just been born, and she, Dawn Chase, was the first human to stand on two legs to look at it.

She felt Ewan pulling at her. "Come on. We're home."

Home under that moon? she thought confusedly. Home in what universe? He dragged her forward a step, and she saw the light beneath the moon, the lantern that Uncle Ridley had hung on the deer horns nailed above the cabin door.

She looked around, dazed like an animal with too much light. "Where's—where did he go?"

Ewan was running across the little clearing, halfway to the cabin. "Come on!" he shouted, and the door swung open. Uncle Ridley stuck his round, hairy face out, grinning at them. The old retriever at his knee barked wildly with excitement.

"There you are!" he shouted. "I knew you'd find your way back!"

"But we didn't," Dawn said, her eyes flickering through the moonlit trees. They cast moon shadows across the pale ground; the air had turned smoky with light. "There was someone—"

"I'm starving!" Ewan cried, trying to wriggle past the dog, who was trying to lick his face. "What's for supper?"

"Bambi!" Uncle Ridley answered exuberantly. That was enough to make the deer Dawn saw at the edge of the clearing sprint off with a flash of white tail. She stepped onto the porch, puzzled, still trying to find him. "Someone brought us home," she told Uncle Ridley, who was holding the door open for her.

"Who?"

"I don't know. He never said. He hardly talked at all. He looked—he was only a couple of years older than me, I think. He had really bright red hair."

"Sounds like a Hunter," Uncle Ridley said. "There are Hunters scattered all through these mountains, most of them redheads. Ryan, maybe. Or Oakley, more likely. He never uses one word when none will do."

"He didn't even let me thank him." She stopped at the threshold, her stomach sagging inside her like a leaky soccer ball at the smell of food. "Where's Dad?"

"He took the truck out to go searching for you. He was pretty worried. There's always some idiot in the woods who'll take a shot at anything that moves. He's probably lost himself now on all those back roads. I told him there's nothing out there to hurt you in the dark. Even the bears would run."

"Bears?"

"But it's best if you don't roam far from the cabin during hunting season. Come in before the bats do, and have some stew."

"It smells great."

He shut the door behind her. "Nothing like fresh venison. Shot it last week, four-pronged buck, near Hardscrabble Hollow."

"Venison?" she asked uncertainly, her throat closing the way it had when he talked about bears.

"Deer."

When she woke the next morning, she was alone. They had all gone hunting, she remembered, even the dog. Earlier, their whispers had half-wakened her. Coffee burbled; the wood stove door squeaked open and shut; bacon spattered in a pan, though it had to be the middle of the night.

"Shh," her father kept saying to Ewan, who was so excited that his whispers sounded like strangled shouts.

"Can I really shoot it?"

"Shh!"

Finally, they had all cleared out, and she had gone back to sleep. Now, the quiet cabin was filled with a shifting underwater light as leaves fell in a constant shower like colored rain past the windows. She lay on the couch watching them for a while, random thoughts blowing through her head. She could eat deer, she had found, especially if it was called venison. She hoped Ewan wouldn't kill anybody. He had never shot a rifle in his life. Uncle Ridley had invited her to come with them, but she didn't really want to be faced with the truth of the link between those wary, liquid eyes and what had smelled so irresistible in her bowl last night. The eyes in her memory changed subtly, became human. She shifted, suddenly finding possibilities in the coming day. She hadn't seen his face clearly in the dusk, just enough to make her curious. The stillness in it, the way it revealed expression without moving. . . . She sat up abruptly, combing her short, dark hair with her fingers. If she stayed in the clearing in front of the cabin, no one would mistake her for a deer, and maybe he would see her there.

She sat for a time on the lumpy ground in the clearing pretending to read, then for another stretch of time on a rock at the edge of the stream that ran past the side of the house, swatting at bugs and watching the falling leaves catch in the current and sail away. She was half-asleep in the sagging wicker chair on the cabin porch, feeling the sun pushing down on her eyelids, when the boards thumped hollowly under her. She opened her eyes.

He didn't speak, just gave an abrupt little nod. Even close, she couldn't see the pupils in his eyes; they were that dark. Again she had the impression of expression just beneath the surface of his face, like a smile just before it happened. She straightened in the chair, blinking, then ruffled at her hair and smiled at him. His skin was the warm brown of old leaves, the muscles and tendons visible in his throat, around his mouth. The sun picked out strands of gold in his fiery hair.

"Ryan?" she guessed, remembering what Uncle Ridley had said. "Or is it Oakley?"

"Oakley," he said in his husky, gentle voice. "Oakley Hunter."

"Everyone's gone," she explained, in case he wondered, but he seemed to know; he hadn't even glanced through the screen door. He sat down on the edge of the porch, his movements quiet, neat, like an animal's.

"Dawn," he said softly, and she blinked again. No one had ever said her name that way; it seemed a word she hadn't heard before. "I stopped by to ask," he continued, surprising her farther by stringing an entire sentence together, "if you'd like to take a walk with me."

Her feet still felt yesterday in them, that endless hike, but she stood on them promptly without thinking twice. "Sure."

He didn't take her far, but it was far enough that she was lost within five minutes. This time she didn't care; she rambled contentedly beside him through the wood he knew, listening to him naming grackles and nuthatches, elderberries, yarrow, maples and birch and oak. She told him about the ungainly turkey; he told her the name of the nut she had thrown at it.

"They only fan their tails for courting," he explained. "Like peacocks."

"How long have you lived here?" she asked. "I mean, your family. You were born here, weren't you?"

He nodded. "There have been Hunters in these mountains for forever."

"Do they ever leave? Or are they all like you?" He turned his dark eyes at her, waiting for the rest of it; she felt the warmth of blood like light under her skin. "I mean—I can't see you taking off to live in the city." She paused, laughed a little. "I can't even see you buying a slice of pizza in the village deli."

"I've eaten pizza," he said mildly. "There are Hunters scattered all over the world." He took his eyes from her face then, but she still felt herself in his thoughts. He drew breath, took another step or two before he spoke. "Every year, in autumn, we have a big gathering. A family reunion. They've been coming for days, now. It begins tonight, when the full moon rises."

"I thought that was last night."

"It seemed that way, didn't it? But one side lacked a full arc. You had to look carefully."

"It was beautiful," she sighed. "That's all I saw."

She felt his eyes again, lingering on her face. "Yes."

"It doesn't seem possible that there could be that many people back here in the hills. Yesterday we didn't see anyone for hours, not even a car. Until we saw you."

"Oh, they're here," he said mildly. "Most of them live in a wood or a forest somewhere in the world. They're used to being quiet. Noise scares the animals and trees; we hate to see them suffer."

"Noise scares the trees?"

"Sure." She looked for his secret smile again, the one he kept hidden in his bones, but she missed it. "You can hear them chattering when they're scared. They get shot, too, along with deer and birds, in hunting season."

"Anything that moves," Dawn quoted, remembering what Uncle Ridley had said. It sounded like a fairy tale: the old trees aware and quaking at the hunters' guns, unable to run, their leaves trembling together, speaking. Oakley had led her into a different wood than yesterday's wood, she realized suddenly. She was seeing it out of his eyes now, a mysterious, unpredictable place where trees talked, and deer lived peacefully among the Hunters. She smiled, not believing, but willing to believe anything, as though she were Ewan's age again.

Oakley gave her his opaque glance. "What's funny?"

"Nothing," she said contentedly. "I like your wood. What do you do, all you Hunters, at the family gathering? Have a barbecue?" She winced at the word after she said it; given their love of animals it seemed unlikely.

But he only answered calmly, "Something like that. After the hunt." She stared at him incredulously; he shrugged a little. "We're Hunters; we hunt."

"At night?"

"Under the full moon. It's a family tradition."

"I thought you said you hated to see animals suffer."

"We don't hunt the animals. It's mostly symbolic."

"Oh."

"Then we have a feast. A big party. We build a fire and eat and drink and dance until the moon goes down."

She tried to imagine a symbolic hunt. "You mean like a game," she guessed. "A game of hunting."

"Yes." He paused; she saw the words gathering in his face, his eyes, before he spoke. "Sometimes we invite people we know. Or friends. We were thinking of maybe asking your uncle. Because he likes to hunt so much. You could come, too. Not to hunt, just to watch. You could stay for the party, watch the moon set with me. Would you like to come?"

She didn't answer, just felt the answer floating through her, a bubble of happiness, completely full, unable to contain a particle more of the sweet, golden air. They wandered on, up a slope, down an old, overgrown road into a dark wood, hemlock, he told her, where an underground stream had turned stones and fallen trunks above its path emerald green and velvety with moss.

She could hear water falling softly nearby. They lingered there, while Oakley showed her tiny mushrooms on the moss, ranked like soldiers, with bright scarlet caps.

"You didn't answer my question," he reminded her, and she looked at him, let him see the answer in her face.

"Yes," she said. Her voice sounded small, breathless among the listening trees. "I'd love to come."

The world exploded around her.

She screamed, not knowing what had happened, not understanding. A crack like lightning had split the air and then a deer leaped in front of her,

233

so close she could smell its scents of musk and sulphur, so close it seemed immense, its hooves the size of open hands, its horns carrying tier upon tier of prongs, some flying banners of fire as though the lightning had struck it, and all of them, every prong, the color of molten gold. She saw its eyes as it passed, so dark she could not see the pupils, only the red flame burning deep in them.

She screamed again.

Then she saw three faces at the edge of the wood, all pallid as mushrooms, all staring at her. Behind her, she heard the great stag as it bounded from the moss onto dead leaves. And then nothing: the wood was silent. The stag left no other sound of its passage.

She heard her father shout her name.

They stumbled toward her, slipping on the moss, Uncle Ridley reaching out to take the rifle from Ewan as he began to run. She couldn't move for a moment; she couldn't understand why they were suddenly there, or where Oakley had gone, along with all the fairy magic of the little wood. Then she saw the stag again in her mind, crowned with gold, its huge flanks flowing past her as it leaped, its great hooves shining, and she began to shake.

Ewan reached her first, grabbing her around the waist, and then her father, holding her shoulders, his face drained, haggard.

"Are you all right?" he kept demanding. "Honey, are you all right?"

"I'm sorry," Ewan kept bellowing. "I'm sorry."

"We didn't see you," Uncle Ridley gasped. "That buck leaped and there you were behind it—thought my heart was going to jump out of me after it."

"What are you talking about?" she whispered, pleading, completely bewildered. "What are you saying?"

"How could you get so close to it? How could it have let you come that close? And didn't you think how dangerous that might be in hunting season?"

"It was Oak—" she said, still trembling, feeling a tear as cold as ice slide down her cheek. But how could it have been? Things tumbled in her head, then, bright images like windblown autumn leaves: Oakley under the tree, the deer watching at the edge of the wood, the great, silent gathering of Hunters under the full moon, Hunters who loved animals, who hated to see them suffer, who understood the language of trees. She saw Uncle Ridley among them, on foot with his gun, smiling cheerfully at all the

Hunters around him, just another one of them, he would have thought. Until they began to hunt. "It was a Hunter," she said, shivering like a tree, tears dropping out of her like leaves.

They weren't listening to her; they were talking all at once, Ewan still shouting into her sweater, until she raised her voice finally, feeling on firmer ground now, though she could still feel the other wood, the otherworld, just beneath her feet. "I'm okay," she managed to make them hear. "I'm okay. Just tell me," she added in sudden fear, "which one of you shot at the deer?"

"It was standing there so quietly," Uncle Ridley explained. "Young buck, didn't hear us coming. Gave us a perfect shot at it. I couldn't take it; I've got my limit for the season. We all had it in our sights, but we let Ewan take the shot. Figured he'd miss, but your dad was ready to fire after that. So Ewan shot and missed and the deer jumped and we saw you."

Her father dropped his face in one hand, shook his head. "I came within an inch of shooting you. Your mother is going to kill me."

"So no one—so you won't go hunting again. Not this season. Uncle Ridley?"

"Not this season," he answered. "And not until I stop seeing you standing there behind anything I take aim at."

"Then it will be all right, I think," she said shakily, peeling Ewan's arms from around her. "Then I think you'll all be safe. Ewan. Stop crying. You didn't hurt me. You didn't even hurt—You didn't hurt anything." He raised his red, contorted, snail-tracked face. You rescued us, she thought, and took his hand, holding it tightly, as though she might lose her way again if she let go, and who knew in what ageless realm of gold and fire, of terror and beauty she might have found herself, among that gathering under the full moon?

Some day, she promised the invisible Hunter, I will come back and find out.

Still holding her brother's hand, she led them out of the wood.

UNDINE

All my sisters caught mortals that way. I have more sisters than I can count, and they've all had more husbands than they can count. It's easy, they told me. And when you get tired of them you just let them go. Sometimes they find their way back to their world, where they sit around a lot with a gaffed look in their eyes, their mouths loosing words slowly like bubbles drifting away. Other times they just die in our world. They don't float like mortals anymore. They sink down, lie among the water weeds and stones at the bottom, their skin turning pearly over time, tiny snails clustering in their hair.

Easy. When it was time for my first, my sisters showed me how to find my way. In our deep, cool, opalescent pools, our reedy, light-stained waters, time passes so slowly you hardly notice it. Things rarely ever change. Even the enormous, jewel-winged dragonflies that dart among the reeds have been there longer than I have. To catch humans, I have to rise up into their time, pull them down into ours. It takes practice, which is why so many of them die.

"But don't worry," my sisters told me blithely. "You'll get the hang of it. When you bring the first one home alive, we'll throw a party."

I had to choose a patch of sunlight in my water and swim up through it, up and up in the light until it blinded me, while I kept a vision of mortals in my mind. What mortals I knew were mostly my sisters' husbands and some mossy-haired, frog-eyed women who had accidentally fallen in love with my snarky water-kelpie cousins as they cavorted among the water lilies in human and horse disguises. But, my sisters assured me, as I moved from our time into theirs my hunger—and my loneliness—would grow. I would be happy to see the human face at the end of my journey. I should not expect to be in the same water there, but it would not be hard at all, they promised, for me to find my way back. I had only to wish and swim.

They gathered so sweetly around me in the water, all languid and graceful, their long hair flowing as they sang me farewell. The singing helped shift me across time; I felt as though I were swimming through their voices as much as through water and light. When I saw the trembling surface of strange water, I could still hear them, the distant singing of water faerie, so lovely, so haunting.

I should have turned at that instant, followed it back. But I felt the odd, shallow depths I had reached. My face and knees were bumping stones and I had to break the surface. I stood up, awkwardly, trying to find my balance in the rocky shallows and pulling my hair out of my face so I could see. I took a breath and smelled it first.

"Yark!" I shrieked. "Gack! What is it?"

I finally untangled the hair over my eyes and shrieked again. Dead fish. I was surrounded by dead fish. Big ones. Hundreds of them, in various stages of decay, wallowing in the water and reeking. They bumped me as I floundered through the stink, their eyes filmy with death where they weren't covered with flies. I wanted to screech again, but I had to breathe to do that. I was panting like a live fish by then, taking short little breaths through my open mouth, trying to get out of the river as fast as I could. The stones were slippery with moss. I flailed, terrified of stumbling and falling into the dead fish. Wearing what I did wasn't helping much; my long dress sagged, wrapped itself around my knees, caught underfoot. At every step, flies swarmed around me from the fish, buzzed into my eyes.

So, half blind, cursing furiously and gasping like a fish, I rose out of the river, and a mortal caught me in his arms.

"What are you doing in there?" he shouted.

I could feel his startled heartbeat, his dry shirt rapidly dampening with me. I opened one eye cautiously. I stood in mud now. I could feel it oozing up between my toes, which didn't improve my mood, but at least I could catch my balance. The mortal I had snared was very cute, with straight golden hair that flopped above one brow, eyes the gentle blue of our limpid skies rather than of the fierce blue-white blaze above our heads. He wore a shirt with a frog sitting on a lily pad and unrolling its enormous tongue to catch a tiny flying horse. A conversation starter, that would have been, if I hadn't just waded out of a river full of one.

I had to answer something, so I said, "I got lost."

"In that dress?"

I looked at it. My sisters had woven it for me out of mosses and river grasses, decorated it with hundreds of tiny bubbles. In this world, it looked like some kind of shimmering cloth overlaid with pearls.

"What's wrong with it?" I demanded, trying to kick away the ribbon of greasy fish scales decorating the hem.

He stared at me, goggling a bit, like the fish. Then his eyes narrowed. "Did you—did you, like, jump off something? After a party? Like a bridge, or something? And instead of drowning you came to in all this—this—" He waved at the appalling river, which was making a sort of gurgling noise as it drained through the fish jammed across it. "What was it? Some guy made you do this?"

I nodded cautiously after a moment. Some guy, yes. I pushed at my hair, trying to make it more presentable. A nasty odor wafted up from it. I couldn't cry—why bother with tear ducts if you are born in water? But I had seen mortals do it, and now I knew why. My first human, and here I was, sinking in mud and stinking while vicious little flies bit my ankles.

Extremely sorry for myself, I sniffed and whuffled piteously, "Yeah. And now I don't know my way home."

"Don't cry—"

"What did you do to all these fish?"

"Me?" he said incredulously. "I just came out here to throw a line in the water. Fishing's great here when the salmon are running. I could smell this all the way out to the highway. I've never seen anything like it."

"Fish can't run," I said crossly; he seemed more interested in them than in me.

"It's an expression," he explained with exasperating patience. "It's what they call it when the salmon swim upriver trying to get back to the waters where they were born so they can spawn."

"Spawn?"

"You know—lay their eggs and fertilize them. Propagate. That's when they're supposed to die." I nodded. That happened to mortals often enough where I lived. "Not like this," he went on. "Not halfway upriver before they've gotten home. And look at this water! It should be deeper and fast-flowing. It's like they couldn't breathe or something in this shallow water. This is all wrong."

He was still fixated on them, staring over my shoulder. I saw his point, though. I could never have dragged him under those pathetic shallows. I sniffed again, to reclaim his attention. His eyes came back to me; he touched my bare arms lightly with his fingers. "Ah, poor kid. What a nightmare. Where do you live? I'll take you home."

I had to think, then, which is not something my sisters warned me would be necessary. "Farther upriver," I said, pleased at my cleverness. I would make him take me to some deep pool where I could lure him under, steal him away from his world, take him back into mine. "But I can't go home like this. Reeking and covered with fish scales. Do you know a place where I can swim it off?"

He considered, torn between me and the dead fish. I rolled my eyes in mortification, hoping none of my sisters had followed to watch. But then, considering myself, I could hardly blame him.

"Sure." He bent down to collect his fishing gear. "I know just the place."

He took me in his truck to his home.

It was a little cottage not far away beneath some immense trees. His dog came out to greet us, wagging its tail politely until it caught a whiff of me. Then it bounded into my arms, howling joyously, nearly knocking me over.

"Whoa!" my mortal said. "Down, Angel. She loves company." Angel was big and golden, with a stupid grin on her face; she acted like she wanted to roll around on the ground with my dress. "Down! My name's Mike, by the way. Mike Taylor. What's yours?"

"Undine." At home we have our private names of course, but to mortals we are all Undines. "Ah—what are we doing here?"

"Undine. Pretty. Come on in. You can wash off in the bathroom; I'll give you some dry clothes to change into. Then I'll take you home. Okay?"

But he wasn't thinking about me as he led me into his house. It was sunny, cluttered and full of dog hair. He waved me into a tiny room which contained a tank, a basin, and a big porcelain mushroom. I had never seen anything like it. Luckily, he turned the water taps on himself. Some gunky water spurted out. And then it ran clear, so clear I had to reach out and touch it, smell it.

"Sorry I don't have a shower, just this tub. The pipes pick up dirt sometimes," he said unintelligibly. "You have to clear them out. There's lots of hot water though. I'll bring you some clothes in a minute. First I have to make a phone call."

I filled the tub to the top, managing to stop the flow before I made a waterfall over the side. As it was, I slopped plenty on the floor when I pulled my dress off and got in. I submerged myself completely, rolling and rolling in the warmth, my hair growing silky again, coiling around my naked limbs. I heard Mike's voice now and then when my ears came out of the water. Fish, he was talking about. Not the mysterious, enchanting young woman he had met on the river's edge.

Dead fish.

"I called the Forestry Department," he announced, breezing in with his arms full of ugly clothes. "And the Fish and Wildlife Department. And—" He stopped abruptly, the absent look fading from his eyes as I stood up in the water. "Oh," he whispered. "Sorry." He didn't move. I hummed softly, lifting my streaming hair away from my neck with upraised arms. The clothes dropped onto the floor. I held out my hand. He stepped into the water, forgetting even that he was wearing boots. The splash we made as I pulled him down hit the ceiling and pretty much emptied the tub, but neither of us cared.

But there was nowhere for me to take him except down the drain.

He lay in my arms afterward, spellbound, contentedly talking, even though he had to balance his drenched boots on the faucets and he was squashing me. I let him ramble, while I tried to think of a way out of our predicament.

"I don't make much," he said, "at the Sport 'n' Bait Shop. But I don't need much to keep up this place, and my truck's paid for, and there's just Angel and me . . . I hunt and fish whenever I can. I love the outdoors, don't you?"

"Water," I murmured. "I love water."

"Yeah . . . That's why this thing with the fish is so upsetting. Turns out it's all political, that's what Fish and Wildlife told me. The water that normally comes downriver got diverted fifty miles upriver. Can you believe that? To water crops in the Saskill Valley, which got hit by drought this summer. Dead crops or dead fish, take your pick. Well, fish don't vote." He had begun to fidget; in another moment he would realize he was lying with his pants down and his boots on in a bathtub with a stranger.

I kissed him, felt his muscles slacken. He babbled on, his voice dreamy again. "You don't have to go home right away, do you? I'll take you home later. We can build a fire, grill some burgers, go for a moonlight swim...."

"Moonlight swim, yes."

"Well, we could have anyway, except that I doubt there's enough water anywhere along the river around here to do much but wade in." He was beginning to brood again. Then this noise rattled through my spell, some kind of weirdness clamoring for attention that made all his muscles tense. His boots jumped off the faucet; he rolled and floundered clumsily against me, groping for balance.

"Sorry, babe, gotta get that. It's probably Sam. She's always on top of stuff like this."

He sloshed out of the bathroom to go talk about fish again, leaving me in a puddle on the bottom of the tub.

That was the last I saw of water until dawn.

Another shrillness woke me when it was still dark. I didn't remember where I was, and something moist was prodding my cheek and panting dankly. Then Mike switched on a light, and Angel, her grin inches from my eyes, licked my face.

"Garf," I said, wanting to cry again because this was not supposed to happen.

"Sorry, babe. Gotta go." Mike pulled a shirt over his head, popped out again, looking hopeful. "Come with me?"

"Will there be water?"

"Oh, yeah."

Which is why, an hour later, I was back with the dead fish, wearing Mike's clothes, standing on the riverbank with a sign in my hands that said PROTECT THE WILDERNESS IN YOU along with dozens of other dour, cranky humans, some wearing badges, others watching us through one-eyed monsters on their shoulders from a big truck labeled KNOX NEWS TEAM.

Mike keeps promising me that soon, soon, we will go out and find that moonlit pool, or that deep, deep sunlit lake, and we will float together, locked in one another's arms, our breaths trailing bubbles behind us as we kiss, and then we will swim beyond the boundaries of mortal love. Soon. But then, on our way to that magical place, the truck will suddenly detour to follow a creek that's turning all the colors of the rainbow and smelling like garbage. Or it will find the lake with the signs along its shores warning of the dangers of swimming here. Then he spends hours on the phone with Sam or Kyle or Vanessa, and then wakes me at dawn to walk in circles carrying a sign. And I still hope, because what else can I do?

But I am beginning to wonder if I'll be stranded here like a fish out of water for a mortal lifetime with this human, sweet as he is, before I can ever swim my way back to that deep, sun-stained pool where I was born.

KNIGHT OF THE WELL

The Knights of the Well came last in the royal procession into Luminum. Their barge was pale green and ivory, the colors of the river; their standard was blue and stone gray, for water and for well. Their surcoats were cloth of gold, their cloaks white for foam, for the moon that drove the waters, bid them come and go. Their hoods were black for the secret dark from which the well bubbled out of the earth, also for humility. Their faces were all but invisible. The city folk crowding the banks of the Halcyon River to watch the parade of brightly painted boats carrying Kayne, King of Obelos, and his court to the summer palace in Luminum, cheered and flung flowers at the still, mysterious figures in the last barge. The procession heralded both the beginning of summer and the ritual, old as Luminum, which would honor and placate the waters of the world, most particularly the waters of the Kingdom of Obelos.

The dozen knights had been standing for hours, it seemed, though the procession had shifted from horses and wagons to boats just outside the city. No one dared move. The small, colorful barge was balanced to a breath, five men on either side plying their gilded oars, the oar master on his narrow perch keeping their time with a brass gong and hammer. The knights were supposed, by the city folk, to be contemplating their awesome function. Most were indeed contemplating water: the last one who had moved impulsively, at the nip of a bloodthirsty insect, had nearly thrown them all into it.

Mingling with the flow of water, the golden drip of sound from the gong, the drift of voices from the other barges, the distant roil of shouts, cheers, scraps of music from the crowds was the murmur of memory the knights passed to one another, trying, as they always did during this part of the journey, to pinpoint why the water-mage had chosen them.

"One of my ancestors was found floating among the reeds in a shallow pond just after she had given birth to a child with webs between its fingers. . . . Family lore has it she fell in love with a water sprite."

"My grandmother flung herself over a cliff into the sea. Her body was never found, though she left her shoes at the place where she jumped. There were prints in the earth beside them that were not quite human."

"There is a lake on our land in south Obelos said to be inhabited by water creatures of a most extraordinary beauty . . ."

Garner Slade, who had been a knight of the king's for three years, and a Knight of the Well since the previous year, recognized most of the hushed voices that came from under the lowered hoods. Not all of the men were knights of the court; a few he only saw at this time of the year: those who left their lands and families at the mage's bidding. The young man who spoke next, Garner recognized as one of them only because he bore the standard that fluttered over their heads.

"I drink water," he said a trifle hollowly. "Sometimes I wash. Sometimes I just stand in a good rain instead. I don't know how to swim. I don't even like water. I'm afraid of it. I'd trade this standard for a beer in a moment. So why would the mage have picked me?"

He had a moment's sympathy. Summer was no further away than a change of expression on the moon's face, a richer hue in the gold that fell freely out of the blue. Even now, heat clung to them as heavily as cloth, beading their faces with the sweat that lured the tiny, malignant pests.

Then came the inevitable: "Clear your mind of such distractions, or we will fail in our task. Contemplate water; allow it to flow into your thoughts, your blood. You will begin to know it instead of fear it. Take care what you say in the same breath as the word, for water will hear; you will offend."

And the crops, Garner thought, will wither on the vine. The sea will open the gates, plunder the ships in the harbor. He blinked salt out of his eyes and contemplated the floating market, the swift, narrow boats drawn close to the banks, decked with flowers and bright ribbons in welcome. The procession was passing through the heart of the city. Ancient stone river houses, interspersed with equally ancient thatched cottages whose garden walls were moldy with bygone floods, offered intervals of shadow cast by the sudden jut of high roofs. Then light, as the rooftops dropped. Then again the welcoming shadow.

Garner's cousin, who had been a Knight of the Well longer than any of them, and who liked the sound of his voice, was still proffering the benefits of his experience. "Our minds must be as waters flowing into one another, pellucid and free of the twigs and sodden leaves of earth. The debris of language. Water speaks; we must listen. Water hears; we must beware."

"I can't hear," Garner murmured finally.

"What?"

"Over the debris of language. A word the river is saying."

Edord paused. The pause was weighted with significance. Garner heard the standard-bearer's breath quiver with suppressed laughter. The oar master, reprovingly, struck the gong a sharp, meaningful stroke. Edord began another word. From the bridge arching across the river just ahead, someone tossed a handful of flowers into the boat.

Garner looked up. For that moment, his face was visible to the world: his dark hair and eyes, his restless, brooding, quizzical expression. He revealed himself as human within the hood, within the solemnity of his status. The young woman who had thrown the flowers flashed a surprised grin at him. The standard-bearer gave a sneeze of laughter, bending to conceal it. The barge rocked; the gong gave a hiccup between beats. For a moment oars flailed; the knights froze. The shadow of the bridge fell mercifully over them.

Then they slid again into light, water lapping with little, agitated river-words against the boat. Garner, standing stolidly, could feel it under the soles of his boots: the thin, thin boundary between wood and water, between dry and wet, between profundity and disgrace.

Even the standard-bearer was silent, the long pennant whipping reproofs into the air, which was stirring suddenly as the river quickened to meet the sea.

Edord opened his mouth.

Garner tried to shut him out, his fair-haired, handsome, humorless cousin with his irritatingly reedy voice that made Garner want to swat at it, as though it had wings and would bite. Edord was the oldest of the twelve, and entirely confident of the mage's choice of him to help balance the powerful, mysterious forces of earth and water. Her choices were varied; at times they seemed wildly arbitrary. Garner, for instance, would not have chosen himself. Despite his good intentions, he was more prone to muddying the waters than placating them. The standard-bearer, affected by nerves and fearful of water, seemed inexplicable. But the mage's ancient, sunken eye, weirdly nacreous, had seen in them both something she needed.

The blunt, craggy walls of the castle guarding the jut of land where the river met the sea revealed themselves above the houses, inns and warehouses along the tangle of city streets. The pattern of the oldest streets in Luminum resembled a wad of thread that had been shoved into a pocket and forgotten. Some said the early roads followed animal tracks, others that their loops and switchbacks were an attempt to confuse the floodwaters, the raging winter tides. Across the Halcyon, where land was diked and drained of marsh water, the younger city was flat as an anvil. Sea walls, gates and sluices, canals and locks, added over the centuries, had tamed much of the flow, trained it into fields, and, more recently, into pipes. But even on the most tranquil of nights, no one completely trusted water not to possess a will of its own. The impulses, secrets, history, the sprites and elementals who swelled beneath its surface, were understood most completely by the mage, who spoke all the languages of water. The rulers of Obelos would sooner have left a sea gate open to a wild winter tempest than neglect the Ritual of the Well.

There was a flourish of brass as the trumpeters in the high walls saluted the king. Edord fell mercifully silent. The castle walls were shrugging out of the city, growing sheer, stark against the blue sky and the sea. Garner could see the stone sea walls curving along the path of the river to front the tide. Tide was turning now, tugging the boats along with it. Ahead, the king's barge began to angle toward the royal dock, along which so many banners and standards and pennants flew that, in a better wind, they might have lifted the dock into the air.

The oar master spoke, slowing the ritual barge until it wallowed, waiting for those ahead to disembark. It took a while. The canopied stairway up the bank to the back of the castle was crowded with courtiers. The oarsmen plied oars expertly, pushing against the tide, then letting the boat creep a little closer as a barge pulled away. They emptied quickly; no one lingered on the dock after the long journey from the west, and all baggage had been left on the wagons coming down the coast road to the castle. Garner's thoughts drifted. He stared at the flowers at his feet, not daring to look up, knowing that his eyes would search for a phantasm, a dream. Petals the color of bright new blood reflected a sudden bloom of pain in his heart. She could have written, he thought. She could have sent word to him privately at the king's winter court, instead of word traveling carelessly from anyone to anyone before it reached him. He hadn't realized, until then, that in her eyes he was just anyone as well. In spite of himself, he raised his head slightly, looked up from under his hood to search the knots of courtiers along the stairs. The scallops along the windblown canopy hid too many faces; he could not find her. He lowered his eyes, found her face again in memory.

Much his return to the summer court mattered to her now, she with her betrothed with his great barking brass horn that bayed so deep it could have drawn whales to the surface to mate with it. She with her head full of water pipes and fountains. No room now for one who had loved her since she was six. Garner made an incautious, despairing movement. The barge shivered; an oar caught a crab, splashed.

"Peace," the oar master pleaded. "Peace. We're nearly there."

"Peace," Edord echoed abruptly, jarringly, "is what we must impress upon the waters of Obelos with our minds, our breath, the rhythms of our hearts. From us it will learn; from us it will—"

"Oh, give it a rest," Garner shouted, exasperated. Somehow he was facing his cousin, not an easy thing to do in a boat crammed with men. Turning, he had shouldered a couple off-balance; they reeled into others; the barge rocked one way and then the other. And then the great crowds on both sides of the river watched with astonishment as the Knights of the Well staggered out of the sides of their barge and tried to walk on water. The wallowing barge scattered its oars, then its oarsmen. The oar master, clutching his gong, fell in last and disappeared entirely as the barge flipped over on top of him.

Garner, descending among the riverweeds, thought he should just settle on the bottom with the snails and stay there. But someone was descending faster than he was within the streaming thicket of weeds. The standard-bearer, he thought in horror, and kicked hard upriver toward him, losing both his boots to the tide. A school of tiny fish flashed past his eyes; it was suddenly hard to see. What he thought was a cloak seemed darker, a cloudy gray shadow fading into the green. He pushed downward. Someone else's falling boot careened off his shoulder. The cloak, billowing and flapping in the current like a live thing, seemed empty as he grew closer, and it began to rise. So did he, with relief, tearing the clinging waterweeds away as he pulled toward the light and air and churning bodies above him, beginning to hear his heartbeat in the surging wash of his blood.

He saw the cloak again, suspended in a long, motionless shaft of light. Still it seemed empty, his eyes told him as he passed it. It twisted slowly among the weeds, the hood turning, turning, until its limp emptiness, shaped by the current, opened to Garner's transfixed gaze.

He saw the face in it.

Breath bubbled out of him. He caught himself desperately before he took in water, felt the aching impulse all through his body. Still he hung there, treading water to keep from beginning the long, slow, irrevocable slide, unable to look away from the strange eyes, shell-white and expressionless in a shifting face as green as waterweed.

A struggling mass of boot and wool and limbs came between them. Garner, started again, lost the last of his breath. Then he recognized the standard-bearer, trailing bubbles and looking terrified. Garner reached out, grabbed his hood and drove them both, with a couple of furious kicks, to the surface. Coming up under the overturned barge, he bumped his head on the edge of the oar master's seat.

He held onto it, heaving for breath. The standard-bearer grabbed hold of an oarsman's plank. Garner, his vision clearing, found himself face-to-face with the indignant oar master. They were surrounded by the swirling cloaks and churning legs of men outside clinging to the bottom of the barge. The weltering tide pulling them toward the sea, the constantly shifting weight on the barge bottom, made breathing difficult for those caught under it. The oar master, gripping his gong with one hand and an oarlock with the other, looked as though he wanted to shove Garner back under the water himself.

"What," he barked, "possessed the mage to choose you?"

Someone outside hoisted himself higher up the barge bottom; the plank the standard-bearer clung to dipped abruptly. He inhaled water, coughing; flailing again, he seized Garner's hair, pushed him briefly down.

Garner hauled them both up again, answered between his teeth, "My cousin would say that I exemplify the chaotic aspect of water."

"Which it is your duty to guard us against!"

"Then the mage must have made a mistake."

"Impossible!" the oar master snapped unreasonably.

Garner rolled an eye at him, still grappling with the standard-bearer, whose sodden hood had slid over his eyes, blinding him. "Then she didn't," he said succinctly. He saw a pair of legs kick away from the side of the barge, and then another. The empty barges must have come to their rescue, he realized with relief, and added, "I might be your greatest hope."

The oar master snorted, inhaled a sudden splash as someone tried to turn the barge over and failed.

"Let go," Garner urged the standard-bearer, who had a death grip with one hand on an oarlock and with the other on Garner's hair. "They've come to help us."

The young man shook his blind head mutely, emphatically.

"Just leave him," the oar master suggested, and vanished under the side of the barge.

Garner treaded water and waited, wondering if the oar master would bother sending anyone to rescue the pair of them.

A little later, as he sat dripping in a fishing boat that had come out to help with the rescue, he saw Damaris finally, on the dock, talking to his sodden cousin, who was gesticulating forcefully. Green, she was wearing, the soft pale green of the waterweed dangling over Edord's shoulder. He would be making very clear to her exactly who had caused the Knights of the Well to become one with the river, of that Garner had no doubt. He sighed noiselessly, regretting the absurd incident, except for dunking Edord. Then, beneath the weave and break of light on the water, he saw the strange, rippling underwater face again, the pale eyes alone unmoved by currents, looking back at him within the waterweeds.

He blinked. The face, or the memory of it, vanished.

One of the water sprites, he guessed, drawn by the odd commotion in the river. The mage would know its name. He raised his eyes from the water again, and saw Damaris and Edord turned away from him, walking up the steps to the palace together. He watched that green until it disappeared within the walls.

In the small, private chamber allotted to him by his rank as knight both of the king and of the Well, he found his baggage and his young squire Inis, who had been attached to him, presumably to learn from Garner's knightly example and experience. Sweet-tempered and capable, he was too polite to comment on Garner's dripping garments, simply helped him out of them and handed him dry clothes. He looked more doubtfully at Garner's bare feet. Garner's family could trace its lineage, in the northern mountains, back past the naming of Obelos. But what with one thing and another, including some disastrous battles with a reigning monarch or two, whom Garner's ancestors considered usurpers, the family had lost its wealth over a century ago.

"Your boots, sir?"

"Waterlogged," Garner answered tersely. "The river ate them."

"Your best boots?"

"Yes."

"Well," Inis said, rummaging. "There's your shoes in here somewhere. Ah, and here's your old patched pair of boots, right under them."

Someone pounded at the door.

It was not what Garner expected: his annoyed cousin, or worse, a summons from the king. It was the impossible, what he would have chosen if he had a say in the various possibilities knocking on his door. It was a request from the Minister of Water for his immediate presence.

Lady Damaris Ambre.

Dazed, he put on the boots Inis handed him and followed the messenger.

The minister was in her official chamber, a lofty corner room just beneath the battlement walls. The side casements overlooked the vast gardens behind the castle, the cobbled path leading down the back of the hill to the city below, with its eccentric tangle of streets cautiously edging closer and closer to the river where it curved around the sudden upthrust of land. From the adjacent wall, the view was of the harbor, the sea walls, the immense gates that protected the inner harbor, the brilliant, unending sea. An enormous table filled most of the room, covered with papers with seals and ribbons dangling from them, letters, lists, meticulous drawings of water projects, maps, schedules, sketches of everything from plumbing pipes to gargoyle-headed water taps. A tray holding pitchers of wine and water and cups stood swamped in the clutter like a drowning island.

Damaris had thrown a black work-robe over her gown; its sleeves were shiny with ink stains. The long, white-gold coil of braid at her neck was beginning to sag, too heavy, too silken for restraints. Leaning over some paperwork on the table, she looked up as Garner entered. The sudden flash of green, the color of river moss, under her heavy, hooded eyelids and pale brows, took his breath away.

She gazed at him a moment, her ivory, broad-boned face the way he remembered it from childhood, open, curious, just beginning to smile. Then she remembered what he was doing there, and the smile vanished. She straightened to her full height, nearly as tall as he, slender and so supple her bones seemed made of kelp.

"Garner," she said in her deep, lovely voice that cut easily through any flow of water or words, "your cousin told me you nearly sank the ritual barge."

"I was told by rumor," he answered recklessly, "that you were betrothed."

"And that has what to do with half-a-dozen gilded oars that went sailing out to sea, and which must be replaced before the ceremony of the fountain?"

"Fountain?" he echoed bewilderedly, wondering how she could be thinking of such mundane details. "What fountain? Of course I didn't mean to overturn the barge."

"Then why did you?"

"I was provoked—"

She held up a hand before he could go on; helplessly he watched a familiar dimple deepen in her cheek as her lips compressed, then quickly vanish. "Never mind. I don't need to know. The water-mage wants to see you. You can explain to her."

Heat surged through him, then, as he remembered the precise moment. His mouth tightened; his eyes went to the sea, where a gull as white as Damaris's brows angled over the dark blue water.

"I was looking for you," he said bluntly, and felt her go abruptly still. "You drew my eyes. You always did. Since I first saw you coming so carefully down those same steps when you were a child, and so was I, come downriver to court in my uncle's company, just docking where you were about to step. You wore green that day, too, and your hair was in the same braid. We met there on that dock. Ever since, I have looked for you there. I was looking today, though I have no right." He looked at her finally, then, found her face as stiff, her eyes as distant, as he expected. "My cousin was lecturing. I lost my temper, and unbalanced the boat. For that, I'm sorry. Is this what I must tell the mage?"

Color flushed over her, swiftly and evenly, from collarbone to brow. "That it was my fault?" she asked with some asperity. "Because I forgot—No, because I didn't know how to tell you?"

"No. Of course not. Let's blame Edord."

"I don't understand. What has Edord to do with this?"

"He opened his mouth," Garner said dourly, "at the wrong time."

She studied him a moment, a line as fine as gossamer above her brows. "I love Lord Felden." Her voice had softened; her eyes shifted away from him briefly. "I discovered that he loves me, too. His music has always enchanted me. We have much in common."

"His horn and your pipes?"

She met his eyes again. "You and I have been friends for many years. Can we keep it that way? Or will you swamp boats every time you pass that dock?" He couldn't answer. The unfamiliar secrets within the green, the fine, clean bones beginning to surface in her face since he last saw her, rendered him wordless. She made a sudden, exasperated gesture, trying to brush away his gaze. "Stop that."

"What?"

"Stop looking at me like that. Just stop looking at me. Garner, just go away."

"Why," he asked her with simple pain, "could you not love me like that?"

She swallowed, whispered, "I don't know. I don't know. Maybe—you were too much my friend. My brother. Maybe nothing more or less than that."

"Damaris—"

"No," she told him firmly. "Go. The mage is waiting for you."

"How much of this do I tell her?"

She shook her head slightly, picking up a piece of chalk, worrying it through her long fingers. She didn't look at him again.

"I think she must already know. She sent for you through me. Now I understand why. Whatever she wants with you, it won't be about the mistakes and mysteries and messiness of love, but about the waters of Obelos. Go and find out."

So he did, feeling as shaken as if he had been bellowed at by the king.

Someone opened the door. Damaris, staring blindly at the chalk in her fingers and contemplating the messiness and mysteries, flashed a wide, incredulous stare at it. But it wasn't Garner back again with his obstinate, tormented eyes to demand impossible explanations from her. It was a stranger, gestured in by a footman.

"Master Tabbart Ainsley, Minister," he murmured.

"Yes?"

"The composer from Sucia."

She blinked. "Why didn't you take him to Lord Felden?"

"I couldn't find the musicians, my lady," the man explained apologetically. "Everything is chaos with the king's arrival. Master Ainsley said he wrote some water music, so I brought him to you."

Speechless, Damaris gazed at the composer, who looked miserably back at her. His face, framed by windblown chestnut hair, was colorless as curds; he swayed a little under the weight of her regard.

"You are welcome," she assured him hastily. "Please. Sit down."

"Thank you," he said faintly, and the footman closed the door. Master Ainsley crept into the nearest seat, which was her drafting stool, and dropped his face into his hands. Damaris, alarmed, poured a hefty cup of wine, brought it to him.

"Are you ill, Master Ainsley?"

He lifted one hand, eyed the wine glumly, covered his eye again. "I could be cheerfully dead."

"Ah," Damaris said, enlightened.

"In Sucia, I was dragged up a canal in a barge. And then floated down a river along with some goats and chickens and a great many noisy children. When we finally reached the ocean I thought, with all that blue space, it would be peaceful."

"But no?"

"But yes." He came out from behind his hands finally, and winced at the sight of the sea in the window. "But how could I enjoy it? The ship tossed me this way, threw me that; my bed fell down; my dinner came up. I was never so happy to see land. Your port looks so calm. It barely breathes."

"We struggle for that," Damaris told him a trifle grimly. "That's why we celebrate our victories so lavishly. And why you're here."

The young man reached for the wine, took a cautious sip. The damp fungal sheen on his face brightened to a healthier shade of white. He looked slight but muscular within his untidy traveler's garb; his eyes, going seaward again, had a blue-green hue much like it.

"Look at it," he said bitterly, nodding toward the spiky forest of masts rising over waters separated and calmed by sea gates and walls. "Somewhere among those stripped tree trunks is my torment. Now they hardly move. Like ships in a painting."

"Would you like to rest awhile?" Damaris asked him with sympathy. "Lord Felden is one of the musicians, as well as the director of the court orchestra which is to play your music. I'll find him; he'll know where you'll be lodged."

He smiled at her, a fleeting but genuine effort that brought even more color into his face. "If I'm not needed, I think I would like a walk first. I've been so confined, these past days. Perhaps you could direct me to the object of your celebration? I would like to be sure that my music is suitable. I've only seen and heard this wonderful fountain in my imagination. And you know how different they are, all the voices of water."

She found herself smiling back at him, trying to remember what Beale had said about his music. She made a sudden decision, removed her work-robe. "I'll take you there. I want to be sure it will be finished in time, that there are no unexpected problems. I'm afraid you must continue to imagine the sound of it, since the water won't begin to flow until the day of the celebration. Nor has it been seen except by invitation. It's been shrouded in mystery for weeks."

The brisk walk through the royal gardens and out the back gate revived the composer even more. By the time they descended the gentler northern slope behind the castle and reached the streets he grew animated, viewing with energy and curiosity the flower boxes in the windows, the brightly painted doors of houses and shops, the costumes of other visitors. He brought to Damaris's attention tapestries from his own country in a shop window, and stopped now and then to exclaim over one or another of Luminum's renowned arts: delicate glass, lacework, water clocks of elegantly painted porcelain.

"You tell time by water?"

"Everything in Luminum is translated into water. It is the first and last sound we hear."

He made another of his fitful stops at the far end of one unusually straight street, glimpsing another blue horizon, another thicket of water traffic. He turned confusedly, walked backward a pace or two, gazing at the castle on the cliff around which the river curled. "Is Luminum an island?"

"Only on three sides."

He righted himself, gestured down the street. "And that?"

"The Halcyon River."

"More water," he breathed, making Damaris smile again.

"That, we worship. It waters our fields, our animals, our city. We dedicate monuments to it, build shrines, offer gifts to those who dwell in it. Your music will be among those gifts. It is finished, isn't it?" she asked practically, and was reassured when the composer nodded.

His eyes were on the concealed object in the square ahead of them, where four streets ended at a broad bed of cobbles. Flowering chestnuts shaded the people hurrying under them as intently and single-mindedly as fish pursuing dinner in the deep. It was a motley mix at this end of the city, where ancient cottages shared the waterfront with houseboats and barges flying pennants of laundry, and the market-boats darted and hovered like dragonflies over the water to sell a loaf of bread, a dozen oranges, before they flitted away to answer the next summons along the bank.

As they grew closer to the hidden object, Damaris heard the sound of hammering. The shrouds, great lengths of sailcloth, bulged briefly and oddly here and there, poked by mysteries within. The work must be finished, she realized, pleased. The scaffolding around the fountain was being dismantled.

"Minister," murmured the guard, rising from the stool on the cobbles where, with the aid of a book, he was defending the shrouds from entry. There was a shout from within; a sudden ridge in the canvas marked the path of a falling plank, which narrowly missed his head. He ducked, breathing a curse. "Are you sure, my lady, that you want to go in there?"

"You're wearing a helmet," she answered briskly. "Go in and tell them to stop for a moment."

The guard slipped between shrouds. Another plank clattered down; they heard laughter among indignant shouting. Then all was silent. The guard reappeared, held apart the shrouds for them.

"Be careful. There are perils everywhere."

There were indeed, Damaris saw: downed tools, swaying planks hammered half free, clinging to others by a nail, the rubble and dust of the sculptor's final touches to his masterpiece. He was still there, tinkering with the very top of the fountain, while he knelt in the basin below it. He grinned down at the minister, saluting with a brush, half his face masked with marble dust.

There were four broad basins, all scalloped and festooned with carvings. The largest, at the bottom, was a twenty-foot platter of pale yellow marble veined with cream. Three mermaids rose to their scaled hips out of the water in the center of the basin, their upraised arms holding the second basin, smaller by five feet. The exuberance of their poses, their alabaster breasts and dancers' arms, was mitigated by taut muscles the sculptor had chiseled to surface beneath the smooth skin. He knew how hard they worked to hold that ton of marble. Their serene smiles made nothing of it. The basin they held was sea green. Three porpoises, slightly smaller than the mermaids, danced upon the surface of the sea, balancing on their noses the third basin, a pale sky blue. A single rosy fish leaped out of its center, a carp by the look of the sinuous fins, standing on its tail and bearing the highest basin on its head. That carried the emblem of Obelos: the white fluted pillar with the water-blue orb upon it. The carp basin also held the sculptor, who was carefully cleaning the ring of holes in the orb, out of which water would rain in a perfect halo to overflow its basin and cascade into those beneath it.

Master Ainsley, who was staring at the massive stonework, closed his mouth with a click of teeth and lowered his head. The sculptor, blowing softly into the holes, had an ear cocked, Damaris noticed, toward their voices.

"Big," the composer pronounced finally, and added, after considering the matter, "Very big."

"As you noticed, we have a lot of water. Will your music be up to the task?"

"I think—" he paused again, finished cautiously, "I think so. I hadn't expected anything so ornate. I've seen such work in the courtyards and gardens of the rich in Iolea, but never so far north in a city square surrounded by chestnut trees.... The water will come from the river?"

"No. The source is the pure water of the Well itself. Water was guided from the underground river into a large holding tank; from there, pipes were laid across Master Greyson's hop fields, with concessions for use as irrigation, along a stone archway across the river, and then buried beneath the banks and run under various gardens and streets, and finally the square. Once the fountain is open, the water can be piped into houses all around the square. So you can see why we planned such an elaborate celebration. Many in Luminum still get their water by lugging a bucket down to the river."

She gazed at the great conduit head, the fountain, with satisfaction a moment longer, remembering months and even years of discussions, plans, legal contracts over property, endless papers she read requesting funds to pay for directors, engineers, pipe-makers, ditch-diggers, shovels and hoes and wheelbarrows, the ceaseless trail of problems into her office, annoyed citizens, leaky pipes, stolen equipment, miscalculations and miscreants.

All finished. Even the carp standing on its tail seemed to be smiling...

A halo of water shot out of the orb the carp carried. In a heartbeat, the sculptor's face and hair were drenched. A mask of wet marble dust opened its mouth in a silent, astonished O. Damaris, her own mouth open, noted dazedly the single clogged hole in the orb. The water, oddly striated, filled the smallest basin quickly and began to run over its scalloped edge in three orderly cascades around the frolicking carp and the sculptor.

The sculptor shouted an incoherent word that freed Damaris from her transfixed state. She drew a sharp breath and whirled.

"Where is the engineer?" she demanded of the staring workmen.

"What is it doing?" Master Ainsley asked confusedly. "Should it be running now?"

"He went up to the castle to see you," one of the workmen told her. "Said he needed to check something. I thought that's why you came here."

She was silent, pulling a vision of the project plans out of memory. The water had filled the carp basin and was flowing cheerfully down among the dolphins. The sculptor, on one knee in the water and clinging to the carp, was groping for a ladder behind him with his foot. It careened as he kicked. The workmen caught it, steadied it for him. He descended finally, cursing ceaselessly, wet as the carp.

"Go down to the river," Damaris said to one of the men. "Make sure no one is in the discharge drain, and that it is covered. When this starts gushing out the flow will be strong. And you—"

"Why," the sculptor demanded, interrupting his own steady stream, "is the water that color? It should be coming directly from the source waters of the Well."

It was, Damaris saw with horror, turning as brown as mud, or worse: as streams running beneath schools sometimes turned in summer when the water grew shallow and the waste from a hundred students tumbled into it from their simple wooden water closets.

The guard was peering through the opening now, drawn by the noises of water and the sculptor. "Stay here," Damaris told him tersely as his eyes widened. "Don't let anyone in."

"What—"

"Don't say a word about this to anyone."

The composer asked helplessly, grimacing at the murk, "Should I revise my music?"

"Of course not." She seized his arm, tugged him away. "It's a temporary problem. A bit of soil in the water main. Most likely. The engineer will fix it easily. Come back to the castle with me; we'll find Lord Felden so he can begin practicing your music."

"I wrote water music, not mud music," he muttered with one last incredulous glance at it before Damaris pulled him out of the shrouds. "Maybe your Well is running dry."

Damaris closed her eyes briefly. Behind them, she caught an unexpected glimpse of the mage's eyes, the swirling hues of mother-of-pearl opening to look at her, and she felt the skin prickle painfully at the nape of her neck.

"Not possible," she told him adamantly, hurrying him along the ancient, colorful, bustling streets. "Human error. The engineer will find it. All will be well. You needn't mention the incident to the musicians. It might weigh heavily on their playing and your music."

"Water," he sighed. "It plagues me still, even on bone-dry streets. Is it cursed, this fountain?"

"I hope not," she breathed. "We would be forced to revise our lives."

"But it is possible?" he asked so shrewdly that she could not answer, only rush him even more ruthlessly uphill until he had no breath for words.

Within the castle, she delivered him gratefully into the care of her betrothed.

"I've been looking for you," Beale Felden told Master Ainsley. "They told me you had arrived and vanished."

"Lady Ambre kindly took me to see the fountain," the composer answered, and did not elaborate, to Damaris's relief.

"Ah." Beale smiled at her amiably but absently. She could almost see the notes and instruments, the faces of musicians crowded behind his limpid blue eyes. As he, if he noticed, might have seen the pipes and conduits in hers, as well as something of her terror. Fortunately for her, he was not particularly perceptive. That was one of the reasons, along with his fair hair, his amiable temper, his ancient title and wealth, that Damaris had permitted him to court her. He added to the composer, "The musicians are all eager to meet you, and see what you've brought us to play for the ceremony."

"I only hope it will be suitable," Master Ainsley sighed; his own eyes seemed to fill with visions of mud.

"I'm sure it will be wonderful," Lord Felden answered. "This will seal your reputation in Obelos." He bore the speechless composer down the hallway. Damaris watched them a moment; Beale seemed to be doing most of the talking. She turned away. She couldn't guard every word the composer said, and, anyway, Beale, if alarmed, would be convinced by the simplest of explanations. A little dirt in the conduit pipe. Easily flushed out. He wouldn't think to wonder who had started the appalling flow in the first place.

She found the engineer pacing as she entered her office; turning abruptly, he nearly bumped into her. They both spoke at once.

"Did you see—?"

"Have you heard—?"

They stopped, studied one another's perturbed faces. The engineer, a lean, muscular, balding man apt to grab a shovel and leap into a trench if work on a project seemed slow, asked tersely, "Is it about the fountain?"

"Yes. Yours?"

"Yes. I was at the river, early this morning, making sure the discharge drain was completely clear before the guard-gate was locked over it. You remember where it is? Parallel to the conduit at that point where it arches across the river near the central bridge—"

"Yes."

"It was just near my head, coming down off the stone archway. So I could hear what was going on inside."

Damaris blinked. "Inside."

"The conduit pipe."

"Nothing," Damaris said after a moment. Her voice shook. "Nothing should have been going on inside the conduit pipe. Why are you here? Why are you not checking the pipe at the source?"

He gazed at her, his brow furrowing. "For what?" he demanded. "What did you see?"

"A great deal of very murky water coming out of the fountain. Isn't that what you heard? Water in flow?"

"No," he said soundlessly. Then he cleared his throat. "I heard voices."

"What?" She stared back at him in horror. "Someone inside the pipe?"

"Singing."

"Inside the pipe?"

"And laughter. Some banging—"

"Children," she whispered, her fingers icy.

"They didn't sound like children. And I couldn't understand a word. Sometimes the pipes themselves seemed to sing. I sent one of the workmen to the Well to check the cap over the conduit pipe, make sure no one had broken the locks on it."

"If anyone had opened the cap to enter it, they would have drowned long before they crossed the river. No one would be laughing."

They were silent again; their eyes slid away from one another, neither wanting to glimpse the doubt blooming there.

"Mud," the engineer said heavily.

"Or worse. I couldn't tell. At least it didn't smell. But where could it possibly be coming from? What did the workman say?"

He shook his head. "The cap was sealed in the water as we left it. Nothing seemed amiss." He paused again, asked her diffidently, "Any word from the water-mage?"

"No. Not for me, at least."

His face loosened slightly. "An accident, then, along the pipeline. I'll have the workmen follow it, check for wet or sinking ground. I'll take a look at the source myself."

She nodded briefly. "And your voices?"

"Echoes from somewhere else, they must have been. The river was misty at dawn; I couldn't see clearly . . ."

She drew breath, loosed it silently, and met his eyes again. "That must have been it. Let me know immediately if you find anything."

He bowed his head, left her listening to the bewildering silence from the water-mage.

The water-mage stood listening as well.

In the rocky, sunken cave where the water ran up out of the secret earth, Eada was little more than a bulky shadow in her black skirts and the veil that hid her long silver hair. She might have been a boulder in the jumble of rock that had broken and cascaded down around the Well so long ago that the shards were growing together again, grain by grain, century by century. The water filled its ancient, rounded pool among the stones with only the slightest tremor at its heart, the little flutter in the center of the pool that spoke of the unseen treasure of water buried deep beneath, in perpetual night. Seemingly without end, it pushed itself up into this silent cave with its little circular roof of sky and light; it gleamed a greeting, then passed into darkness again, down a narrow, shallow bed of stones, pushing more quickly now through its ancient waterway to find the light again, beyond the cave, where it bubbled up and pooled beneath the open sky.

That pool was where the city dwellers came to worship. They brought gifts, dropped wishes into it in the form of coins or words written on thin strips of metal. They crowded around it during the ritual, under the first full summer moon.

The knights ringed the Well beneath the ground; the king stood on the earth above, drank water from a gold cup, and dropped coins and jewels the color of blood into the wellspring. Near the natural pool above, and fed by it, a great marble tank had been built, a pretty thing surrounded by broad walkways, flowering vines, fluted pillars with little fountains perpetually offering water to the worshippers. Beyond it, the water flowed free again, very briefly, offering itself to insects, mosses and reeds, birds and wild creatures before it dove underground again, vanished back into the dark. Around this open water, the city dwellers watched the ritual, flooding beyond their human boundaries once a year to honor the mysteries of the Well, and to drink, after the king, the pure water out of the earth.

The water welling up out of the underearth made no sound.

The water welling up out of the underearth should have made no sound.

The mage, standing in the shadows, kept listening for silence from the sunlit pool. An ancient, familiar silence there should have been in that cave, as old and peaceful as the dark. Instead, there were half-words, like water emptying down a drain; there were hisses, a gurgle like a laugh that echoed against the walls, a sudden splash that left no ripple behind it. The language of water, she recognized. But who spoke? What was said?

She heard a step in the low passageway that led from the Well to her dwelling. The walls echoed suddenly, as though a stone had spoken. Eada looked quickly into the water, saw nothing but the insouciant reflection of the sky.

"Mistress, the knight is here," Perla said. She was a slight young girl, the daughter of a market-boater, used to the vagaries of water, who had come to peer into the cave one day and stayed to give the old mage a hand with this or that. She might have been part water sprite, Eada guessed. She feared nothing that poked its head unexpectedly out of the Well, and didn't mind running errands between the underearth and sky.

A hesitant step in the stone chamber beyond told Eada how far the knight had gotten. Her odd experiments, her trifles, had slowed him in her workroom. She played with water in all its forms, even ice in its season. In tanks, she kept strange fish and other river creatures Perla and her friends found; she studied most for a moon or two before she sent them back. Scholars and witches from all over Obelos sent her the odd instrument, the unusual crystal that might interest her.

Perla was hovering, looking, with her pale hair and scant, restive limbs, like she might sprout wings like a dragonfly if she touched the earth another minute. "Shall I stay, mistress? Or shall I go buy bread?"

"Go," Eada said, shooing the sprite away and found her slow way around the stony edges of the pool, and down the passage into her chambers. They were roofed above the earth by domes of stone and wood studded with crystals that caught the daylight and drew it underground in mellow, shimmering shafts. Entering her workroom, the mage found that the knight had indeed been slowed by her playthings; he was toying with a tiny windmill on the table, turning its blades with his forefinger.

"Better to blow it," Eada suggested, and he started.

"I wasn't sure it worked."

"Try it."

He blew gently. The slats turned; the mill wheel, driven by the cogs and pistons within, drew up water from a shallow pan, flicked it into a chute that fed it neatly into a pot of basil.

The knight grunted, almost smiled. But he wasn't in the habit of it; Eada could tell by the clouds that gathered immediately to engulf the simple moment of pleasure. The mage reckoned that she had not been that young in at least a couple of centuries.

He looked at her silently then, uneasily. Well he should, she thought. Living in the water-cavern, she had become a shapeless, bulky thing: a boulder with legs and great slab hands. Her neck had vanished somewhere; her white head balanced on her shoulders. Strange colors had seeped into her eyes from what she had seen. Witch-lights, Perla called them; they fascinated the child. But Garner Slade was not a child; he had a good idea of what was worth fearing.

"Did it speak to you?" she asked, and his eyes widened. He was quick, though; she'd seen that when she chose him.

"No. It only looked at me." He hesitated, ventured a question. "What was it?"

"Something that wanted you to see it. You," she repeated with emphasis. "Garner Slade. Your eyes."

"How did you—how did you know?"

"I was watching, in the Well. I'm mage, so I can do such things with water."

"And you saw—"

"Everything. I see through all your eyes." The knight opened his mouth, then closed it, a red tide rising in his face. "That's how I choose the knights," Eada continued. "I must be able to see. The young man who thinks he dislikes water sees it with such clarity.... And your cousin loves it, though he might have trouble loving anything human."

"I'm sorry," Garner blurted. "I'm sorry I lost my temper."

"Ah, but look what you found. Look what you saw. Something is wrong in the waterworld, and we need to know what. Since you were the one to look trouble in the eye, you're the one to help me. If we have offended the water realms, if some strange mage is churning up things better left on the bottom, if the kingdom itself is in danger, we need to know." She turned without waiting for him to answer. "Come."

Perversely, now that she wished to show, to illumine, the Well made no sound; not a ripple or a chuckle disturbed it. The bright face of the pool was blank and still. She waited, the knight a breathing shadow beside her. No one even glanced up from underwater to see who was there. Finally, without comment, she led him back into her workroom, where she rummaged through her books and manuscripts. The knight, looking confused, finally spoke.

"Was there something I should have seen?"

"I couldn't see anything either," she said absently. "They're teasing our eyes; they knew we were looking. They were whispering and laughing all morning before you came."

"Who?" he asked bewilderedly. "Who?"

She showed him.

"I drew these on my travels all around Obelos, when I was young," she said, turning pages slowly in the bound book she had made of her sketches. "I wasn't even a water-mage then. I didn't know that's what I wanted to be. I only knew that I never wanted to be far from water. . . . Some of these have been given human names. Others are seen so rarely they have no names in our world."

Many she had drawn from memory, a brief glimpse of the face within the waterfall, among the flowers along a brook, the shadowy creature swimming with the school of fish. Others she saw clearly; they had human names: the kelpies, the water nymphs, the naiads, and nereids and undines, the mer-people. Some spoke to her in various ways, touching her with pale, webbed fingers, showing alarming teeth in warning, singing to her, beckoning. There seemed a different face for every stream, every pond and branch water. She drew as many as she could find. Some stayed to watch their own faces flowing out of her ink jars onto paper. They knew their human names, and had learned to speak to humans for their own purposes. They did not consider Eada entirely human. They didn't try to entice her underwater, or into their arms. They questioned her, gossiped about other water creatures, told her where to find the shyest, the most secretive, the wildest.

They spread her name throughout the water-web of Obelos. When the dying water-mage in Luminum searched for his successor, he heard the water speak Eada's name and summoned her.

"And that's when I finally realized what I am," she told the speechless knight, who was staring at the wide-set eyes and languid mouth of the face peering up from under a water lily. "Now you know what you'll be looking for."

He came to life again. "What?" he asked huskily.

"That one will make you forget your own name when you look at her."

"What is it you want me to do?"

"I need your eyes. I need you to follow the waterways of Luminum, looking for such as these. Look into every rivulet, every puddle, every rain barrel, every place where water gathers. See what you can see. You'll be my eyes; I'll be behind yours, watching, listening. I must know what is troubling the water creatures. Go swimming if you have to. That worked for you earlier."

"The creature seemed more inclined to let me drown than talk to me."

"Well, some are like that. Just do your best. I'll help you in any way I can. We need answers before moonrise tomorrow, or the Ritual of the Well will become the disaster your mishap on the river portended."

"That soon," he breathed.

"And let Damaris know what I've told you to do."

He gazed at her, seeing what she knew he would. "Must I?" he asked a little explosively. "I'm the last man she wants to see. She's the Minister of Water and you're the water-mage. Shouldn't you tell her?"

"I'm hoping you will," she only said. "Be careful of teeth, and don't fall in love with anything waterborn."

He drew breath, debated over any number of replies. Then he loosed it with a huff and a toss of his hands, and made his way back out of her caverns and across the threshold of day.

....

Faced with another encounter with the annoyed Minister of Water, Garner found the most labyrinthine path possible back to the castle. Follow the water, the mage had instructed. So he did, beginning with the irrigation ditches along the broad fields beyond the river. Seeing anything in them but gaudy insects and weeds seemed unlikely. The sudden glimpse of a splintered darkness beneath the surface made him start; his horse gave an uneasy snort. Then he saw the blackbird swoop past him, its shadow flying behind it in the ditchwater. The ditch ended at a canal with its sluice gate closed. He rode along the canal for a while. Nothing disturbed the water; nothing spoke. He watched it carefully, remembering that the mage watched as well. Remembering, too, the lovely eyes beneath the lily pad, he could not help looking for them among the clustering green on the still, sunlit water. But nothing beckoned; nothing lured; the only face he saw in the water was his own.

Nearer the river, he dismounted to thread his way at random through the streets of the city. On that side of the river, they fanned evenly away from the water toward the fields. The cross streets, cobbled with fieldstones, were equally straight. Except for the ancient houses along the bank, this part of the city was newer, tidier, and, he discovered, eagerly awaiting the pipes that would connect it to the massive conduit from the Well, send its water flowing into the houses.

"The minister promised us water by the end of autumn," a tavern-keeper told Garner, who had stopped to peer into his rain barrel. It was positioned beneath a clay gutter-pipe; water poured out of the wide mouth of an ornate, hideous face that, despite its chipped nose, reminded Garner of one of the sprites in the mage's book. He gazed with interest into the water. But nothing gazed back at him, with or without teeth. "They have to wait until after harvest to go digging up the fields. I've waited years, but it's hardest to wait that one more season." He paused, watching Garner curiously. "Something your lordship wanted?"

Garner nodded, realizing what. "A dip into your barrel?"

"Help yourself."

Garner filled the cup dangling from its chain, drank, felt the sweet rain branch through him in all its secret rills. *How can I possibly?* he wondered tiredly. *How can I find what the mage needs? I might have just drunk the answer down.*

"They say the Well is as pure as rain," the tavern-keeper commented reverently. "We'll hear it singing from that fountain across the river in a day or two."

Damaris had said something about a fountain, Garner remembered. He let the cup drop. "Is it important, the fountain?"

The man cocked a brow. "Where have you been?"

"With the king at the winter court."

"Ah. Those with pipes and without take their water from the river, even the king. No telling what you might find in it, especially toward the end of summer before the rains come. The fountain will draw its water from the Well itself. Can't get much cleaner than that. Straight out of the bones of the earth. . . ."

"Where is this fountain?"

"Just across the central bridge, up the street and in the square. Nobody's seen it yet. It'll be unveiled and let run after the Ritual of the Well. That'll be something to celebrate."

Garner left him gazing with anticipation in the direction of the square. He continued his meandering way through the streets until one led him to the river, ending at the dock where the market-boats loaded their wares. There he could see distant chestnut trees where the streets ended, and the smudged blur of part of some huge thing standing among them, the unwrapped gift to the city. He debated crossing for a closer look. Then he envisioned the Minister of Water with the same impulse at the same time, and the two of them running into one another under a tree. Not only would he be forced to give Damaris the unpleasant message from the mage, he must present her with the last thing she wanted to look at: his face.

He turned instead, went downriver toward the sea, and the place where he had seen the water creature.

That side of the river was wilder, thinly populated; the city tended to cluster around its stronghold and its bridges. Here the fishing boats docked, coming and going with the tide. Here the river quickened as it curved around the headland, broadened to meet the sea. A massive watchtower guarded the castle across the water. Garner had spent some months in it when he was younger, learning how to use his weapons. There was little river traffic now. The fishing boats were still out at sea.

The royal dock where Garner had so ignominiously disembarked that morning still ported its pennants and scallops, but the few barges tied there were all empty.

Garner dismounted at the river, stood watching the water while his horse drank. The bank was low there. The water of the little inlet lapped softly along mossy tree roots and tangles of bramble and wildflowers. Afternoon sun lay gently on the shallows, a rumpled cloth-of-gold, stirring languidly in the backwash of deeper currents. The pennants fluttering like colorful leaves across the water drew Garner's eyes. He saw Damaris in memory, several years earlier, coming down those steps to welcome the returning court. Garner, who had accompanied one of the king's knights as his squire, had been transfixed by the sight of her. She had grown quite tall and slender over the winter. She moved like water, he thought. Like kelp, every frond graceful, swaying dreamily to the slightest touch of tide. He felt the moment when her eyes met his. She laughed and waved; he could only stand there, forgetting to move even after the barge had docked.

He drew a soft breath, forced his eyes away. No one stood there now, and anyway, all her welcomes were for someone else. Lord Felden, with his wealth, his horn, his absent-minded humming, his amiable disposition. He gave all his passion to his music, Garner had heard, when news of the betrothal reached the winter court. His mother, who reigned in his rich house south of Luminum, must have reminded him that no amount of copious outpourings of beautiful music would transform itself into an heir to his title and fortune, no matter how hard he blew.

Her eyes met his.

Garner started, feeling the implosion like a silent lightning bolt all through him. Those eyes, as green as river moss, watched him just above the surface of the water. Her pale hair floated all around her like the petals of some extravagant flower. In the next moment he caught his breath. It was not, could not possibly be Damaris, silent as a wild thing, her nose under water, and from what he could see, naked as an eel.

A river creature, he realized, his pulse quickening again. Sunning in the shallows, breathing water like air as she gazed at him. He wondered whether, if he spoke, she would vanish with a twist and a ripple, like a fish.

But he had to risk it. "You startled me," he said.

She lifted her face out of the water then, revealing a familiar, charming smile, a slender neck, the curves and hollows of her shoulders. He wondered if her skin was that golden everywhere.

"I know," she answered. Her voice was light and sweet, a purl of water. She raised her fingers; he saw the webs between them, delicate, iridescent. She pushed lazily at the water, the light. "Come join me."

"I don't dare," he said somberly.

"Then I'll leave you."

"No—Don't do that."

"Then come in with me. We'll talk."

That face drew hard at him, so familiar, all its smiles for him, promising all he wanted.

"You're a dream," he breathed.

"So? Don't you take pleasure in dreams?"

Don't fall in love, the mage had warned him, *with the waterborn.* . . . She was there, he remembered, starting again. In his head, watching out of his eyes. He sighed noiselessly, relieved to have the choice made for him.

"The water-mage sent me," he said carefully. "She wonders if we have offended the water folk."

She flicked water toward him again, not answering, only looking at him out of that face she must have pulled out of his thoughts. Was her true face, he wondered, what he had seen under the water that morning, watching him?

"If we have, tell us what to do to make amends."

She smiled, raising both hands out of the water, fingers stroking the air like wings, beckoning.

"I'll show you . . ." he heard, but how he couldn't imagine, for she had already vanished.

He stood a moment longer, waiting for her, feeling a curious emptiness, as though it truly had been Damaris and he had turned away from love.

Damaris, he reminded himself, or the mage did, urging him along. Reluctantly, he mounted again, rode to the watchtower dock to summon the ferryman.

A dozen market-boats had ventured down that far; they swarmed around the dock, selling bread, strawberries, cheese, ale and savory pasties to the men in the tower. Garner bought some meat and onions skewered on a stick and roasted on a little brazier balanced on a shelf on the prow of the boat. It seemed precarious, but fire rode easily over the swell and dip of water. The boatman, his face seamed with an endless labyrinth of wrinkles, lingered at the dock to thread more meat and turn his skewers.

Garner, watching him as he ate, asked impulsively, "Have you seen anything strange in the water?"

"Strange? You mean like mermaids and such?"

"Anything out of the ordinary."

The man shook his head. But his mouth widened into a gap-toothed grin at the same time; he chuckled soundlessly, waving a skewer at the bees. "Only what everybody saw this morning."

Garner felt himself flush but pursued the matter anyway. "What?"

"You didn't see? It happened near the bridge, where the market-boats are thickest. A man in one of the fancy houses along the river pushed his head out of the vent in his private water closet, crying that something was in there laughing at him. Then the water closet slid right down his wall and into the river. For a few moments, we all thought it would float at the head of the king's procession. But it stuck in the mud and got pulled ashore before the king had to see it. The man came out cursing his leaky pipes that had rotted the wood. But a water pipe wasn't what terrified him. You could see that in his eyes."

"What was it, then?"

The old man shrugged. "Water sprite, likely," he said calmly. "They get frisky sometimes just before the ritual. We make our living on the water; we've learned to placate them, leave gifts in the river—flowers, beads, floating candles, little carvings—so they don't toy with our boats. But I've never seen them go that far before. Up pipes and into someone's house."

Garner finished his meal hastily, disturbed, and rode to the shallows beside the dock, where the ferryman, a lean man with his head hooded against the wind, sat alone on his raft, watching the currents.

"Between tides," he remarked cryptically. "Easy journey."

Garner led his horse on; they were the only passengers. The ferryman glanced up and down for traffic, then gave a cry. High-pitched, inarticulate, it sounded across the river like some wild water bird calling to another. At the royal dock a giant spool began to turn. A pair of ropes attached to the front of the raft rose slowly through the water to the surface and tautened. Another spool turned on the watchtower dock, loosing the raft cables. Garner felt it begin to move.

The ferryman plied his pole, kept the raft from drifting. Garner stood stroking his horse, watching the great stone pile loom above them until it filled the sky. Its shadow slid over them, mid-river.

"She get the message yet?" the ferryman asked, shifting his pole.

"She—" His thoughts had strayed; he couldn't imagine what they were talking about. "The water-mage?"

The ferryman flashed him a glance. "The mage. The minister. Either." Garner stared at him. He looked back, long enough this time to give the knight a clear view of his spindrift face, his shell-white eyes. The ferryman smiled then, a quick, tight smile. "Guess not."

The cables on one side of the boat snapped, whipped the water with a vicious hiss. Garner ducked, clinging to his horse's reins. On the other side, the rope dipped underwater, pulling the raft down with it. He felt his boots fill again with water. The raft tilted like a door opening into the riverworld and he went through it for the second time that day.

Beale would not go away. Damaris, desperate to find her engineer again and inquire about the fountain, kept seeing her betrothed in her doorway, no matter how many times she paced around the table. His pleasant, thoughtful voice went on and on; his eyes, seeming to follow her spiral path, saw nothing disturbing in it; walking around and around a table must be simply what she wanted to do.

"Chairs," he said, "for fifteen musicians. The little gilt ones. To be placed, I think, beside the fountain and facing it. The music is, after all, a gift to the fountain. Don't you agree? The king, I believe, is planning to step out of the royal barge near the square and proceed up one of the streets to the fountain. I'm not sure who else will make up the procession. The musicians, of course, will not come down by water. The Minister of Ceremony has not yet decided exactly when to unveil the fountain: before or after the king's arrival. In either event, the musicians will already be there. I don't think I've told you this: Master Ainsley plays a very sweet flute and will be joining us to perform his own composition for the first time."

Master Ainsley, Damaris thought, chilled. Who must still wonder if he'll be playing mud music.

"Beale," she said desperately.

"Not to leap ahead, since there are so many details to consider, but I am so much anticipating our journey after the celebration to my estate, where you will finally meet my mother. As I've told you, she's much too frail to make the journey to Luminum."

"Beale."

"She is eagerly awaiting our arrival. So is my sister, who used to be one of the king's musicians until our mother's health—"

"Beale!"

He stopped, seeing her finally, his fair brows raised. "What is it, my love?"

"If—if there should be—if something should go wrong—"

"What could possibly go wrong? You're intelligent, wonderful, young enough to bear twenty grandchildren for my mother, your family and history are impeccable, you look like a water nymph, my mother will adore you."

She closed her eyes, tried to keep her voice steady. "I meant with the fountain."

"The fountain. What could go wrong with the fountain? You let the water flow; it comes out the holes; we play. Simple as breathing."

She opened her eyes, saw, over his shoulder, a bad dream coming toward her down the hall, its bare feet squelching watery footprints on the marble. She gave a hiccup of astonishment, and closed her eyes again, hoping it might go away.

"Beale. Excuse me, but I must find my engineer."

"There is such a charming analogy between the holes in the fountain, and those in our instruments," he said with sudden enthusiasm. "Don't you think? One flowing water, the other music; both necessary for life, I would argue, though no amount of music would—Now, I wonder, could an instrument be fashioned that could flow with both water and music at once? What would it look like? Surely—"

The face of the nightmare was beside him now: the Knight of the Well running water like a leaky pipe. His dark eyes were furious, but that she understood. It was the fear in them that brought her fingers to her mouth. Be careful, she pleaded silently to him. Be discreet.

Beale turned; even he must have felt the exudations of emotions and dampness. He stared, amazed, at the knight. "You seem to be dripping."

"I fell in the river," Garner said shortly, and otherwise ignored him, holding Damaris's eyes with his disquieting gaze.

"Again?" she said through her fingers.

"The ferryman tossed me in. This was after I spoke to the nymph—"

"Stop," she said sharply, and, to her relief, he veered away from that.

"I have a message for you from the water-mage."

"Nymphs and water-mages and Knights of the Well," Beale murmured. "Sounds like a tale that should be set to music. Does it not? A small, perfect cycle of compositions—"

"Beale," Damaris interrupted explosively, "I must hear Eada's message in private. Please."

"Oh." He glanced with surprise at the doorpost against which he leaned. "Of course." He moved himself, but only to advance with a touch of deliberation into the room, where he positioned a kiss firmly on the cheek of his betrothed. "Come and tell it to me when you're finished here." He left finally, passing Garner with a careless nod and a laugh. "You must tell me your nymph story in more detail later. Don't forget."

"Come in and close the door," Damaris said tightly. "Don't drip on my papers. Tell me what the mage said."

"Something is wrong in the waterworld. She sent me searching everything from ditchwater to the river to find out what. She told me to tell you this."

"She did."

"Do you think I wanted to come back here?" he demanded. "To interrupt your intimate conversation with Lord Felden? To make a fool of myself drenched and barefoot in front of you both?"

"No," she admitted. "Anyway, it wasn't very intimate. Anyway," she said more firmly, "what did you mean about the ferryman? He had an accident, taking you across the river?"

"It wasn't an accident, and he wasn't human."

"Oh," she whispered.

"He sank the ferry deliberately. I nearly got kicked by my horse flailing in the water before I could grab its mane. We swam across together. I didn't have a chance to question anything among the waterweeds. I lost my boots. Again. Whatever is going on among the water people is becoming dangerous to humans."

"Well, did you find anyone to ask?"

"I asked the water nymph. She just looked at me out of your face and refused to answer."

Damaris felt behind her for the edge of the table, held on. "My face," she said faintly.

"You had been on my mind," Garner sighed. "I think she—whatever it truly was—must have seen it in my thoughts."

"I see." She chose words carefully, as though they were stones across a swirling current. "You didn't—I've heard such nymphs are—are difficult to resist."

"Of course she was," he said bluntly. "But I also had a water-mage looking out of my eyes, and after this morning, I was wary of going anywhere near you. Or anything that looked like you. I didn't want to come here now. But I'm beginning to be afraid for Luminum."

"Yes." Her fingers tightened on the wood. "So am I. We had what looked like muddy water coming out of the fountain earlier today. Before anyone had uncapped the conduit pipe at the Well."

He gazed at her silently, some of the anger in his eyes yielding to bewilderment. "Do you have any idea why?"

"Because we have run pipes out of the Well itself?" she guessed. "But we began the project years ago, and nothing has bothered us until now." She paused, eyeing his plastered hair, his sodden clothes, his naked feet. "Garner, be careful. They seem to be using you as a—a conduit for their messages."

"Yes," he said quickly. "The ferryman asked me if you had gotten it."

"What?"

"The message."

She felt the blood leave her face. "He said that. If I had—"

"The mage or the minister," Garner amended himself. "I assumed he meant the Minister of Water. Maybe not." He moved restively. "I need to get out of these wet clothes and continue my search. Do you have any suggestions? You know the waterworld as well as any human can."

"I'm beginning to feel that I don't know it at all.... I may understand more after I speak to the engineer. But, Garner, what will you do for boots?"

He shrugged. "Steal a pair from my cousin."

"Be careful," she said again, and he looked at her a moment, silently.

"You be careful, too," he warned, and followed his own soggy path back out.

Soon after that, she received the first message from the engineer. He had checked the conduit line from fountain to Well, and seen nothing amiss. But something, he assured her, was. On that disturbing note, he ended, but she didn't have long to wait before the next messenger came, and the next. Garner's was not the only sodden body to appear in her office. Sprites had invaded the water pipes of Luminum, and they showed no respect, not even to the king, whose luxurious water closet, fitted with cushions, scented linens, and bowls of flower petals, had somehow popped its ornate taps completely off to spew river water all over the carpets. There were similar disasters throughout the city, in those houses and inns fortunate enough to have private systems. The harassments extended beyond pipes, Damaris learned. Fishers found their boats immobile in mid-current, or completely overturned. Sluice gates between canals and irrigation ditches were randomly opened or shut, causing herds of pastured animals to find themselves shank-deep in water. Mill wheels ground to a halt for no reason anyone could see. Damaris, fearing for the dikes, sent riders out to check for breaches. The harbormaster came himself to tell her that a dock had floated out to sea.

"Why," she demanded incoherently of him, "can't they just put it into words? Why must water speak for them?"

"I don't know, Minister," he sighed. "I'm only hoping the sea gates don't start talking."

Beale wandered back in the midst of all this to invite her to the rehearsal, after supper, of Master Ainsley's music. She stared at him incredulously, then remembered what he was talking about.

"Music. Yes. For a little while. But Beale—"

But he was already leaving, trumpeting, in his resonant baritone, what must have been the horn section to Master Ainsley's piece.

She saw Garner again finally, taking his place belatedly among the knights in the hall for supper. He was still alive, and he looked dry; other than that she couldn't draw conclusions. She watched him, hearing Beale only when he stopped speaking. Then she would shift her attention quickly back to him.

"Beale," she said carefully, during one of his brief silences. "Are you aware of the water problems in the city?"

He shook his head. His eyes, she realized suddenly, were on the knights' table also. "You seem distracted," he murmured, in a rare moment of discernment she could have done without.

"I am," she said quickly. "I have been hearing all day long about disturbances, restlessness in the water."

His face cleared; he asked with a sudden chuckle, "You mean the king's water closet?"

"Yes, that, too. And—"

"I heard they had to bail out the royal bedchamber before the water was stopped. You keep staring at that knight. The morose one with no manners."

"He's a Knight of the Well, on the water-mage's business. I need to talk to him after supper. I'm beginning to be very worried."

"Oh," he said complacently. "Is that all. I was beginning to think—No matter. It's probably just a storm."

"What?"

"The weather seems to be changing. I heard the wind rise as I came to supper. An early summer storm, nothing more; it will no doubt blow over by morning." She opened her mouth just as he pushed back his chair and stood up. "I beg your pardon, my dear, but we have so little time to practice. You will join us, won't you, before too long? You must hear Master Ainsley's composition; it is wonderful. The voice of water itself . . ."

She had to wait for Garner until the king and his nobles rose from the dais table; then the knights were permitted to leave. Garner, watching for her, came to meet her as the elegant court swirled around the king to welcome him. He looked exhausted, she thought, as well as a bit wild-eyed, haunted by sprites.

"Anything?" she demanded.

He shook his head. "Nothing that makes any sense. Fountains refused to flow, or poured like waterfalls all over the streets. Rain barrels overflowed as though they were fed by secret springs. Public water closet doors stuck fast; I helped tear several open to free those trapped inside. Pipes leaked; people were chased out of their houses by water."

"Did you meet any other water creatures?"

"I heard them singing out of buckets people dropped on their way back from the river. I searched along the river, and on my way to the Well. But, perversely, they hid from me."

"You saw Eada again?"

"I tried to, but she was nowhere to be found, either. I saw your engineer."

"More than I did," she said grimly. "Did he have any messages for me?"

"Only that he could find—"

"Nothing amiss," she guessed, and he nodded.

"He told me to tell you that the fountain was clean, completely dry. The scaffolding is down; the debris cleared; the work is ready to be unveiled."

"If we dare," she sighed. "Well. That's something."

"A trick," he suggested somberly.

"Maybe. But if anything goes wrong, it will go wrong first tomorrow night at the Ritual of the Well. They won't wait for the water music the day after." He was silent, so completely baffled, she saw, that he had forgotten to be angry. She added, "At least you didn't fall in the river again."

"Maybe I should," he murmured. "Maybe I should go back, find that nymph with your face and listen to what she has to tell me."

"Lies," Damaris said succinctly. "Like her face."

He was silent again, blinking at her out of heavy, bloodshot eyes, as though he couldn't remember the difference between the minister and the nymph. She shifted abruptly; he raised his hand to his eyes, rubbed them wearily.

"I'm too tired to think. I'm going to rest a little, for as long as the mage will let me."

"Let's hope the night will be more peaceful than the day."

She went to the music room, where the musicians, Master Ainsley, and Lord Felden sat on their gilt chairs in ranks according to their instruments. Beale smiled at her, pleased.

"Welcome, my lady. We are just about to go over it again."

Damaris sat down. He lifted his horn and nodded his head. As they played the first light, charming flurry of falling water droplets, she heard the storm begin.

A summer storm, Beale had said. Warm, noisy, clearing by morning. But nothing was predictable that day, not even water coming out of a tap. Damaris left as early as she could, throwing Beale an apologetic smile without quite meeting his eyes. In her office, she studied the tide tables. Rare for a summer storm to be destructive. As rare, she thought dourly, for a water bucket to sing. And that night the moon was nearly full, the tide would be high, and late, and everyone would be sleeping as it rose . . .

She made her decision, wrote a note, affixed her seal of office, and sent it to the harbormaster.

Close the sea gates now.

The mage heard the first falling notes of rain on the river, on the sea. She was a shadow beside the Well, night-dark, motionless as the ancient tumble of stones around her. Her blank gaze was fixed upon the water. She saw nothing; she saw everything. Her mind was a fish, a ripple, a current running here, there, everywhere: through pipes, along ditches, in ponds, canals, down the river flowing to the sea. She listened, wondered, watched.

Snatches, she heard: underwater whisperings. Brief as the gurgle of water down a drain, some were, and as coherent. But she had been watermage for many decades. She understood the ways of water creatures, and many of their words. When she didn't understand, she went farther, her mind seeping into another like water, filling every wrinkled crevice of it until she saw, she spoke, she understood.

What she guessed at last amazed her.

Her surprise cast her thoughts back into the still old woman she had left at the edge of the Well. For a long time she sat there, contemplating the fragments of this and that she had pieced together. A word repeated many different ways, an odd detail washing up against another, an underwater face seen through as many kinds of eyes as were in the water, now a colorless blur, now a bright, startling mosaic of itself repeated in a single eye, now as nearly human as it could get . . .

"Well, I never," the mage said in the dark, and, a little later, "All this fuss . . ."

The Well turned suddenly vivid, bone-white, as though the moon had fallen into it. The mage gazed at the water, astonished again. Then the thunderbolts pounded all around her, trying to shake apart the boulders. She drew fully into herself for a moment, hearing the rain hiss down through the open roof onto the Well; then she felt it. She grunted; her thoughts slid back into the water. She rode the river current down until down became up as the salt tide pushed upriver. She borrowed bodies, then. There were many, she realized, and all swimming against the tide, making for the sea.

She saw it as they did: the massive gates across the harbor, sluice gates lowered, hinged gates fashioned to open outward with the outgoing sea and close fast when needed, with the help of the incoming tide. The tide had barely begun to turn, but they were already shut.

She came slowly back to herself, feeling as though, between rain and river and sea, she must be wet as a puddle. She whispered, as she pulled herself to her feet, balancing on one stone, then another, "Good girl."

She moved through the torch-lit cavern of her workroom, into the chamber beyond, which had a bed, and a hearth, and warm, dry clothes. She put them on and moved into the tiny kitchen. She found Perla there, windblown and barefoot, stirring something savory in a pot over the fire.

"The knight came, mistress."

"Did he?" She warmed her hands, remembering him like a dream: the knight looking into her cave, she seeing nothing out of his eyes. "Did he leave a message?"

"No."

"What are you doing here, child? Didn't you see the rain coming? You should have scampered home."

Perla answered only with a brief, wild grin at the thought that a storm should be something to avoid. She brought Eada a bowl of stew, bread, and some late strawberries. The mage ate absently, mulling over what she had glimpsed underwater.

"Who's to say?" she inquired finally, of nobody, she realized. The child had gone somewhere, maybe home, maybe out to watch the lightning. "Not I," she answered herself, and rose with sudden energy to clear the table. "Not for me to say . . ."

For a long time then, she sat beside the Well, half-dreaming, half-dozing. She heard rain dripping off reeds and waterweeds, dimpling ponds, sighing in gusts over the restless sea. In her thoughts, or her dreams, she allowed herself to be carried along by impulses. They went against the tide, she realized: push against flow, drive against mindless drag. Mute and innocent as a polliwog she went along, seeing little beyond a silken, singing dark running against the tide. Then the tide caught the shadowy travelers, sent them swirling, tumbling in its grasp, flung them toward stones, toward the moon. They melted down, fingering themselves between stones, slithering, flattening themselves, easing around, sliding under vast slabs of wood, finding ways through the heave and swamp of tide, clinging, climbing, up and over, into the calm on the other side.

And then they began to push back at the tide.

Eada woke as though she had heard, across the city and river and fields, the sound of moored ships banging recklessly against the wharves, straining at their cables, masts reeling drunkenly, swiping at one another.

She opened her eyes, just as she felt Damaris, in her own bed, open hers, stare into the suddenly chaotic night.

Damaris, the mage said to her. *They have opened a gate.*

"I can hear it," Damaris said aloud. The mage, riding her mind, looking out of her eyes as she sprang out of bed, felt the cold stones under her feet, and the slap of wind and rain as she pushed a casement open.

In the harbor ships and boats heaved and tumbled on a tide that was trying to tear away the wharves. Some, anchored in deeper water, had already begun to drift, meandering a choppy, heedless path toward other ships, toward warehouses and moored boats. Little rain-battered blooms of fire moved quickly along the harbor's edge; some met to confer, parted again; a few vanished, doused under a wild burst of tide.

The great harbor bell in its massive tower began to boom a warning, accompanied by the high, fey voices of ships' bells careening madly in the waves.

I'll be right there, Eada told the Minister of Water, and was, quick as a thought, far more quickly than any of the Knights of the Well her thoughts had galvanized awake along the way.

The tide was still dancing its way into the open gate, which trembled mightily under the onslaught, but couldn't bring itself to close, locked, as it was, in the grip of many invisible hands. The sprites recognized the mage, who was barely visible, and who looked more like a battering ram than herself. She wedged herself against the gate and pushed back at them: an enormous snag caught against the gate, her feet its root ball in the sand, her head and shoulders its broken trunk rising above the weltering. She could hear the hisses and whispers in the rain, the spindrift.

"You'll have to sort things out another way," she told them. "Drowning Luminum will not explain anything to humans."

The longboats were casting off from the wharf, rowing against the tide. Some of her knights were among them, the strongest, the most fearless, straining against the surge to reach the gate. Their boats rode low under the weight of huge chains, which they would lock into the iron rings on the inner side of the gate, so their pulling could help the tide push it shut.

If the water-mage could only coax it free from the stubborn grip of the waterworld.

She saw, in a vivid flash of lightning, the world out of Garner's eyes as he rowed.

The sprites have gotten hold of it, she told him. *That's what you must pull against.*

She gave him a crazed glimpse of the formless swarm inside the gate jamming it open. Eada felt their strength pitted against her power. The power of persuasion would be even stronger, she thought, if only she could think of what to say.

And then she knew.

How they understood something shaped like a battered old tree trunk, she wasn't sure. Maybe they just picked the impulse and the image out of her head. *Take what you want at the Ritual of the Well,* she told them. *Until then, let the city be.*

The gate shifted; the tree trunk slid. They were gone, she realized. Vanished like the last thinning rill of a wave into sand. Water pushed the gate; the men pulled their chains, plied their oars. The trunk, angled sharply now, and underwater, prodded at the gate as it moved a few more feet. The gate closed finally; tide built against it, but could not enter. The tree trunk, finally level, floated to the surface and vanished as well.

Garner, standing at the prow of one of the longboats, struggling with wet, numb hands to unhook all the chains from the ring, nearly fell overboard yet again when the mage appeared beside him. She freed the chains easily, and passed them back into the boats alongside them. Garner stared at her, worse for the wear, she noted, thoroughly soaked again, and just waking as from a nightmare.

"What happened?" he asked hoarsely. "We couldn't budge that gate."

"I made a bargain."

The boat lurched, turning; he tumbled into a seat, took up his oars. Eada sat in the prow on the pile of chain; the knight's incredulous eyes were telling him there was no room, between him and the pile of chain, and the sea, for anything bigger than a broom straw.

"Or a shadow," she told him.

"What?"

"I need you to do something for me."

"Now?"

"Well, no, not exactly at this moment. When it seems appropriate. You know far better than I how these things go."

He pulled his oars, blinking rain out of his eyes, as though, if he could see her more clearly, she might make more sense. "Exactly what kind of bargain did you make?"

"We've got something they think is theirs. I told them they could have it back at the ritual."

"And you want me to—"

"Find it." She put a weightless hand on his shoulder, patted it. "Don't worry. Just go along as you do. How do humans put it? Follow your heart." He stared at her, his mouth hanging open to any passing wave, as she nodded. "Oh, and tell the Minister of Water what I've just told you. That's all."

Above his head, she saw that the winds were busy shredding cloud, uncovering stars, and then the glowing moon, which illumined the tattered roil, turning cloud to silk and smoke before everything blew back into black.

"But I have no idea—"

"Magic," the mage breathed, enchanted, and vanished.

Garner fell into the sea and woke.

He pulled himself out of the dream of dark, cold, weltering water, and blinked at his squire, who was reverently examining the ceremonial garb.

"For tonight, sir," he told Garner, who needed no reminding.

He sat up, holding his head together in both hands, while pieces of the extremely early morning's adventure came back to him. What had the mage said to him? Something he was supposed to find? Something he was supposed to tell Damaris . . . He groaned softly.

Inis murmured sympathetically, "A short and noisy night, sir.... At least you didn't lose your boots this time. My boots." He brought Garner a cup of watered, spiced wine, and added, "Your ritual tunic has a couple of stains on it, but only in the back, and your cloak will cover them. Everything's dry, now."

"Let's hope it stays that way," Garner muttered. "See if you can get me a pair of boots made by this evening, and you'll have yours back."

"Yes, sir," Inis answered simply, having grown used to the vicissitudes of knightly endeavor, especially Garner's.

"Do I have anything decent left to wear? I have to talk to the Minister of Water." He saw the rare trace of anxiety cross his squire's face. "Have you been hearing tales?"

Inis nodded. "From everywhere in the city. And even in the palace. Your cousin, Sir Edord, was found climbing into the well near the stables yesterday. He said a woman was calling to him, and he had to rescue her. He fought, but they managed to pull him out before he got far."

Garner, musing over possibilities, breathed, "Pity..."

"Sir?"

"The mage spoke to the water creatures last night while we were having a tug-of-war over the sea gate. She made some kind of truce with them. Things will be much quieter today."

"And the ritual?" Inis prodded shrewdly.

Garner shook his head, completely mystified. "All we can do is trust that the mage knows what she's doing."

He couldn't begin to guess what Eada wanted him to find. All he could do was send a page ahead to request an interview with the Minister of Water, and hope that the mage had revealed a few more details to Damaris. The Minister of Water, summoning him immediately to her office, seemed neither surprised nor displeased to see him. She hadn't slept much, either, he guessed; her braid was becoming unraveled and her eyes seemed huge, luminous.

"Eada told me to give you a message," Garner said.

"Another one?" she marveled. "Why doesn't she speak to me?"

"I have no idea."

"She wants you to speak to me," Damaris answered herself promptly. "But why?" She gazed at him, as perplexed as he; he restrained himself from taking the braid she was picking apart out of her restless fingers, and folding her hands in his own to calm them.

"I don't know. She said that we have something the water creatures think belongs to them. She promised that, if they left Luminum in peace until the ritual, they could claim it then." He paused. She was absolutely still now, her eyes lowered, her fingers motionless. "Oh," he added, remembering, "and she wants me to find this thing. Whatever it is. Do you have any idea what she's talking about? Where do I begin to look for this nameless, vital thing?"

She raised her eyes finally. "Why you?" she asked again, her brows crumpled, her tired eyes trying to look so deeply through his that he wondered if she were trying to find the mage in his head.

"Because we have known each other most of our lives? Because I can hide nothing from you, so if I know something that will help us, you will know it, too? Because despite all my blunderings and rashness, there is nothing I wouldn't do for the Minister of Water? I don't know. Is any of that likely?"

She swallowed, looked down again, quickly. "As likely as it is unlikely."

"What should I do?" he pleaded. "Where do I begin? It must be something that the water creatures want badly, judging from the ways they have been harassing us."

"And why now?" she wondered. "What's different now?"

"You're betrothed." She stared at him. "I'm sorry," he said hastily. "I'm sorry. It was the first thing that leaped into my head. Of course, that has nothing to do with water."

"Garner—"

"You have every right to please yourself, and I have no right to torment you about your decisions. I promise I will stop. Just tell me where to go, what to look for—"

"I don't know!" she cried, so fiercely that he started. "I don't know. Garner, just go away and look for something. Anything. I have to think." He opened his mouth. She shook her head wildly, and he closed it. "If I think of anything useful at all, I will send for you, I promise. I promise. Go."

So he went, following the paths of water as he had the day before, hoping at every moment for a whisper from the mage, a message from the minister. Both were silent. So were the water people, he realized as the day passed.

Water behaved like water in pipes and buckets, stayed mute and did not sing. Fountains splashed with decorum; sluice gates remained as they were set; mill wheels turned placidly. Everyone waited, Garner felt.

But for what?

At dusk, he returned to the palace to dress. Inis gave him new boots, buckled his sword belt and brightly polished spurs, pinned the bright silver disc of the moon that drew all waters onto his cloak. They joined the other knights and squires in the yard where the procession was forming behind the king.

The townspeople lined the streets, carrying torches and drinking vessels. They were subdued, murmuring, laughing only softly, for the ritual was ancient, vital, and, the previous day had warned them, by no means predictable. After the king, his consort, his courtiers, the royal knights and the Knights of the Well with their torch-bearing squires had all passed, the townspeople fell in behind them. The procession grew slowly longer and longer, a river of people flowing down the twining streets of the old city, past the shrouded fountain in the square and across the bridge to the broader streets that changed, beyond Luminum, into the wide, rutted, uncobbled wagon roads between the fields.

Garner rode silently, his eyes on the gentle uprise ahead, already marked by torches thrust into the earth around the opening above the Well. It was growing very dark. The pillars and walkways of the outer pool were lined with fire as well, where the city folk would gather to drop their gifts and wishes, and dip their cups to salute the moon. The full moon, rising in leisurely fashion out of the sea, had been following the procession for some time, arching higher and higher among the stars. By the time the king and the knights gathered around the Well itself and began the ritual, the moon would already be regarding its own perfect reflection in the water beneath the earth.

The king reached the hillock finally and drew aside. Courtiers, warriors and city folk all waited, while the Knights of the Well dismounted and filed underground through the mage's doorway. Eada drew them one by one to their positions around the Well. No one spoke, not even Edord, who usually had some appropriate exhortation ready for the occasion. Even he looked apprehensive, Garner noted, after his adventure with the nymph in the stable well. Garner himself wanted nothing more than to drown himself in the nearest tavern until dawn. He had found nothing; neither mage nor minister was speaking to him; he foresaw nothing but disaster.

The king's face appeared in the water beside the moon. He stood above them on the stony crown of the hill, alone between water and moon; torches on either side of him illumined his face. He would address the Well, giving thanks for the generosity of its waters, pay tribute to the moon that drew such pure waters out of the earth. Garner heard a quick intake of breath beside him, from the newest of Eada's knights. He was seeing for the first time the gathering faces of the underwater creatures, blurred, distorted, many of them paler than the moon, or tinged the colors of water.

Garner looked down at them morosely. They didn't look happy, either, the way they milled and turned in the water, flicking so close to the surface that they left ripples in the peaceful pool. If they had been human, he would have said they were pacing.

Eada murmured something incomprehensible. Water splashed back at her, an unprecedented occurrence. The king had just begun the traditional phrases, which had lengthened, like the night's procession, through the centuries. Along with dropping the first words into the Well, he dropped a handful of gold coins, and a carefully faceted jewel. They fell in a rich little shower, lightly pocking the water.

The jewel shot back out of the water, smacked him on the shin.

He stopped mid-word, dumbfounded. His face, above his golden beard, grew bright, somewhere near the color of the jewel. He looked torn between continuing the ritual, and fuming at his water-mage, who was just standing there, as near as Garner could tell, doing nothing. A gold piece ejected next from the water, struck a rock beside the king with a tiny, musical clang. Another, cast higher, was caught in midair. It seemed as though the moon itself had reached out long white fingers to claim it.

It was the Minister of Water, moving into the torchlight. The king stared at her, as did the knights; even the moon seemed to take more than a passing interest in the proceedings.

The king found his voice first.

"Lady Ambre," he said brusquely. "Why are they rejecting our gifts? Can you explain?"

She nodded. Garner, seeing again the green-eyed, foam-haired nymph in the river, felt his heart twist like a fish in his chest.

"My lord," she said ruefully, "I believe they want your Minister of Water to acknowledge her heritage." The king's brows tangled; his mouth dropped. "I don't," Damaris continued, "entirely understand the disturbance, but if it will ease the tensions between our worlds, I will claim my connection with both. My mother is human. My father, evidently, is some kind of water creature. Since I have no markings of the waterborn, only a fascination with waterworks and an ability to spend an impossible amount of time under water, I was able to conceal that side of me. Until now. Now, before you all, I claim the waterborn as my kin."

The king closed his mouth wordlessly, looked again into the Well, where the accumulated coin of countless rituals, tossed lightly out of the water, caught fire as they fell, and were tossed again, as quickly as they hit the water, like a little golden rain of cheers.

"They seem," he observed cautiously, "to be pleased with that. But why now? Why disturb the entire city of Luminum over this? Why ravage my water closet?"

"My lord, I do not know."

"Eada?"

She shook her head. "Nor I. Shall I ask them?"

"Please," said the king. But it was not his answer she wanted. The water-mage gazed at the Minister of Water, one sparse brow cocked questioningly. Damaris looked down at her silently, her face as expressionless as the moon watching over her shoulder. They were speaking to one another again, Garner realized. And about time.

Damaris came to life again, answered the water-mage with a little, decisive nod. "I'll go to them," she said. "I owe them that courtesy."

Then she was gone, gliding down a shaft of moonlight, it seemed, to fall with scarcely a ripple into the water. The king gave a cry; Garner managed to swallow his. He froze, his eyes on the thin, fading ripples crossing the moon's reflection. Nothing, he decided, could make him move; he would stand there, watching the dark water, turning himself to stone if need be, until she returned to earth.

"Where did she go?" the king demanded. "She'll drown!"

Eada patted the air, as though his head were beneath her hand. "Hush, my lord," she said. "I'm listening."

"To what?"

"To them talking. She doesn't understand their words; I must translate what I can."

"But—"

"Shh."

The king was silent finally, staring into the Well, as they all were, and then at the mage, then back at the water, trying, as they all were, with his fixed attention to raise a sign of life from it. Garner, unblinking and scarcely breathing, grasped at what he could understand of the mage's language: her quick nod of comprehension, followed by suddenly raised eyebrows, and then a mew of surprise. *What?* he shouted silently. *What?* But nothing. Yet. The knights waited soundlessly beside him, as though if they listened hard enough they might hear, within the trembling waters of the Well, the language far older than their own.

Finally, a pale, wet head appeared above the water. Damaris drew herself out onto the rocks with such ease and grace she seemed scarcely human. Garner saw the water nymph again, and felt his own powerful urge to walk across water to join her. Shifting around him, unsteady breathing, told him he would not be alone.

Then she shivered slightly and turned human in his eyes.

"Well?" the king asked harshly, unsettled himself, it seemed, by this vision of his capable Minister of Water.

"My lord," Damaris began, then gave up, gesturing helplessly to Eada. "I understood so little. Except that they were pleased that I had come to meet them in their own world."

"Yes, they were," the water-mage answered. "Very pleased."

"What did they say?" Damaris and the king asked together.

"They told Damaris that her father has found his way back to the great deep from which all things flow and to which all return."

"I guessed that," she said softly. "I am sorry. I would like to have known him. I was never brave enough to admit his existence before."

"Well, it seems that he was the powerful ruler of the realm beneath the river. He has many children, and since such water creatures like their rulers to live a long time, it is the youngest child, not the oldest, who inherits the realm. That would be you."

"Me," Damaris said blankly.

"Yes."

"But I can't—I could never—"

"Of course not. You'd not last a day under water, which would surely defeat their intentions. But by their own customs, and out of honor to your father's wish, they were duty-bound to ask you first. To do that, they had to get your attention."

"Which I never, ever wanted," she breathed. "I only wanted to be human."

"Yes."

"So they tried to speak to me in the only language we have in common. Water."

"Yes."

"But the mage understood them," the king interrupted. "Why could they not just explain all this to Eada, so that she could tell you?"

The mage was silent, letting Damaris answer, which she did, drawing herself to her feet so that she could turn and look up at him.

"Because, my lord, they were angry with me. They wanted to do me this great honor, give me this gift from my father. But I refused to hear them. I made use of their water realm, but I gave them no honor, not even the simplest courtesy of recognition. I rejected them, pretending to everyone that I am only human. I ask your forgiveness for the deception, and for being the cause of all this trouble."

"You are more than human," the king amended gruffly, and raised his voice, to make her status very clear to those courtiers who might be forming doubts about the matter. "You do us honor to refuse a kingdom for the sake of Luminum. I would hate to lose our dear friend, and our very gifted Minister of Water."

"Thank you, my lord."

"Is that all, then?" he added with a touch of anxiety. "Can we get on with it?"

"You may continue the ritual," the water-mage told him. "They are content."

After the king and his knights had drunk from the Well, and then from the pool, Garner looked for Damaris. She was nowhere in the crush of city folk and courtiers filling their cups around the pool and drinking vociferously to the moon, the Well, to Luminum and to the eagerly awaited water pipes. He found her sitting where the king had stood, well away from the noisy crowd, gazing down at the Well. Someone was with her, Garner realized, just before he walked into the torchlight. He recognized the light hair, the deep, easy, unruffled voice, and stopped, trying, for once, to be courteous, to turn and disappear.

But Lord Felden's words unraveled his good intentions.

"Of course we cannot marry," he was saying. "You understand that, I'm sure." Damaris's answer was inaudible, even to Garner's straining ears. "I can't risk having an heir with webs between its fingers who might spend all its time in the fish pond."

"Of course not."

"My mother will understand completely."

"Yes."

There was a short silence, during which Lord Felden refused to take his leave.

"I wish I could," he admitted unexpectedly. "I've grown very fond of you. If only I were not the eldest, with the title and responsibilities—"

"But you are," the naiad on the rock at his feet said firmly. "You must do your duty. Besides, our marriage might interfere with my work, and you heard what the king said." She lifted a hand to him. "Let us stay friends."

"You're not—ah—offended?"

"No. You will continue to enjoy the benefits of my work, and I the beauties of yours. Which should not be troubled tomorrow by so much as a misplaced drop of water from the fountain."

Still he paused, for which Garner had to give him credit, much as he wished him gone. "You almost make me fall in love with you all over again," he said huskily.

"It's the water nymph in me," Damaris said evenly. "Don't take it seriously."

He went off finally, a little hurriedly, after that. Garner, motionless and awkward in the shadows, wondered if he should as well; he had no reason to suppose she would be grateful for his presence. But he took a step toward her anyway. She turned, and he watched her expression change as he emerged from the night.

"Garner," she sighed.

"I don't want to disturb you if you would prefer to be alone."

She shook her head, gesturing him to join her. She was still wet, he realized, and trembling a little in the midnight air. He took his cloak off, put it over her shoulders.

"Thank you," she said, huddling herself into it. "Thank you for noticing that I am cold. I wanted to see you."

"Really?" he marveled, sitting down beside her.

"To apologize. Did you hear any of my conversation with Lord Felden?"

"Enough," he admitted. "Are you sorry?"

"Beale offered me everything I thought would make me completely human. The wealthy noble, the title, his children—I could hide safely behind him for the rest of my life."

"Are you sorry?" he asked again.

She stared down at the reflection of the moon, which was beginning to disappear as it drifted toward the underground stream.

"I would have wronged us both," she said simply, "if I had married him. I didn't understand that until tonight. I didn't understand how little in love I was." She looked at Garner then, wryly. "You saw how wrong it was, I think. That's why you were so angry with me."

"You were angry with me."

"For seeing far too much."

He was silent, gazing into the pool. Somewhere in his idle thoughts a child with Damaris's eyes and fingers webbed with dragonfly-wings dove without a ripple into a sunlit pond.

Damaris tossed a tear of gold into the Well; the image in his head blurred, faded.

"What was that?" he asked.

"One of the king's coins. I found it in the grass."

"Did you make a wish?"

She smiled at him, untangling her feet from her wet skirt, shifting to rise. "You can have the wish. All I want now is a drink of water."

So he took it, tossing his heart into the Well after the coin, and walked with her to join the celebration.

WHAT INSPIRES ME
Guest of Honor Speech at WisCon28, 2004

A FRIEND ASKED ME recently, "What inspires you to write?" She is a writer herself, so I knew she wasn't asking me, "Where do you get your ideas?" She would know that ideas are as random as shooting stars; they come while you're cleaning the bathtub, or watching *Four Weddings and a Funeral* for the ninth time, or in the morning when the last bit of your dream is fraying away, just before you open your eyes. You see it, then, what you've been searching for all these weeks or months, clear as day; you look at it and think, "Oh. Yeah," and open your eyes. That wasn't what she was asking. And that was why I couldn't answer; I could only sit and stare at her with my mouth hanging gracelessly open, because all the answers that sprang immediately to mind answered the question she hadn't asked.

Such as, well, money. Money is an enormous and entirely respectable source of inspiration when writing is your sole means of support. I did the math recently and was astonished. I've been writing for forty-two years, since I sat down one morning when I was fourteen and wrote a thirty-page fairy tale. I sold my first novel when I was twenty-three, so I've been published for thirty-three years. Which means I've been supporting myself by writing for over three decades. My agent swears that I'm most inspired when I'm broke. As when, during one financially dicey period, the cesspool of the 130-year-old house I had bought in the Catskills gave up the ghost one spring on the first day of May. It is a day indelibly etched in memory, because I had a guest with whom I was trying to kindle the fires of romance, my cesspool was backing into my bathtub, and I remembered then that my plumber and his wife, who threw a Kentucky Derby party every year, and everyone who worked for him would be three sheets to the wind by the time the horses galloped out of the starting gate.

After the race was won and my guest had gone home, and I finally got someone interested in my problem, I had something else to worry about. My next-door neighbor, the minister for the elegant stone Dutch Reform church across the street, had walked over a mossy patch of my back lawn when I moved in, and told me that was where my cesspool was. I expressed mild interest and then forgot about it. Before that I'd lived for a quarter of a century in California, where nothing much was older than the Gold Rush. I understood apartments with white walls and shag carpets, or apartments that had done a little dance with the 1906 earthquake and refused to fall down. I had never needed to know what a cesspool was, or how it might affect my life. That morning I stood in the backyard and watched half a dozen hefty young guys unbury my cesspool, and I wondered uneasily how personal was this going to be, exactly? Would they, for instance, see my tampons floating around in the murk? What they unearthed first caused them all a great deal of interest. It was the passenger door to an ancient pickup truck somebody had laid down to cap the cesspool. There seemed to be a ritual involved here: the men could not lay the door aside until they had first figured out the make and model of the pickup truck. I waited; they sorted it out to their satisfaction, and moved it to uncover the source of my problem.

To my surprise, I saw a very neatly constructed little fieldstone well, a perfect circle of stones running down into the earth, holding, to my relief, what seemed nothing less innocuous than the average mud-puddle. It was a gorgeous day in early spring, with lots of blue sky and budding leaves, and a good strong, sweet wind that probably saved the day. A shovel, inserted into the puddle, only went down a few inches. The well was pronounced dead, and was buried again. Being, as I said, temporarily out of funds, I borrowed money from my mother and repaid her a couple of months later for my new system with what was probably the delivery payment for *The Book of Atrix Wolfe*.

A steady accumulation of detail over a length of time is also a good source of ideas. For instance: music. I had followed it across country: friends who had played in a band in and around San Francisco also moved to the Catskills and played there in homespun places called the T-Bar, the Pine Hill Arms, Larry's Place. I sat on maple barstools drinking whatever passed for white wine, and thought about all the variations on the theme of relationships a band and its groupies go through in time. Outside, a snow squall might be covering the country road, making the night seem very dark and very old. Left to my own devices, I was more inclined to blunder my way through Bach and Chopin on the piano. I learned soon that if you tossed a stone in pretty much any direction in those small mountain villages, you would hit a piano player. Or an aging fiddle-player, keeping up the traditional tunes of the region. A friend down the road played all of those things—Bach, rock, and fiddle. He also played recorders and from him I learned how much fun it is to play music with someone else. We played recorder and keyboard sonatas by Handel and Telemann. I took a fiddle class briefly, and met the wife of a missionary of some brand of faith I never quite figured out. She and her husband had traveled widely in Eastern Europe; she had once danced in a nightclub with a Russian general; she gave me a piece of the Berlin Wall for a wedding present. We played sonatas of violin and piano, and actually performed, during one fiercely hot summer day when my fingers felt like sausages on the keys, for the residents of the village retirement home. Which had once been the country home of the railroad baron Jay Gould's daughter. Who had built the elegant Dutch Reform church with the Tiffany windows next door in hope that the gesture would somehow ease her father's way into heaven. Whose pulpit was graced, each Sunday, by the minister who had told me where to find my cesspool if I ever needed it. Who, later, scandalized the village by having an affair with—well, never mind. Music. I don't know if the residents of the rest home were impressed by our performance or not, but I was certainly grateful when it was over.

In a crying need to get out of those mountains for a bit, I registered for a music class offered at Juilliard to the community at large. To this day I wonder if Juilliard realized that the Catskills was part of its local community. The subject was World Music, which I didn't know much about. It was held every Thursday evening from seven to nine, from late September to early December. To get to it, I would drive for an hour and a quarter out of the Catskills, across the Hudson River, to another tiny village called

Rhinecliff, which boasted a little train station with two tracks. I would board an Amtrak train there. After an hour and forty minutes, the train would pull into Grand Central Station, and I would step into an entirely different planet. The huge buildings, the noise, the smells, the languages, the music, as varied as the languages, offered at every street corner were mind-boggling, intoxicating. By day, I explored the city; in the evening I sat in a classroom listening to weird instruments, exotic music. Afterwards, I would reverse the journey, moving farther and farther out of the enormous, intense hothouse of civilization until the roads became narrow and solitary, mountains hid the river and the city lights, and I reached the strange point in my drive home where I felt that I had somehow traveled so far that I had left the real world, real time behind. I had passed into the realm of Sleepy Hollow, the Otherworld, which was just a little farther than anyone should go.

The final class was held in the Indonesian Consulate so that we could learn about the gamelan. I had also learned, on those Thursday explorations, enough about the subway system to find my way there and back again, which gave me no end of satisfaction. Later, I would put that journey from one tiny world into a huge, complex and noisy world, those details of bar and classroom and my amateur efforts at music, into a fantasy novel: *Song for the Basilisk*.

A Looming Deadline can also be a galvanizing source of inspiration. I got married for the first time at age fifty-three, which is statistically highly improbable or maybe even impossible, but what the hey. It seemed like a good idea at the time, and still does. Because it was easier for me to plan a wedding 3000 miles from where I lived than it was for my mother, in a wheelchair with Parkinson's, to get on a plane, and because both our families were for the most part scattered between San Francisco and Puget Sound, Dave and I got married in a small town on the Oregon coast. Over the internet I found the only department store in the town of Bandon that hadn't burned down in the devastating fire of 1936, and which had been turned into a charming guest house, with five bedrooms, a hot tub that didn't leak into the living room unless you filled it too high, a potbellied stove for an altar, a big kitchen, and enough space for seventy-five chairs. Since JPs don't travel in Oregon, I commandeered a good-natured Presbyterian minister to marry us, and asked my dearest friend along to cater.

Meanwhile, Dave started to dismantle his own life of thirty-four years in New York, pack up the house and the memories for our trek west. This was the summer of 2001.

We flew out a week before the wedding to prepare. Preparation involved things like cleaning the scales with a garden hose off five huge salmon a fisherman friend of my mother's had given us, driving the byways to gather wild sweet pea vines along the roadside for decoration, peeling enormous quantities of potatoes while my siblings, who came from Puget Sound, and Reno, and Coos Bay, unpacked guitars and flutes and tried to remember the words to "The Wedding Song" which they had played for one another's weddings way back when we were all young.

The day itself was quite delightful. During the month after the wedding, we spent a week looking for a house to rent, flew back to the Catskills to close up my house and say goodbye to friends, get Dave's possessions into a moving van, and then took off back across country in separate cars—Dave in his sleek black jet-propelled Talon, and me in my gerbil-driven Chevy Metro, with two cats in the back who were so totally not amused. We couldn't dawdle; the moving van was somewhere on the road with us, making for the rental house. As with the wedding, most memories are blurred. Others are indelible. The rear end of the Talon. The tornado in Iowa. The rear end of the Talon. The eerie badlands of South Dakota, full of ancient, sleeping gods. Losing sight of the rear end of the Talon on the empty, rainy highway across Wyoming. Realizing that I had been married for scarcely three weeks and I'd already misplaced my husband. The devious places the cats found to hide themselves every morning in motels—under blankets, under beds that seemed riveted to the floor—to avoid being put back into the cat-carrier. Driving up a gentle slope in Montana and finding myself at the top of a dizzying mountain in Idaho, with nowhere to go but down, and the rear end of the Talon so far ahead of me I thought it would be in Oregon a day before I got there. Driving from the gentle, tangled woods of the Catskills, with their modest slopes of 3000 feet, into the spectacular vastness of the west, where mountains look down at you from 10,000 or 14,000 feet, shrug a few boulders, and ask, "What did you expect?" A friend, visiting me once in the Catskills, commented of them: "Mountains higher than these are unnatural." But I'm half-Swiss; my forebears came down out of the Alps to settle in Oregon, and I knew why: they felt at home.

Another indelible memory: waking very early on the last morning of our journey, our first morning in Oregon, turning on the news while the coffee brewed, and watching the Twin Towers fall.

Later that day, stunned and groggy, we reached the town where we would live, tracked down the key to the rental house, and settled in to wait for the moving van, which we had managed to outrace. I'm not sure how long it was afterwards—I think it was after we finally got a bed and pots and pans—when I began to consider seriously the Looming Deadline.

It had been a year away when I began searching for a place to get married. It had been over six months away when we got married. When I looked again, it was four months and small change away. I had thirty-nine typed pages and a contract stating I would send the completed manuscript in by February 1, 2002. I knew where I wanted the novel to go, but I couldn't seem to shove it past page 39. I couldn't find the point of view I needed to examine the life and motives of a man who wanted to conquer the world. I did the usual: sacrificed small rodents to the moon, offered my soul to demons in exchange for inspiration, did some research. Nobody wanted the rodents or my soul, and the research into ancient conquerors seemed barren. Finally, out of the blue, a young girl stepped into my head, opened her mouth and told me where that part of the story began. I finished *Alphabet of Thorn* in three and a half months, the fastest book I'd written in thirty years.

Certainly the Looming Deadline provided the crucible in which inspiration and imagination fused to give me what I needed. But none of these things—money, experience, deadlines—answers the question I was asked, because the question was not about inspiration or ideas at all.

The question was about drive, motivation: What possessed you to write eight or ten entirely different fantasies in ten or twelve years? What compels you? How could you? Why would you want to? Ever since I was young, the imagination, like the raw stuff of magic, has seemed to me a kind of formless, fluid pool of enormous possibility, both good and bad, dangerous and powerful, very like the magma in a volcano. And I envisioned myself sitting on top of this mountain of magma, spinning it into endless words, visions, imagery, controlled and useful, to keep it from bursting out in its primitive shape to devastate the landscape. At first, I felt very precariously balanced on top of my private volcano, spinning word and image into tales as quickly as I could to keep up with the unstable forces I was trying to harness. Lately, I've been feeling rather at home there. The magma level has gone down a bit; I've done some satisfying work. I can slow down, maybe, take a longer time to think what I want to make now. What I set out to do about fifteen years ago was to write a series of novels that were like paintings in a gallery by the same artist. Each work is different, but they are all related to one another by two things: they are all fantasy, and they are all by the same person. That's all I wanted to do. And now I'm reaching the end of that series.

I have no idea what will come next.

WRITING HIGH FANTASY

THE FORMULA IS SIMPLE. Take one 15th-century palace with high towers and pennants flying, add a hero who talks like a butler, a wizard with fireworks under his fingernails, and a Lurking Evil that threatens the kingdom or the heroine, and there you have it: high fantasy in the making.

And there we have all had it up to the proverbial "here." How many times can you repeat the same plot? But how can you write high fantasy without the traditional trappings, characters, and plot that are essential for this kind of fantasy?

So I am forced to ask myself the same question when I begin a new fantasy: How can it follow the rules of high fantasy and break them at the same time?

The Hero

In writing the *Riddle-Master* trilogy, my impulse was to be as deliberately traditional as possible: a ruler leaves the comforts of his castle to learn from wizards how to fight a Lurking Evil that threatens to destroy his land. The hero, the magic, the danger are after all elements of fantasy as old as storytelling. But how do you give the Generic Hero—who only has to be highborn, look passable, and fight really well to be a hero—personality?

I discarded quite a number of auditioning heroes before settling on

Morgon, Prince of Hed, ruler of a tiny island, who liked to make beer, read books, didn't own a sword, and kept the only crown he possessed under his bed. He did not talk like an English butler, he knew which end of a shovel was up, and only a penchant for wanting to learn odd things kept him from being a sort of placid gentleman farmer. That small detail—among all the details of a prosaic hardheaded life that included farming, trading, pig herders, backyard pumps, and a couple of strong-willed siblings—became the conflict in his personality that ultimately drove him from his land and set him on his questing path.

Before I let him set forth, I placed him against as detailed a background as I possibly could. I wanted the reader to see the land Morgon lived in and how it shaped him before he left it and changed himself. So I let him talk about grain and bulls, beer and plowhorses, and his sister's bare feet, before I let him say fairy tale words like *tower, wizard, harp,* and *king,* and state his own driving motivation: to answer the unanswered riddle.

THE HEROINE

In *The Sorceress and the Cygnet,* my questing hero found himself falling literally into the path of my questing heroine. She is, in one sense, the princess in the tower whom my hero eventually rescues; in other words, she is very much a piece of the familiar storytelling formula. But she has imprisoned herself in a rickety old house in a swamp, trapped there by her own obsession with the darker side of magic.

As she defines herself: "I have been called everything from sorceress to bog hag. I know a great many things but never enough. Never enough. I know the great swamp of night, and sometimes I do things for pay if it interests me." She has pursued her quest for knowledge and power into a dangerous backwater of mean, petty magic, from which, it is clear to everyone but her, she must be rescued. The language she uses, like Morgon's, covers a broad territory between palace and pig herder's hut. Her wanderings have freed her tongue.

In the same novel, I also used a female point of view—that of a highborn lady—to contrast with the more earthy, gypsyish, view of my hero.

She is a female version of the "friend of the hero"; she frets about the sorceress, gives advice, and fights beside the sorceress in the end. She is perhaps the toughest kind of character to work with: genuinely good, honest, and dutiful. Making a point-of-view character both good and interesting is a challenge. Traditionally, a "good" character has a limited emotional range, no bad habits to speak of, and a rather bland vocabulary. As the "friend of the heroine," she is also a sounding board for the heroine's more colorful character.

I deliberately chose that kind of character because I wanted to see how difficult it would be to make her more than just a device to move the plot along its necessary path. She turned out to be extraordinarily difficult. I wanted her to be elegant, dignified, calm, responsible....

To keep her from fading completely into the plot, I constantly had to provide her with events that brought out her best qualities. Keeping her dialogue simple kept her uncomplicated yet responsive as a character; it also moved the plot forward without dragging along the unnecessary baggage of introspection. She is meant to observe and act; the language should not be more complicated than she is.

THE LURKING EVIL

Traditionally, the Evil in fantasy is personified by someone of extraordinary and perverse power, whose goal in life is to bring the greatest possible misery to the largest number of good honest folk. Sauron of the *Lord of the Rings* trilogy, Darth Vader of the *Star Wars* trilogy, Morgan le Fay of *Le Morte d'Arthur* are all examples of social misfits from whose destructive powers the hero and heroine must rescue humanity and hobbits and the world as they know it.

The problem with the Lurking Evil is that as social misfit, it might become far more interesting than the good and dutiful hero. Yet without proper background and personality, the Lurking Evil becomes a kind of unmotivated monster vacuum cleaner that threatens humanity simply because it's plugged in and turned on. I have trouble coming up with genuinely evil characters who are horrible, remorseless, and deserving of everything the hero can dish out. I always want to give them a human side, which puts them in the social misfit category.

In my *Riddle-Master* trilogy, I used various kinds of misfits: the renegade wizard Ohm, who was motivated by an unprincipled desire for magical power; the sea-people, whose intentions and powers seem at first random and obscure, until they finally reveal their origins; and the ambiguous character Deth, who may be good and may be evil—and who keeps my hero off-balance and guessing until the end of the tale.

In *The Sorceress and the Cygnet*, I used much the same kind of device: allowing my hero to define characters as evil until, in the end, they reveal that the evil is not in them, but in my misguided heroine. I do this because evil as a random event, or as the sole motivation for a character, is difficult for me to work with; it seems to belong in another genre—to horror or mystery.

Jung says that all aspects of a dream are actually faces of the dreamer. I believe that in fantasy, the vanquished evil must be an aspect of the hero or heroine, since by tradition, evil is never stronger than the power of the hero to overcome it—which is where, of course, we get the happy endings in high fantasy.

Magic

If you put a mage, sorceress, wizard, warlock, witch, or necromancer into fantasy, it's more than likely that, sooner or later, he or she will want to work some magic. Creating a spell can be as simple or as difficult as you want. You can write, "Mpyxl made a love potion. Hormel drank it and fell in love." Or you can do research into herb lore and medieval recipes for spells and write: "Mpyxl stirred five bay leaves, an owl's eye, a parsnip, six of Hormel's fingernails, and some powdered mugwort into some leftover barley soup. Hormel ate it and fell in love."

Or you can consider love itself, and how Mpyxl must desire Hormel, how frustrated and rejected she must feel to be obliged to cast a spell over him, what in Hormel generates such overpowering emotions, why he refuses to fall in love with Mpyxl the usual way, and what causes people to fall in love with each other in the first place. Then you will find that Mpyxl herself is under a spell cast by Hormel, and that she must change before his eyes from someone he doesn't want to someone he desires beyond reason.

The language of such a spell would be far different from fingernails and barley soup. The Magic exists only in the language; the spell exists only in the reader's mind. The words themselves must create something out of nothing. To invent a convincing love potion you must, for a moment, make even the reader fall in love.

Why?

Why write fantasy? Because it's there. Fantasy is as old as poetry and myth, which are as old as language. The rules of high fantasy are rules of the unconscious and the imagination, where good quests, evil lurks, the two clash, and the victor—and the reader—are rewarded.

Good might be male or female; so might evil. The battle might be fought with swords, with magic, with wits, on a battlefield, in a tower, or in the quester's heart.

At its best, fantasy rewards the reader with a sense of wonder about what lies within the heart of the commonplace world. The greatest tales are told over and over, in many ways, through centuries. Fantasy changes with the changing times, and yet it is still the oldest kind of tale in the world, for it began once upon a time, and we haven't heard the end of it yet.

PATRICIA ANNE MCKILLIP was born February 29, 1948, in Salem, Oregon. She attended the College of Notre Dame, Belmont, and San Jose State University in California, receiving a BA in 1971 and an MA in 1972 in English.

Her first publications were short children's books: *The Throme of the Erril of Sherill* and *The House on Parchment Street* (both 1973). Her first novel for adults, *The Forgotten Beasts of Eld* (1974), won a World Fantasy Award.

McKillip's science fiction and fantasy novels include the *Riddle-Master* trilogy: *The Riddle-Master of Hed* (1976), *Heir of Sea and Fire* (1977), and Locus Award winner and Hugo and World Fantasy Award finalist *Harpist in the Wind* (1979); Nebula Award finalist *Winter Rose* (1996); Nebula Award nominee *The Tower at Stony Wood* (2000); World Fantasy Award finalist *Od Magic* (2005); Mythopoeic Award winner *Solstice Wood* (2006); and Mythopoeic Award winner *Kingfisher* (2016).

McKillip's other books include non-SF children's book *The Night Gift* (1976); adult contemporary novel *Stepping from the Shadows* (1982); and shared-world novel Brian Froud's *Faerielands: Something Rich and Strange* (1994), a Mythopoeic Award winner. Her collections include *Harrowing the Dragon* (2005); *Wonders of the Invisible World* (2012); and Endeavour Award winner *Dreams of Distant Shores* (2016). McKillip received a World Fantasy life achievement award in 2008.

Patricia McKillip was living in Oregon when she passed away in May of 2022.

Ellen Kushner is the author of acclaimed works of literary fantasy, an award-winning audio book narrator and stage performer, the past creator and host of public radio's national series *Sound & Spirit*, and a popular teacher and lecturer. Her novel *Swordspoint*, considered the progenitor of the Fantasy of Manners, is the first of an achronological series of two more novels, many short stories, and the collaborative serial *Tremontaine*. A fourth novel is in the works. Her novel *Thomas the Rhymer* won the World Fantasy Award and Mythopoeic Award, and is in the Gollancz *Fantasy Masterworks* series.

Kushner lives in New York City with Delia Sherman and a great many theater and airplane ticket stubs. They teach at the Hollins University MA/MFA program in Children's Literature.